A Mask of Flies

A Mask of Flies

MATTHEW LYONS

NIGHTFIRE

TOR PUBLISHING GROUP
NEW YORK

A MASK OF FLIES

Copyright © 2024 by Matthew Lyons

Interior art by Shutterstock.com

A Nightfire Book
Published by Tom Doherty Associates / Tor Publishing Group
120 Broadway
New York, NY 10271

www.torpublishinggroup.com

Nightfire™ is a trademark of Macmillan Publishing Group, LLC.

The Library of Congress Cataloging-in-Publication Data is available upon request.

ISBN 978-1-250-88981-2 (hardcover)
ISBN 978-1-250-88983-6 (ebook)

Our books may be purchased in bulk for promotional, educational,
or business use. Please contact your local bookseller or the Macmillan
Corporate and Premium Sales Department at 1-800-221-7945, extension 5442,
or by email at MacmillanSpecialMarkets@macmillan.com.

First Edition: 2024

Printed in the United States of America

0 9 8 7 6 5 4 3 2 1

For my family—thanks for showing up.

*I believe the common denominator of the universe
is not harmony, but chaos, hostility, and murder.*
—Werner Herzog

Don't you wish you never, never met her?
—PJ Harvey

PROLOGUE
The Glass Storm

The sound of her mom moving back and forth in the living room woke her, but she didn't open her eyes until she heard the bedroom door creak wide.

The beam of the flashlight was bright and brilliant white, almost painful. It sliced through the shadows like a blade, carving a narrow path through the darkness that poured through the little bedroom's single window. Curled up under the covers against the early-winter chill that had suffused the cabin, Annie stirred and rolled over just in time to feel her mom's sure, steady fingers alight on her shoulder, shaking her the rest of the way awake.

"Annie, get up," Mom said, the forced hush in her voice failing to disguise a rising panic. "We have to go."

Annie kicked the blankets away as she rose, rubbing sleep from her eyes with the backs of her bandaged-up hands. She could hear the wind groaning against the walls of their little cabin, the soft pit-a-pat of fat blackflies beating themselves against the glass, trying to find a way inside.

"Mom? What's going on?"

In the back glow of the flashlight, she squinted at her mother and felt her heart falter, the machinery inside her chest sputtering and spinning uselessly. She didn't recognize this version of her mom: dressed in her pajamas and bathrobe, eyes wide and bloodshot, crowded by runnel-deep crow's-feet above heavy purple bags, pupils drawn down into pinpricks so small they nearly disappeared. Her hair, firework red like Annie's, was tangled and windblown, and her mouth was drawn into a long, thin grimace that left her lips pale scars in the dark. Annie thought she might've been crying.

"Mom?"

"It's not safe here, Annie. We have to go," Mom said again, her voice hardening like the ground in January. "Now." She took Annie's wrist to pull her from her bed. Her fingers were cold and stiff, her grip too tight, too insistent.

Instinctively, Annie tried to free herself, but Mom held her fast. The chilly cabin floor bit into Annie's bare feet as she slid from the warmth of her bed and looked uselessly around her room for some reason, some explanation as to why her mom was acting this way.

"Mom, wait—"

"Put your shoes on, Annie." Mom's voice was stern, brooking no argument. "I'm not joking."

"What's going on, though?"

But Mom was already walking out of the room, feet creaking the floorboards as she moved.

Following her out, Annie watched her mother hurriedly pull on her boots, not even bothering with the laces. Annie wanted to beg her to stop, slow down, explain what was going on, please, but she didn't have the words. Her thoughts were muddy from sleep, and anyway, it was clear from how Mom was acting that they didn't have time for questions.

This was just like before.

Annie didn't like thinking about before. It was too scary, too confusing, more like a half-remembered nightmare now than anything she'd actually lived through. There had been screaming in the darkness, and crying, and so much blood, and that terrible white-black light . . .

Chewing on her lower lip like a wad of Fruit Stripe, Annie went to the far side of the living room and stepped both feet into her worn old tennis shoes. Outside, something scratched at the walls of the cabin, the sound bony and brittle. Annie jumped, and her fingers fumbled on her shoelaces, her hands awkward around the edges of the bandages covering her palms. Blood was oozing through the gauze again.

When the scratching sound came once more, she had to bite back a whimper.

Outside, the San Luis Valley was cosmically dark, the distant hills and black mountains carved from shadow, looming so high that Annie thought that they'd come crashing down to flatten her at any second. Overhead, clouds had snuffed out half the stars in the sky, the darkness bleeding perfectly between the firmament and the hills, making it impossible to tell where the sky ended and the earth began. The air bit into Annie's skin with needle teeth and she wrapped her thin arms around herself, trying to hang on to some small amount of warmth, but her secondhand Ninja Turtles pajamas did less than nothing to keep the cold out.

Together, Annie and Mom quickly scuffed down to their four-door Jeep Cherokee, parked at the head of the deep wheel-rut path that served as the sprawling property's front drive, its white paint speckled with dried mud. Mom led Annie around to the passenger side and opened the front-seat door for her to climb in.

"What do we do when we're in trouble, Annie?"

"*We follow the stars,*" Annie parroted as she settled in, her half of the call-and-response Mom had drummed into her head ever since she could remember.

"That's right, we follow the stars. Seat belt," Mom commanded.

Annie did as she was told. Mom clapped the passenger door shut, then circled around to the other side of the Jeep. Dropping herself behind the wheel, Mom put a hand into the pocket of her robe, then laid a strange heavy something—dull and angular and black—atop the dash. A hard, freezing wire wriggled through Annie's chest at the sight.

Is that—?

"Mom . . . ?"

She'd seen revolvers mounted on the pegboard behind the counter at the sporting goods store in town, but she never thought of her mom as somebody who would actually buy one. Behind the wheel, Mom shook her head stiffly, dismissing the question, and cranked the key in the ignition, urging the Jeep to life. She hit the headlights and reversed away from the cabin hard, pulling a hasty two-point turn in the dirt.

Pebbles and rocks pinged against the Jeep's undercarriage, pin-balling off the metal as the tires spun over the rough road. The night crowded in around them. In the passenger seat, Annie twisted in place, watching their cabin recede into the distance, hunting the shadows for some sign as to why they were leaving in such a hurry. They hadn't even turned off the lights inside.

Annie didn't want to leave, and she especially didn't want to leave like this, unsure of where they were going or when they'd be back, but she wasn't about to ask, either. There was too much going on. Everything was already bad enough without her making Mom mad with questions that probably didn't matter. So she kept her mouth shut and dug her slender little fingers into her knees and held on for dear life. She looked back at the cabin again, staring into the darkness that filled up the space between the roof and the sky, trying to understand, trying to make it all make sense.

And then, in front of the cabin, the darkness shivered and trembled, and opened dead-white eyes to stare back at her. Annie cried out and pressed her face to the seat back. When she looked again, the eyes—and the blurry shadow-thing that had surrounded them—were gone.

What . . . ?

Behind the wheel, Mom stomped on the gas pedal. The Jeep's engine roared louder as the speedometer crept past fifty. Annie's breath hitched in her chest.

The dirt road led them down-down-down, curling back and forth between the steep, grassy hills that kept their property hidden from sight. Annie knew there were five switchbacks before they made it to the two-lane highway that connected the cabin property to the rest of the world, and she counted them off inside her head as they passed them by: *one, two, three, four.* Twisting around in her seat, Annie realized that she could already see the blacktop from here, a thin, poorly kept road that snaked through the low foothills, just beyond the deep ravine that traveled the far edge of their property.

Mom took the last bend without slowing, whipping around the dusty ridge at speed. And then it was right in front of them. The shadow-thing. For a moment, it looked like a woman standing in the middle of the road—thin, bony shoulders underneath curtains of stringy black hair, staring straight ahead at them with those horrible, deadglow eyes.

It looked like—

Annie screamed, and Mom screamed with her, jerking the wheel hard to the left as she floored the gas. The engine ground and whined, and the Jeep peeled off the dirt road and went hurtling across the rocky terrain toward the ravine. But the shadow-woman was already in front of them again, and the ravine was coming up quick—too quick.

They were going to crash.

Oh god, they were going to *crash*.

Annie had half a second to look over as her mom floored it, aiming the Jeep at the shadow-woman, and idly thought, *She's not wearing her seat belt.* But even at six years old, Annie could see that it was already way too late. So she shut her eyes tight and curled herself into a ball as the Jeep plowed over the shadow and smashed headlong into the far slope of the little gorge.

Metal twisted and snapped as the Jeep folded in on itself like a crushed soda can. Glass exploded all around her in a blue-green flurry. Shards sprayed against her chest and arms, and she heard herself wailing, trapped inside the storm. The Jeep's tires rasped against the hard winter soil, unable to find purchase.

Somewhere both nearby and very far away, tiny explosions slapped at the darkness—were those gunshots? Annie tried to look around, tried to see what was going on, but her eyes were filled with red. Beside her, Mom screamed again, a bright, horrible noise that split the night into a million pieces before being cut painfully, wretchedly short.

That was when the darkness inside Annie's head took her, and nothing hurt anymore.

For a little while.

When she came to, she could smell gasoline staining the air, drip-drip-dripping out of the car, slithering up her nostrils. She blinked and blinked: her eyes burned bitterly, that red curtain still pulled obstinately across her field of vision. She wiped at her face with shaking hands, clumsily trying to push the blood away. Every window in the Jeep was shattered or smashed out, and through the cracked windshield, Annie could see smoke leaking up from underneath the crumpled, gore-covered hood. It looked like they'd run over a waterbed filled with blood and just kept going.

Behind the wheel, Mom was still. Her head had smacked the steering wheel in the crash, opening up a deep red frown in her forehead. Blood ran down the side of her face and soaked into her clothes. The look on her face was horrible, wide-eyed, open-mouthed. She'd died screaming. Beside her, the driver's-side window was gone.

A chill wind blew through the Jeep, and for a moment, Annie thought she could hear a whispering on the breeze, a kind of soft, nauseating *SssUusSuSuss* that corkscrewed something awful inside the base of her skull, made her feel like she was going to throw up. Through the bright electric spiderweb of the shattered windshield, Annie saw something—slight and misshapen with glowing white eyes—shift and move atop the edge of the ravine.

Fear thundered in her heart anew, but she blinked and the shape was gone, just another shadow in a valley flooded with them.

Annie was alone.

She released the seat belt that still somehow held her in place, and it snapped away from her, lashing like a cobra as it spooled back into its mechanism. Looking down, she saw that the gun was still in Mom's grasp. Annie's wounded hands shook as she peeled her mother's fingers away from the grip. It was still warm from her skin. Holding the big revolver in one small hand, Annie tried the door handle next, but the door wouldn't budge. It had fused shut in the crash.

Forcing back a fresh surge of tears, Annie looked around the interior of the wrecked Jeep. The window in the hatchback had been blown out like the others, leaving only a ragged hole behind, ringed in pulverized safety glass. Maybe she could squeeze through that? On shaky limbs, she began crawling over the seats.

She tossed Mom's gun out first, then climbed after it, tumbling head over heels through the broken window until her sneakers crunched on dirt and pebbled glass. Half-blind in the dark, Annie searched the cold winter ground for the awkward shape of the pistol. Taking it in both hands, she held it close to her chest like a rosary, clutching tightly onto the last bit of warmth her mom had left in this world as she stumbled away from the ditch. All around her, the valley was silent and still.

Numbly, she walked back to the dirt road and followed the slope down to where the wheel ruts met asphalt and kept on going. After a while, she saw headlights in the distance, and she began to run.

I

*Outer
Darkness*

1

She ran.

Shotgun slung over her back, lock-top bank bag weighing down her shoulder, Anne sprinted down the alley behind the First Durango Savings and Loan, feeling the cold November air slash at her lungs and arms. Inside the confines of her rubber mask, she could still smell the gunfire and the blood and the panic sweat like they were being pumped straight into her nostrils. Steam clouded her face with every breath, suffocating. With her free hand, she tore the mask from her head and threw it into the nearest dumpster. Stupid fucking clown face. She kept running.

In the distance behind her, she could still hear the bank's alarm wailing against the gray morning, but it sounded like the shooting might have stopped for the time being.

She didn't know who killed that first guard, didn't see where the shot had come from or who'd pulled the trigger. All she knew was that one second everything was going according to plan, and the next, a bullet had obliterated the guy's face, reducing it to a messy blur of blood and bone. Anne didn't even register the sound of the gunshot until it was way too late to do anything about it.

That was when everyone started screaming and running. In the fray that followed, a couple of the other guards managed to snatch their guns back, then started blasting the place up like it was the O.K. Corral. Everything fell apart in fast-forward.

Merrill had been the next to die—one of the guards put three slugs in his front when he wasn't looking. He'd dropped to his knees, groaning and pawing at his chest as it seeped blood, uncomprehending. A fourth bullet deleted most of his head a moment later, and just like that, poof, no more Merrill. Like the world's most fucked-up magic trick.

Anne's brain went into full panic mode after that, a starving rat locked in a tiny cage as the bank turned into an abattoir, a hole in the world filled with dead people. Jessup started shooting. Travis started shooting. Anne started shooting. People ran for their lives. Somebody pulled the fire alarm. Beyond the marble walls of the bank, police sirens started to swell. How the fuck had the cops shown up so fast?

At least Anne hadn't killed anyone in there. Her pistol, a Glock 17, hadn't even cleared the waistband of her jeans, and she'd only used the twelve-gauge to buy herself some space, keeping the other guards where they were long enough for her to grab the bag and get out. But for a fleeting second, she entertained the possibility that maybe—just maybe—she'd been the one to shoot the first guard. All it would have taken was a misplaced ounce of pressure on the trigger, the tiniest lapse in attention and the slightest jerk of her finger. Was it possible? Sure, anything was possible. But had she done it?

No. She told herself no. Despite the unholy fucking mess that first bullet had left the guard's head in, it was clean and sterile, nearly hospital quality, compared to what her shotgun, a weathered but well-cared-for Remington 870, would have done. If she'd made a mistake, if her finger had slipped, the twelve-gauge would have turned his skull into a fucking salad bowl, a moon crater filled with blood and flecks of bone.

Somewhere not too far from where she stood, helicopter blades thumped at the air. She turned her face upward, searching the drab, cloud-scraped sky for the shape of the police chopper, but she couldn't see anything. Yet.

She kept moving.

Following her mental map away from the bank, Anne cut through the alleys that lay beyond, switching back and forth again and again, making herself hard to follow. They'd gone over this part a dozen times or more: half a mile away from the Savings and Loan, idling at the edge of a lonely little parking lot behind a derelict 7-Eleven, Joanie, their driver, would wait for them in an unmarked van with the doors unlocked. Once they were all in, she'd hit the road, driving the speed limit out of town, and then they'd just keep going until the Durango PD was little more than another shitty memory.

Except, when Anne stepped free of the last alley into the desolate old lot, there was nothing there. No one. Nothing. Not even an oil spot on the asphalt.

The van was gone.

The plan was simple, as far as bank robberies went. At 10:15 a.m. Mountain Standard Time, Anne, Jessup, Merrill, Travis, and Gemma would enter the front doors of the First Durango Savings and Loan wearing masks, carrying guns. Merrill would hit every security cam in the lobby with a burst of black spray paint, then he and Anne would run crowd control while Jessup, ever the showman, calmly addressed the tellers and patrons. Standard line, really: nobody moves, nobody gets hurt. Everybody knew the deal.

After that, Anne would hang in the lobby with Jess and Merrill while Trav and Gem took the bank manager back to unlock the vault, where they'd drill open a few choice safe-deposit boxes and relieve them of their contents. Back in the lobby, Cathy, their insider, would play good hostage, emptying the bait cash from the teller drawers into pillowcases and setting a good example so her clueless coworkers would stay on the straight and narrow until it was over. There was no keeping the alarms from getting tripped, but as always, Jessup had done his homework: response times for high-priority emergency calls in the city of Durango averaged about eleven minutes, give or take. As long as everything went according to plan, they'd have the job done in five.

By 10:20, they'd all be hell and gone again, and a whole lot richer than they'd been an hour before. A clean operation—no fuss, no muss. And for a couple of minutes there, yeah, it was all going exactly how it was supposed to. The machine was running as intended.

But then someone did the stupidest thing possible and killed one of the security guards.

A cold spike punched through Anne's middle as she stood there at the edge of the parking lot, grasping at mental straws, trying to slow her racing thoughts.

Why the fuck was the van gone?

Joanie Perez was a seasoned driver who'd been running with them for most of a year and a half. She'd proven her skills time and time again—she could drive with the best of them, but maybe more importantly, Joanie was steady. Reliable. She didn't spook easy, and she didn't make last-minute decisions if she could help it. There was no way in hell she'd have left Anne and everyone else behind to get eaten by the cops.

Not unless she thought they were all dead.

Fury and confusion boiled inside Anne's skull. It wasn't supposed to be like this. They had a plan in place to keep this kind of shit from happening. Everything was going so fucking wrong.

But standing here like an asshole, wishing Joanie wasn't gone didn't make it so. Anne was on her own, and she had to keep pivoting. That was the only way she was going to stay alive now.

She'd ridden into town with Jessup in his robin's-egg-blue Oldsmobile Ninety-Eight, a full-on land yacht straight out of 1970 that, for whatever reason, he prized more than just about anything else in the world. It was a brutal old luxury beast, a Sherman tank in automobile form with whitewall tires around bare black wheel hubs instead of hubcaps because, in Jessup's words, it looked mean. Anne and Jess had stashed the sedan in a dark, lonely side alley where it could go unnoticed for a couple of days, until Jess came back to pick it up. Anne cross-referenced her mental map again: unless she was totally turned around, it was only a few blocks away.

She could probably make it. But she had to move—now.

Keeping to the alleyways and side streets, Anne retraced her steps from the empty lot, moving as fast as she could without drawing too much attention to herself. Thanks to the mask, nobody inside the bank had seen her face, and she was pretty sure she hadn't gotten any blood on her, but the Remington across her back would definitely raise questions, even in southern Colorado. People tended to notice people wandering around carrying shotguns and bank bags full of cash. She kept the Remington slung over one shoulder, gripping it by its stock so it sat along the line of her arm. It wouldn't hold up to scrutiny, but it might buy her a second or two's head start if anybody clocked her.

She forced her breathing to slow, trying to get her pulse back under control as she went. Panic wasn't useful now. She had to stay clearheaded. So she walked instead of running, and as she did, she went through the list of her people, trying to take stock of what she knew and what she didn't, who was alive and who wasn't.

Jessup. Travis. Merrill. Gemma. Joanie. Cathy. Iris.

Me.

She herself was alive; she knew that much for sure. And since Joanie and the van were both missing in action, odds were good that she'd gotten away—no way the cops would have had time to tow the Caravan if they'd pinched her after things went south. Fair shot that Iris was probably safe, too; as their resident fixer, Iris Bulauer could get her hands on anything—guns, burner phones, extra muscle, whatever—any day, any time, faster and more reliable than DoorDash. But she never got her hands dirty with the actual work if she could help it. She operated behind the scenes and made sure everything went according to plan. She'd also been married to Travis, Jessup's second-in-command, for basically ever.

Setting Iris aside, Anne turned her thoughts to the others—Jessup, the closest thing to a leader that their crew had, had been in the lobby with her when the shooting started. He'd put down the guard that killed Merrill, but after that, things got blurry. She hoped to hell that Jess had made it out okay. He was a good boss. A good friend.

So who did that leave? Travis and Gemma had taken the bank manager back to the vault, but as soon as that first shot rang out, Travis had reappeared, gun in hand, another magic trick, ready to rain hell down on anyone unlucky enough to get in his way. As for Gem, she was long gone by the time Anne got out. Vanished into thin air. It made sense: Gemma Poe had always been a survivor. Probably cut and ran the second the alarm started howling.

As for the dead? Well, there was Merrill. No question about that.

But had she seen anyone else get dropped? She couldn't be sure. She thought she might have heard Cathy scream as she ran for the door, which made her feel like shit. Last she'd seen of the woman, she was hiding under one of the teller stations, eyes glazed and blank, hands shaking uncontrollably. Shock. Anne wasn't exactly surprised. Cathy Sleator was a civilian, a woman Jessup had met at a bar and prized open with charm and tequila and promises of a hefty cut of the take once everything was said and done. She'd never fired a gun in her life, let alone had to keep her head down and shit together as people died all around her. She'd just wanted to get back at her boss, some pencil-mustached little creep with a wandering eye who kept cutting her hours. They'd promised her this was going to be an easy job, five minutes in and out, clean as a whistle. Not a drop of blood shed.

Now look what had gone and happened.

Anne had tried to drag Cathy out of the bank when she finally cut and ran, but the woman wouldn't budge from her hiding spot. So she left her there. Anne wasn't about to risk her own neck trying to save someone who didn't want to be saved. Maybe Cath had made it out all right, but maybe not. Anne couldn't get her hopes up about it. Not now. Not while there were so many chainsaws left in the air that needed juggling.

Between buildings and down alleyways she moved, staying as far away from the main streets as she could. She moved silently, ducking from shadow to shadow, her shoulder groaning from the sheer weight of the bank bag in her fist. She couldn't lug this shit much farther, but if she was remembering right, Jessup's Olds was right around the next corner. Up ahead of her, a shot rang out— POW! Acting on instinct, Anne pressed herself against the nearest wall and inched her way down to the alley break, spine tight against the cool brick.

Holding her breath, Anne peeked into the alley. The Oldsmobile was parked halfway down—with a pair of uniformed Durango PD officers standing beside it, one old, one young, both with service weapons drawn. Jessup was on the ground in front of them, slumped awkwardly against the front wheel of the Ninety-Eight, his long black hair pooling around his shoulders like an oil spill. He was bleeding, too. A red lake burbled out from underneath his body and spread across the asphalt.

Anne stood there and blew air through her nostrils in a slow stream. Considered her next move. The world was falling apart. Jessup was hurt, maybe even dying. She didn't have a lot of options here, and they all seemed to end with her going through these cops one way or another. Great. That was just great.

Anne adjusted the weight of the shotgun over her shoulder and drew the Glock from her belt. Then she was moving up the alleyway toward the cops and Jess. She didn't slow as she approached, didn't bother hiding her footsteps or the guns or the heavy canvas bag bursting with cash, none of that. She was out of time to waste. Whatever she'd stumbled on to here, it ended now.

The younger cop—average height, pasty-white with dark hair, only a few years younger than Anne herself—saw her coming, but he was too slow, too green, too nervous. He froze. Sucked for him.

Wordlessly, Anne brought the nine millimeter up and pulled the trigger. The older cop never even saw it coming.

The Glock kicked in her fist, and the old cop's right knee exploded into a bright red bloom that went splattering across the blacktop. Screaming through bared teeth, he toppled over, clutching at his ruined leg with both hands. The fool wasn't ever going to go tap dancing again, but he'd live.

Another shot rang out, and Anne heard a stray bullet spang off the brick wall at her back. The young cop had found his courage, after all. Twisting in place, she zeroed the Glock dead at the kid's brainpan, hand steady. Plenty of better folks than him had taken a shot at her before without walking away. Shithead was bullying a dragon and didn't even realize. She glanced down at the police-issue SIG in his shaking hands.

"Put it down," she said. "Now."

Panic washed over the young cop's face as he realized the world of shit he'd found himself in.

"Won't tell you again," Anne said.

Anne saw the gears of internal calculus turning behind the kid's eyes. He knew how this was going to go now. Same way things like this always went. He dropped his gun.

Good boy.

"Kick it away," Anne said, then nodded to his partner, pain-blind and bleeding. "His, too."

The young cop did as he was told. Anne gestured to the ground with her pistol.

"Down. Now. Cuff your hands behind your back. Tight."

It took the guy some doing, but he managed it after a second, freeing the silver handcuffs from his belt and click-clacking them tight around his wrists without looking. Beside him, the older cop was still wheezing and whining like a dog that had been run over by a truck as he clutched desperately at his shot knee. Blood gushed freely between his fingers and pooled on the ground underneath him.

"You're Heller, right?" the old cop groaned. A thick cord of drool ran down his chin from his frenzied panting. "Right? Anne Heller?"

Anne felt her face go hot and red at her name. The cop showed her a mouthful of crooked yellow teeth. The calm in his voice was a put-on, a performance forced through the pain, but the grinning cruelty of it all was real. "Somebody dimed you out. You, and Lees here"—he kicked at Jessup's feet with his good leg—"and all the rest of your shitbag friends."

Anne studied him, searching his face for a quaver or a twitch, some tell that he was bluffing. Normally, she would have written it off as standard-issue cop bullshit, but he knew her name. Between that and the way all those sirens had shown up so quickly back at the bank . . .

Tumblers and gears clicked into place inside her head. Yeah, okay. Shit. Someone had tipped the cops off and kicked the plan to hell. Somebody had fucked them. Maybe it wasn't such a bad thing that Joanie had taken off and left everybody behind.

She knelt in front of the old cop. Tucked the muzzle of her Glock underneath his jaw.

"Who?" she asked, her voice soft, almost gentle. "Who called it in?"

The cop's smile grew like a cancer. "Fuck yourself," he said. "Even if they told me, which they didn't, you think I'd tell a thieving, murdering piece of shit like you?"

Anne stared knives at him, but she didn't move, didn't say anything else. Trying to reason with a cop was like trying to argue with a drunk hog. She was just wasting time now. Her hand tightened around the Glock's grip and she swung her arm like a rat trap, bricking the ceramic-and-steel pistol's broadside into the cop's face with a flat, meaty CRUNCH. His head snapped to the side, and he dropped.

Down on the street, more black-and-whites screamed past the alley, barreling toward the Savings and Loan. No doubt the first responders had made their way inside by now, so it wouldn't be long until they turned their attentions outward, searching for the remaining perpetrators. Which meant she only had a couple of minutes, max.

Anne went to Jessup and jostled the side of his head, patting one unshaven cheek hard enough to land like a light slap. Nothing. She pulled his hands away from his belly, revealing the wellspring of blood beneath, bubbling out from a little black poke-hole in the center, just above his navel. This close up, she could see that he hadn't just been shot the once—there was a second bleeding hole high up in his shoulder. Except she'd only heard one shot. Which meant the other had to have happened back at the bank. Fuck. She didn't have time to think about it right now. Jess's keys were on the ground beside him, slowly being swallowed by the blood pumping out of his body. She didn't know where his gun was. She patted his face again.

"Jess? Jess, wake up. Come on, it's me," she said. He didn't stir.

She laid two fingers along the side of Jess's cold, clammy throat, searching for a pulse. It was faint, but it was there. She plucked his keys off the ground and went to unlock the Ninety-Eight. Snaking an arm under both Jessup's armpits, she dragged him over and eased him into the back seat, feeling his blood leach into her clothes, hot and sticky. Once she got him situated, she covered him with a battered old squall jacket she found stuffed in the footwell, its navy blue long faded. It wasn't exactly great camouflage, but it would probably hold up enough if they passed by a highway cop. And if they got pulled over? Well. She'd deal with that if and when it happened.

Her gaze went back to the two cops on the asphalt. She still had questions, and plenty of them. Between his obvious attitude problems and shot-up knee, the older one wasn't going to be much help, but could be the kid knew something about something. Maybe he'd even overheard a name during the buildup to the total fuck show that this day had turned into. At the very least, he'd make a decent insurance policy if push came to shove. She knelt next to him and pressed her gun against his neck.

"Up," she said.

Wordlessly, the guy rose. Anne led him to the back of the Olds, popped the trunk, then cracked him in the back of the skull with the Glock, just once. He made a weak coughing sound, then fell forward into the waiting trunk beside the spare gas cans and didn't move again. After moving the two heavy fuel jugs behind the passenger seat—no way in hell was she about to deal with that cop spilling gasoline all over the interior of Jess's car in some misguided escape attempt—Anne circled back around and slipped the handcuff keys off the kid's belt, then clapped the trunk shut and headed for the driver's-side door. In the back seat, Jessup recoiled from the noxious stench of the gasoline next to his face, then moaned softly underneath the ruddy jacket and went horribly still. Anne hoped he wasn't dead. She really hoped he wasn't dead.

Wiping Jess's blood from the teeth of the car key, she slid it into the ignition and cranked it. Under the hood, the engine roared like some caged beast. Sitting low behind the wheel, Anne glanced over her shoulders, checked her mirrors, then dropped the Ninety-Eight into drive and let it roll out of the alley without touching the gas pedal. She hung a left at the next street, heading northeast, away from the bank and the city center and every cop in the entire goddamn world.

She didn't know where she was going, because if someone had talked, she sure as shit couldn't go back to the safe house. Badges were probably watching it with eyes peeled. Same went for her apartment and everybody else's, too. Everything was compromised. Nowhere was safe. That went double now that she'd kidnapped one of Durango PD's finest and used a nine-mil slug to kneecap another.

The cops would be watching the highways, but maybe they hadn't clamped down on the side roads just yet. Could be they were still looking for a busted old van. If she was lucky, she could get out of town while the cops were looking the other way. Out of town was a good start. She'd figure the rest out after that. She'd come this far. She thought she could probably go a little further.

2

She drove home.

She didn't know what else to do, didn't know where else to go, so she made for the valley. Through the rocks and trees and mountains along Highway 160, she drove them east past Chimney Rock, through Pagosa Springs into Del Norte and the eastern border of the San Luis Valley, some eight thousand square miles of rough, ancient terrain underneath a sky so big it was like it had been ripped open by some cataclysmic explosion.

In the daylight, the valley was beautiful: stark and sprawling, painted in deep greens and rich browns, its brushstroke hills and knifepoint peaks slashed this way and that above a wide-open expanse dotted with farmland, tiny towns, and dead, bone-dry gulches. Telephone lines and highways crisscrossed the countryside in sporadic intervals, darting between the quavering orange lights of the lonely, tree-buffeted homesteads that stood resolutely against the grassy, windswept vistas. The weather could turn on a dime here, bounded between the serrated Sangre de Cristo Mountains on the east and the rolling San Juans to the west, a perfect basin of endless sunlight punctuated by the punishing thunderstorms and snowfall that blanketed the full of the land when they came—which they always did.

At night, the San Luis Valley might as well have been the dark side of the moon, all shadows and sawtooth edges raking at the infinite sky above, like ink spilled across dark velvet in an uneven zigzag pattern. You could *feel* the sunset coming on out here, out where the people weren't; it clawed at the skylines, ripping away the day until the night was everything, the night was all. Its totality reduced the valley and all its geologically primitive beauty to a memory of a memory, a lacuna where the ground used to be, with only the legions of stars that twinkled distantly overhead left to show which way was *up*.

Webbed with secluded county roads and ill-kept dirt lanes, the landscape was primarily divided along its highway lines, the 285 and the 17 running north to south, and the 160 and the 112 cutting east to west. North of the New Mexico border, there were only a few ways in and out of the valley itself—through Saguache and Villa Grove up north, Del Norte to the west, or Fort Garland to the southeast, just beyond Blanca Peak's massive, imposing shape. That was it. Four routes in and out of an area that was bigger than the states of Connecticut, Delaware, and Rhode Island combined. It left the valley's sheer enormity feeling somehow both perfectly isolated and like you were never entirely alone—as if there was always someone watching you from afar, just out of sight.

Anne's apartment was in Pecos, a modest little burg nestled at the far southeastern corner of the valley, and as she'd burned hell out of Durango, she'd momentarily entertained the idea of heading that way, despite knowing that was about the dumbest choice she could possibly make. If the cops knew her name, doubtless they'd have eyes on her place by now. Probably they were watching the whole town, just in case she tried to sneak in the back way or some shit.

No, heading down to Pecos was off the table for now. Maybe forever. She didn't know yet. It wouldn't be the first place in the valley she'd turned her back on for good.

White-knuckled around the wheel of the Ninety-Eight, she toed the gas pedal deeper as they raced east along the blacktop, urging the heavy old beast's speedometer north of seventy. She pulled her burner phone from her pocket and checked the screen: *No Service*. Not like she'd really expected any different. Even in the little towns like Hooper and La Jara that dotted the valley's grassy sprawl, cell service was spotty at best. Out here in the reach? Forget about it. She tossed the cell onto the seat beside her and locked both hands around the steering wheel again.

In the rearview mirror, beyond the mountains and low hills, Anne watched the sun dip closer and closer to the horizon, staining the sky a brilliant purple-orange as afternoon shifted into evening. It was going to be dark soon. She checked over her shoulder—Jessup was still asleep in the back seat, his chest softly swelling and falling with each rickety breath. Blood pooled in the royal-blue upholstery beneath him and went streaming down the vinyl trim in thick, dark stripes. He was going to need some kind of medical attention soon if he was going to last much longer. Gunshot wounds were not to be fucked with, even if by some miracle the bullets hadn't clipped anything vital.

Without thinking, she checked her cell again. Still nothing. Not exactly a shock. Just ahead, she could see a little one-pump gas station sitting along the side of the highway, rendered in chipped stucco and peeling white paint. Windows dark. No cars in the parking lot. The place was abandoned. But maybe there was a pay phone. She checked her mirrors again, scanning the horizons for the telltale beetle-shapes of other cars, but there was nothing. Just more lonely highway slicing through scrubby plains underneath a gray-smudge sky. Anne toed down the brake and popped her turn signal on.

Out front, the station's lone pump sat beneath the flickering, half-blown lights of the old, corrugated awning, its little digital readout glowing resolutely through the patchwork scratchiti marring its plastic screen: WEED WOLF, LECK, GET FUCKED. Anne rolled past it and parked the Olds around the side of the station next to a pair of rusted-out old dumpsters. Sitting behind the wheel, she checked the station's corners for security cameras, but of course there were none. She glanced over her shoulders again: no one on the highway, no one cresting the horizons. Nobody around for miles. Idling beside the little station house, Anne flipped on the car radio and turned the knob back and forth until she hit a news station. A woman's voice said:

"Details are still emerging about the bloody bank robbery in downtown Durango earlier today that left seven dead, with one Durango police officer in critical condition and another one missing. In a press conference just minutes ago, Police Chief Melissa Graves had this to say . . ."

Sneering, Anne snapped the radio off again. She didn't need to hear the cops' side of the story to know how fucked things had gotten. She cut the Ninety-Eight's engine, dug a handful of quarters out of the ashtray, and stepped out of the car, burner in hand. Her body groaned in protest. She'd been sitting in the aftermath of her adrenaline dump for too long. She twisted back and forth, trying to stretch some of the stiffness out, but it was futile.

Halfway down the building, a lone pay phone was bolted to the stucco, white on blue on gray, covered with trash, ancient wads of gum, more graffiti. WEED WOLF, whoever they were, had been here, too, etching their nom de guerre into the damaged metal housing with a nail or the point of a pocketknife, just below the words *THERE IS STILL SOME DIGNITY LEFT TO LOSE* scrawled in looping silver Sharpie. On the outside of the little cubby, someone had pasted a Missing Persons poster, requesting any information on Dean Garritsen, who'd apparently gone missing from Alamosa back in June. There was a photo of the guy at the top; he was a good-looking kid, but good-looking wasn't nearly the safety net most people thought it was. Especially not down here, where it seemed like sometimes the ground just came alive and ate people up. Whenever it happened, the authorities would always trot out the same tired explanations—the missing got lost camping or hiking and never made it out; they were attacked by wild animals; they fell in with one of the many fringe religious groups up in Crestone and just left their old lives behind. Anne didn't doubt that those stories were true sometimes, but she knew better than most the bigger point that the official accounts tried so hard to ignore:

The valley was a hungry place. And it had plenty of teeth to go around if you weren't careful.

Standing in front of the phone, she rubbed at her face with open hands, pressing the knotty, purple-bubble-gum scars on her palms against her eyes until starbursts lit up behind the lids. She'd had those scars since she was a little kid, a grotesque memento from some ill-fated adventure that she couldn't remember anymore. Thick and knurled, they covered the majority of her palms like spills of India ink, impossible to miss. She'd been so ashamed of them when she was a kid. As a teenager, she'd taken to wearing long, Victorian-style riding gloves to try to hide them away, but that had just earned her the high-school nickname "that girl who wears the gloves," shunned by everybody but the friendly goth kids and the one Mormon girl in her class who once confessed to Anne a quiet-yet-fervent conviction that everyone on earth was trapped in outer darkness, her church's version of hell. As she'd gotten older, the scars had gotten less important, less embarrassing, or maybe she'd just made her peace with them. They'd always been there, they'd always be there. That was really all there was to it.

Shaking off the memories, she clapped her quarters down on the metal shelf next to a beer bottle and a torn condom wrapper, then clicked her cell to life. She navigated over to CONTACTS, and the seven phone numbers stored there, nameless. She deleted Merrill's and Jessup's numbers straight off. That left five. She dropped a pair of coins into the pay phone's slot and dialed the first—straight to voicemail. She killed the call, fed the phone another pair of quarters, and punched in the next number. Second verse, same as the first. She dialed, and she dialed, and she watched her coins dwindle away two by two by two as generic robot voices told her to *leave a message after the tone.* Then there was just one number left.

She dropped her last two quarters into the pay phone and slowly dialed the last number on the list, the direct line to Travis's burner. It rang once, twice, three times. He wasn't going to answer. He wasn't going to fucking answer. Shit. *Shit.* He wasn't—

Click.

"Hello?"

Relief crashed through Anne's body in a wave. Someone else had made it out. Thank fuck.

"Trav, it's me," she said.

A pause, then: "Hell's Bells, Jesus. Where are you?"

Anne bristled. *Hell's Bells.* She hated that nickname, but she bit back her frustration. They were alive. That was what mattered.

She searched the countryside for a street sign or some identifying landmark, but there wasn't anything. Just long, empty country roads and dead, dry grass underneath cat's cradle power lines.

"On the road," she said. "Few hours east. You?"

"Safe. Anybody else with you?"

"Jessup," Anne said.

There was a pause on the other end of the line that Anne didn't like.

"Good, yeah, good," Travis said a second later. "You hurt?"

"No. Ran into a couple of badges on the way out. Dealt with them."

"You dead 'em?"

Anne took a breath and considered all the bad it would do, telling Trav that she'd kidnapped a cop.

"Nah. Kneecapped one. You run into any problems?"

"I mean, yeah. Had to shoot my way out. Few of the bank guards got in my way, one civilian. Typical good guy with a gun. Did what I had to, and I'm for damn sure not losing any sleep over it." Trav paused. "What about Jessup James? He make it out okay? Lost track of him in the fuckaroo."

Jessup James. Travis and his cutesy fucking nicknames.

Stop it. Breathe. Focus on what's important.

Turning back to glance at the Ninety-Eight, Anne rubbed at her eyes with her free hand. Her first impulse was to tell Trav the truth, that Jess was in shit-poor shape after getting shot not just once but twice, but she held back. There was something in Trav's voice that was setting her off-balance, some edgy lilt that hadn't been there before, a little too eager, a little too nervous. Trav had been peachy keen, sounding like he was talking about Sunday brunch instead of a bank robbery that had gone all to shit until he'd brought up Jess. Something was definitely off here.

"He's fine," she lied. "Fuck happened to you, anyway? I thought the plan was to meet back at the van, wasn't it? But then everything went to shit, and Joanie was gone by the time I got to the lot."

"Plans always go to shit," Travis said. "That's what plans do. Fuck d'you expect, Heller? I mean, come on. I know strategy isn't exactly your thing, but at least try and keep up, huh?"

Anger pulsed hot and shaky behind Anne's face as the cold wind lashed at her. On the very fucking short list of people she had to justify herself to, Travis Cade was not. She didn't report to him. She was alive, and Jess was too, at least for the time being, and despite everything else, she'd somehow managed to not bring any more murder charges down on their heads. What the hell else did he want from her?

"Look, fuck it," Travis said a second later, exasperated. "Whatever. It's fine. We're all alive, nobody's pinched, and we walked away richer, didn't we? That's what counts."

"Not all," Anne corrected him. "Merrill got it. Back at the bank. One of the guards popped him when everything started falling apart."

"Right, no, yeah, I saw that," Travis said. "Shit roll. Merrill was a good guy."

He wasn't wrong—Merrill had been working with Jessup for a couple of years now, and despite what he did for a living, he was sweet. Soft-spoken, sensitive, kind, he'd never killed anybody in his life, and he definitely didn't deserve to die like he did. He didn't deserve to die at all.

On the other end of the line, she could hear Travis sucking his teeth.

"Look, I don't want to be indelicate here, but did you see what happened to the bag from the vault? We only made it out with the take from the teller drawers," he said.

"Yeah, I got it with me," Anne said. She looked back at the Olds again. "Grabbed it on my way out. Safe and sound."

"That's great," Travis said. "I'm really glad to hear it. Thank you."

"Mmm. Who's *we*?"

"What?"

"You said, *We only made it out with the take from the teller drawers. We*," she emphasized. "Who else is with you?"

"Iris, Joanie. A couple of hired guns Iris knows, folks we can trust. They're watching our backs until all this shit blows over."

"Where?"

"Safe house," Travis said, a little too quick. "New place, somewhere nobody's going to come looking."

"Great. The hell happened to Joanie, anyway? When I got to the pickup spot, she was long gone. Van, too. So what the fuck?"

"Yeah, she told me she had to scramble. Guess the cops were sniffing around a bit too close for comfort."

"Shit. What about Gemma? Cathy?"

"Gem's in the wind, far as I can tell. No word from her, but there's nothing about her on the news yet, so that's reason to hope, I s'pose. I'm, ah, I'm not sure about Cath, though. Didn't see."

Nerves fizzed at the base of Anne's skull as memories of how she'd tried to pull Cathy screaming and crying from her hiding place materialized in her mind's eye. She felt like such an asshole for leaving the woman behind, but there was no world in which Anne was going to stick around and wait to get pinched or killed on her account, either.

She drummed her fingertips against the pay phone's metal casing.

"Listen, Trav, you hear anything about a tip-off?"

For a second, Travis went quiet. "What?"

"A tip-off," Anne repeated. "Cops I ran into, one of them said somebody dimed us out."

"Huh. I mean, probably bullshit, right? Cops love to talk."

"Doubt it. They knew my name, man. Jessup's, too. That sound like bullshit to you?"

On the other end of the line, Travis sighed. "Look, I don't know anything. All right? Just that shit went south and now we have to deal with it. Merrill's gone, probably Cathy, too. So with Jess shot and you on the fucking lam, our options are looking a little—"

Wait.

"Trav, how'd you know Jessup got tagged?"

Travis didn't say anything for a long, empty moment. Gears turned inside Anne's head, relentless, but she resisted her better instincts and didn't hang up. The hiss of the empty line was deafening.

"What?"

Anne's fist tightened around the handset of its own accord. "I didn't say that Jessup got shot, Trav. And you told me you lost track of him in the fracas. So how'd you know?"

He wouldn't, her brain whispered at her. *Unless he's the one who pulled the trigger.* Her stomach turned at the thought. After another endless second, Travis cleared his throat and said:

"I mean, you just told me. Like a minute ago. You said, *Jessup got hit.* Come on, don't act like a fucking psycho about this."

As if she didn't know what she did or didn't say. Gaslighting prick.

"Listen, Hell's Bells, I don't know what—"

Grinding her molars, Anne clapped the handset back into the cradle hard enough to make her hand ring. It was fucking Travis. Of course it was fucking Travis. It made sense: he was a fair shot with a gun and a decent thief, but his true talent had always lain in taking advantage of chaos, kicking up dust and turning it to his benefit. Call the cops, shoot Jess plus a guard or two for good measure, then grab the loot and skip away grinning while everybody else fought it out. The whole thing reeked of Travis's bullshit, top to toes. And if Iris and Joanie were with him, it was a fair bet that they'd been in on his little side play, too. Iris was no surprise, but Joanie? Well, that one stung a little. She didn't know what Trav and Iris had promised Joan to turn traitor, but maybe a bigger cut of the take was all it took. Except whatever their big master plan was, they'd screwed up—they didn't have the take, and they'd left Anne alive.

Poor fucking them.

Her eyes drifted over to WEED WOLF again, scratched deep into the oxidized surface of the little metal cubby. Stepping back from the pay phone, she turned in a slow, graceless circle, staring out at the empty fields all around her as rage pulsed in her temples. Miles southeast, farther into the valley, she could just make out the glowing lights of a town rising against the coming night. Monte Vista, maybe.

Overhead, the clouds swirled and churned. The wind pulled at her clothes and blustered in her face as the storm that had been looming overhead for hours finally started to roll in proper. Anne's body shuddered with a sudden rush of vertigo. It felt like she was trapped on the roof of a collapsing building, feeling the floor go out from underneath her feet as the beams and bricks crumbled all around her in a shower of catastrophe and ruin. By the time the dust settled, there'd be nothing left of what had been there before, just a smoking hole in the ground where a life used to be.

That feeling got worse as she stood there, the truth sinking into her spine like some incurable disease: with Gemma missing in action and Jessup shot, probably dying, there wasn't anyone else that she could call. She was well and truly on her own now. Panic bubbled and spat inside her skull, burning oil in a searing-hot pan, but at the heart of all that noise sat a cool, calm realization: She was going to kill Travis Cade the next time she saw him. Him, and Iris, and Joanie, and whoever else had hitched their wagon to his turncoat fucking star. The decision came as easily as drawing breath, autonomic, absolute. Travis was already dead. It was just a matter of when reality caught up with him.

Beside her, the pay phone started to ring. Anne recoiled from the sound, so loud in this big, blustery emptiness, her heart suddenly beating a tarantella against her ribs. The asshole was trying to call her back. Of course.

Baring her teeth, she yanked the handset from the cradle and clapped it back down, then she did it again, and again, and again until she heard the plastic crack. Whatever it was Travis had to say to her, she didn't need to hear it. She let the broken handset hang by its wire. *THERE IS STILL SOME DIGNITY LEFT TO LOSE* stood out bright and silver on the pay phone's weathered housing.

All alone, Anne turned her face to the dead-gray sky and screamed.

3

"What was that?"

Iris Bulauer glared at her husband and laid both of her hands flat on the weathered kitchen table, feeling its scars and scratches and the places where the finish had worn thin, trying to center herself. Just like everything else in this shabby little safe house, the old table was way too beat up to be called an *antique*—time and use had done their damage, just like they always did. Nothing ever lasted. Everything fell apart eventually. On the other side of the table, Travis looked back at her, burner still in hand, dumbly confused at her anger.

"What? Call got dropped. I'll just call her back," he said.

Iris traced her fingertips over the wounds in the wood, trying to keep her breathing calm. She loved him, god knew she loved him, but Christ, he could be slow on the uptake sometimes.

"She knows, Trav."

Travis dropped the phone to the scarred-up tabletop and scoffed.

"The fuck she does. She wouldn't have called at all if that was the case."

"Not before, maybe. But now? Yeah, she knows. Hundred percent."

Travis's face wrinkled. "How do you figure? Come on, I played that shit clean. Two steps ahead at all times."

"*You just told me. Don't act like a fucking psycho*," Iris mocked. "You don't think when you talk—that's your problem. You know that, right?"

"Babe, she doesn't know, okay? I'm telling you."

"She hung up on you, Trav. That doesn't tell you something? You heard what she said. Cops talked. She knows someone dimed. And apparently, Jessup's still alive, which, wonderful, great job there, genius. What do you suppose he's going to tell her? Huh? You really think he's just going to forget you putting a bullet in his belly?"

Travis screwed his eyes up in thought. "Nah. She doesn't know anything about us for sure. Could have been anybody. Fucking *anybody*, Riss. Like, what about Gemma? She could have pulled some shit, right?"

Iris nearly laughed in his face. The only thing less likely than Anne Heller letting any of this go once she cracked it was Gemma Poe flipping on them or going to the cops. Even if they tried to sell that line to Anne, there was no way she'd ever buy it. Iris had seen the way that those two stole looks at each other when they didn't think anyone else was watching.

"No, love. Not likely. Come on, be realistic," she said, shaking her head. Who was he trying to sell this weak crap to? Her, or himself?

Travis sighed, blowing out his cheeks, making a show of it. He leaned back in his chair and ground his knuckles into his eyes. Iris shook a cigarette loose from the softpack on the table in front of her and lit it with a match, blowing smoke. Maybe the nicotine would help steady her shredded nerves.

She'd been apocalyptically pissed when Trav had walked in and announced that he'd flipped the script and put a bullet in Jessup in the fray at the bank—doubly so when he'd laughed it off, like it was some joke, no big deal. Another piece of her carefully curated plan blown to hell on a whim by her dear, impulsive husband. What was worse, as if it could have possibly gotten worse, he didn't even have the money. When she'd demanded an explanation, all he'd said was, *C'mon, babe, I saw an opportunity. What, did you want me to wait or something? I'll figure it out,* in that shitty, patronizing tone he used when he thought he knew so much better than she did. As if all of reality was nothing more than the Travis Show, and everyone else on the planet was just a side player. The only thing that had kept her from blowing up at him then and there was the thin, rotten hope that it had been a killing shot, that Jess wouldn't survive to tell the tale. Alas, no such luck.

Out in the living room, the TV blared with yet another episode of *Shark Tank*, watched mindlessly by Joanie and Caff and the rest of the guys he'd brought along with him. Iris hated *Shark Tank*. As far as she was concerned, it was everything wrong with the world wrapped up in tidy little forty-five-minute episodes, fetishizing capitalism and deifying the ultrarich to keep the underclasses dumbly loyal to a system that was rigged against them from the start. Playing by the rules only ever served the assholes who already had all the money; the only way to get what was yours in a world like this was to take it. So fuck *Shark Tank* and fuck everybody who bought into its bullshit myth. Might as well have been eating brain cancer for breakfast. But she wasn't about to ask Caff to turn it off or change the channel. He and his guys were doing them a favor, after all.

Iris and Caff went way back; he'd been the first person she'd called after the debacle because he was smart, he was efficient, and best of all, he'd work on credit. Caff had rounded up a few other guys, hard-assed ex-military types who owed him a favor or felt like his rep was enough to go on, and they'd all met up at the safe house, an anonymous ranch-style in an anonymous subdivision of an anonymous suburb. So far, the work had been easy—stupid *Shark Tank* reruns and heating frozen breakfast burritos up in the shabby old microwave—but Iris couldn't ignore the fact that Caff and his guys were working on IOUs. Sooner or later, she and Travis were going to have to deliver.

Across the table, Travis scooped up the burner and started thumbing something into the keypad. Iris raised an eyebrow.

"What are you doing?"

Travis didn't look up from the phone's screen. "I'm calling her back."

Sudden panic flared in Iris's head. *"You're—"*

A couple of Caff's guys perked up and glanced over at her outburst. Iris smiled sweetly at them and forced her voice down to a level of calm she under no circumstances actually felt.

"Trav, what the hell would you do that for?"

But Travis wasn't listening. He lifted a single condescending finger in her direction without looking. *Sorry, just one second.* It made Iris want to burn his face with the cherry of her cigarette. All this noise was his fault, after all. He was the one who'd jumped the gun back at the bank, he'd drop-kicked her plan to matchsticks. She'd done her best to let it go, move on—there was no use in fussing over what could or should have been, right?

But him acting like this right now was more than she could deal with. So, slowly, calmly, she rose from the table, then went outside to the back porch, where she sat down in the gray winter light and chain-smoked cigarettes until her hands started to go numb from the cold.

She'd get it figured out eventually. With or without Travis's help.

4

The sun set just as they rolled into town, sinking all the way past the San Juans and bathing the streets and alleys in a blood-red dusk that made Anne's skin crawl. Monte Vista was one of those spots—like so many small towns in the valley—that got a little bit haunted at night, where light and dark cascaded into each other and left everything soaking in suffocating twilight. It was a quiet place, really: one high school, two grocery stores, two pharmacies, a couple of gas stations, one veterinary clinic, and one drive-in movie theater. Boasting a population of less than four thousand, it was the kind of town where eventually you ended up getting to know everybody, if not by name, then at least enough to recognize their faces. Anne was a stranger, and with her blood-filled shirt and huge old land yacht, she was sure she'd stand out like a sore thumb.

She didn't want to be here. She didn't want to do this. But she didn't have a choice. Not if Jess was going to have any chance of making it through the night. So, nerves crackling stubbornly in the tips of her fingers, Anne carved a path through Monte Vista to the scuzzier of the two pharmacies, a run-down megamart with a flickering sign out front that read MAGGIE'S PHARM 24 HOURS. She nosed the Ninety-Eight into a spot in the far corner of the lot, back where the sallow glow from the streetlights didn't reach, back where you might not even see the car at all, unless you were really looking for it.

There was a rustle of movement from the back seat. Anne turned to look: sprawled across the bench and still bleeding, Jessup was watching her, eyes wide and glassy.

"Hey, Heller," he croaked.

"Hey yourself. How you feeling?"

"Bad," Jessup said. Then, abruptly, "It was Travis. Back at the bank. Shot the first guard, then me. Blew it all up." Wetting chapped lips with his tongue, he sucked air and let out a rough, damp cough. "Guessing he's the one that dimed us out to the cops, too. Grinning prick."

Fury pounded through Anne's brain at the mention of Trav, and she struggled to resist the overwhelming urge to put her fist through the driver's-side window.

"He'll get his," she seethed, opting to not mention the phone call and Travis's unwitting confession. At this point, it wasn't going to change anything and it certainly wasn't going to help shit. "My word on that."

In the mirror, she saw him make a face, half-amused and half-heartbroken. "Yeah, I don't doubt it. You hear from Gem yet?"

"Nah. Still radio silence," Anne said, shaking her head.

"She'll call," Jess reassured her. "You know her. She'll be fine."

Sitting in the dark, Anne felt her face grow hot, and was silently thankful that Jess couldn't see.

"Sure," she said noncommittally. "It's whatever."

"*Riiight.* Whatever you say, man. So what's the plan here?" He nodded at the pharmacy at the other end of the parking lot.

Anne's eyes darted out the windshield at the glowing MAGGIE'S PHARM 24 HOURS sign, its faded neon shining softly over the empty streets.

"No plan. Just going to go in there for a couple of things."

"Things like what?"

"Things that'll help me take a couple bullets out of someone," she said humorlessly. "You've still got the first aid kit in the glovebox, right? With the suture kit and the forceps and everything?"

Jessup groaned and wheezed. "Yeah, last I checked. But you know it's a risk, right? Going in. They're gonna . . . fuckin' . . ." He drunkenly trailed off.

Anne made a blunt *hmmnn* sound in the pit of her throat. Of course it was a risk. No shit it was a risk. But she was almost out of moves and still had to keep dancing until the music stopped.

A panicked, insistent thumping came from inside the trunk. Guess the cop had finally woken up, too. In the mirror, Jessup's eyes widened.

"The fuck is that?" he asked.

Anne studied him in the rearview, his face blanched and slick with sweat, his slender body looking more like a scarecrow with every passing minute, some gaunt burlap sack tied haphazardly into the shape of a man.

"Nothing you have to worry about," she said.

He shook his head, but didn't push it. "Okay. Whatever. Fine. Where are we, anyway?"

"Monte Vista," she said.

"Right," Jessup coughed. "And where the hell is Monte Vista?"

Anne sighed.

"San Luis Valley."

"Wait, like Pecos? We heading to your place?"

Anne shook her head. It had been awhile since she'd had anyone over to her apartment, and tonight was absolutely not the night to change that. The last time, Gem'd finally been emerging from the divorce that had been tearing her life apart for the better part of six months, and Anne, already well head over heels for her—her looks, her intelligence, the lacerating wit that she wielded like a rapier—had invited her and Jess over for celebratory drinks. Gem's ex had been a douchebag since day one, and with him out of the picture, she already seemed so much happier, the smile on her face like the sun rushing through the clouds after a thunderstorm. All Anne wanted to do was bask in the warmth of her light. Jessup, not an idiot by any measure, gathered what was going on pretty much immediately but, being a decent guy, didn't make a thing out of it.

A couple of gins turned into a couple more as they traded war stories and personal histories, and eventually, after no small amount of prodding from Gem and Jess, Anne had cracked and told them what had happened to her mom. She'd made a total mess of the story, of course—she wasn't even really sure what she believed about that night anymore. It was all so tied up in trauma and pain and childhood misunderstandings, she couldn't say for certain what was true and what she'd misremembered or dreamed up and passed off to herself as fact. But to their credit, neither Gem nor Jessup called her fucking crazy.

All in all, it had been a good night. But the good nights never lasted. Not really.

"Absolutely not," she said after another second. "Isn't safe. Gotta find somewhere else we can hole up for a while 'til shit settles down."

A dull spark lit up behind Jessup's eyes as she watched him, a new plan starting to pull itself together inside his head. He was pathological.

"I mean, if we're already in the valley, couldn't we—?"

"No," she said, cutting across him. She knew where he was going with this, and it wasn't an option. "Just no, Jess."

"What, then? You're the one that dro—" A coughing fit racked his body, damp and messy. A fresh glurge of blood spilled over his lower lip. "—drove us here," he finished, wiping at his mouth with the back of one hand.

"Not for that. Even if we did head up there, which, again, we *aren't going to fucking do*, cops're going to find it eventually. It'd give us what, a day? Maybe two?"

"As compared to what? How much time do you think we have on our side right now, exactly?"

"Nope, nonstarter. Sorry. We'll find a motel or something. Pay in cash. Pay extra, if we have to. Plenty of places around here that cater to them that don't want to be found."

"Cops'll be watching the motels, Heller. The highways and the motels and the bus stations and everywhere else. They'll check everything. You know they will. Run, hide, or fight, right?"

Run, hide, or fight, in that order. Chapter 1, verse 1 in the Book of Jessup. His golden rule to staying alive if you decided to live your life with a gun in your hand. She'd heard it a million times: you ran until you couldn't run anymore, then you hid until they found you, and when they did, you made them wish to high hell that they hadn't. They were doing the running right now. Hiding came next. She knew it as well as he did.

"We'll find something," Anne said. "Okay? Someplace they aren't watching."

"That's exactly what I'm saying."

"Jesus, Jess, can you *please* just—"

She caught herself before she snapped at him. She knew why he was asking—going to ground up at the old cabin made perfect sense, from his perspective. But he hadn't been there that night. He didn't know how bad it had really been. If he did, he wouldn't in a thousand years have dreamed of asking her to go back. So no, they weren't going up there. Better to pull a Butch and Sundance with the Colorado State Patrol and let the chips fall where they may.

In the back seat, Jessup's eyes drifted shut again, his breathing tidal and shallow. Guess that meant the conversation was over. Anne studied the pharmacy's glass front underneath its flickering yellow lights and hoped that nobody inside paid too much attention to the news. Maybe their descriptions, names, sketch artist renditions, mug shots hadn't gone wide yet. Yeah, and maybe she'd won the lottery without buying a ticket, too. One thing was for goddamn sure, things were going to get a lot worse before they got any better.

She tightened her fists around the wheel until the bones stood out through her skin, and exhaled in a slow, sharp stream. Then she killed the engine, stepped out of the car, and went to the back for the bag. Kneeling down beside the wheel well, she pulled the zipper open and, for the first time, beheld the take. If Jessup was right—and at this point, she had zero reason to doubt him—there was nearly a million and a half dollars in there. It sure felt like it; the bag had to weigh thirty pounds or more. Quickly, she grabbed a couple of crumpled hundreds, then closed the bag back up and stashed it. Sweeping the squall jacket off Jessup, she pulled it on over her bloody shirt, zipping it halfway up to hide the worst of the stains before kicking the door closed and crossing the empty lot on foot.

Inside, Maggie's Pharm was basically empty, except for the bored twentysomething wearing a dirty green smock behind the cash

register, and the middle-aged security guard who stood watch beside the sliding doors. The cashier, all tattoos and piercings under a shock of fading Oompa-Loompa-green hair, didn't look up
at Anne when she stepped inside, too distracted by her phone, but
the guard, a pornstached little freak who must have weighed a
hundred pounds soaking wet, perked up as soon as he laid eyes
on her. Was that recognition or just standard-issue rent-a-cop self-
importance? Anne couldn't tell, but then she wasn't going to stick
around long enough to find out, either.

Hunching her shoulders up around her ears, she made for the
back of the store, trying to play anonymous, just another forgetta-
ble face during another boring graveyard shift. Hopefully. Anne
wove around the overnight-inventory boxes in the dusty, high-
shelved aisles and paused to scan the hanging directory for *First
Aid*. Aisle 2. Other side of the store.

She turned a corner and looked behind her and felt a flood of
panic spiders go scrabbling up the back of her neck. The musta-
chioed security guard was trailing her at a medium distance, pretending to examine something on one of the endcaps, probably
congratulating himself for being so subtle about it: *You're a real in-
vestigator now, Jerry.* One of his hands lingered deliberately by his
hip and the semiautomatic pistol holstered there. Great. Amazing.
That was just fucking fantastic.

Automatically, her fingers went to the pull on the jacket's zipper. She didn't think any of the blood underneath was showing,
but she zipped the jacket all the way up to the pit of her throat just
in case. Probably the little wannabe wouldn't notice anything off
unless he managed to get in real close, but there was no sense in
taking any chances.

Anne turned down the next aisle, cutting a serpentine path toward
aisle 2, trying to keep space between her and the rent-a-cop. Walking
by the makeup counter, she passed a rack of cheap T-shirts—mostly
gaudy soccer-mom bullshit bedazzled with stupid crap like *Live,
Laugh, Love*, or *Oh, Look, It's Wine O'Clock*. Near the end of the rack,
she found one in her size, a pale blue V-neck with Porky Pig on
the front, *That's All, Folks!* printed in cursive above the goofy little

swine's grin. Better than nothing. She snapped it off the hanger and beelined for the restrooms.

Inside the ladies' room, fluorescent lights hummed and buzzed above a row of four stalls, all empty. A line of sinks sat opposite them, underneath a scratched old mirror that looked like it hadn't been cleaned since last year. Anne locked the door behind her, then shucked off Jessup's oversize jacket and her blood-soaked tee. She hung the jacket on the door hook, while the ruined tee went in the trash. A few dots of red had leached through the shirt to stain her sports bra, but it wasn't nearly as bad as she'd expected. She ran the faucet over a handful of paper towels and started swabbing the rusty smears from her skin. It didn't need to be perfect, just passable.

When the worst of the bloodstains were gone, she pulled the Looney Tunes shirt on, shrugged Jessup's coat back around her shoulders, and checked herself out in the mirror: not bad. Not great, but not bad. She drew her Glock from her belt and checked the breach, the sights, the magazine. She was short a round from where she'd hobbled the cop back in Durango, but she really wasn't worried about that. She still had fourteen left in the clip plus one in the pipe, and two spare magazines waiting for her in the car. She slid the gun into place at the small of her back and let Jessup's coat fall loosely over it.

Next she pulled her burner from her pocket and, switching it on, watched the display fill up with notifications: text messages from Travis, text messages from Iris and Joanie, five missed calls from numbers she didn't recognize at all. She held her thumb down on the power button until the screen went dark, then slid the battery and SIM card from the back, folded them up in a paper towel, and stomped on them until they were powder. She flushed the debris down the toilet, snapped the crappy little clamshell phone in half, tossed the pieces into the trash atop her bloody shirt, and pulled the plastic liner from the aluminum bin, meaning to knot it off and carry it out with her. No sense in leaving evidence behind.

Then someone knocked on the restroom door.

Panic jolted through Anne's body, tremulous and electric, and she froze in place. For a moment, everything reverted to its previous stillness, as if she'd simply imagined it. A heartbeat later, the knocking came again.

"Open up, ma'am," the rent-a-cop called from the other side of the door. "I know you're in there."

Anne didn't move. A second later, there was the jingle of keys and the click of metal against metal as the lock disengaged itself. The door swung open to reveal the little security guard standing in the hallway beyond, key ring in one hand, the other still resting near his gun. The name tag underneath his cheap plastic badge read *Orrin*.

"Excuse me. This is the women's room. You can't be in here," Anne said, faking outrage, faking innocence.

"Don't do that," Orrin said. Something shaky flickered in his eyes, a kind of nervous, unstable energy that Anne didn't trust. "Just don't, okay? Now step back. Back, I said."

Anne stepped back, and Orrin followed her in. The door swung shut behind him with a hollow *clunk*.

"I know you. You're all over the news," Orrin said. He gestured to the trash bag in Anne's hand. "Drop it."

Anne let the bag fall to the floor. She looked the little man up and down, trying to calculate the odds of her clearing the Glock from her waistband before Orrin drew his own iron. They weren't exactly good.

"I'm sorry, but I really don't know what you're talking about," she said.

"Yes, you do," Orrin replied. His eyes narrowed, and his fingers tightened on the butt of his pistol, but he kept it in its holster. For now. "Don't lie, okay? Just . . . don't. Put your hands up. Now."

Anne raised her hands slowly. "You're making a mistake here."

"I told you, don't do that!" Orrin snapped, the shake in his voice giving way to a shrill bark, like a scared Pomeranian. His hand twitched on the grip of his gun. "I'm not making a mistake. You're you, I know you are. I saw your face. So just . . . stop. Okay? We're going to go back to the office and we're going to call this in, and then we're going to sit tight until the police get here. Understand?"

Anne nodded. "Okay, yeah. Fine. Whatever you want. Let's just stay calm, okay? No need for this to get out of hand."

Rage bubbled in Orrin's face as he took a step closer, then another, and another, until he stood mere inches from her face.

"I—am—calm," he said. His shitty breath reeked of stale coffee and cigarettes. Sweat collected at his brow and in his armpits. Anne could tell by the way his eyelids twitched that he'd already gone full kernel panic, his system dumping adrenaline to try and stay one step ahead. He probably had some experience with that pistol of his, but Anne figured he was a weekend warrior at best, a range lizard who'd never had to put all of his so-called training to the test.

Retail guards like him—retail guards and most cops, really—typically came in two flavors: Angry and Nervous. The Angry ones were predictable, pretty much pathetic fucking white guys across the board with something to prove, living out some bullshit cowboy fantasy that made their weird little dicks feel big. Paper tiger motherfuckers. Anne knew how to deal with them. It was the Nervous types—like Orrin here—that you had to look out for. Nervous types were unpredictable, liable to make brainless, panicked decisions out of some desperate sense of self-preservation. They just wanted to live long enough to see home again and didn't particularly care who they had to shoot or choke-hold to death to get there.

Except Orrin had already tipped his hand and didn't realize it. He'd said it himself: he hadn't called the cops yet. Probably wanted to be the one security guard that proved to the world that security guards weren't a joke. Maybe looking for a way into the local PD himself. She didn't know what the little freak would do if—when—things went south here, but she knew she wasn't going to end this day arrested, and she for damn sure wasn't going to die in this stupid fucking Porky Pig shirt.

So when Orrin moved, so did she. And she was faster.

His shoulders twitched, telegraphing his draw; like clockwork, Anne stomped a foot down on the man's instep, hard. Something crunched inside his shoe.

Orrin yelped and fumbled for his gun—slapping his hand away,

Anne yanked the pistol, a cheap little Ruger, free of its holster, then smashed it into his dumb moustache.

Orrin's head snapped back; his eyes went funny. Anne hit him again, clapping the flat side of the Ruger into the man's face as hard as she could. She felt his nose pop open. A waterfall of blood erupted down his mouth and chin. She clubbed him once more, and this time he dropped, hitting the scuffed bathroom tile in an awkward heap.

Standing over the felled rent-a-cop, Anne righted his pistol in her hand and locked the slide back, kicking the chambered round free. She ejected the magazine next and slid it away with her foot as her hands worked quickly, popping the lockpin out and whisking the barrel from the grip, tearing the pistol down to its component parts in seconds, rendering it useless. She dropped the pieces of the Ruger in the bunched-up bin liner with the rest of the trash and took it with her while Orrin mewled and bled on the floor.

Back in the store proper, she jagged up aisle 2, moving fast but not running, pulling supplies off the shelves and pegboard hooks as she went: gauze, medical tape, jug-size bottles of isopropyl alcohol and hydrogen peroxide, an extra-large tube of Neosporin, a box of saltine crackers, a jar of peanut butter, and as many bottled waters as she could carry. Dropping everything in the plastic trash bag, she moved purposefully toward the pharmacy's cash registers and the sliding glass doors beyond. The cashier watched her from behind the register. The girl, with her tattoo-covered arms and metal-filled face, met Anne's gaze, defiant. Tough girl. Anne studied her expression, trying to suss out what she'd seen, what she knew, and what she only suspected. Maybe she was wondering why Orrin wasn't back yet, or maybe she was running her own mental calculus, trying to figure out how fast the cops would get here after she made the call.

Anne laid both of the crumpled hundreds from her jeans pocket on the counter between them and slid them over to the girl's side with two stiff fingers. When the girl tried to take them away, Anne held them in place.

"What are you going to tell the cops when they get here?" Anne asked.

The girl studied her face for a moment, then shook her head.

"I didn't see anything," the girl—her name tag read *Allie*—said. "I was on my phone the whole time."

"What about Orrin?"

Allie scoffed. "Orrin's a creep. He's always trying to fuck the girls that work here, bragging about his friends who were on the news like we're supposed to be impressed or something. I don't listen when he talks."

Anne smiled, despite herself. She was starting to like this girl. "This place have security cameras?"

Allie shook her head. "None that work. Manager's a cheap asshole. He told me I had to work Christmas this year," she said.

"Sounds like a real prick," Anne told her. She let the girl take the hundreds.

"Did you . . . ?" Allie's voice was a mousy squeak. Anne fixed her with a hard, questioning stare. The girl flushed a deep, embarrassed red. "Did you really do it?" she asked, finally finding her courage. "Did you really take all that money like they said?"

Anne breathed out slow. "Some of it."

She turned to leave.

"Badass," the girl said behind her.

The automatic doors slid open, and Anne stepped out into the freezing November night beyond. Her nerves thrummed like live wires under her skin. She breathed deep and exhaled in a rush, watching her breath billow and swirl in front of her face as she moved through the shadows toward the car. Thirty seconds later, she was gone.

They disappeared into the night.

Anne sank her foot deeper on the accelerator and let the highway roll them away from Monte Vista and Maggie's Pharm and Orrin the creepy incel security guard and whatever other problems still lay in wait for them. The Oldsmobile's engine rumbled and roared as they picked up speed. At the northern edge of town, she wove around a pickup truck and a busted old minivan and hurtled faster into the night, not slowing, not stopping. Nights were different out here than they were anywhere else; in cities, night was part of the natural light-dark cycle of the earth's rotation. But in the valley, night was vast and carnivorous, an infinite living blackness that could decide to chomp down and swallow you whole in an instant.

Too many mistakes. She was making too many mistakes, too many shitty decisions. But dumb mistakes and shitty decisions were all she had to work with right now. Every move was a wrong one, every choice potential suicide. There was no clean way out of this. So maybe it wasn't about making the right choices now so much as it was about making the least bad ones available, the ones that wouldn't end with them pinched or dead.

Reaching down, Anne flipped the car radio back on and surfed from station to station, trying to find something that wasn't news, Jesus-freak jabbering, or plastic country-arena-pop bullshit, trying to distract herself from the decision she knew in her heart she'd already made. Jessup was a know-it-all asshole sometimes, but he wasn't wrong. They had to stop sooner or later, and when they did, they needed somewhere safe, somewhere isolated. Somewhere they could see the cops coming from a mile off if they really had to.

After a few more seconds of fruitless channel hopping, she switched the radio off and listened to the silence. They were in the belly of the beast now, deep in the heart of night, away from the lights and the noise, out beyond the edge of forever.

Fuck.

She rolled her head back and forth from shoulder to shoulder until the joints in her neck popped. She didn't want to do this. She really didn't want to do this. But she didn't have a choice. Not anymore.

At the next intersection, she whipped the car north and stomped on the gas. She didn't need to slow down, didn't need to consult a map. She could have made the drive with the headlights off in full dark if she had to. She knew the way back.

5

Shadows loomed long across the snow-patched ground as the Ninety-Eight wound its way past the sagging fence and up the dirt road, over the hills and through the woods, deeper and deeper into the valley's ancient darkness. At the edge of the property, Anne stopped the car and cracked the window to listen: Through the emptiness and the desolation, the valley was so undeniably *alive*. All around them it buzzed with life, the clicks and chitters of insects, the scuttle of rodents across the scree and soil, the hush of the wind and the birds through the branches overhead. The valley was empty; the valley was so full.

She drove on.

The car's tires thumped over the metal grate that served as a bridge across the ravine that split the southern side of the property like a long, crooked scar. Anne kept her eyes locked straight ahead, resisting the urge to search the ground for the place where the Jeep had crashed—the place that her mom had died. She had bigger concerns right now than slaking some harebrained, fucked-up sense of nostalgia. Jessup was still bleeding out. She leaned a little heavier on the gas pedal, and the Ninety-Eight roared forward around the next switchback, tires spraying rocks as they sawed against the dirt.

The drive up north to the old property hadn't taken long, though Anne kind of wished that it had: She'd have loved a little more time to get her head around what she was about to do, where she was taking them, what she was heading back into. But maybe if she'd had more time to think about it, she would have turned around, tried to find somewhere else, anywhere else. A campground, a back road, the dirt lot of a trailhead, anything. But second thoughts were a luxury she couldn't afford anymore. Despite everything inside her screaming in protest, this place was the best option she had, and what was worse was, she knew it.

Ahead of them, the old wheel-rut road snaked around the base of one of the low hills and disappeared from view. Anne cranked the wheel as she navigated the switchbacks, left then right then left again, keeping the car steady as gravel pinged and bounced off the car's undercarriage. They were almost there now.

Despite living nearly her whole life in the valley, Anne hadn't been up to the old property since the night her mom had died. She thought she'd turned her back on it for good, left it to crumble in the past. The memories of that night were too painful, too ugly, too sad for her to want to relive. After the crash, little Annie had marched for what felt like hours through the cold, her mom's pistol in both hands, until someone had found her on the roadside and brought her back to civilization. She barely remembered the long walk or the person that had found her, small and sobbed-out in her Ninja Turtle pajamas on the roadside, but she still remembered everything that had happened at the cabin that night with perfect clarity. Every moment was burned into the surface of her brain like a ranch brand—right up until the point that she climbed out of the Jeep's blown-out back window. After that, it was as if she'd blinked and found herself in the hospital, surrounded by beeping machines and concerned-looking adults in colorful scrubs.

Eventually, the police came and told her what they knew while the doctors stood quietly by, listening with tangled expressions on their faces. They told her that her mom was dead. Anne—still *Annie* then—told them that she knew that part. They explained to her that a kindly old rancher had found her on the side of the road and brought her back to his home to sit with him and his wife until the ambulance arrived. It dawned on her then that this was the first time in her life anyone had ever spoken to her like she was a grown-up and not just some little kid. They asked her what had happened all the way out there in the dark. She didn't offer an answer because she didn't have one to give. The grown-ups asked her where the gun had come from. She told them that she didn't know. It was only half a lie. When they explained that it had most likely been a mountain lion that killed her mom, she didn't argue. She knew enough about grown-ups already to know that they wouldn't believe the truth, anyway.

The worst part, other than her mom being dead, was that her memories of life before the cabin were at best fractured, and more often than not, missing entirely. It was as if whole chunks of her life had just been deleted from her head, black holes where there should have been something. She had a vague sense of living up in the woods with her mom before the cabin, driving around the backcountry in their Jeep, the occasional nightmare of a light burning underground. But that was it. The doctors didn't seem worried at the time—she'd hit her head pretty bad in the crash, after all—but as she'd grown up, her memories of early childhood hadn't returned. They were just gone.

For two days, Annie had lain in that hospital bed, attended to by social workers and pediatric nurses and a nice lady detective who wouldn't let the other police officers talk to her unsupervised. They all told her they were trying their best, that everything was going to be okay, and Annie made noises like she believed them, even though she didn't. When she woke up on the third day, there was an old woman sitting on the side of her bed. She had gray-white hair done up in a tight curlicue perm above a pair of big Gloria Steinem glasses on a button nose. Her fingers were long and graceful, like a piano player's. She smiled when she saw Annie roll over to face her, a warm, loving expression that crinkled her eyes up at the corners. She looked familiar, but Annie didn't know why at first.

"Hi, Annie," the old woman said. "I'm your grandmother. My name's Evelyn Heller. Your mom is my—*was* my daughter."

A tangle of snakes exploded in Annie's belly. She started to bawl. Even now, twenty-five years after the fact, she remembered that sobbing fit so well that she could nearly feel it rolling her insides around like a cement mixer. Grandma had taken her home not long after that; there was no one else to volunteer, no other family, no friends, no will, nothing. Beverly Heller had died and left behind a chilly void in her place, a wound in the shape of the woman that had been there only days previous.

Growing up in Grandma's house had been all right, if strained; it quickly became clear to Annie that Mom and Grandma had never really gotten along and that it had been years since Grandma had to take care of anyone but herself. The old woman had done her best, Annie knew that, but at the end of the day, they were two strangers trying to make the best of a shitty situation neither of them had signed up for.

Once, when Annie was still little, Grandma had asked if she wanted to make the trip up to the cabin, *to pay her respects*, but even then, Annie had bucked against the notion. She was still too angry, too heartbroken, and—if she was being honest—too scared. Her nightmares were still haunted by what she'd seen up there that night, and it wasn't some dumb mountain lion. With time, those wounds, that pain, it had all scabbed over and calcified into a kind of cold aversion. As far as she was concerned, the property and the cabin had died with her mom, wiped off the face of the earth by the finger of some uncaring god in an act of backhanded mercy. But driving up the hill now, tonight, she was shocked at how fresh the hurt bristling underneath her skin felt. As if her mom had only died yesterday. As if all her scars meant nothing.

And then, just like that, there it was.

The cabin sat low and hunched underneath the looming sky, nestled in the place where the hill began to slope up toward the next plateau and the rock-laden forest and the mountains that lay beyond. Time hadn't been kind to it: Where Anne remembered safety, warmth, refuge, now stood a pile of crumbling logs and planks hanging unevenly around the doorframe like hunched shoulders astride a boxer's battered face. The cabin had taken one hell of a beating in the decades she'd been away. Anne gawped at it through the foggy windshield, trying to tell herself that it was just another safe house, a place for them to hide. Nothing more. She studied the darkness that surrounded the dumpy little lodge and for a moment thought she saw a pair of glowing white eyes slowly hinging open deep in the shadows to leer back at her.

She blinked, and they vanished.

Crossing her arms atop the steering wheel, Anne let her head fall forward, burying her face in her forearms and shutting her eyes so tight that she saw white-purple starbursts behind the lids. Just another safe house. A place to lie low until the storm blew over. That was all.

She cut the Ninety-Eight's engine and stepped out of the car, dirt crunching under her sneakers. Cold winter air raked at her arms and her face; she pulled Jessup's coat tighter around her shoulders and drew the shotgun from the footwell beside the gas cans in a loose two-handed grip, letting it sit lazily across her hips. She took a deep breath, tasting the frost and the pine on the air, savoring it, trying to anchor herself inside her own body. Then there was nothing else to do but see if the front door was locked, or if she was going to have to kick it in.

To her surprise, the knob turned easily in her hand. The cabin door swung silently open as light from the car's headlamps illuminated the motes of dust that danced inside like fireflies on the wind. Anne held her breath as she stepped through the door, walking heel to toe, keeping her steps silent as she swept the Remington from corner to corner, hunting the darkness for any sign of movement. But the cabin was grave-still. No one had been here in a very, very long time.

Anne breathed in again, deep and slow. Underneath the close, murky dust smell that seemed to emanate from every plank and board, the scent of this place was staggering in its familiarity, soft and earthy with just a hint of sweetness. It wasn't particularly impressive as far as cabins went—two bedrooms, a living room with a stone fireplace and a long box of ancient hearth matches, a kitchenette cluttered with empty cans and plastic cartons, and a single small bathroom—but standing here after all these years still punched Anne square in the heart. Memory after memory of that night lit up inside her head, unbidden. Ungently, she shoved them back into the furthest corners of her mind, where she could safely ignore them for a while longer. *Just another safe house.*

Moving quickly through the rest of the cabin, she cleared the bathroom, the closets, then the bedrooms, the blankets and sheets atop the mattresses still rumpled and tangled in disarray. Framed art prints twenty-some-odd years out of date hung on the walls above familiar furniture that Anne hadn't thought about in decades but still somehow remembered every detail of. Little plug-in space heaters stood in the corner of every room. She lingered in the doorway to the second bedroom—*her* bedroom—for a long, harrowing moment, trying to reach back in time to the girl she'd been, back before her entire life had been detonated, trying to give her some warning of all the horror and the pain and the bullshit that was waiting for her just down the road. But the past never answered when you called. That was what made it the past.

Back in the living room, Anne leaned the shotgun between the stone hearth and its fire poker, long-handled brush, and matching ash pan, then turned and saw something that she hadn't noticed before: a plain white envelope, left on the coffee table in the center of the room, caked in the dust of decades. Sweeping her fingers through the grime, Anne scooped up the envelope, angling it in the glow of the Oldsmobile's headlights so she could read the single cursive word that had been inscribed on it:

Annie.

What the actual fuck? She read the word again and again as if she were expecting it to change, say something else, but the letters stayed stubbornly in place. This hadn't been here that night. Someone had been up here since then. Someone had left this for her.

Her fingers trembled and her heart lurched as a tiny voice in the back of her mind urged, *Open it. Just open it. See what's inside. You know you want to.*

And the thing was, that voice was right. She did want to. More than just about anything, she wanted to. But she had other things she had to handle first. After all, this envelope, and whatever waited for her inside its folds, had lain here for years by now. She figured it would probably be fine waiting a little bit longer still.

Folding the envelope in half, she pocketed it and went outside to first start up the old generator with the fuel cans from the Ninety-Eight, then fetch Jessup. Her knees shook under his weight, but after a few minutes, she managed to walk him into the cabin and lay him down on the big bed in her mom's bedroom beside the heavy-duty first aid kit from the car and everything she'd taken from Maggie's Pharm. Working silently, she unwrapped everything piece by piece, sterilized it all with the isopropyl, then went digging for lead.

The bullet in his shoulder was easy; the one in his belly was harder. Jessup wouldn't stop squirming, trapped in fluttering half consciousness, whimpering and shuddering at her every touch, to the point that Anne finally had to hold him down to keep him still. Once she'd extracted both bullets, she disinfected his wounds again and stitched him up as best she could. The sutures weren't exactly hospital quality, weren't even *good* by any measure of the word, but they were probably decent enough to keep him alive for another couple of days. Just until they could get him to a doctor who wouldn't immediately call the cops.

She double-checked the bandages to make sure they would hold, then took the first aid supplies out to the living room and went back to the kitchen to grab Jess a couple of bottled waters. They were room temperature, but shit, water was water. They'd do. She left them on the bedside table next to his face so he'd see them when he woke up. Whenever that was.

The cop was next.

Glock in hand, she popped the Ninety-Eight's trunk and stood back. The cop inside looked plenty worse for wear after spending most of the day handcuffed in the trunk of a car, but beyond that, he seemed fine.

"Out," Anne said, coldly, gesturing with the pistol.

The cop didn't say anything, didn't move. He just lay there folded up and stared at her, eyes wide in the blue moonlight. Anne sighed and forced herself to not point the nine millimeter at his face.

"I didn't drive you all the way out here to kill you, if that's what you're thinking," she told him.

The cop chewed his lip, doubt scratched all over his face.

"I can leave you out here, if you want. Gonna get cold tonight, though," Anne said, annoyed. She really was trying to be as decent as she could about this, but if he wanted to be an asshole, she could play that game, too. She waited for him to move. He got there eventually.

The cop rose slowly, unsteadily, and tottered out of the trunk in a daze. Anne stayed out of reach in case he decided to try and run or make a play for her gun. He stumbled to the side, then planted his feet and craned his neck toward the sky.

"Where are we?" he asked, voice craggy.

Anne blinked at him. Didn't say anything.

The cop shook his head. "Maybe it doesn't matter," he said.

"Yeah, maybe not." She nodded toward the cabin. "Inside," she said. "Now."

She followed him at a distance, keeping the gun trained on his spine. In the living room, the cop paused and looked through the door into the big bedroom. His eyes went wide when he saw Jessup.

"Is . . . is he dead?"

"You'd better hope not," Anne said, swiping an empty orange juice jug off the kitchen counter. "Other room, come on."

She shoved him through the other doorway into the little bed-room that used to be hers. Standing beside the beaten-in twin mattress, he looked back at her; Anne pointed at the metal bed frame, then tossed the plastic jug onto the floor and passed him the handcuff keys.

"Cuff yourself to the bed, tight," she said. "Hands in front of you. I'm not coming in here to help you go to the bathroom or whatever."

"But there's not a bathroom in here," he protested.

Anne showed him a thin, joyless smile. "That's what the jug is for."

"Oh. *Oh*," the cop said, his voice heavy with understanding. "Oh, god."

He eased himself down to sit on the floor next to the bed and used the keys to pop the cuffs from around his wrists, then threaded the chain through the frame and fastened them back in place with a mechanical zipper click. Anne snapped her fingers at him.

"Kick them back. Now."

Awkwardly, the cop kicked the handcuff keys across the floor with the heel of his boot. Anne knelt and pocketed them.

"Now what?" he asked.

"Show me," Anne said.

The cop leaned back and used both arms to rattle the handcuffs hard against the metal. They were secure. He wasn't going anywhere. Good. She pitched a shoulder against the doorjamb and crossed her arms, letting the Glock dangle down by one elbow.

"What's your name?" she asked.

A defiant, angry look crawled into the cop's eyes. "Why do you care?"

"I don't," Anne said honestly. "Just trying to be polite. But we don't have to do that if you don't want to. Probably easier that way."

"You shot my partner," the cop sighed.

"Just in the knee. And for the record, you guys shot first. Remember?" She jerked her head toward the other side of the cabin, and the bedroom, and Jessup. "So as far as I'm concerned, you both got off light."

The cop's expression darkened.

"Come on, out with it," Anne said. "Unless you want me to call you *cop* for however long we've got left together."

After a second, he sighed and relented. "It's Louis," he said. "Greene. But everybody just calls me Dutch."

"Why?"

"It's what my parents called me. Same as my dad. He was Louis Greene Jr., and everybody called him Dutch, too. I guess I just inherited it."

Anne made a *hmm* sound in her throat. "Shitty inheritance."

"I guess. But it's mine, so."

"All right. Dutch. Nice to meet you." She turned and started to walk away.

"What about you?" the cop called after her.

Anne stopped. Didn't turn around. "What about me?"

"You got a name?"

"Pretty sure you already know it, right?" she said. "You and every other cop in Durango."

"I guess, yeah. But as long as we're being polite. Right?" His voice had turned soft, almost conversational. Decidedly un-cop-like. She didn't trust this prick further than she could throw him, but unarmed and handcuffed to a bed, what was he going to do?

"It's Anne," she said. "My name's Anne."

"It's nice to meet you, Anne. You been doing this long?"

"Are you interrogating me now, *Dutch*?"

"Just trying to be friendly."

Anne scoffed. "Sure."

"Well, I don't know what people usually do in these situations," the cop said. "Should I be begging for my life? Telling you I have a family, something like that?"

"You think it would help?" She started for the door again.

"I have a sister," the cop said. Anne stopped in her tracks and turned halfway back. Was he really pulling this shit right now?

"Danielle," the guy went on, the expression on his face naked and diffident. "My sister's name is Danielle. She's got a husband, a kid. Kinsey. Kinsey's eight. She plays a lot of Nintendo and likes Taylor Swift. What about you? D'you have anyone?"

"Nope," Anne said. "Nuh-uh. No way."

"No as in *no*, or . . . ?"

"No as in *this conversation is over*," she snapped. "Now try and get some sleep. Or don't. I don't give a shit. And don't be a fucking ass-hole tonight, okay? I'm already running low on reasons not to shoot you."

"I'm telling you, you really don't want to kill me," Dutch said.

She looked at him. "Did I say anything about killing you?"

Realization creeped into his expression. "Right. You got it."

"Good night, Dutch," Anne said.

"Sleep well, Anne."

Anne sucked her teeth and walked out before the cop could say anything else.

In the living room, Anne went to the hearth and pulled the wrought iron handle in the wall to open the flue, but it wouldn't budge.

Goddammit. She'd been planning on starting a fire to warm the place up, but something was blocking it from inside the chimney. Probably crows' nests or a tangle of dead squirrels or something. It made sense—old mountain spots like this could fall into disrepair after a single season, forget about twenty-five. Whatever. At least there were the space heaters.

Once they were all running, coils glowing orange in the gloom, Anne crashed down on the busted old couch in a heap. Exhaustion had hit her like a truck doing eighty-five on the interstate. What a profoundly fucked-up day this had turned into. She could still hear the gunfire inside the bank, the screams, Merrill dying scared and confused, traitor fucking Travis smirking on the other end of the phone. It all wailed louder and louder inside her head until the wailing was all she could hear.

She rubbed at her temples and breathed slow until the din ebbed away, replaced by the gentle, tidal thumping of her heartbeat. Digging in her back pocket, she fished out the folded envelope with *Annie* written on the front. The handwriting was unfamiliar, but it was neat and tidy, rendered in the kind of controlled loops that Anne had always associated with her elementary school teachers. Turning it over, she saw that the flap on the back was unsealed; or maybe the glue had dried out and come unstuck at some point while the envelope sat waiting for however many years. Gently, she eased it open to find a single sheet of yellowing paper tucked inside, inscribed with a few short lines written in the same neat, spruce script:

Annie,

If you're reading this, you need to get out of here as soon as possible.

The cabin isn't safe. Watch your back, and don't trust anyone.

The Passage is everywhere.

— Aunt Lisa

Below the signature, this Aunt Lisa person had drawn a sketch: three stars, interlocked along their edges. The shape of them together like that kind of reminded Anne of a crown.

And who the fuck was *Aunt Lisa*? Anne didn't have an aunt named Lisa. She didn't have any aunts or uncles at all. Beverly had been an only child, and it wasn't like Anne had ever known her dad; to hear Grandma tell it, the man had been some fly-by-night shitbag back in the day who'd amounted to little more than a sperm donor before jumping ship. Anne supposed it was technically possible that he, whoever he was, had a sister named Lisa, but what were the odds of that being the case, really? Infinitesimally low. And what the hell was *the Passage*? What did that even mean? Anne didn't know what she'd been expecting, but it certainly wasn't this.

Surrendering herself to the fact that she wasn't going to figure any of it out tonight, Anne refolded the letter, tucked it back in the envelope, then tossed it on top of the coffee table in a little plume of dust. She'd deal with it later. Right now, her eyes burned, her legs were brittle and unyielding, and her back was sorer than she could ever remember it being. Every atom in her body screamed for sleep.

She rubbed her eyes with the fingers of one hand and felt exhaustion pull at her from the darkness, a kraken rising out of the deep to drag her down into the drowning depths like an unsuspecting galleon. She'd been going full tilt since this morning, and now she was completely gassed. Nothing left in the tank but a few fleeting fumes. Sliding her Glock from her waistband, she laid it atop her chest, resting her finger across the trigger guard, careful not to thread it through. Last thing she needed right now was to put a bullet through her own face because she had a bad dream or some shit.

She was just going to close her eyes for a minute. That was all. Just long enough to collect her thoughts and try to come up with a new plan now that the old one had blown up in such spectacular fashion. Just for a few seconds, no more. All she—

6

"There's something out there."

Curled up on the lumpy old couch, Anne unfolded herself and sat up, setting her Glock on the coffee table beside the letter while she rubbed at her face with both hands. Christ, she was stiff. Her body ached from the cold, the joints all swollen, her muscles frozen and knotted. Sleeping on the couch without a blanket hadn't done her any favors, space heaters or no. Through the bedroom door, she could see the cop coiled where she'd left him, still handcuffed to the bed frame. Dark circles under his eyes, skin sallow and waxy. She doubted he'd slept at all.

"What?" Her voice was flat. Uninterested.

"Last night," he said. "I heard something. Outside. But like, close. Really close." His eyes were gummy and leaden with insomnia, but there was something hiding underneath that dullness, something sharp and uneasy. Something scared.

"Okay, sure. Something like what?"

"I don't know," he replied. "But I'm pretty sure it was scratching at the door."

A wince of panic pulsed in Anne's guts, a nightmare from the past rising up through the mist. Shaking it off, she fixed him with a weary stare.

"Probably just an animal," she said. "Just the valley. Plenty of wildlife out here that isn't used to humans. Things sound different when people aren't around."

"Maybe, I guess."

"Yeah, well, maybe you dreamed it or something, what do I know."

She rose and shuffled into the little kitchenette to start searching the cabinets for coffee. Even if it was years stale at this point, it would be a hell of a lot better than no coffee at all. She found an ancient can of Folgers instant underneath the sink—peeling back the gritty plastic lid, she brought the can to her face and breathed deeply, smelling the black crystalline powder inside. Definitely stale, but any port in a storm. She took the old kettle from the stovetop and filled it with water from the tap, then set it to boil.

The fatigue from the day before was still there, stitched deep into her body, stubborn in its insistence. Waiting for the kettle, she stretched out as best she could in the little space, then checked the clock on her phone—Jesus, she'd been out for nearly nine hours straight, but she didn't feel like she'd rested at all. More like she'd just barely managed to not die of exhaustion for a little while longer. She peeked into the main bedroom—Jessup was still, but then he moaned and shivered in his sleep, recoiling from some nightmare. Okay, so, not dead. That was good. Atop the stove, the kettle started to whistle and whine.

The coffee was bad—really bad—but it was hot, and it was black, and it was bitter, and that was all Anne needed right now. After she'd greedily drained her mug, she fetched the still-hot kettle and fixed herself a second and, against her better judgment, made one for the cop.

"Thanks," he said as she passed him the steaming cup. Leaning forward, he sipped his coffee and nodded toward the bed.

"You know, you can sit down, if you want. I won't mind," he said.

Anne considered that, then slowly eased herself down to sit on the edge of the mattress, just out of his reach in case he tried something stupid. She curled both of her hands around her coffee cup, trying to pull some warmth from the chipped ceramic into her scarred-up palms.

"That wasn't bullshit, before," the cop told her between sips, face grave. "Last night. I heard it. I don't know what it was, but I heard it."

"Scratching at the door," she said.

"Yeah, exactly."

Anne rolled her eyes and sipped her own coffee. "Like I said, probably an animal or something. Lot of those out here."

"Didn't sound like any animal I ever heard."

"What'd it sound like, then?"

"I told you, I don't know. Just sounded like it was big."

"Big. Right. Sure."

Draining her cup, Anne stood. She was already sick of this conversation.

"Well, you let me know when you figure it out, okay?" she said, and left.

In the big bedroom, bright orange-white sunlight spilled through the window, turning the thin curtains into burning tissue paper. Closer up, Jessup still wasn't in great shape: his skin was wan and sweat-dappled, his clothes soaked, his eyelids bruise-purple. The bandages looked like they were holding up okay, though she knew she was going to have to change them pretty soon. Gently, she laid a hand across his forehead, feeling for a fever. Definitely still warm, but not nearly as hot as he'd been last night. For now, Anne let him sleep. She watched the gentle ebb and swell of his rib cage underneath the blankets for another moment, then turned to pull the curtains the rest of the way shut. Under her feet, one of the floorboards creaked and gave, just the tiniest bit.

What . . . ?

She lifted her foot and looked down. In the glare of the morning light, she could just make out a small, rectangular impression cut into the grain of the planks next to the molding, between the bed and the side table. It was well hidden, the planks around it only the slightest bit uneven. She probably would have missed it entirely if she hadn't stepped right on top of it.

Kneeling, she traced its outline with a finger, then softly drummed her knuckles against it, careful not to wake Jessup. Hollow. She laid her hands flat against the panel and pushed until it popped loose and came away entirely, revealing a dusty little hidey-hole no bigger than a shoebox. Anne set the false plank aside, then leaned down to peer into the tiny cubby.

Inside, she found an old VHS cassette, carpeted in dust, just like the rest of the cabin. Pulling it out, she brushed the tape off and turned it over in her hands again and again. It was unmarked but for a peeling label along its spine, ten digits that had to be a phone number scribbled into the paper, probably a half-hearted attempt at *If lost, please return to . . .*

Experimentally, she thumbed at the recessed button on the side of the cassette, hinging back the guard panel to make sure the magnetic tape inside the shell was intact. Everything seemed okay, but Anne didn't really know shit when it came to outdated media formats. When was the last time she'd laid eyes on one of these things, let alone a VCR to play it? It had to have been years. They didn't even have a TV up here. Setting the tape aside, Anne checked the hidey-hole again, but there was nothing else in there. Weird.

Outside, she heard the unmistakable sound of an engine, and of tires crunching against dirt: distant at first, but getting louder, and fast.

Someone was coming up the road.

Someone was here.

7

Cops.

The word drummed inside Anne's head again and again in an infinite death-spiral: *cops-cops-cops-cops-cops-cops-cops.* Her heart leapt into her throat and stayed there as her hands crackled with nerves. Fucking police. Of course they'd found out about this place. Of course they'd run her down like a pack of wolves following the scent of blood. She imagined the Colorado State Patrol rolling up to the cabin in force, peacocking in black tactical gear, ready to make a grisly spectacle of bringing them to justice for the news.

She put the tape down and went to the living room for her Glock, hugging the shadows. Instinctively, she swept her spare magazines from the squall jacket and pocketed them. Pressing herself up against the cold cabin wall, she peeked an eye up around the edge of the nearest window.

A rattletrap pickup—faded red, rusted out around the wheels—meandered up the road toward the cabin and rolled to a stop a couple dozen feet from the front door. It idled for a moment, tailpipe spewing smoke, then its engine cut and two men climbed out: both white, middle-aged, and soggy around the midsection, decked out in busted jeans and moth-picked flannel. That was where their similarities stopped. The one on the left was short and stout, with a bushy handlebar mustache and caterpillar eyebrows to match, while the one on the right was built like a lamppost, tall and thin and bespectacled, the midmorning sun shining off his bald, liver-spotted pate. The tall guy was holding a shotgun, a weathered old break-action, while his friend wore a bolt-action rifle with a cherry stock over one shoulder. No badges, no radios, no pistols on their hips.

Okay, so not cops. Probably. But whoever these assholes were, Anne had no doubt that they thought pretty highly of anybody wearing a badge. She knew the type: self-righteous old pricks who popped a weird rubbery one for law and order, as long as law and order didn't stop them from going hunting whenever and wherever they liked.

But this property didn't belong to them. Anne didn't give a fuck if people decided to go poaching, but she gave all the fucks about being left the hell alone. Especially up here. That was the whole point of the place.

"What's going on?" Dutch called out from the second bedroom, eyes wide and worried.

Anne threw him a lethal glare and crossed her lips with one finger, waving him off with her gun hand. In the big bedroom, Jessup was still passed out, drenched in blood and sweat. That could either be a good thing or a real fucking problem, depending on how the next few minutes went.

Out of the corner of the window, she watched the two men approach the cabin on foot. Didn't seem like they'd clocked the Olds yet, parked around the side like it was, but it was only a matter of time. She had to handle this *now*. Staying low and moving fast, Anne went to the hearth and grabbed the Remington. She racked the pump, checked the breach, then set it next to the front doorjamb just in case.

Taking a deep, slow breath, she tucked her Glock into the waistband of her jeans, then pulled the door open and stepped out onto the porch to meet the two men. They stopped in place when they saw her, sharing a quick look.

"Help you?" Anne called out.

"Uh, yeah, hey there," the short one, Lefty, said. His brows crowded his eyes, making his expression hard to read. "What are, ah, what are you doing all the way out here?"

"I was about to ask you the same thing," she said, unsmiling.

They tensed. Righty's hands tightened around the shotgun. Anne pretended not to notice.

"Just came out here to do some hunting," Righty said, raising the break-action without pointing it. His voice was nearly a full octave lower than his friend's. "How about you?"

"I don't think that's really any of your business," Anne said. "Maybe you two should find somewhere else."

Lefty scoffed and mugged a shitty little grin. "Excuse me?" he chuckled.

"This isn't your land," Anne said.

"Is it yours?" Righty asked.

She didn't say anything to that. The men shared another look that she couldn't quite parse. Righty looked back at her, brows knitted tight underneath his shiny scalp.

"What's your name?" he asked.

"Does it matter?"

"Sure it does," he replied. "Always important to introduce yourself to new people. Here, we'll go first, okay? My name's John, and this is Norris."

Lefty—*Norris*—scoffed, then horked a loogie and spat. John ignored him.

"What about you?" he asked.

"Look," Anne sighed. "We really don't need to make this into a thing. So how about you two get back in your truck and drive. Okay? Don't care where. Just not here. Then we can forget we ever met each other. This never even happened."

Norris snorted again, but Anne didn't see what was so fucking funny.

"Just tell us your name, sweetie," Norris said. John—who Anne was quickly coming to think of as *the reasonable one*—elbowed his friend in the ribs, but Norris persisted. "That's all we want. Then, sure, we'll be on our way, no problem."

Anger frothed in Anne's head like smoke from a broken engine. *Sweetie.* Fuck you twice. Without blinking, she drew the Glock from her waistband and let it hang down by her thigh.

"Last chance," she said, her voice turning hard and icy. "Go."

The men bridled at the sight of the pistol; Anne could feel the needle on their shared anxiety burying itself in the red from here. Norris's hands went to his hunting rifle as he ground his heels against the dirt, but no way he was getting that thing off his shoulder before Anne put him down.

"Look, I'm sorry, okay? Sorry about him," John said, stepping forward and clearing his throat. "We, uh, we don't want any trouble, really."

"Makes three of us," Anne said. She nodded toward their truck, and the dirt road beyond. "I'm not going to say it again."

The men shifted in place. John still hadn't taken his eyes off Anne's Glock, but Norris stared straight at her, either playing at courageous or just too dumb to know when he was batting way out of his league.

"And what if we say no?" Norris asked. "What then?"

Anne raised the Glock and pulled the trigger. The shot slapped the air, deafening, and one of the pickup's headlights exploded in a spray of broken glass. Both men yelped and recoiled, then twisted back to stare at her, wide-eyed.

She didn't lower the gun. She didn't breathe. She just waited for them to either make their move or get the fuck out of there. It didn't take them long to choose. John and Norris shared another furtive look, then quickly turned tail and climbed into the pickup's cab. It spun a donut in the grit and hauled ass away from the cabin. Anne watched it kick up a loose rooster tail of dirt as it receded into the distance, engine steadily Dopplering into nothing as the truck disappeared past the switchback hills. Anne stood there, gun hand steady until she was sure they were gone.

Back inside, Jessup was awake again, propped up against the headboard in her mom's room. He studied Anne with wet, heavy-lidded eyes as she stalked through the door, both his hands pressed flat against the mattress.

"They're going to be a problem," he said, his voice a damp wheeze. He'd watched the whole exchange from the bedroom window. She shook her head.

"If they were going to make a thing of it, they would have."

"I don't know," Jessup told her. "Assholes like that have a real long memory. And you shot at them first."

"I shot their truck," she corrected.

"You really think they're going to make that distinction?"

"They're just hunters," she said. "Poachers. Fuck them."

"Didn't seem like hunters to me." Jessup coughed.

"Yeah? And what'd they seem like to you?"

Jessup's eyes twitched. "Dunno. Not hunters," he said again. "But whoever they were, you'd better hope to hell that they don't go and call the cops, either."

"Doesn't matter," Anne mused. "We're going to be out of here long before they decide to pull that card."

"Yeah." Jessup frowned at the wound in his belly. "Sure."

Anne slid the Glock back into her waistband and watched him as his gaze wandered around the bedroom, taking it all in.

"So this is it, huh? Your mom's old place?"

"Yep."

"It's nice," Jessup told her. "Well. Maybe not *nice*, but I can see how this would have been a good place to grow up. Quiet, you know. Peaceful and all that."

Except I didn't grow up here, Anne thought bitterly. *This is just the place where my mom died.*

She sat down on the edge of the bed and patted Jessup on his unshot shoulder. He raised one hand and let it fall on top of hers, giving it a reassuring squeeze. His skin was clammy and cold, chicken skin fresh from the fridge.

"How you holding up?" Anne asked.

"Not great," he told her. "But I've been worse and made it through."

Anne sincerely doubted that. But she didn't press the issue.

Jessup hacked and wheezed, strings of fresh blood speckling his chin. "Don't suppose you thought to pick up smokes, did you? I'd just about stab someone in the face for a Marlboro right now."

"Sorry, wasn't exactly high on my shopping list."

"Fuuuuuck," he said.

"So, what, you think they were Travis's?" she asked, pointedly changing the subject.

"What?"

"Those *not-hunters*. What are the odds that they're on Trav and Iris's payroll?"

Jess's eyes glinted again, more nervous than she might've ever seen before. "Not sure. Probably pretty good. What d'you reckon?"

"I don't know. Maybe could be his," she said. "Maybe not. I don't think Trav knows about this place. Not like I ever told him."

"What about Iris? You ever tell her? Give her any reason to get curious?" A shuddering belt of coughs escaped Jessup's lips, but his eyes stayed fixed on hers.

"Mm. Maybe. Can't say for sure."

"Well, for both our sakes, let's hope you didn't." He had a point. Travis walked around all day every day telling himself that he was a genius, but his wife was the one with all the angles. Iris paid attention, picked up on shit when you thought she wasn't listening, filed it all away for future reference. If anybody else in their crew other than Anne, Jessup, and Gemma knew about this place, it'd be Iris fucking Bulauer.

Jessup's expression softened around his eyes as he watched her, bright and curious as ever.

"You know, you're surprisingly calm about this, Heller. What's going on?"

She let her hand fall away from Jessup's and looked down at the floor, the hidey-hole, the VHS tape. Thought again about telling him about the phone call at the gas station, but decided against it. They'd have plenty of time to talk about it later, when he was upright again. They could come up with a new plan, get ahold of Gemma, and then they'd all deal with Travis and Iris, together.

"Just . . . Try and get some sleep, okay?" she said. "I'll be back to change your bandages later. Figure out next steps after that."

She knelt to pick up the cassette, then walked back into the living room, feeling Jessup's eyes between her shoulder blades as she went, studying her, trying to piece her together like a puzzle. Just like always. When she looked back again, he was already snoring, deep asleep and lost to the world. Anne envied him that. In the other bedroom, she could see Dutch watching with a curious expression on his face. She ignored him.

She went to the kitchen and made herself a plate of saltine-and-peanut-butter sandwiches, then scarfed them all down like a starving raccoon feasting on a derelict trash can. Her stomach rumbled and growled in response—this wasn't nearly enough to keep her going, but then, two full steak dinners wouldn't be enough after the last couple of days. She dropped down on the dingy old couch and pulled out the letter from Aunt Lisa again, skimming through it three times without really reading a word. Whatever. She'd try again to make sense of it later. Once they were the hell out of here.

Tomorrow, they'd get moving. She and Jessup definitely, maybe Dutch, too. Or maybe she'd leave the cop here to starve until John and Norris finally came back. Whatever. Bright and early, she'd pile everything into the Ninety-Eight, and then they could get the hell away from this place and never, ever think about it again. Let the mountain take the land back, tear the cabin down to logs and rubble. It didn't matter anymore.

Tomorrow, they were getting out of here. Tomorrow.

8

As he slept, Jessup dreamed that he was following a voice.

Tender yet insistent, it whispered through the frozen wastes, buoying him along in its gentle embrace and leading him effortlessly over rocks and between the trees. It had been there when he'd opened his eyes, a filament wire of sound stitched through the lonesome fabric of night, so faint that he'd barely registered it at first. But once he realized it was there, it was impossible to unhear it.

—*sSsSuuUsSuUusSuSussSuSsss*—

It beckoned him out of bed and through the little lodge, rendering his every movement rubbery and alien, as if his body were no longer his own. It wanted him to follow. Jessup had never been so sure of anything in his life. So he obliged.

Wrapping the bloody blankets tight around his scarecrow shoulders, Jessup had chased the wispy ghost-voice into the night, quietly easing the cabin door open and stealing out into the freezing darkness. He didn't know how far he'd gone since then, but given the drunken way his legs threatened to buckle underneath him now, he thought maybe it had been a long time. His skin ached from the cold, his lips were chapped, his head was pounding. The bullet holes in his front felt like they were tearing wider with every step he took. He'd never had a dream that hurt like this before.

Limping over the rough, rocky terrain, Jessup chased the voice up the hillside and into the trees, around lichen-furred stones and over ankle-breaker gulleys, deeper into the wild dark. The farther he went, the louder the whisper grew, humming and buzzing through the underbrush, at times almost loud enough for Jessup to make out words before fading back into the hushed drone of the mountain. As if the whisper were simply another part of the land-scape, a chilly piece of an otherwise indifferent whole.

As Jessup climbed farther up the pine-laden hill, the ground grew steeper, causing him to first slow, then stop altogether as he tried to catch his breath. His chest and legs burned, his face and hands now long numb. Steam billowed from his lips in huge white gusts as his heart hammered at his ribs. He turned in place, squint-ing against the night, trying to get his bearings. The forest had surrounded him when he wasn't looking, rising up in narrow black towers that stabbed at the sky, blotting out the stars entirely. There was barely room enough to breathe out here.

Jesus Christ, how far had he gone?

Cocking his head in the scant moonlight, Jessup listened for the whisper and heard it rise once more, slicing through the night like an eel through black waters. It filled him from the inside, pressing on his chest like a warm, sure hand—but then the pressure dis-appeared, and instinctively, he recoiled, twisting on the balls of his feet as he tried to keep his balance, suddenly unmoored from gravity itself. He felt his foot catch on something hard and twisted, half-buried in the soil, and he went tumbling forward. His hands slapped the ground, and rocks bit deep into his palms as his teeth clacked together. The impact lit the wounds in his chest up like fireworks on the Fourth of July.

He didn't know how long he lay there, waiting for the agony to pass, but as he did, he realized that he could still hear that faint, brittle voice in the darkness, the softest exhalation of breath in be-tween the shadows and the trees.

No. Not breath. Not a whisper. A buzzing of flies.

—ssSsUsSssUusSuSussSuUsusSsssss—

Jessup's skin crawled at the sound as his bloodied stomach twisted itself into tight, painful knots. Face down in the dirt, he braced his cut-up palms against the soil and drew a shaking breath against the nausea. The night air burned his lungs, but he forced himself to not launch into a coughing fit for fear of throwing up. Somewhere close by, he thought he heard a footstep. Then another.

"Is . . ." he moaned softly, weakly. "Is someone there?"

At first, the night was still. But then he heard it move, heard it breathe, heard it sigh, insectoid: ⏐

"... *sSssusussuSusssSuuUSsssomeone* ..."

Jessup's heart clanged. Soft explosions of white light popped and danced in his field of vision. The throbbing inside his head got worse.

Over his shoulder, something moved.

Raising his head from the icy soil, he twisted around to look, studying the darkness, the shadows of the trees overhead and the lopsided silhouettes of the rocks. At first there was nothing, but then it moved again, and Jessup saw.

It was a shape unlike any he'd seen before—as if the shadows themselves had come alive and taken form, coalescing into something far more terrible than the sum of their parts. It moved like liquid, it moved like oil, like hatred, like fear. It loomed over him as it slithered across the hard winter ground, shifting and changing, warping like a body in a fun house mirror, all teeth and bones, tumors and fingers and bloody gray skin bouqueted with filthy tufts of hair. He felt waves of heat pouring off its terrible mass, as if its very presence were burning the air around it, baking an uncontrollable fever into its essence.

Still prone, Jessup scrambled on bloody hands to get away from the roiling shape, trying to draw breath, but his chest was frozen, gear-locking his lungs, keeping his heart from beating. The night was on him now, and the last thing he saw was the hunched, misshapen shadow opening empty white eyes as it unfurled itself before him.

He opened his mouth—

9

The scream split the night like an axe through an unsuspecting skull. Anne was up and moving in an instant, suddenly all of six years old again, jolting awake in the dark of the cabin, scared to death without knowing why. Glock in hand, she turned in place as she wiped crusts of drool from her cheek, listening so hard that her ears started to ring. But it was all just silence again.

She hadn't imagined it. She hadn't. Someone had screamed, she knew that for sure. She cocked her head and closed her eyes, searching the quiet for some echo, something that might confirm that she wasn't just crazy or dreaming. For a moment, she thought she could hear whispers on the wind.

"What was that?"

Dutch's voice was small and frail, riddled with nerves. She looked at him, stooped there in the little bedroom, still cuffed to the bed frame.

"Anne, what was that?" he asked again. Whatever it was, he'd heard it, too. So she wasn't crazy. Wasn't dreaming. Okay. Shit.

"Don't know," she said. "Something."

"Something," he echoed. "Okay."

A chill wind blew through the living room and kicked Anne square in the chest. Panicked, she hit the lights and nearly screamed.

The front door was hanging wide open. Bloody footprints tracked across the hardwood, leading out. In her mom's room, the bed was empty.

Oh god. Jessup.

Anne didn't even think about what she was going to do next. She just stomped her feet into her sneakers, grabbed the Remington from its place by the front door, and took off running.

"Hey, what are you doing?!" Dutch wailed, rattling his hand-cuffs against the metal bed frame. "Anne, what the hell?!"

She ignored him. She had to get out there. She had to find Jess.

Death-cold air lapped at her skin as she hurtled out of the cabin and into the night beyond, the pupils of her eyes wide as dimes. The bloody footprints ended in the dirt just a few feet beyond the front porch. Shit. She glanced down the hill toward the road and the switchbacks, then up toward the tree line and the rocks and the plateau that lay beyond. She headed up.

"Jessup?!" she called out. "Jess, I'm here! I'm coming!"

Over scrub and rocks, in between the straggly dead trees that dotted the hillside, up and up and up to where the stones stood huge and imposing, she ran, sucking frigid air between bared teeth. The cold scraped at her lungs. Panic seethed inside her head. Thunder rolled faintly in the middle distance, menacing, but she kept run-ning toward it. He was out here. She just had to find him and bring him back.

Anne dashed up the hill, pumping her knees as she bounded over the cracked and rough landscape, but her legs were already so fucking tired. Had the slope always been this long, this steep? She couldn't remember exactly, though she knew logically that it must have. Back when she'd been a little girl, the hill behind the cabin had seemed like a mountain unto itself, a sheer cliff face shooting up from the ground to pierce the sky, impassable, impossible. The memories were jumbled and incomplete, but she thought she re-membered afternoons spent outside the cabin, looking up the hill toward the shadowed tree line and the plateau beyond, wondering what was hidden all the way out there, just waiting to be discov-ered. Her mom had warned her off from venturing too far into the wildlands of the property, said there were animals out there, animals and other things best left well alone, and Anne had always listened.

Until tonight.

Overhead, stars twinkled in the darkness, spinning and danc-ing around one another in a slow, incomprehensible ballet. Anne remembered that half-blurred sky. It was exactly the same as the night everything had gone to hell, the night Mom had woken her up stomping back and forth through the cabin, rousting her awake with that cold, firm voice.

Annie, get up. We have to go.

Mom had never sounded like that before; at least, not that Anne had ever heard. She'd cried for a week when she realized that it was one of the last things her mother had ever said to her. There was grit in Beverly Heller, a well of toughness that Anne, in her childhood innocence, hadn't recognized until it was already gone with the rest of her. Maybe that was partially to blame for who Anne had grown up to be, as if robbing the rich and starting shit with cops could somehow prove that whatever vein of iron that had run through her mom hadn't died with her, out in that ravine, the life snatched out of her heart by some unseen predator.

Anne had never really known for sure what to believe about that night. After all, she'd been a sleepy kid when it had all gone down, and the official story, the one the cops and park rangers had told about a starving mountain lion running loose, made sense on paper. Outside all the cities and highways, Colorado was still wild at heart, a vast expanse of untamed hinterlands brimming with animals to which killing came as naturally as breathing, wolves and mountain lions and black bears and more. There was every reason for her to believe their version of the truth, but Anne could never quite manage it.

Because mountain lions didn't stand on their hind legs.

Their eyes didn't glow dead white in the dark.

Whatever had destroyed her life all those years ago, whatever the truth was, the fact remained: She'd already lost her mom to this fucking place. She wasn't going to lose Jessup to it, too.

So she ran.

She ran until her chest burned and her head swam with exhaustion, until the shotgun hung heavy as a millstone in her hands. Finally slowing, she shuffled to the side, pitching her shoulders against one of the hillside's massive stones as she paused to catch her breath. Her pulse droned in her temples. Her legs were wet cement. She couldn't keep going like this, but she couldn't stop now, either. Not while he was still out there.

Farther up, beyond the plateau's edge and well into the trees, the thunder crashed again, so much louder than it had been only moments before. It was a familiar sound, a low, cacophonous rolling deep in the hills, but overhead, the skies weren't telegraphing rain. There wasn't a storm cloud around for miles.

The thunder crashed again, nearly on top of her now, and she finally realized what it was that she was hearing.

That wasn't a storm.

It was a stampede.

Her whole body went numb at the realization; she spun back around to stare up the rocky hill just in time to see a black wave of antlers and hooves and fur surging out of the trees, elk and mule deer and pronghorns and more. There were dozens of them, hundreds, drenched in shadow, eyes glassy with panic, stomping and snorting and screeching and clacking as they hurtled over the plateau's edge, barreling straight toward her.

Anne choked back a scream and pressed herself against the rock, crouching to make herself as small as she possibly could, hiding from the flood of animals roaring toward her. The sound of it was massive and terrible, crushing in its enormity, an oncoming typhoon of noise and flesh and frenzy. Anne clutched the Remington to her chest, and for a single, perfect second, there was nothing. She was alone. And then the stampede was on top of her.

It crashed through the night like a never-ending explosion, pummeling the soil and kicking up a thick cloud of dust that swallowed Anne whole. Angular, fur-covered bodies shredded the ground around her, tearing dead brush from the ground and branches from trees with great, dry cracks that sounded like gunshots. Stones and pebbles flew like shrapnel. For the second time in three days, Anne found herself trapped in a war zone.

Her heart pounded inside her chest like it was trying to punch through her ribs and escape. She could feel the sheer heat of the animals as they rushed by, turning the air to soup, thick and putrid. It stole the breath from her lungs and the thoughts from her mind until all that was left was the noise, the heat, the storm, the panic.

Huddled there against the rock, Anne felt her body start to rebel, her every impulse telling her to make a break for it, to try to escape this sudden hell, but she held fast. If she moved now, she'd get dragged under and trampled to death in an instant. So she made herself into a statue, jaw clenched, hands so tight around the shotgun that her fingers started to lose feeling.

Then, as fast as the stampede had come, it was gone. Cold, stinging air slashed at Anne's skin as the choking dust started to dissipate and ebb away on the breeze. Silence crept in around the corners, a little bit here, a little bit there, until the silence was all Anne could hear. Still hunched against the massive stone, she watched the cataclysmic wave of animals surge down the rocky slope, past the cabin, and into the low switchback hills and endless miles of untouched Colorado wilderness that lay beyond.

Finally, Anne rose to her feet. She drew breath with shaky lungs, then turned back toward the trees and screamed Jessup's name. Her voice bounced off the hills and echoed away, but there was no response. She shouted for him again and again. Still nothing.

Without thinking, she started up the slope once more. It only took her a minute to crest the plateau's ridge into the tree line. Darkness crowded in around her, swelling like the tide. Trees scraped at the starlit sky above, tattering the moonlight and shrouding the path ahead. All around her was the aftermath of the stampede, soil divoted by pounding hooves, arm-thick branches snapped like toothpicks, trunks hacked and harrowed by antlers and tusks. She stood in the middle of that great destruction and felt dread bloom in her stomach anew.

This was suicidal. She knew enough to know that for certain. She didn't have a light, didn't know where she was going. She wasn't even wearing a fucking coat. Winter nights were hard in the valley, and like an asshole, she'd gone sprinting out of the cabin dressed only in a T-shirt, jeans, and tennis shoes. If she got turned around all the hell back here, she'd freeze to death before the night was out. Jessup or no, she had to turn back.

Hurt and embarrassment burned in her chest as she stumbled out of the trees and back down the hill toward the stooped little cabin. The shotgun was so heavy in her shaking hands, but she didn't dare let it go. Right now, it was the one thing tethering her to this world, the only thing she was sure was real anymore. Even the stampede seemed so far off already. As if she hadn't just somehow narrowly avoided death, yet again.

Back at the cabin, Anne turned to cast one last look up the slope, toward the trees and the impenetrable shadows that waited beyond. The urge to call out for Jessup one last time rose in her chest, but she tamped it down. He was gone, and there was nothing else she could do about it now. Not until it was light out.

Wait until daybreak. It's only a couple of hours away now. You'll find him. He'll be okay.

Everything's going to be okay.

Back inside the cabin, Dutch stared at her from the second bedroom, worried and wide-eyed.

"What the hell was that?" he demanded.

She ignored him. He asked again, louder. Glowering at him from the doorway, she pulled the bedroom door shut with a hard click, then laid the shotgun across the coffee table and slumped down on the couch.

Eventually, sleep came for her. It didn't last.

10

Anne woke with the dawn, eyes swollen and crusted with tears. She was still in her clothes, sneakers tight on her feet, jeans and dumb Looney Tunes shirt stiff with dried sweat. Her whole body ached from the cold. The space heaters had switched themselves off at some point last night, else the genny had hitched just enough to cut their power. She rose from the beaten-in old sofa and went to the big bedroom. The blanketless mattress was still soaked in blood, the stain massive and revolting. Jessup was still missing.

Shame, toxic and vile, churned in Anne's belly as she stood there in the doorway, staring at the vacant bed. Another empty space in the shape of someone she cared about, spirited away in the night by this fucking place. Her mind fired ceaselessly with all the things she should have done differently: She should have stayed out there, gone deeper into the forest, brought Jessup back. But fucking coward that she was, she turned tail like a scared little girl and left him out there, in the dark, in the cold. Just like her mom.

She had to get out there. She had to find him. Or, more likely, what was left of him.

"Hello?" she heard Dutch call from the other bedroom. "You there? I, uh, I have to pee again."

She crossed over and pushed the door open. Inside, the cop was still cuffed to the bed frame, looking plenty worse for wear.

"Hi," he said. "I have to pee, and the, uh, the jug you gave me, it's full, so . . ."

Anne stared at him for a long, empty moment, glanced askance at the plastic jug on the floor, brimming with the guy's piss and who knew what else, then dug in her pocket and threw him the cuff keys.

"C'mon, s'go," she said, and nodded to the jug. "Bring that, I don't want it stinking up the place. Dump it in the toilet while you're in there."

Wordlessly, he unlocked himself from the bed frame, then refastened the cuffs around both his wrists, arms in front, and underhand-tossed the keys back to her. She walked him and his revolting jug out into the living room, watching the way his shoulders knitted themselves tight when he saw Jessup's bloody footprints smeared across the floor.

"Where's . . . Is that what . . . ?"

Anne shook her head. She wasn't in the mood for it this morning.

"Don't," she said, voice icy.

She toed the bathroom door open, then stood aside to let him in. A second later, Anne heard the telltale sound of liquid hitting water, first from the jug, then from the cop. She tried to ignore it.

"Look, I'm sorry to ask, but . . . that was him last night, wasn't it?" Dutch said. "Jessup, I mean?"

Anne didn't respond. She didn't need to. He'd seen the footprints, he'd watched her bolt from the cabin in the middle of the night. No way he'd missed the terrible thunder of all those animals breaking from the trees, running for their lives like they were trying to get free of a wildfire. Animals only ever ran together like that when they were trying to escape something.

"Anne?"

"Shut up. Stop wasting time," she snapped.

She pulled on Jessup's squall coat while she waited for the cop to finish pissing and zip up. When he emerged from the little bathroom, he gave her a confused look.

"What are you doing?"

"*We're* going to find him," Anne corrected. "He's out there somewhere."

Dutch's eyes went wide.

"Wait, what? No. I'm sorry, but maybe no? Yeah, no, I'm not gonna, no. I'm not doing that. Sorry, but—we don't know what's out there," he said. "I'm not going out there. I'm just not."

With a sigh, Anne slid the Glock from her belt and pointed it at his face.

"Did I give you the impression that you have a choice in the matter?"

Dutch's shoulders fell. Anne gestured with the gun to the front door.

"Stand over there," she said. Dutch did as he was told.

Anne slung the Remington over her shoulder and tucked her Glock back into its place at the small of her back, then shoved him toward the door. He walked out. She followed.

Outside, the morning had risen cold and misty and corpse gray, the sky blurred with hematoma clouds that hung too close to the earth, claustrophobic. They walked uphill for near half a mile before they found the trail of Jessup's blood in the hoof-turned soil, arcing off toward the plateau and the tree line. Silently, they followed it over the ridge, back to the edge of the place where the rocks and trees grew closer together. The forest was huge and dense back here, the trees blotting out all the sunlight, leaving the ground in perpetual shadow. They slowed as they approached, their footsteps suddenly so loud against the tranquil, freezing morning.

Anne didn't want to go in there. But she knew she didn't really have a choice. Not if she wanted to bring Jessup back. And she wasn't turning around until she did just that. She nudged Dutch in the back with the muzzle of the shotgun, then the two of them headed into the trees.

They tracked Jessup's bloody footprints until they came upon a rickety fence threaded crookedly between the trunks. It wasn't much more than a few skeins of rusty barbed wire wrapped around a string of crumbling fence posts, but as far as fences went, it did the job well enough. On the ground, Jessup's trail turned sharply left, following the line of the fence deeper into the thick underbrush. Anne studied the hoof-and paw prints that had been pressed deep into the soil and remembered the feeling of the stampede in her chest, the way that it had pummeled the air and stolen the breath from her lungs. Those animals had been running from something. She just didn't know what, yet.

Deeper and deeper they drove into the forest, following the fence as it meandered through the trees until they finally came to a place where they found a bundle of tattered rags mounted on the wire. Except they weren't rags at all.

Jessup hung in a bloody mess, suspended face down by his throat and wrists in a grotesque parody of a ten-point buck mounted on some hunter's wall. Even at a distance, the smell of him was awful, foul and sickly sweet, drawing fat flies that alighted on his arms and back and neck and skull like black fur, picking and eating and fucking and buzzing.

Dutch moaned, "Oh god, fuck, oh my *Jesus*—" and stumbled back. A second later, Anne heard him vomiting. Her stomach turned sour at the sight of her dead friend, but she swallowed back the bile that rose in her throat and made herself look. She needed to see this. She owed him that much.

Jessup's scalp had been ripped all the way back from his skull and hung down his neck in loose flaps like the peel of a banana, while thick red-black sludge drip-drip-dripped from the ragged, empty hole that used to be his face. More flies hummed and frothed inside the bloody crater, orgiastic. From where she stood, Anne couldn't tell if Jessup's visage had been smashed in or torn away, but she supposed that either way, the result was the same. Holding her breath, she stepped in close and peeled back the bloody rags of his shirt, exposing the messy, finger-thick runnels that ran down his spine, weeping thick, clotted gore.

On the underside of his body, his belly was ruptured, loosing pearly, glossy loops of intestine that dangled from him like sausages in a butcher's shop. His legs had been ripped down to scraps, all the way to the bone. Farther up, some of the fingers were missing from his hands, his wrists and neck dotted with starbursts of little black scabs where the barbed wire had bit in. Anne stared at those little cluster wounds until she finally understood what she was seeing: he'd hurt himself trying to get free.

Whatever had mounted him here had done it while he was still alive.

She was moving before she was fully aware of what she was trying to do. Anne bunched her hands in the rags of Jessup's shirt and started to pull, but he wouldn't budge. Shifting her weight, she reached underneath his bulk to get a better grasp on him, trying to avoid touching the wreath of viscera that loped from his open belly, and pulled again. Her hand slipped. One of the sharp jabs on the fence bit into the pad of her finger, drawing blood. She sucked air through her teeth and pressed her hand tight against her leg.

"What . . . what are you doing?" Dutch coughed, still keeping his distance.

Anne looked back at him. "Come on," she said. "Help me with him. Please."

The cop stayed where he stood. Panic started to churn inside Anne's head.

"Dutch, *please*."

Reluctantly, Dutch wiped the puke from his lips and joined her by the fence, holding his cuffed wrists out expectantly like a Dickensian orphan. *Please, ma'am, I want some more*. With fumbling, disobedient fingers, she produced the keys from her jeans pocket and unshackled him without a second thought. She wasn't worried about him trying to run; if he did, she'd put a bullet in his brain and leave him up here for the crows and coyotes. She was all out of fucks to give.

Except he didn't try anything—he didn't take a swing at her or make a break for it; he just stood there, rubbing at his wrists while pointedly not looking at the obscenity mounted on the barbed wire. Anne couldn't begrudge him that. She'd have done the same thing, if she felt like she could.

Jessup's body was heavy and awkward, nothing like the straw figure she'd carried into the cabin a couple of days ago. No, this version of the man was all soft parts and broken edges, a cold bag of Jell-O and bones spilling apart where the stitches had snapped. It took some doing, especially with Dutch insisting on working blind, eyes shut against the horror in their arms, but they finally managed it, pulling Jess off the fence and dropping him to the ground in an awkward, wet slump. Looking at him now, Anne suppressed the urge to scream. This was all her fault. She'd abandoned him to the night and the cold and the wild, and look what had happened.

Nearby, the blanket from her mom's bed hung from the lowest branch of one of the scarred-up trees, the foul red stains that had soaked it through already dried to rust. Together, they pulled it free and laid it flat on the ground, then rolled what was left of Jess on top. His body seemed so small like this, all bent up and mangled, as if he were missing some essential part of himself, some piece that made Jessup *Jessup*.

Anne folded the ruined blanket over the top of him and started to drag him back to the cabin.

They buried him in a shallow hole out front, digging the grave in a dead grassy patch beside the wheel-rut road with a pair of rusty old shovels they found lying in the dirt around the back of the cabin. The frozen ground made the going slow, but with both of them digging, they more than made up the time. Stubbornly, Anne kept one eye on Dutch as they worked, waiting for him to make a move and swing the shovel at her head or something, but he never did. More than anything, the cop just seemed like he wanted to get it over and done with.

Together, they poured what was left of Jessup into the earth, then tossed the blanket and the bloody sheets on top and piled him over. They worked quickly against the cold until finally Anne stood at the edge of the filled-in hole, looking down at the freshly packed soil, feeling fat beads of sweat roll down her spine underneath her shirt and coat. Jess had always been there for her, the closest thing she'd had to family since Grandma died. He was genuine, brilliant, and troubled; she hadn't given it much thought before now, but the fact of the matter was that he was probably her best friend in all the world. Not that the competition was particularly stiff. And now he was gone. She wiped tears from her eyes with the back of her hand, then marked the head of the grave with a single fist-size rock, scratching a ragged *X* into the stone with the point of her folding knife.

Like Anne, Jessup was an unbeliever; he wasn't religious or even spiritual (which Anne had always felt was kind of a cop-out, a safe way of saying you didn't believe in God without actually having to admit that you didn't believe in God), but burying him here, like this, without any ceremony, just felt *wrong*, somehow. Marking the rock wasn't much, but it was all she had right now.

Back inside, Anne cuffed Dutch to the bed frame once more, then collapsed onto the couch to watch the sun sweep down across the sky, staining the jagged Sangre de Cristos as red as their namesake before disappearing beneath the horizon. When the cold outside got to be too much, she cranked the space heaters up to max and left them that way, holding her scarred hands out to their flickering ceramic warmth, trying to force some life back into her frozen digits, blaming herself, hating herself. It was no better than she deserved. No matter how she looked at it, she bore responsibility for Jess's death.

She'd made the choice to drive them up here. Whatever it was that Jessup had run across in the reach, it never would have happened if Anne hadn't dragged him out to the cabin. Inwardly, she admonished herself: She should have been smarter. She should have kept a closer eye on him. She should have known better. This place was death. She'd known that since she was six years old. They never should have come here.

Out of the corner of her eye, she caught Dutch watching her from the small bedroom. Sprawled on the floor, his eyes were dark and beady underneath a creased brow, giving Anne a glimpse of what he'd look like as an old man, all hunched over and angry. Day by day and blow by blow, this world would beat all the kindness and decency out of him, until the only things left were his rage and insecurity. Just like every other cop.

"What?" Dutch asked, his voice dripping with exhaustion.

Anne shook her head. "Nothing. You just look tired, is all."

His expression fell. He looked like he was going to start crying. Anne was surprised to find her heart going out to him. Despite her best efforts, she was actually starting to like the guy. Could be that he was still just waiting for his chance to take her down, or get away, or whatever cops were supposed to do in situations like this, but Anne sort of doubted it. There was a gentle decency to him that was uncommon in most people, let alone police. He was still a fucking hostage, but he clearly wanted to get out of this shitty situation alive just as much as she did, and at this point, she figured if he played his cards right, he—

Knock, knock.

Anne froze.

Someone was at the door.

In the little bedroom, Dutch's eyes went wide, the unspoken question written all over his face: *What the fuck?* Anne shook her head—*Don't know*—then crossed her lips with a single finger: *Ssshhh.* She rose from the couch and silently lifted her pistol off the coffee table as she stole over to the front window, taking deep, measured breaths to try to calm her rabbiting heartbeat.

She hadn't heard any tires on the road, hadn't seen the flash of headlights against the cabin's façade. She hadn't heard anything but the buzzing of flies outside. There wasn't zero chance that someone had walked all the way up the switchback hill from the blacktop, but she knew the terrain, knew the Valley. It wasn't exactly likely. Even if there was a whole SWAT battalion out there waiting for the signal, there'd have been some sign. Engine noise from the highway, the crunch of dozens of tac boots against the ground. Something. Anything.

No, odds were good that whoever it was out there was all alone. But who the fuck was it?

She took another breath. Curled her other hand around the Glock's grip and steeled herself, inching closer to the window frame. Just a little peek. That was all. She'd figure out what to do after that.

Just one peek.

In a single, fluid motion, Anne eased the curtains to one side and looked out the window and nearly screamed.

It was Jessup.

A cold blade punched through Anne's guts as she stood there, looking at him. *Him.* Not dead, not mangled, intestines safe and sound inside his belly, face still fixed on the front of his head. But the longer she stared, the more she realized that something was *off* about him, something wrong, something that she couldn't yet put a name to. It was there in the way he held himself, not tall and graceful and easy but hunched and uncomfortable. It was in the way his eyes sparkled white in the darkness, too pale, too bright.

No. No, no, no, no, no.

A crushing black wave rose from the base of her skull at the sight, raw and electric. Her stomach churned and heaved. Her vision blurred. Her hands started to shake. She'd felt panic before, she'd felt dread, but never anything like this, at once welling from within her and without. Part of her, but at the same time, so entirely not.

It looked like Jessup, but it wasn't. Jessup was dead and buried. She still had the mud underneath her fingernails to prove it. That thing was just wearing his face. She stood there staring numbly at him—*it*—through the window, and after a moment, it turned and smiled at her with a mouth filled with too many teeth, a bear trap ready to snap down at any second.

"Annie . . ."

Its voice was all wire and wood, a mangled Chuck E. Cheese animatronic gasping its last artificial breath. Black flies and fat white maggots crawled all over the thing, across its face and eyes, up and down its neck, seething out of its warped mouth. Anne's chest shuddered. She was definitely going to scream.

"Annie . . . open . . . the . . . door . . ."

The thing's hitching, gasping voice swarmed her, less a sound than a commandment from the darkest corners of her own mind.

Was she hearing it or thinking it? Both? Beyond that voice and the screech of blood and panic inside her head, she thought she could hear Dutch in the other room, shouting something like *What the fuck?!* but that hardly mattered now. Nothing mattered now.

On numb stick legs, she felt herself lurching toward the door.

11

She came out shooting.

She didn't mean to, didn't really even know it was happening until it was too late to take it back. One second, she was standing by the window, mind reeling at that horrible imitation of her friend, and the next, she was throwing the front door open and unloading her Glock into its stolen fucking face, all fire and fury and death.

It happened in snapshots, strobing in the muzzle flare of her nine millimeter. *Flash*: the first bullet tore away a chunk of its forehead in a bloody spray. *Flash*: the next shattered its jaw in a shower of brown teeth. *Flash*: a ragged hole appeared in the side of its chicken-skin throat, spluttering black muck. *Flash, flash, flash, flash*. Anne didn't stop pulling the trigger until the thing hit the ground and went still.

She stood over the impostor, empty Glock still smoking in her hand, barely feeling the chill wind digging into her bare arms and face. Heat poured off the thing's crumpled, bleeding form like a sickness. She didn't know what the hell it was—but she knew those eyes. They'd haunted her nightmares ever since she was six years old, waking up in the hospital with dead spots in her memory.

Automatically, Anne whisked the spent magazine from the pistol's grip and clapped one of her spares into place, snapping the slide back into position with a twitch of her thumb. She could feel the red panic still spinning inside her skull, whirling at dizzying speeds, only barely controlled.

It wasn't him. Whatever the fuck it was, nightmare, memory, some horrible combination of the two, it wasn't Jessup. It might have been wearing his face, but it was a hollow imitation at best. A subpar copy. Stealing a glance away from the ruined body, Anne looked over to the place where she and Dutch had buried her friend—the soil freshly packed, untouched since they'd piled the last shovelful on top.

"Anne? *Anne!*"

Dutch's voice sounded so distant, even though he couldn't have been more than twelve feet away from where she stood. She turned toward the cabin and the light spilling out through the open door.

"I'm okay," she called back, her voice ragged and raw. "I'm . . . It's okay. I think it's okay."

She looked back down at the impostor's body. Its eyes were open again. Staring right at her.

Oh, fuck—!

The Glock bucked in her free hand as the creature launched to its feet, bleeding from all the holes she'd already blasted into its mass. A web of red, razor-thin lines sprouted at the corners of its horrible mouth, then split apart and spread, revealing rows and rows of rotten teeth ridged atop belts of blood and bone and sinew and yellow globules of fat that all quivered together around a devouring, empty gullet that looked like it went on and on into black infinity.

It was revolting, hideous, atrocious, but underneath all that, it was just fundamentally *wrong*. Faces didn't do that. Faces never did that. The wrongness of it all was so colossal, so all-encompassing, that it was the only thing Anne could register. Every other sensation, every emotion, her fear, anger, revulsion, they were all obliterated in its inescapable glare. Her brain was short-circuiting. She was having a panic attack.

That was when it struck, lashing one twisted hand out to drag its gnarled, yellow razor-claws through Anne's exposed forearm in a spray of blood and shredded skin. For a moment, a blinding flare of nauseating black-white light erupted behind her eyes, there and gone again. Anne shrieked in pain and jerked her arm away, pressing it to her chest. The impostor shivered and shook and snorted, and its eyes went wide, frenzied. Anne threw herself backward as darkness flickered around the corners of her vision. She was going to black out. She felt her feet go out from under her just as consciousness fled her body.

12

Dutch didn't see any of it, but he heard plenty.

He heard the panicked half-gasp catch in Anne's chest after she pulled the window curtain back. He heard that broken-rattle voice from outside, calling her by name. He heard the door fly open and the flurry of gunshots that followed.

He heard Anne call out to him, saying she was okay. Then he heard her scream.

Panicking, he yanked his cuffed wrists against the bed frame, looking for a way to force a weak spot in the chain. He hadn't known Anne long, but he knew enough to be sure that she wasn't the type of person to scream if she didn't have to. Whatever was out there, it was beyond serious. He had to get loose and help her, if for no other reason than the fact that once whatever it was finished with Anne, odds were good it would come for him next. He yanked on the handcuffs again, but it was futile. There was no way in hell the chain was going to break . . . but maybe he could squeeze a hand through.

Shifting around to brace both legs against the little metal bed frame, he screwed his jaw tight, twisted his hand into a spearpoint, and started to pull it back through.

The metal bit into his wrist as if it had teeth, pinching and bruising. He pulled until he felt the skin above his hand split and peel back and his shoulder felt like it was going to pop loose from its socket. But still he kept pulling, screaming through his teeth, feeling the delicate bones inside bow and warp. For a second, he didn't think it was going to work, but then, inch by painful inch, his blood-slick hand started to slide through the cuff. *Just a little farther, come on, please, come on . . .*

The metal edge bit deeper, dragging long red smears down the back of his hand. He pulled again and felt something inside *give* just a little bit more; not exactly a *snap* but not far off, either. Pain, blunt and crushing, leapt up his arm, and a second later, his hand finally slipped free of the cuff and he found himself sprawled on the cabin floor, gasping for air as he bled.

Lurching to his feet, Dutch stumbled out of the bedroom and swept the shotgun off the coffee table, the handcuffs still dangling from one wrist as he turned to look at the bleeding, humanoid creature stooped just beyond the doorway. At first, he didn't understand what he was seeing. Anne was on the ground, trembling in half consciousness as the thing ran one long-fingered hand up her wounded arm, sniffing at her like a wolf inspecting a fresh kill. Dutch pitched the twelve-gauge's stock into his shoulder and lined up the iron sights on the malformed thing, then drew a sharp breath and held it. He pulled the trigger.

The shotgun blast caught the monster full-on in the chest, blowing it away from Anne in a spray of gore. Freed from the impostor's grasp, she scrambled away in slow motion, eyes still wide and uncomprehending. Dutch racked the shotgun's pump, kicking the spent shell from the breach, and planted his feet to line up his next shot, but it was too late. The thing was already up again—and rushing him.

13

Anne's senses returned to her just in time for her to see the impostor—roaring, chewed up by bullets, furious—crash through the cabin doorway and into Dutch, sending him flying. She'd been out for only a few seconds, but it felt like much longer, an empty space, another perfect void where consciousness and memory should have been.

She rolled over onto her front, bracing her free hand against the cold winter soil, and rose unsteadily, head woozy and swimming. On her feet once more, she wheeled her Glock up at the impostor's back as it stalked toward Dutch, ready to pull him apart at the seams. She didn't even really bother aiming this time. *BLAM, BLAM, BLAM*—the gunshots hammered loudly against the silent night, punching fresh holes in the thing's shoulders until the gun clacked empty again. Shit.

Standing over the fallen man, the impostor roared and spun to face her. It had managed to hang on to some semblance of Jessup's visage despite the bullets and the damage they'd done, but its face was hardly an imitation now; it was a cruel mockery. Its chest hung in gory tatters, blown apart by the twelve-gauge, its flesh riddled with holes. The fingers on one hand dangled like grisly wind chimes, suspended precariously by stringlets of torn skin beneath broken spurs of bone. But it wasn't the wounds that held Anne's attention, it was those blank eyes. Dead. Unmistakable.

"I remember you," Anne said.

The wounded thing shivered and lurched toward her, the skin of its stolen Jessup-face peeling back from its spiderweb mouth, giving way to a second one waiting underneath, bulbous and imprecise, a drunken, misanthropic sculptor's approximation of a human profile. Seeing it change, Anne's instincts took over. She moved for the cabin door, feinting right then going left, weaving around the impostor at top speed.

This was a bad idea. This was a very bad idea. But she was fresh out of good ones.

She dashed through the doorway and vaulted over the couch, keeping it between her and the impostor, not that the busted old channel-back would stop the thing if—when—it charged her.

Screeching, gushing flies and blood in equal measure, the impostor lumbered after her, snapping its nightmare jaws, its movements halting and herky-jerky. It was wounded, but wounded wasn't nearly dead.

Against the far wall, Dutch was splayed on the floor, eyes lolling under heavy lids, Remington still cradled in both hands. For a second, Anne thought about making a play for the shotgun, but she'd already seen enough to figure that another load or two of buckshot would only minimally slow the impostor down while maximally pissing it off. She needed something a little more potent.

Snatching the mostly-full bottle of rubbing alcohol off the coffee table, she spun the cap off and splashed it in the impostor's face, drenching it. The thing paused midstep, and for a second, Anne thought she could see the slightest hint of confusion in its broken expression. Good.

Anne snatched the long, dusty box of hearth matches off the fireplace, lit one off the striker strip, then held the flame to the cardboard. The box caught almost instantly, going up like a road flare as Anne hurled it at the mutilated creature.

There was a gasp of air like a sharp, deep inhalation as the alcohol caught, bursting into orange flames across the impostor's body. The fire spread fast, and the thing recoiled, shrieking. Anne clapped her hands to her ears and stumbled away from that piercing scream as the burning impostor thrashed backward out of the cabin, dragging a snail trail of flames behind it.

Outside, the impostor, the un-Jessup, the whatever-it-was, thrashed and contorted, folding over itself again and again, trying to snuff out the fire that was steadily consuming its body. A fresh wave of flies and maggots burst from its burning form in sheets as its cacophonic screech grew somehow louder, more insistent. There was a flash of bright white eyes in the center of its hideous mass, incandescent with pain and hatred, and then, with a final shudder, the impostor turned and ran.

The thing's desperate screeching gave way to a deafening drone of a thousand insectoid wings beating against the night—Anne could feel the sound in her back teeth, like chewing on aluminum foil. And then it was gone. The maggots left in its wake dug into the soil as the flies rose like some dread shadow then scattered, disappearing into the darkened sky above.

Everything was silent again. Everything was still. Misjudging a step backward, Anne went tumbling onto her ass, staring uncomprehendingly at the place where the impostor had stood only moments before. In a daze, she hung her head, trying to make sense of it all.

There was a sound from the other side of the room. Anne looked over and saw Dutch slouched there, bathed in yellow lamplight, one maimed wrist bleeding freely, an empty handcuff dangling from the other.

"Are you okay?" he asked, staring blankly at her right arm, and for a second, she didn't understand what he was talking about. Then, she remembered: The impostor had shredded her forearm. The wounds there were deep and bloody, the skin hanging in ribbons above split flesh, but she could still move her hand and her fingers without too much pain, so maybe the damage wasn't as bad as it looked. She sure fucking hoped so. She'd never learned to shoot with her left.

"Come on," Dutch said, his voice raw and wheezy. "Let's . . . We should . . . get patched up, and . . . we have to . . . We can't stay here."

Anne nodded, but didn't dare speak. There was nothing else to say, and she didn't want to start screaming again.

★   ★   ★

Together, they cleaned and bandaged each other's arms, then packed up the little that they'd brought with them into the Ninety-Eight's oversize trunk. There wasn't much: the shotgun, the first aid supplies, the bank bag. The Glock found its way back to its familiar place in Anne's waistband, and Aunt Lisa's letter went back in her pocket. The VHS tape she kept with her—it had been her mom's, and she wasn't about to take her eyes off it if she could help it. Carefully, she slid her bandaged arm into the sleeve of Jessup's squall jacket and shrugged it the rest of the way on, zipping it tight like a Kevlar vest. Everything else in the cabin they just left, lights on, door hanging wide open. What did any of it matter now? This place wasn't hers, hadn't ever been. So let the valley take it back, let time and weather wear it down and rust it through; let the forest spread and grow through the floors and walls to rip it all the way down to the stones.

In the driver's seat of the Oldsmobile, Anne curled a hand around the top of the steering wheel and pitched forward until her forehead touched her knuckles. Exhaustion rattled through her every nerve and muscle, urged on by the post-adrenaline-rush drop that had hung on ever since she watched that horrible fucking thing, the nightmare, the impostor, whatever, thrash away and disappear burning into the night.

Her mind wandered back to the burst of light inside her head as the thing had raked at her—migraine-bright and nauseating, not white and not black and yet too much of both. She could still feel the aftershocks of it pinballing around inside her stomach; like she'd been snared by a live wire or something. She'd never had something like that happen to her before, and if she were lucky, it wouldn't ever happen again.

But they hadn't killed it. She wasn't nearly so deluded or arrogant as to think otherwise. They'd hurt it for sure, sent it packing, but it wasn't dead. It would come back, probably twice as angry. She didn't plan on being here when it did. Bone-tired or not, they had to go. Now.

Beside her, there was a clank of metal and a squeal of hinges as the passenger door swung open. Anne straightened in an instant, knuckling at her eyes as Dutch climbed into the seat beside her.

"You get everything?" she asked.

"Yeah, I think so." He rubbed idly at his own bandages. She'd wrapped the fingers he'd hurt getting free—wasn't sure if they were broken or dislocated or what, so she'd settled for taping them up and hoping for the best before she turned her attention to the torn-up skin circling his wrist. Like her shredded arm, they'd disinfected it and wrapped it tight with what was left of the gauze— the wounds underneath were too shallow and too messy for the kind of stitches that Anne, a trained medic by no measure of the word, could manage. There'd be a thatch of scars there, eventually, but that couldn't be avoided. They'd just needed to stop the bleeding. It wasn't supposed to be pretty.

"Are you okay?"

Anne paused. How could she even begin to answer that question? She thought about laughing in his face, riposting with some cutting remark, but then remembered that he'd seen all the same crazy things she had. However not okay she was, Dutch couldn't be that far behind. So she swallowed her venom and shrugged.

"No," she said.

Sliding the keys in the ignition, Anne started the Oldsmobile up, the big V-8 roaring to life under the hood like a dragon roused from its slumber. Anne let it idle for a second, relishing the sound, then reached down and pulled the knob for the headlights. The sedan's dash lit up in a warm orange-yellow glow as the car's high beams slashed through the gloom ahead, transmogrifying the trees that loomed overhead into an army of billowing ghosts above the rocks and soil and spindly, straggly underbrush. Anne breathed out, watched her breath steam the glass beside her face, then wiped it away with her bare hand. From where she sat, the cabin looked so small, now. So shabby. Nothing like the place she remembered, but maybe nothing ever was, really. The lights inside would stay on until the generator ran out of gas; after that, it was up to the valley what became of it. She was done here.

Beside her, Dutch snapped his lap belt into place. Anne didn't bother with hers. She dropped the engine into Drive, pulled a quick U-ey in the dirt, and for the second time in her life, fled her mother's cabin with little more than a gun and the clothes on her back.

II

Rattler

14

They drove until the needle on the gas gauge hovered just above E, then pulled off into a lonely little one-pump filling station on the side of the highway, its cracked lot weakly illuminated by a single overhead light. The convenience store windows were dark behind accordion grates, but it looked like the pumps took credit cards. Anne recoiled at the thought. Credit cards meant a digital paper trail. Meant cops. But there wasn't any other option that she could see. It was either this, or they drained the Ninety-Eight's tank dry, ditched it on the side of the road, and made their way on foot, but that really wasn't a choice at all. They had to keep moving. There were way worse things out there than the cops.

She killed the engine. Looked over at Dutch. "You got a credit card?"

"Uh, what?" The cop's face was incredulous.

"Credit card," Anne said again. "Plastic. For the gas."

"Oh, um. Yeah, yeah, sure," Dutch said. He dug in his pocket for his wallet and thumbed out an orange card from its folds. Held it out to her. Anne took it without a word and stepped out of the car.

Standing beside the pump, she swiped the card, then knelt by the back end of the Oldsmobile and hinged the license plate down to uncap the gas tank and fit the nozzle in place. While the tank filled, she returned to the driver's seat, leaving the door open as she waited. She held the credit card out to Dutch without looking.

"Thanks," she said.

He took his card back, watching her in the pale glow of the sedan's dome light.

"What?" Anne asked.

"Nothing," Dutch said. "I guess I'm just wondering what our plan is. What are we going to do?"

Anne kept her eyes straight ahead. "I don't know who you're talking about. There is no *we*. Me, I'm going to go get my shit from my place, and then I'm going to get the fuck out of here. Out of the valley, out of Colorado. Maybe out of the country, I don't know. As far as I can get, as fast as I can get there."

"What about me? What about the . . . that thing?"

"What about it? What about you?" Anne snapped, suddenly irritated at the naked frailty in his voice for mirroring the frailty she felt inside, the fear she couldn't allow herself to look at just yet. Maybe ever. "You go back to your life, Dutch. Back to Kinsey and your sister and whoever the fuck else. Call your buddies with the badges and billy clubs and tell them I let you go. Tell them what you saw up at the cabin, or don't. I don't really give a shit. You do whatever the fuck you want, but me, I'm gone."

"They're not going to believe me. Not about any of it. They're either going to think that I'm fucking crazy, or worse, that I was in on the whole thing from the start. They'll string me up for everyone to see, and then they'll throw me in the deepest, darkest hole they've got, and they'll forget all about me," he told her. "Listen, I've been thinking a lot about this, and all I want is to just go back to my life. But I can't. No matter how many ways I try to put the pieces together again, they don't fit anymore. Not after all this. I'm just as fucked as you are at this point. No question."

"Not my problem."

"Anne, please."

In the low glow of the single light overhead, she finally turned to look at him and studied his expression, the unalloyed fear that had settled deep in his eyes. He wasn't wrong—about any of it. There was no way in hell he was going back to his old life now, whatever that had looked like before. Even if he somehow managed to dodge charges, he was done being a cop. He'd never escape the shadow of this mess. They wouldn't let him. For a moment, she entertained the thought of saving them both the trouble and shooting him in the face right here, right now, then dumping him on the roadside somewhere and vanishing forever. But she knew in her heart she wasn't going to do that. He'd helped when he didn't have to; he'd saved her life, blasting that thing with the shotgun like he did. Law enforcement or not, that had to count for something.

"Fine," she said after another moment. "Whatever. Fine. Let's just get the fuck out of here and we'll figure it out. Okay?"

"Yeah," Dutch said. "That's great. Good. Thank you."

"Mm."

At the back of the Ninety-Eight, the pump thumped and shut itself off. Anne got out, replaced the nozzle in its cradle, capped the tank, then got back in and started the car without another word.

She hated this. But at least she didn't have to hate it alone.

The town of Pecos, Colorado, wasn't much to look at, as far as towns went. Even by San Luis Valley standards, it was small, comprising six or seven main thoroughfares crisscrossed by another three or four cutting perpendiculars across the city limits. It was ramshackle, too—it didn't have any of the small-town charm of Monte Vista or Alamosa's collegial vibes; likewise, it hadn't experienced the tourist-hipster explosion of Salida, with its brewpubs and dispensaries and overpriced vinyl-and-coffee shops. To anyone looking in from the outside, Pecos was essentially a wide spot on the road, a place to fill up on gas and snacks before getting the hell out again. The people who lived here had drifted in from parts unknown, looking to take advantage of the quiet living and the cheap rent; else they were longtimers, locals who had grown up around these parts and weren't planning on leaving any time soon. People minded their own business in Pecos, kept their heads down, and didn't pretend to be friendly when they weren't. As far as Anne was concerned, it was basically perfect.

Anne scanned the darkened windows of every building they passed, searching for movement, for some sign of life, all her nerves on high alert for anything that would give her cause to return to the highway and never look back. She knew she shouldn't have come back here. But there were things she couldn't leave without. Not if she was going to have any chance of getting away clean and living with herself.

Anne pinned the speedometer a few miles below the limit as she drove past the church and the bank and the liquor store to the far side of town and the shabby little apartment complex that she called home. Over the front doors, the words PECOS PARK ARMS were rendered in spindly, 1940s-imperial-style lettering. Anne nosed the car around the corner, then looped back up again to park at the head of a dusty access road a block and a half away. She killed the lights and the engine and sat there behind the wheel, watching, holding her breath, trying not to blink. Beside her, Dutch followed her gaze toward the darkened building.

"Are we going in there?"

Anne rubbed at her face with one hand. "I am. You're not."

"Why not?" Dutch's voice was smeared with reproach.

"Because I don't know what's waiting for me in there. Could be cops. Could be one of Travis's guys with a shotgun. I can't say for sure."

"All the more reason for you to not go it alone. Come on, we talked about this. I'm with you. Right?"

Anne looked him over in the darkness. His eyes were wide and guileless, nearly electric with anxiety. She understood then: When he talked about her not going it alone, he was really talking about himself. He didn't want to be left on his own. She couldn't blame him. Not after what they'd seen. Not after it had nearly killed them.

"Yeah, okay," she said, scooping the VHS cassette up off the bench seat as she kicked the door open. "Come on. Let's make it quick."

They went in the back way, taking the service door beside the dumpsters to the fire exit stairs. Anne went first, taking the steps two at a time until she reached the fourth floor. She eased the door open and stepped out into the carpeted hallway, moving fast and keeping her head down. Up ahead, Anne heard a dead bolt turn and saw a face appear in the gap of a chained door. It was the old woman who lived two apartments down, a bitter old bat who kept what sounded like sixty Pomeranians and clearly thought of herself as the building's resident hall monitor. Anne met the old woman's glare and faked a smile; the old woman didn't return the courtesy. Not that Anne had expected any different. The woman slammed her door tight as they passed, and that was fine by Anne. She didn't plan on sticking around any longer than she absolutely had to—just enough to close up shop and get the hell out of Dodge for good.

Sliding her key into the lock on her door, she eased the dead bolt back and hit the lights as Dutch followed her in. Her apartment wasn't much to look at, outfitted for function rather than form: a small kitchen with little counter space to spare between the microwave and the coffeemaker; a thrift-store couch facing a coffee table and a cheap flat-screen TV; a thrift-store dining table cluttered with a dusty, aging desktop computer, a legion of empty coffee cups, tools, and a few guns in various states of disassembly.

There was movement atop the sofa, a dark flash of striped gray fur and big green eyes. Murphy, Anne's chubby, grumpy tabby, regarded the two of them from his perch, unimpressed. Anne went to the big cat, nuzzling one hand against the side of his face. Murph yowled in protest for a second, clearly pissed off about being left alone for so long, but after a second, he warmed to her like he always did and hopped up into her arms.

She'd first found Murph when he was just a stray kitten, a terrified little thing hiding curled up in the back of a garage one winter, his big green eyes wide and frightened, flicking every which way as he scanned nonstop for possible threats. The world was full of them when you were so small and on your own. Anne had looked around for any sign of other cats, maybe even the little guy's mom, but he was alone. Cold. Scared. It had taken him a little while to let Anne get close, but he'd started purring like a tiny little chainsaw the second she had scooped him up in her arms. The two of them had basically been inseparable ever since. People had always been complicated to Anne. Cats were easier. And as far as cats went, Murph was the best.

Standing with the big chunk in her arms, Anne caught Dutch looking, eyes wide, face impassive. Whatever he might have been expecting, she had a feeling that this wasn't it.

"What?" she asked.

"Nothing," Dutch said. "Just wouldn't have taken you for an animal person, that's all."

"Yeah, well. Plenty of shit you don't know about me," she said, shifting the cat in her arms so he sat with his front paws over her shoulder. "This is Murphy."

Awkwardly, Dutch raised a hand as if to wave to the cat.

"Hi, Murphy," he said.

Anne nodded toward the short hallway leading to the back of the apartment. "You should get changed. That uniform's starting to stink like shit. There's some clothes in the back of my closet that'll probably fit. Go grab whatever. Bathroom's across the hall. We don't have a lot of time, but if you want to rinse off, I'm not going to stop you. Shower's a little creaky, but it runs fine after it warms up."

"Yeah, all right," Dutch said, then excused himself down the hall.

Anne watched him go, first to her bedroom, then into the bathroom, holding a handful of old clothes. It was strange, having Dutch here—having anyone here, really, but a cop more than most. Gem would probably shit bricks if she found out.

A second later, Anne heard the shower start to run at full blast. Setting Murphy down, she quickly went to work. The desktop was first. She yanked the power cable from the back, then took a small screwdriver from the clutter and opened the tower's plastic case corner by corner. With a quick jerk of her arm, she pulled the hard drive from its slot, then unscrewed it and scraped the point of the screwdriver across the silver platters inside, thoroughly destroying all the data. Next she popped out the circuit board and snapped it in half against the edge of the table. She'd kept the computer totally air-gapped ever since she brought the thing home, but she wasn't about to give the cops any more evidence than she already had.

In the kitchen, she stood on her tiptoes to pull the little drab-green lockbox off the top shelf of her pantry, then fetched the hazard-yellow squeezy bottle of Ronsonol from under the sink. Unlocking the box, Anne looked inside to examine its contents: bank statements, fake IDs, an envelope thick with cash, receipts, prepaid phones and credit cards, a handwritten list of contact numbers—all their burners—and a copy of her fugazi lease. The apartment wasn't in her name; she'd worked out a deal with the landlord for four hundred over the monthly, asking to sidestep the standard background and credit checks and add a fake name on the lease. That had been what, five years ago already? It had been a sweet deal for everybody involved, up until now. She almost felt guilty, splitting in the middle of the night like this, but the landlord would be fine; over the course of five years, Anne had put—she did some quick mental math—an extra twenty-four grand in his fat fucking pocket, tax-free. She figured that would probably go a long way to easing his pain. And if it didn't, fuck him. Landlords were all leeches and scum, anyway.

She pulled a fresh burner phone from the box, still in its thick plastic vacuum-mold packaging, then took the envelope of cash, the contact list, and her best fake ID, and left the rest. Setting the box in the sink, Anne upended the Ronsonol over its contents, squeezing the bottle's soft plastic sides once, twice, three times. When everything inside was well soaked with lighter fluid, Anne climbed up on a chair and ripped the smoke detector out of the ceiling, then lit a match and tossed it into the little tin box. The contents went up in an instant, smoking something terrible. Anne slid the window over the sink open to give the noxious fumes somewhere to go, then went to the hallway closet for the cat carrier and her backpack.

Back in the kitchen, she snuffed the flames with a towel and ran the faucet over the charred remains, then threw the fake ID and the cash into the backpack—the total inside the envelope seemed so paltry, compared with what was inside the bank bag, but at this point, every little bit helped. Wherever she ended up, she was going to have to live off the take for a while. But it wasn't just her and Murphy, either. Like it or not, she had Dutch to worry about now, too. And Gemma. Wherever she was.

Anne's heart lurched, thinking of Gemma again. She hadn't seen what had happened to her after shit hit the fan back in Durango; didn't know if she was alive or dead, but if she had to wager, she'd bet every cent on Gem. Cautious, smart, stubborn, Gemma Poe was a survivor through and through. If anybody had made it out, she had.

Anne used her pocketknife to slit the plastic off the fresh burner, clicked it to life, then laddered through the short, handwritten contact list to the third number labeled *GP*. She thumbed it into the keypad, then punched Call and braced the phone between her ear and shoulder as she filled her backpack with the VHS tape, food for Murphy, a few spare boxes of ammo, her lockout kit, and a couple of other things from around the apartment. Unsurprisingly, the call went straight to voicemail. A blank robotic voice recited the number to Gem's burner, then played a harsh *BEEEEEEP*.

"Hey, it's me," Anne said. "I got out okay. Fucking mess. I, uh. Okay. Stats." She paused, trying to think about how to say what came next. Anne had never been great at talking on the phone, and she had to be extra careful now not to use any names. "J's . . . gone," she said, eventually. "M, too. That grinning prick and his bitch wife burned us, but I don't know, you probably figured that out already. Driver's with them. I'm at my place, I've got your . . . yeah. Your part. Give me a call back when you can, just so I know everything hasn't gone all Godzilla. I really hope you're okay. All right. Bye."

She hung up and looked down at the cheap little Nokia in her palm. *Godzilla.* She couldn't help but smile. A private joke between her and Gem that went back years to one of their very first jobs together, an armored truck robbery that had gone sideways when one of the guards decided to be an asshole and make a play for his radio. Anne and Gem had cut bait then and there, hiding out in a nearby shitball second-run theater, which, on the night in question, was hosting a kaiju double feature: the original 1954 *Godzilla* back-to-backed with *Godzilla vs. Destoroyah*. Over a tub of stale popcorn and a couple of fizzless fountain drinks, they'd gotten to laughing about hypothetical worst-case scenarios and what-ifs, agreeing as the final credits rolled that in the whole galaxy of *it-gets-worse* developments, "Godzilla arriving on the scene to fuck shit up" was probably the very worst either of them could imagine. That night was one of Anne's very favorite memories, gorging herself on trash snacks and stealing glances at the shimmering silver screenlight reflecting off of Gemma's beautiful brown skin, and ever since, *Godzilla* had become their go-to code word for apocalypse-level scenarios that couldn't be unfucked. It meant burning everything to the ground and getting gone forever, because the only other option meant dying like an idiot. And for them, more often than not, *getting gone* meant New York.

As far as Anne and Gem were concerned, New York, or somewhere like it, was the ultimate getaway plan, a city big and far away enough that even if everything went irreversibly wrong, they could just disappear into and never look back. It meant the end of their criminal careers, a chance to start over and do something else, be someone else. They were careful to never talk about it when Jess was within earshot; he would have been so hurt even to consider the notion of the two of them jumping ship. But if Anne were honest, she kind of liked it that way. There was something special about having a secret that was only hers and Gem's—something to hang on to even in her very darkest moments, somewhere to pull hope from when hope was in short supply.

Shaking off the memory, Anne returned her attention to the backpack and the ancient video cassette tucked inside. She fished it out again and turned it over in her hands, inspecting the phone number inscribed into the label on the bottom of the casing. She hadn't given it a second thought back at the cabin, but now ran the pad of her thumb over the ballpoint numerals furrowed into the paper. It was just a phone number. It probably didn't even work anymore. What could the harm be?

Swallowing back her nerves, Anne clicked her burner to life and dialed the number, digit by deliberate digit. Her thumb hovered over Call for a breath, then two, then three as her heart thundered inside of her rib cage. Fuck it. She pressed the button and held the phone to her ear.

The line buzzed and clicked, then started to ring: once . . . twice . . . three times . . .

Then someone picked up.

"Hello?" a crackly, static-shredded voice said on the other end of the line. *"Annie?"*

Her heart jumped into her throat and she felt her face go hot. She killed the call and clapped the phone to the countertop just as she heard someone shift in place behind her. When she turned to look, she found Dutch standing at the mouth of the hallway, hair wet from the shower, dressed in a chambray work shirt and battered khakis over his heavy cop boots. He'd changed the bandage around his wrist, but the blood was already seeping through. He'd really ripped himself up, but Anne was thankful that he had. She'd have been dead otherwise. Standing there, he eyed her curiously.

"All good?" he asked.

"Yeah. Fine," Anne said, shaking her head. She tossed the burner and the VHS into the backpack, along with Aunt Lisa's letter. Pushing a loose lock of red hair away from her face, she went and scooped Murph up, then slid him into his carrier alongside a blanket he'd long claimed as his own, plus a couple of her old T-shirts for warmth.

"Nothing to worry about," she said, zipping the cat carrier tight. She quirked her eyebrows at his new clothes. "Nice duds."

"Thanks," he said, brushing a dove wing of dust from one of the sleeves. "Whose are they?"

"Jessup's," she said.

Dutch fixed her with a questioning look, a raised eyebrow. "Wait, really? I didn't know that you two—"

"Not like that," she said, her voice clipped. "Not at all. I'm not . . . into guys. He just stashed a couple of things here for when he got too drunk to drive home and had to sleep on the couch."

"Oh, great," Dutch said. "Dead man's clothes. Cool."

"Don't make it weird, okay? Better those than walking out of here with a fucking blood-smeared badge pinned to your shirt. Lady down the hall already saw us come in. What'd you do with the uni?"

"Stuffed it in the back of the bathroom cabinet, underneath all the towels and shit," he said.

Anne nodded. "Smart."

"So, is that it? We on our way out?" Dutch's tone was bright with excited, almost academic, curiosity. Anne's first impulse was to take offense, but thinking about it, she kind of got it, too. She sincerely doubted that he'd ever had to consider torching his whole life and getting the fuck out at top speed. That kind of thing was SOP for people in Anne's line of work, but Dutch was a cop seeing the other side of the street for the first time. Of course he was going to be curious.

"Just about, yeah," Anne said honestly.

"Okay," he said. "Need me to carry anything?"

Anne waved him off. "I got it. Just be on the lookout for anything weird."

He smirked. "What, like swarms of flies, dead people walking around like it's no big deal?"

"I was thinking cops, but yeah, those too," Anne said, feeling the barest whispers of a smile prick the corners of her mouth. Inside her head, her nerves threatened to spike at mention of the impostor, the thing, whatever it was, but she was surprised to find Dutch joking about it actually . . . kind of helped.

She zipped the pack shut and slung it over one shoulder, then hefted Murphy's carrier and took one last look around her spartan little apartment, making sure she hadn't missed anything. The desktop was dead, any records connecting her to anything burned to a crisp in the sink. Everything else that mattered she was taking with her.

She wanted to feel nostalgic for this place, but she just couldn't. This apartment, this town, it had always been a way station, a home in name only. Purely liminal. A space in between, some place for her to crash and keep her head down until the next job. Walking away from it now was like getting rid of a wall calendar from last year. It was never meant to be permanent.

She turned off the lights and walked out.

They took the stairs as quick as they could, feet spinning down the steps like a waterfall. Around and around they went, taking the floors at speed, third, second, ground-floor landing, toward the service door—

Anne's heart nearly stopped.

There was a cop waiting for them at the bottom. He was older, out of shape, sweaty, nervous, but the pistol in his hand was trained squarely at Anne's heart.

She heard footsteps behind her, then felt the barrel of a gun kiss the back of her head. The old woman's face flashed across the backs of Anne's eyes, pinched with scowl lines in the chain-locked gap between her door and the jamb. The mean old asshole had called 911, no doubt about it. Anne wanted to rage, wanted to scream, but forced her emotions to stay in check. These small-town badges had them dead to rights, and odds were good that they were just looking for a reason to let shit pop off. She wasn't about to give it to them.

"Pecos Police Department," the cop at the bottom of the stairs said. "Get your hands up. Now."

Setting Murph's carrier by her feet, she stood straight and raised her hands high. Beside her, Dutch did the same.

Fuck.

15

Ungently, the two cops relieved Anne of her backpack and her gun, then led her and Dutch out of the building in handcuffs, perp-walking them down the alley to the back of their waiting black and white. Without being too obvious about it, Anne hazarded a glance up the street at the Ninety-Eight, still parked at the corner of the access road. Either the cops hadn't noticed it yet, or they had and were planning on coming back for it later.

In the back seat of the cruiser, Dutch leaned forward, getting close to the Plexiglas barrier to address the badges on the other side.

"Listen, I'm a cop," he said. "Durango PD. Louis Greene, *G-R-E-E-N-E.* You can look me up, okay? I'll explain everything."

Anger boiled in Anne's belly, but at herself more than at Dutch. Of course he was going to pull that card the second he was able. He was a cop. Self-preservation was the name of the game. Shit, she'd probably have done the same in his position. She was just pissed that she'd given him the benefit of the doubt.

The younger cop, the blond one who had stuck her gun to the back of Anne's head, tapped something into the cruiser's dash computer, and made a *hmn* sound as she scanned the screen's digital readout.

"Checks out," she said to her partner. "That's him. Warrant and all."

Beside Anne, Dutch bristled. "Wait, what? What warrant?"

The older cop glowered in the rearview.

"Aiding and abetting," he said with a smile that didn't reach his eyes. "Turns out, there's consequences to being a collaborating piece of shit. Your ass is all over the news, *Officer Greene*. Or hadn't you heard?"

"No, hold on, there's been a mistake," Dutch stammered. "I didn't, I mean, no, come on, you have to listen, please—"

"Save it," the older cop said. "We'll take your statement back at the station, but right now, I don't want to fucking hear it. You're a disgrace to the badge."

"I didn't do anything wrong!" Dutch roared. Beside him, Anne nudged him with a shoulder, then met his eyes and shook her head slowly, deliberately: *Don't bother.* If there was a warrant out on him, no amount of arguing or bitching was going to make a difference. Cops were all absolutists, the ultimate in-group. Either you were with them, or you were their enemy. That was how it had worked since time immemorial, and it wasn't about to change because Louis Greene III wanted it to be so. Best thing they could both do now was shut the fuck up and let the wheels of justice grind on until an opportunity presented itself. After another second, Dutch's shoulders fell, and all the air went out of him. His head sank. His eyes slid shut.

It wasn't far to the station, no more than a few blocks, but that didn't stop the cops, high and hard over their apparent win, from making an entire thing of it, running the cruiser lights the whole way, a victory parade of one. Anne watched the soggy cop in the rearview mirror as he drove, studying his eyes until he caught her staring and mad-dogged her back, eyes narrow and pissy between the mottled folds of his crow's-feet and frown lines. Anne showed him her winningest smile. Somebody had a little temper on him. That was good to know.

The Pecos police station wasn't particularly impressive, a small, squat stucco building that made it adorably clear just how unprepared the PPD was for anything bigger than issuing speeding tickets or pinching local teens for shoplifting shit from the dollar store. Anne had been in 7-Elevens bigger than this place. There were a few desks near the front, just beyond the counter, outfitted with outdated desktop computers and piled high with clutter. On the wall next to the holding cells, someone had painted the words *Pecos Police Department—Where You Matter!* in amateur cursive. Cute. Insane, but cute. Those holding cells were interesting, though: iron-barred cages set in the far back corner of the station that Anne guessed had probably been in use since the 1940s, maybe even earlier. There was someone rucked out and snoring in the cell on the right, probably a drunk sleeping off a few beers too many at the local watering hole. Whoever he was, she was willing to bet he was likely a regular here at the Hotel Pecos.

Anne didn't say a word as the soggy cop, smiling and self-satisfied, set Murph's carrier aside and led her back to the cells. Uncuffing her, he shoved her into the cage on the left. The iron bars slammed shut between them with a heavy *CLANG*.

"You sit tight, Miss Heller," he said. "And don't do anything silly now. We know all about you."

"Go fuck yourself, *Reno 911*. I want a lawyer," she snapped back, rubbing gingerly at her mauled arm. In all the hubbub, the cops had torn it open again—blood was already soaking through the gauze in messy crimson patches.

The cop's smile curdled like milk, and he walked away. Anne watched as, on the other side of the bullpen, the blonde handcuffed Dutch to the steel eyelet bolted into the nearest desk, then sat down to take his statement. Stepping back from the cage door, Anne lowered herself onto the cell's cold metal bench/cot and stretched out slowly and methodically as she tried to roll the tension from her shoulders, the weary ache from her thighs. Unsurprisingly, the last few days had left her body a knotted-up mess.

This wasn't her first time behind bars—far from it. First time she'd been thrown in holding, she'd been, what, not even sixteen? Got caught shoplifting a whole stack of CDs from the local Kmart. They hadn't been anything special—she hadn't even wanted them, really. She just wanted to see if she could do it, taking them into the last stall in the ladies' room near the back of the store, then ripping off the cellophane wrappers and throwing them in her school backpack. The manager had been waiting for her the second she stepped out. He decided to make an example of her: marched her back to the office and called the cops, then had her led away in cuffs, the whole song and dance. Probably thought he was scaring her straight or some shit. Pathetic.

That was the first, but it hadn't been the last by a damn sight. On a long enough timeline, it was practically a prerequisite for the job. So being stuck in another cage right now? This shit didn't faze her. These small-town cops had gotten lucky, that was all. The only thing left was to wait and see where the chips fell. Maybe Dutch would dime on her, maybe he wouldn't. Shit, maybe he was spinning these badges a tale so tall it would somehow clear both of their names. But she kind of doubted that last one.

In the next cell, the snoozing drunk farted, then shifted in place and started snoring louder. Anne ground her teeth and kicked the bars between them until the guy rolled over, his snores momentarily muted. Then she lay down and stared at the ceiling, counting the pockmarks in the drywall tiles one by one. Wasn't like she had anything better to do right now. Might as well get comfortable.

16

She'd been lying there for nearly two hours by the time the station door swung open.

Outside, the first faint, blue-orange wisps of dawn grasped for the valley as the sun grew closer and closer to cresting the horizon. Anne watched that glow as another Pecos cop, neither young nor old, shuffled through the door into the bullpen, framed in shadow and early daybreak, shoulders hunched around his ears, hands hanging limply at his sides like he didn't know what to do with them. His dark hair sat in a greasy tousle above a pale, moony face and a red, corded neck. The guy looked like he hadn't showered—or slept—in days. Anne felt a cold spike of panic rising up between her shoulder blades, driving itself past her neck and into the base of her skull. She knew his type—angry, microdick insomniacs who stayed up all night pounding gallons of coffee and fistfuls of confiscated Adderall, treating their shitty little boondock precincts like their own personal bad-cop playgrounds. Badges like him were always, always trouble.

Dutch and the blond cop, fresh off what must have been their third or fourth go-around of Dutch's account of the last three days, glanced over at the guy, but neither said anything. They just went back to the task at hand:

"Okay, so when you say that you heard this . . . animal . . . speak . . . to her? From outside the cabin? What do you really mean by that?" It was almost funny; for an hour now, she'd kept hammering at Dutch with the same questions, like eventually he'd get sick of giving her the same answers and change it up to something a bit more palatable.

Anne wasn't shocked that the girl was having a hard time understanding, let alone believing, the story that was coming out of

Dutch's mouth. She'd have thought he was full of shit, too. He might as well have told her that Frankenstein or the Wolf Man were after them. But to his credit, Dutch sighed and leaned forward in his chair, obviously searching for some remaining shred of patience, then started to walk her through the story a fourth time, like it would make any difference. At this point, Anne was more amazed than anything that the cop hadn't gotten sick of hearing it and thrown Dutch in the cells with her and the still-sleeping drunk.

"Hey, you missed some real shit last night, Nicholson," the soggy cop called out from the other side of the bullpen as the insomniac moved to stand in the center of the station. "You remember that bank robbery out in Durango that went all to shit a few days ago? Caught ourselves one of the perpetrators last night, trying to blow town. One of her neighbors called it in. All we had to do was sit tight and wait for her to walk right into our hands, if you believe it. This job's too goddamn easy sometimes, I'm telling you. Check her out, cell A."

The soggy cop jabbed his ballpoint pen in Anne's direction. Anne showed him a middle finger that he didn't see, then turned her attention back to the insomniac, Nicholson, fully expecting him to play to type: Next he'd come sauntering over to the cage with a shitty smile and some half-baked quip that he, in his limited fucking cop intelligence, thought was clever. But Nicholson was just standing there in the center of the bullpen. Staring at her.

Inside his carrier, Murph shirked back and hissed at the guy, his hackles standing straight up along the ridge of his spine. The panic between Anne's shoulders swelled.

Nicholson shambled over to the cages, his footsteps heavy and uneven on the cracked tile, and came to a stop in front of Anne's cell, his face nearly pressed against the bars. She could feel the flushed heat coming off him from here, rising from his greasy, unwashed skin in waves. The smell of him—stale, filthy sweat and raw meat—made her stomach turn in knots.

On the other side of the cage, Nicholson smiled, his mouth hanging half-open like a panting dog's, and ran his hands back and forth across the painted iron bars like he was strumming a harp. His tongue hunted at the corners of his dry, cracked lips, back and forth, back and forth. Anne rose from the cot and stood in the center of the little cell, staring the prick down, refusing to show him a goddamn thing beyond the depths of her contempt. The panic didn't matter. The fact that he was bigger than she was, stronger than she was, and armed to the teeth didn't matter. Cops, even the so-called good ones, were all bullies at heart. Predators born and bred. The only way to deal with them when they got hungry was to show them you weren't scared, that attacking you was going to go just as bad for them as it was for you. She didn't think that this psycho was going to try anything with the other two badges present, but she couldn't be sure. Cops—small-town cops especially—got bored real easy, and when cops got bored, or pissed, or horny, or insecure, people around them had a nasty fucking habit of dying ugly. So Anne held her ground. Kept her back straight, her head high, her expression stony. Stared Nicholson right in his ratty fucking eyes, daring him to blink first. Which he did.

Which was when his eyes turned dead white.

Oh, fuck.

"Annie . . ."

Jessup's voice came warbling out of Nicholson's throat, that same sickening, mangled mockery. Her skin crawled, and her stomach flopped. How the hell had it followed them here? How was that even possible? Across the bullpen, Murph's frantic hissing grew louder, crescendoing into a high-pitched, panicked yowling.

The breath caught in Anne's throat like a fist, and she threw herself back from the bars—not fast enough. The impostor thrust a hand through the cage and caught her wounded arm in a brutal, viselike grip. The thing's touch was excruciating, all thorns and fangs. Every system, every function in her body seized and contracted at the sheer *wrongness* of it all. Her skin froze as it burned, like the worst fever she'd ever had. The air in her lungs grew foul and viscid, too thick to breathe. Pressure mushroomed behind her forehead, and she shut her eyes against it as fragments of a distant memory boiled up through the barbed panic inside her skull.

—agonizing, nauseating black-white light, filling her up from some-where else—

—pain blazing through both of her hands, up her arms, into her chest—

—screaming without end—

A second later, Anne felt the thing's claws rip into her skin, flensing away the sodden bandages, piercing the flesh beneath and drawing fresh blood as it dragged her back to the present. She screamed.

On the other side of the cage, the impostor's pale eyes bulged, fixed on the rich red blood coursing down Anne's arm and pouring off her fingertips. The creature shivered and yanked more insistently, panting and wheezing as its grip tightened nearly hard enough to crush the bones inside her arm to powder. Anne had seen the thing go frenzied like this before, and then she realized: it was the blood. Her blood was driving it crazy. Fuck. *Fuck.* The thing probably had her scented all the way up at the cabin; all it had to do now was follow the smell.

Anne thrashed and tried to pull away again, jamming her heels against the lacquered concrete floor for leverage. It wasn't working. On the far side of the bullpen, Dutch and the other cops were on their feet, faces agape with shock and horror, clueless, useless. Anne screamed again and saw the blond cop start forward, brushing past the still-chained Dutch, drawing the big silver .357 from her belt. She raised the revolver in shaking hands as she closed the distance between them, leveling it square at the impostor's back.

"Hands . . ." The blonde gasped. "Stop . . . stop it! *Nicholson, stop it!*" Her voice quavered and cracked like a fourthgrader giving her first public speech. The creature paid her no mind, still clutching on to Anne through the bars like it was trying to tear her arm from its socket.

Then the cop did the dumbest thing she could have possibly done: she pulled the trigger.

BOOM.

The big revolver kicked hard in the blonde's hands, blowing a bloody hole through the impostor's side. With a hiss, it whipped around to face her and screeched, the noise like drywall nails against plate glass.

BOOM. BOOM.

The cop pulled the trigger again and again, the gunshots painfully loud in the little bullpen. The thing stumbled, releasing Anne's arm as blood and meat burst from its hide. Awkwardly, Anne threw herself out of its reach, pinwheeling backward until the backs of her knees caught the edge of the cot and her legs buckled, dropping her painfully to her ass.

On the other side of the bars, flies jetted angrily from the shape-shifter's wounds, taking flight to swarm around the rest of the thing's hideous mass as it charged the cop, knocking the gun out of her hands and crashing onto her like a tidal wave. They hit the ground as one, and the blonde screamed—just the once, that was all she had time for—as the creature began to tear her apart in a vicious flurry of claws and teeth.

A few feet away, the soggy cop stumbled to the side, eyes wide and uncomprehending as he watched his partner die ugly. Anne waved her bloody hand at him, trying to signal his attention. When he finally looked over at her, she mouthed the word *keys* at him, miming turning a key in a lock. It was only then that she realized that the poor old bastard was alone in the bullpen. Where the fuck had Dutch gone? Had he cut and run already?

The cop's face knurled and contorted into a knot of revulsion. Anne could see in his eyes that the shock of the last few seconds was wearing off, replaced by horrible, wretched clarity.

"Nicholson, what the fuck are you doing?" the cop bellowed, as if that would do anything at all. Squaring his shoulders, he raced toward the bloody obscenity on the floor and grabbed at the impostor as if to intercede, trying to drag the thing that he still thought was Nicholson away from the dead blonde.

For a moment, Anne thought to scream, *No, don't!* at the poor asshole, but it was too late. He was already dead. He just didn't know it yet. The cop's face blanched with distant, animal fear, as if his brain had suddenly and unexpectedly shit itself out of his ears, and the impostor wheeled on him, its face and neck hinging back and erupting into that bottomless moray gullet. Trapped inside the cage, finally Anne realized what that mouth reminded her of: a Pez dispenser. Her stomach turned at the thought.

The cop sucked air like he was going to scream, too, but the creature was already on him. It curled its warped hands into his chest—not just his shirt but his *chest*, shredding the flesh underneath to cherry Jell-O—then threw him across the bullpen, toward the holding cells. His back crunched against the cage door, and he dropped to the ground, hard. Half a heartbeat later, the shapeshifter was digging into him.

The cop flailed and thrashed under the thing's twisted bulk, screaming his heart out, not that it helped him any. There was a wet ripping noise as the impostor tore deeper into his flayed chest, and then the screaming stopped entirely. Blood coursed out from underneath the cop's mangled form, spreading across the hard floor in a ruby tarn. A second later, the creature rose to its full height again and turned to regard Anne through the bars once more, drenched in blood, panting and chuffing.

Frantically, Anne looked around the cage, searching for something, anything to defend herself with, but it was futile. She was trapped in here. Helpless. Dead. The impostor's bloody smile grew wider as it reared its malformed head back. *CLANG!* The thing banged its twisted face against the bars, smashing what remained of its nose flat with a soggy *CRUNCH*. Then it drew back and did it again, and again, and again, splitting its forehead and cheeks open in thick, bloody furrows. Gore sheeted down the thing's face, but it kept beating its head against the cage as it grasped for her, the sound of its skull drumming against the bars loud and rhythmic, like some kind of horrible, fucked-up metronome.

"Hey!" The shout came from the other side of the bullpen—Dutch.

He stood in the station doorway, staring straight ahead with panic-wide eyes, handcuffs dangling from his abraded wrist. Anne didn't know how the hell he'd gotten free—maybe he'd swiped the cop's keys when she'd stood, or maybe it didn't really matter. What did matter was what Dutch held in his other hand—the blonde's .357.

He raised the pistol, leveling it at the shape-shifter's misshapen head. Then he pulled the trigger.

The bullet tore a fist-size chunk of blood and bone from the thing's skull, but it stayed stubbornly upright, swaying in place as more flies fountained from the wound, their buzzing sharp and furious. Shaking off the impact of the gunshot, the impostor started toward Dutch, its footfalls heavy and juddering. Dutch's face went blank with fear, and he stumbled away—guess his plan started and stopped with the cop's revolver. Anne watched him twist and run, legs spinning underneath him like cartoon wheels as he sprinted from the station. The impostor gave chase, nearly blowing the doors off their hinges as it crashed through into the waiting early-morning beyond.

Silence flooded in around Anne, punctuated by hiccupping panic breathing in the next cell. She glanced over her shoulder and saw the drunk, no longer asleep, curled up in the corner of his cot, expression confused and frantic.

"What the . . . what fuck . . . fuck was . . . the what the . . . that was what . . ." The words fell out of his mouth all runny and slurred, a scrambled mess of nerves and drunksleep. After a second, his eggy, bloodshot eyes found Anne's.

"What the *fuck*?" he cried, his voice hoarse and torn. Anne only shook her head at the guy. She didn't know much more than he did, and at this point, what few answers she did have would only make things worse.

Dropping to her knees, she snaked an arm through the cage's bottom bars, reaching for the nearest dead cop and the cell keys hooked on his belt. Dipping her hand into the man's still-warm blood, she closed her fingers around the key ring, but it wouldn't detach itself from the little clasp on his belt. She tried again, but her fingers slipped, too wet, too slick. She couldn't get a good grip. Wiping her hand on her pants, Anne gritted her teeth and tried again as anxiety screamed inside her head. The shape-shifter was going to be back any second now. Either she got out now or she wasn't going to get out at all.

Come on, come the fuck on . . .

Finally, she found a surer grip on the clasp, pressing the latch back and snaking a single finger through the key ring—she yanked it off the dead man's belt and stood, reaching through the bars again to unlock the cage door from the other side. Shoving it open with a rusty groan, she stepped out into the bullpen and quickly gathered up everything the cops had relieved her of: backpack, Glock, Murph. All here. Good. Kneeling, she put her face close to the carrier's mesh zip-front, blinking slow at her cat.

"Hey, hey, it's okay," she said, struggling to keep her voice down. "I'm going to get us out of here, all right? Just gotta give me a second. Then we'll go. I promise."

Inside the carrier, Murph yowled again, then met her eyes and slow-blinked back at her, seeming to calm, even if only a tiny bit. She could feel the blood trickling down her ripped-open arm, rolling down her wrist and the blade of her hand to spatter on the floor. She'd have to patch that up later. Right now, she just had to get out of here. Outside, someone screamed.

"Hey, hey!" the drunk called from the other cell. "Let me out of here, come on!"

She went to the cage door, meaning to fit the key into the lock. Then she heard a tattered panting coming from behind her.

The shape-shifter was back.

It stood in the ragged hole that used to be a doorway, drenched in fresh blood, its face hanging in tatters around its grotesque maw. It leered at Anne with those blank eyes and hunched down like an Olympic sprinter, twisted claw-hands twitching madly, and she knew it was going to charge her just like it had the cops, just like it had Dutch. She dropped the cop's keys and the rest of her stuff and slid Murph's carrier to the side with her foot. There was no sense in putting him in the way of any more harm than she had to. She moved slowly, taking a step to the side, then another, and another. The thing tracked her movements, eyes following her curiously across the bullpen as she moved toward the open cage in a

few long, measured strides. She kept her hands down at her sides,
breathing deep as the vague shape of a plan started to form in her
head. It was a marvelously fucking stupid plan, but with no guns,
no fire, no Dutch, it was all she had. And she was only going to get
one shot at it.

With a shriek, the impostor broke and ran, bounding across the
bullpen, barreling right for her. Despite her every instinct shouting for her to *run, move, get the fuck out of the way*, Anne waited
until the last possible second, until she felt the thing's sickening
heat staining the air in front of her face—then hurled herself to
the side. The creature's bulk blasted past her and went hurtling
into the cage at her back. It crashed hard against the cinder block
wall at top speed, knocking itself into a momentary daze, and
Anne kicked the cell door shut as hard as she could—trapping the
hideous thing inside.

Got you, asshole.

Snarling and snapping and retching, the impostor threw its
bleeding, deformed frame against the door over and over, trying
to knock it off its hinges, but the heavy iron bars wouldn't budge.
It was stuck. Anne had never been so thankful for the existence of
jail cells in her life. She rose to her feet and brushed the grit from
her jeans and palms, watching the creature press itself against the
cage door, fitting its massive, bear-trap mouth between the bars to
gnash its teeth at her.

"Oh god, oh fuck shit, fuck me, fuck shit!" the drunk wailed
as he pressed himself against the other door. "Let me out, please!
Please, fucking *please*!"

It was a mistake. Now trapped, the impostor whirled around to
face the drunk in the next cell, its white eyes aglow with malice
and hunger. *Move! Get away from the bars! What the fuck are you doing?*
Anne shouted at the guy inside her head—but of course he couldn't
hear her. He just stood there, shaking with fear as the creature's
long, ropy arms shot through the bars and sank their claws into the
soft meat of his throat with a spray of blood. The guy screamed, but
the sound was cinched off in an instant, like water from a kinked
garden hose.

The impostor started to pull. The drunk slammed against the bars like a rag doll, hanging in the shape-shifter's terrible grip a full foot off the ground. More blood spurted from the man's face as a damp crunching sound filled up the bullpen. Anne stared on, unsure for a moment what she was seeing. She could hear bones snapping underneath the guy's skin; then he started to shake as if he were having a seizure. What the fuck was it doing to him? It was only when the man's shoulders folded back like the flaps of an envelope and a fresh glut of blood started to stream from the crown of his fractured skull that she understood: the monster was pulling him through the fucking bars.

A high, nasally whine rose from the drunk's chest, a sound of desperate, throttled anguish. It was the last noise he would ever make. His skin split against the iron, peeling away from the red musculature underneath in loose, rubbery sheets as his body contorted and ripped and began to slide through. The man came apart in bloody hanks that barely registered as human: a mangled arm here, a leg torn from its socket there, ribs and organs pulped as they were dragged through the bars like soft cheese going through a sharp grater. The sound of it was awful, and the impostor shivered with pleasure as it pulled the man to gory ribbons, painting the floor red and purple with the mess of his insides. Anne could only stand there and stare, breath caught in the pit of her throat.

"Oh my *fuck*," someone groaned from the other side of the bullpen. Anne turned to look. Dutch. He gapes at the hideous scene, panting like he'd just run a twenty-mile marathon at top speed. "Are you—?"

BANG. A massive impact rocked the cage door, rattling it on its hinges. The blood-drenched impostor dropped the remains of the drunk to the cement floor and pressed its mangled face against the bars once more. Then it started to push. Anne watched, uncomprehending, until she saw the skin stretched around the thing's head start to tear and bleed, revealing stripes of red, maggot-ridden flesh underneath. Guess the dead guy had given it an idea. Its grinning cheeks peeled back and tore away underneath the pressure, revealing foul teeth planted in pale gums around a long, sore-covered tongue that hunted back and forth, slurping at the air. It pressed forward harder and harder, shattering its own body to force its way through, bones bending and popping, giving way to something else, some other form, some other mask.

Anne heard herself shouting, *"Go, go, go, go—!"* as she grabbed Murph and all her shit and backpedaled across the bullpen, Dutch hot on her heels.

Then they were running again.

17

Freezing air slashed at Anne as she sprinted through the early morning, scouring her arms, her face, her neck all the way down to the bone. But she barely felt it.

It had followed them—followed *her*, tracking the smell of her blood out of the hills and into the world. And now here she was again, fleeing yet another bloodbath toward parts unknown. This was getting to be a habit.

The wheels inside her brain spun freely, trying to find purchase, trying to catalog what she knew—or thought she knew—about the thing chasing her: It was tough, and it was fast, and it was deadly. It killed without hesitation. Bullets slowed it down, fire seemed to hurt it, but more than anything, both just seemed to piss it off. It wore people's faces like masks, but they weren't perfect; its disguises were good enough for it to get in close, but not good enough to pass the smell test. Plus, it was smart enough to hide in plain sight until it had a chance to strike. So whatever the fuck else it was, it was a hunter. Maybe more than any of the rest of it, that was going to be a problem.

Together, Anne and Dutch made a break down the block and down another, their footfalls heavy and loud as they pounded the asphalt. Somewhere far off, Anne could hear sirens, growing louder. Their fracas at the station hadn't gone unnoticed. She couldn't tell yet if those sirens meant fire, EMTs, highway cops, or something else, but it didn't really matter. The best thing they could do now was get out of Pecos as fast as they possibly could.

They sprinted up the nearest alley, heading for the next street over, but when they burst onto the sidewalk, headlights exploded from the corner of the block, trapping Anne and Dutch both in their beams. There was the roar of an engine, and a big dark SUV, a late-model Chevy Tahoe, burst from the shadows, swerving around them to screech to a halt in the middle of the blacktop. Instinctively, Anne's free hand went to the Glock in her belt as her mind went to every other threat in the world that wasn't a shape-shifting atrocity: Travis, Iris, cops, FBI, ATF. Whatever the fuck it was, they'd handle it, because at this point, it couldn't be any worse than the bleeding nightmare they'd left tearing itself apart in the station cage.

The Tahoe's passenger-side window slid down with a swishing hum. Behind the wheel sat a beautiful, intense-eyed woman, dressed in a long coat over a dark T-shirt. Her long braids were tied back into a loose chignon, and there was a singularly pissed-off expression scribbled across her face. Anne's heart nearly stopped with relief at the sight of her.

Gemma.

"What did you get yourself into?" Gemma demanded, her tone sharp, clipped. She jabbed a finger at Dutch. "And who the fuck is he?"

Anne raised her hands, placating. "Gem, he's a friend," she said, glancing over her shoulders, checking the shadows. Nothing there. For now.

In the distance, the sirens were getting closer. Gem jerked a thumb back at the sound.

"That's you, right?"

"Kind of, yeah. It's hard to explain," Anne said.

"Oh, I'm sure it is. Get in, c'mon."

Gem punched the automatic locks and Anne yanked the passenger seat door open, then paused. What about the Ninety-Eight? What about the bank bag? Anne looked back at the alley behind them, then over at Dutch.

"Jessup's car," she said, meeting his eyes.

"Shit, yeah, right," Dutch said. He held his hand out. "Here. Give me the keys. I can follow you."

Anne's shoulders tightened. Was she really about to trust Jessup's car and the entire take from the bank to a fucking cop? But then again, did she really have a choice? Gem, cautious goddamn

Gem, wasn't going to let a stranger into her car, let alone ferry him to wherever they were going. Plus, Dutch had come back for her, hadn't he? He could have broken and run at the police station, but he came back. That had to count for something. Besides, it wasn't like every shadow of a plan hadn't gone clean out the fucking window already. They were just making shit up as they went now. Anne didn't love the idea of Dutch taking the Olds, but it was the best option that they had.

Anne nodded to herself and slapped the Ninety-Eight's keys into Dutch's waiting hand, then climbed into the front seat of the Tahoe, balancing Murph's carrier on her knees. Standing by the open passenger door, Dutch looked at Gem.

"Just need to know where I'm going."

Gem fixed him with a cold stare. Anne knew what she was thinking; she'd seen that same stern crease notch Gem's brow too many times over the years to not: she didn't know this guy, didn't have any reason to do anything but leave him in the dust. Feeling nerves hum and buzz in her stomach like she'd swallowed a wasp's nest, Anne reached a hand out and laid it on top of Gem's. Held it there until she looked over at her.

"He's okay," Anne said. "I promise."

Frustration flared in Gem's eyes, then cooled. She looked back at Dutch.

"Fine; it's the Happy Trails Motel, 6466 Main Street in Mott. Room 117. I'm not writing it down for you."

Dutch nodded. "No, I got it—Happy Trails, 6466 Main. Mott. One seventeen. See you when I see you," he said, then turned around and hoofed his way back down the side street, heading in the direction of the Oldsmobile. Anne pulled the car door shut and watched him go. Inside his carrier, Murph yowled once, then lay down and curled up with a huff.

"Here," Gemma said, and held out a roll of paper towels, giving it a little shake. Anne's face twisted in confusion.

"You're bleeding," Gem explained, glancing at Anne's wounded arm.

Oh. Right. That. Anne tore a large handful of sheets from the roll, then pressed the wad to the seeping gashes just below her elbow.

"You sure about him?" Gemma asked, nodding out the window. "Like really sure?" Her brown eyes shone in the moonlight.

"About as sure as I can be, yeah," Anne said. "Like I said, it's complicated. I'll explain on the way."

"Explain when we get there," Gemma said. She dropped the Tahoe into Drive and stomped on the gas.

The big SUV took off like a shot. Gemma cut the corner at speed, grinding the tires against the pavement, and then they were barreling out of town, away from the sirens and all the dead people and that horrible fucking monster-thing. Idly, Anne found herself checking the speed limit signs as they whipped by, irrationally worried that they were somehow going to get caught in a speed trap or something. But who the hell was going to pull them over? Every cop within fifteen miles of this place was already dead.

Leaning forward, Anne mashed her purple-scarred palms against her face as hard as she could, trying to force some—any—clarity into the ash pile of her brain. Christ, she was so fucking tired. It felt like she hadn't slept in years. She hadn't had the luxury.

"How far is it?" she heard herself asking Gem. "Wherever it is that we're going."

Gem drummed a beat on the steering wheel with her thumbs. "Other end of the valley. Hour and a half, probably. Maybe less. You should close your eyes, try and get some z's, maybe," she said. "No offense, but you look like shit."

"Gee, thanks," Anne replied, her voice all acid and exhaustion. "It's been kind of a rough night."

"I'm sure it has been. And you can tell me all about it once we're clear, okay? I'll get us there, wake you up if whatever." Gem's tone was stiff, but not unkind. All business until she knew they were safe. Just like always.

Anne slid down in her seat and let her head thump softly against the window. She sincerely doubted that she'd be able to get any sleep with all the fear and adrenaline coursing through her system, but still, it was probably worth a shot. She rubbed at her eyes and listened to the sound of the wind around the SUV, the engine thrumming underneath the hood.

Near the far edges of the valley, she could see the sun starting to come up over the hills again.

18

The Happy Trails Motel was in bad shape.

Little more than an off-brand Super 8, it was a long, slouched, L-shaped single-story, all its rooms facing the parking lot where an ancient neon sign rose high above the sidewalk, reading HAPPY TRAILS MOTEL: NIGHTLY RATES, FREE HBO, ICE, and then in smaller letters just below that, VACANCY. The doors were all worn and scarred, no doubt from years of being pounded on and kicked in by drunk or jealous (or both) husbands, pissed-off dealers, or cops. Heavy, narrow bars bolted over every window made sure the glass underneath stayed musty and caked in grime. Studying them now, Anne's mind flitted to the police station and the way the monster had pressed its face so hard against the cage that the skin had torn like bloody tissue.

In the next lot over sat a seedy strip mall with a few storefronts that hadn't yet been boarded up: a check-cashing place, a ram-shackle 7-Eleven, and nearest the motel, a shabby, filthy little liquor store. A handful of folks stood around the front of the liquor store, probably waiting for the door to unlock at 8:00 a.m. Anne didn't blame them. Didn't seem to be much else to do around here but drink yourself into oblivion, anyway. Places like Mott, Colorado, were tailor-made for the lonely and the lost. Anne herself had spent more than a few nights in spots just like this one, either waiting for the go-ahead on a job, keeping an eye on some unsuspecting mark, or casing a place from a safe distance.

Standing on the gravel of the motel's lot, Anne heard Gem step out of the Tahoe behind her. Following her over to room 117, she watched her produce an electronic keycard from her pocket and swipe it against the lock. Anne was honestly a little impressed that the people who owned this place had actually sprung for a semi-current security measure.

"C'mon," Gem said.

Inside, 117 was just like every other motel room Anne had ever seen in her life: two broken-in queen mattresses separated by a lamp-topped end table, an old cathode-ray TV on a heavy wooden console against the opposite wall, a mini fridge, a small table and single chair next to the door, plus a modest bathroom in the back. The bed nearest the door was still made, the sheets neat as a pin, while the other was rumpled and tossed, recently slept in. The trash can in the corner overflowed with fast-food wrappers and drained plastic water bottles. A half-empty seven-fifty of Martin Miller's gin and a sleeve of plastic cups sat on the table by the musty window, beside what looked to Anne like a contraband police scanner. Gem had been listening to cop chatter. Probably how she'd managed to find Anne and Dutch back in Pecos. It wasn't the most luxurious hideout, but it was better than her mom's dust-blanketed old cabin, and it was a hell of an improvement over a jail cell.

"Nice place," Anne said, setting her stuff down on the nearest bed.

"Thanks," Gem said, smirking. "You know, the concierge has a bit of an attitude, but I have to say, the sommelier is just world class."

Anne flicked a fingernail against the bottle of gin with a hollow *ting*. "No doubt."

Gem shut the door behind them with a soft click and threw the chain lock into place.

"You been here since everything went down?" Anne asked, rubbing at her eyes again. "Kind of looks like you were going Godzilla on me."

"I mean, that was the idea, but plans change, right?"

Anne looked up at her and felt something cold and stiff churn in her belly. There was a gun in Gem's hand, a sleek nine-millimeter FN High Power. Gem didn't point it at her—not yet, anyway. Instead, she just let the stainless steel pistol dangle down by her hip, held casually but confidently in one slender hand. Anne's eyes went wide, but she forced her face to stay placid.

Gem smiled and shrugged. "Sorry. But you get it."

She did. Anne didn't know what Gem had been through over the course of the past few days, but if she had to guess, it had been a whole lot of silence—fertile soil for your worst fears and assumptions to take root. If the tables were turned and she were in Gem's position, she'd be doing the same exact thing. She looked down at the nine again. Gem specialized in operations—opening electronic locks, getting past security systems and firewalls, shit like that—and mostly carried a gun as a formality, but standing here now, Anne had no doubt that she'd use it in a heartbeat if she felt like she had to. Anne gestured toward the nearest bed without moving her hands.

"Can I sit?"

Gem nodded. "Sure, whatever. Just . . ." She gestured with the gun.

"No sudden movements. I get it." Anne sat on the edge of the mattress and kept her hands where Gem could see them.

"Tell me what happened back in Durango," Gemma said. "Walk me through it."

"I told you. Travis burned us. Him and Iris and Joanie. Called the cops. Kicked the plan to shit. Tried to take the money for themselves."

"Yeah, you already gave me the CliffsNotes version. Sorry, not good enough. I want the whole story. Now," Gem said, her voice hard as stone.

Anne flexed her hands, open and shut, open and shut, running her fingertips over the pilled polyester blanket, timing it with the tidal rhythm of her breathing, trying to figure out where she should even start. The cabin? The bank? Before that? After? The last few days were so mixed up. She'd tried to keep everything in apple-pie order, but it was too much. Too crazy. Her memories were all just broken glass inside her head at this point. So maybe it didn't matter where she started.

She swallowed against the lump in her throat, and then she began walking Gem through everything as she understood it: the way the bank job had ended, Dutch, the phone call with Travis,

Maggie's Pharm, the cabin and Jessup, the impostor, the shit show in Pecos, every last crazy piece. She didn't mean to, but once she started, it all just came spilling out in a rush, like gravel pouring from a slashed-open bag, and when she was done, it was all she could do to press her face into her hands and breathe slow until her pulse started to ebb back toward normal.

"Jesus," Gem said after another second. "I mean, just, wow. That's, uh. I mean . . ."

"You don't believe me," Anne said with a joyless laugh. She wasn't shocked. If she'd been in Gemma's place, she'd have thought she was completely full of shit, too.

Gem made an exasperated face. "It's not that. It's just, it's a lot, okay? I mean, come on, I know you understand. I'm trying to keep up here, I really am. But I'm not the kind of person who buys into the supernatural. You know?"

"I'm not, either," Anne grumbled.

"But for what it's worth, I do believe you about the Travis stuff. Him and Iris. Sucks about Joanie, but, I dunno. We all make our choices. And for the record, I'm still extremely not happy about you throwing in with a fucking cop—"

"Dutch is okay," Anne told her. "Really. He had plenty of chances to fuck me over and didn't. Trust me, I don't think he's exactly eager to head back to the land of law and order right now." She'd seen how the cops back in Pecos had treated him once they'd figured out who he was, especially with a warrant out on his head. *You're a disgrace to the badge,* that was what the soggy cop had sneered at him. No way was Dutch getting welcomed back into the long arms of the law as anything but another two-bit criminal.

"I guess we'll see about that, right? Too late to do shit about it now, anyway. It's already done. As for the . . . other stuff? I don't know, man. I'm not sure what to believe exactly, but whatever the fuck it was, I believe you saw *something* up there. Can that be enough for now?"

Anne met her eyes and realized that maybe the worst part of living through the unbelievable was that nobody believed you when you told them about it. They just looked at you like you were fucking crazy. That was what stung most: Gem *knew* what had happened to Anne's mom. Against her better judgment, she'd told her and Jessup everything—the blood, the horror, the white eyes floating in the darkness, all of it. And yet, even after Anne's worst childhood nightmare showed up in the flesh to try to kill her, Gem still thought she was full of shit or crazy or both.

"Sure," Anne lied, trying to stuff the hurt deep down where she didn't have to look at it too closely. "Whatever." She glanced toward the back of the room. "Look, I'm going to go take a shower, clear my head. Are you going to shoot me if I stand up?"

"No, of course not," Gemma said, tucking the High Power into the folds of her coat. There was a tired, down note in her voice that hadn't been there before. "Go. Do what you gotta. Shampoo and soap and towels are in there already. Help yourself to whatever."

"Yeah, good," Anne said, rising from the bed, cat carrier in hand as she moved toward the back of the motel room. "Thanks, Gem."

In the bathroom, Anne shut the door and unzipped Murph's carrier to let him out into the small, tiled space. He padded out slowly, unsure but curious, his green eyes big and bright as coins. Anne had half expected him to go running for the underside of the toilet, somewhere to hide, but he didn't. He just looked up at her, confused and indignant. Maybe the grumpy tabby was a lot more resilient than even she'd given him credit for. Anne ran the shower until it was screaming hot, then stripped down and stepped into the blistering spray, letting it scald the filth and blood away from her skin, purging the aches and exhaustion from her body.

Once she was done, she used one of the stiff, cardboardy towels from the rack to dry off while Murph figure-eighted around her ankles. Changing back into her clothes, she toweled her hair dry, wrapped her wounded arm in a hand towel, and shuffled barefoot out into the motel room proper, where she found Gem sitting at the table, reading Aunt Lisa's letter. She'd spread the rest of the contents of Anne's backpack out across the made bed, the boxes of ammo, the burner phone, the fake ID, her keys, the envelope of emergency cash, and finally, the VHS tape. Gem's High Power sat on the table next to the gin, seemingly forgotten as she read.

"You usually go through people's stuff like that?" Anne asked, biting back a fresh swell of anger at the presumption.

"Only when they tell me the kind of crazy shit that you just did," Gem said, resolutely not looking up. A tiny flare of hurt fired off in Anne's belly at that. "What's the Passage?"

"The what?"

"*The Passage*," Gem said again. "This Aunt Lisa person talks about it in the letter. *The Passage is everywhere.* That mean anything to you?"

"No, nothing. You?"

"No, never heard of it. You didn't look it up?"

Anne shook her head. Shrugged. "Had bigger problems."

"Yeah, no, I get that," Gem said. "Give me a second." She produced a smartphone from her pocket and clicked it to life. The screen was blinding in the dim little motel room. Anne came up short at the sight of it.

"What are you doing with that?" she asked.

"Googling," Gem replied, as if it were the most obvious thing in the world. "What do you think I'm doing?"

"I mean, that's not a burner. You can't get burner smartphones. Not how it works."

Gem smiled patiently. "Yeah, true, but you *can* buy a dead person's social security number off the internet for, like, ten bucks. Far as Verizon—and the government—are concerned, this line belongs to Brenda Lynn Barseghyan."

Something unclenched inside Anne's chest. "That's . . . that's actually really smart," she said.

"Right? I'm just full of surprises," Gemma said with a faint smile as she tapped at the screen in her hands. "Okay, found something. Here."

Gem tossed the phone over. On the screen was a blog entry titled "THIS WEEK IN FRINGE CHRISTIANITY: THE PASSAGE OF DIVINITY."

A minor (but nonetheless interesting) entry into Colorado's history of fringe religious groups is that of the Passage of Divinity Evangelical

Church, later known as the Passage of Divinity, or more simply, the
Passage. Based throughout the entirety of its existence in Colorado's
San Luis Valley, the Passage found its stride, as so many Colorado
cults do, in the small town of Crestone, before picking up and moving
camp to the nearby ghost town of Cabot. Founded in the city of Alamosa
in early 1954 by a trio of Korean War veterans who returned home
seeking refuge from the violence they'd witnessed, leadership of the
Passage was eventually assumed by a charismatic young veteran of
the Vietnam War—

The Passage was a fucking cult? Anne tapped the address bar
at the top of the screen and searched for "Cabot Colorado." There
weren't many results, mostly mentions on local-history blogs with
names like *Ghost Towns of Colorado* and *Abandoned Centennial State.*
She clicked on the first result, a decent-looking academic blog titled *Colorado Mines: A Rich History:*

The town of Cabot, Colorado (originally known as Ballmer's Hope to
match its central mining claim farther up its modest mountain gorge),
located in the shadow of the San Luis Valley's Blanca Peak, was settled
in 1898 by George Ballmer, a miner and industrialist originally out
of St. Louis, Missouri. However, five years after its founding, Ballmer
brought on a partner to help him expand and industrialize his mining
operation, one Timothy Allen Cabot, formerly of San Francisco. They re-
named the town to attract fresh mining talent, and for over twenty years
following, the Ballmer's Hope Mine and the town of Cabot flourished,
bringing continuing prosperity to the small town and its inhabitants.

However, tragedy struck Cabot in the summer of 1924 when an
accidental explosion in the lowest shafts of Ballmer's Hope took the
lives of nearly a hundred men and left the mine itself too dangerous
and unstable to continue working in. In the weeks and months that
followed, Cabot was slowly abandoned and eventually left to the wil-
derness that surrounded it.

Anne scrolled down to a couple of grainy black-and-white pho-
tographs. In them, smoke rose from the mine's entrance in a thick

gray-white plume; two men, drenched in dust and blood, stumbled away from the mine wearing tattered clothes and thousand-yard stares. One of them was badly burned, his skin scorched and blackened, bubbling up in terrible, glossy blisters. The other was missing an arm, his face hauntingly vacant as blood geysered from the torn socket. Jesus fuck. She closed the tab and tossed the phone onto the bed beside her.

"You ever hear of this place? Cabot? Guess it's some kind of ghost town or something."

Gemma shook her head. "Not that one, but the whole state's filled with those," she said. "Half of 'em aren't even on the maps anymore. They just got abandoned and forgotten after they died, then swallowed up by the wilderness. Same old story. You think this is connected to, you know, what you saw up at the cabin?"

"I don't know. Maybe," Anne said. "Here." She held a hand out for the letter. Gem passed it over, and Anne read through it again.

"You never told me you had an aunt," Gemma said.

"I didn't know." Anne nodded to the bottle of gin on the table underneath the room's single window. "Any chance I could get some of that?"

"Sure, help yourself," Gem said.

"You want?"

Gem's face broke into a soft, sad smile. "Sure. Seven thirty in the morning, why not? Not like I have anywhere else to go right now, anyway." With a faint *mrrrowl*, Murphy ambled up beside the bed and hopped up into her lap. Instantly, Gem's hands went up like she no longer knew what to do with them. "Oh. Uh. Okay. Hi, cat."

Gem had never warmed to Murphy much, but Anne got the sense that was more out of a lack of experience with cats than any kind of strongly-held antipathy. Gem just wasn't a cat person, and that was okay. Nobody was perfect.

Smirking a little too much at Gem's discomfort, Anne poured a couple of fingers of gin into a pair of plastic cups and passed one over. They toasted silently and drank deeply as Murphy settled down to curl up on Gem's thighs. There'd always been a natural chemistry between her and Gem; a kind of quiet, unspoken gravity that Anne tried to not look too closely at, because if she did, it started to hurt. Gem was everything Anne wasn't, smooth and collected and calculating in all the ways that Anne was rough and brutish and impulsive. She was funny and fearless, a natural tactician, one of those people who played her cards so close to her chest that you never knew exactly what she was holding, or if she was even holding any cards at all. She balanced Anne out in all the ways she'd never known she needed, and if things were different, if things hadn't gone all to hell, maybe there could have been something there. But Anne figured that any chance they had of romance was pretty much off the table at this point. Someday, maybe. If they somehow managed to make it through this nightmare alive, Anne might finally get her shit together enough to tell Gem how she really felt.

"It really is good to see you," Anne said after a moment, easing herself down onto the edge of the bed again.

Gemma showed her that same little brokenhearted smile as before. "Yeah. You, too. Glad you got out all right."

"Likewise." She took a deep slug off her gin and studied Gem's face, trying to figure out how to ask the next thing, but really there was no way but to just ask. "So. What happened to you back in Durango after everything fell apart?"

Gem gave her a knowing look, then nodded and went quiet for a second, collecting her thoughts. She always thought before she spoke. Anne admired that. Envied it.

"I knew for sure that something had gone wrong when I heard the alarm," Gem said, staring down at the drink in her hands. "That's what alarms mean, right? But . . . I don't know. I think I had a bad feeling about this one from the jump. Something was just *off* about Travis and Iris, you know? You remember when Jess walked us through the plan."

Anne remembered. Trav and Iris had spent so much time smirking and whispering among themselves that day; Iris almost completely disinterested, Travis poking holes in the plan and prodding at Anne until she'd stormed off just so she wouldn't shoot him. She'd written it off as bog-standard Travis fuckery at the time, because she'd had to. You needed to focus before a job, and you had to trust that the people you worked with knew how to handle themselves. Doing anything else was an easy way to get your ticket punched by some insecure wannabe-hero shithead with his concealed carry permit.

Anne swirled the gin around in her plastic cup, then knocked it back in a single fiery gulp. "Yeah. What about Joanie? Was she off, too?"

Gem shook her head. "Not that I noticed. She was nervous, but you know Joanie. Nervous is basically her happy place. The day we went in? Dunno. Everything seemed fine, I guess. Merrill was in his headphones before he got his mask on, psyching himself up to go play Big Bad Bank Robber, you know. You and Jess were getting your game faces on, too. But yeah, Trav and Iris definitely seemed weird."

"Weird how?"

Gemma shrugged. "Just a tiny bit wrong, you know? Like an off-key note in a song you've heard a million times. You might not notice it right away, but it's there, throwing the rest of the tune off-balance. It was how he kept looking at her, like he had a secret he couldn't wait to share, but she wasn't having it. She was basically ignoring him, which, even for Iris, seemed a little cold. Anyway, when we got to the bank, everything was going according to plan, until it wasn't. Took the bank manager back to the vault with Trav, and the thing was, the guy was playing ball. He didn't want to die, and he sure as fuck wasn't going to be a hero. He just wanted to see his kids again. Hard to blame him for that.

"He filled the bag from the safe-deposit boxes, and Travis took the bag back out to the lobby. All according to plan, right? But that wrong note, man. I was zip-tying the guy's wrists when the alarms got tripped and all the shooting started. I cut and ran then and there." Gem drained the rest of her gin, then poured herself a refill. "Ran until I was sure I was clear, then made my way back to my SUV and got the hell out of Dodge. Basically been holed up in here since."

"And then I called," Anne said, filling in the rest. She held her cup out to Gem for a top-off—a double this time.

"And then you called. Figured you wouldn't have done something like that unless you absolutely had to. You always did have a way of playing it safe. Respect that." She downed the rest of her drink in one go. "Which makes me wonder just why in the fuck you think you can trust a cop at all. Time was, you'd have put a bullet in his head and left him up at the cabin with the rest of the wreckage."

Anne winced. She'd thought Gem was a bit too quick to drop it before. She should have seen this coming. Frankly, it was impressive that she'd had held back this long.

"I need you to be honest with me here: What are the odds that he called his buddies on the force the second he was out of sight? Like, truly."

Anne rubbed at her face. "I don't know," she said honestly. "Probably not high. He saved my life up at the cabin. He came back for me in Pecos. He didn't have to do that."

"He's still a fucking cop," Gemma countered.

"He's good people."

"No cop is *good people*, Anne. Not first, anyway. Every cop you've ever met is police first, human being second. Probably third. Come on, you know this shit. Why am I having to explain it to you?"

"He helped me bury Jess," Anne said. "He was good about it, Gem. He didn't have to be, but he was. Plus, cops put a warrant on him, too. Guess they think he was in on shit from the jump."

"Guilt by association? That's your litmus test? Really?" Gem was incredulous.

"Kinda, yeah. Cops are carnivores, right?"

Gem's eyes narrowed. "They are." Out of anyone, Anne knew she didn't have to explain that fact to her.

"That's exactly my point. They go where the red meat is, and if they put a warrant out for him, too, he must be looking a lot like dinner. He's solid. At least solid enough to not act completely suicidal."

"I really hope you're right," Gem told her. "Because at this point, the alternative is probably him rolling up with a SWAT team in tow."

Sour fingers dug at Anne's stomach. Gem did have a point; Anne didn't know for sure what Dutch was planning, or what he'd done once he was out of her orbit. Could be he'd gone back to the cops, but it was just as likely he'd taken the money and the Ninety-Eight and ran for the hills. She almost wouldn't have blamed him if he had. He'd seen the same shit she had and come out the other side. Getting gone while the getting was good probably looked like a way better choice than getting mauled to death by some shape-shifting fucking monster. He'd spend the rest of his life with a warrant out on him, but it was still a lot better than dead.

Gem leaned back, rubbing at her eyes with the backs of her thumbs. "Jesus Christ," she sighed. "What an absolute disaster."

Anne nodded and shot back the rest of her gin. "Yup, some real Godzilla shit, huh?"

Gemma smirked, but it was an expression completely devoid of humor or joy. "You're super not wrong about that."

On the other side of the door, they heard tires crunching across gravel. Still curled up on Gem's lap, Murph roused and looked around, trying to source the sound. Setting her cup down next to the gin bottle, Anne stood, went to the room window, and looked out to see the Ninety-Eight in all its baby-blue glory grumbling across the lot.

Dutch was here.

19

They went outside to meet him. Anne could feel Gemma tensing as Dutch switched off the Oldsmobile's big V-8 and stepped out—not a great sign, but she hadn't pulled her gun and shot him, either. It was a start.

"Hey," Dutch said, giving the Happy Trails a quick once-over. "Nice place."

"Were you followed?" Gem asked, arms crossed, voice stern.

Dutch shook his head. "No. Don't think so, at least."

Gem narrowed her eyes at that.

"You sure you didn't call anybody? Friends on the force, maybe? Didn't tell anyone where you were going?"

"No," Dutch replied, voice deathly serious. "I just put the keys in the ignition and drove. Speaking of—here."

He tossed the car keys to Anne. She plucked them out of the air with one hand, then went to the back of the Ninety-Eight and eased the trunk open. Inside, she found her shotgun, the first aid supplies from Maggie's Pharm, and the bag from the bank, exactly as she'd left them. She took the bag and the first aid supplies and left the Remington as Dutch circled the car to stand next to her. From where they stood, Anne could see Gemma studying them, eyes curious and cautious.

"So . . . what did you tell her?" Dutch asked, jerking his head toward Gem.

Anne hoisted the bank bag up over her shoulder. "All of it," she said. "Everything."

Dutch's eyebrows went up. "Everything? How'd . . . how'd she handle that?"

"She thought it sounded fucking crazy," Gemma called to them, her voice just a little too loud. Dutch turned red and twisted in place to face her.

"Just crazy? That's all?" he asked.

Gemma's face was like stone. "What do you want me to say, cop?"

Dutch's shoulders fell. "I don't know," he sighed. "Listen, I—"

"No, you listen," Gem said, stepping forward, her voice hard as quenched steel. "Between your day job and every bugshit thing *she*"—she jerked a finger in Anne's direction—"told me about, I've got basically every reason in the world to not be here right now, but here I stand none-the-fucking-less. I'm not the unknown quantity here. Far as I'm concerned, the second we left you back in Pecos, you called your boys with the badges and guns and spilled your guts all over the floor."

"Okay, then shoot me," Dutch said, a kind of resigned calm that hadn't been there before sliding into his voice.

Gem faltered. "The fuck?"

Dutch shrugged, guileless. "Seriously. I'm here, car intact, same with your money. I don't see any other cops around, do you?"

Gem didn't say anything to that, but she didn't stop listening, either.

"I didn't call anyone, didn't see anyone, and even if I had, what do you suppose I'd tell them? How would I even begin to explain it all? Also, not sure if you've heard, but they think I was in on that shit you guys pulled back in Durango. You know what they do to cops who get labeled traitors? They crucify them and leave them to rot in the sun. So no, I didn't call anyone. I just drove. Like I said I would," Dutch explained. "But I get it. I don't blame you, I really don't. So if you still don't trust me after all that, yeah, shoot me. Take me inside, stick my head in the toilet, put a gun to the back of my skull, and pull the trigger. You won't even have to clean up the mess. You'll just have to flush."

A blistering, electric tension arced between the two of them, making the gossamer little hairs on the back of Anne's arms stand at attention. Dutch kept his eyes on Gemma as she stared him down, an Old West gunslinger waiting for the signal to draw.

Gemma was the one to break the silence.

"We'll see," she said. "I hope for your sake you're telling the truth. I'd hate to have to dig a shallow grave out here somewhere, but to be honest with you, I've already done harder things this week."

"Jesus, Gem . . ." Anne started, but Dutch held up his hands, placating.

"No, I get it," he said. "I'd do the same if it were me. No big deal. I'm happy to earn my keep."

Gem snorted something like *sure*, then turned and walked back into the motel room. Dutch and Anne followed. Inside, Dutch sat down at the table. Anne shrugged the cash bag off her shoulder, then opened up the first aid supplies to start rebandaging her shredded arm.

"Okay, you're going to make a mess of that," Gem said from where she sat on the edge of the unmade bed. "You suck at first aid. Come on, let me." Anne sat down beside her, handing the bandages over and letting her work. Gem's hands were cool and sure, and Anne sat as still as she possibly could, secretly savoring her touch.

Gem jerked her head toward the bottle on the table without looking away from her task. "You want a drink, cop? Help yourself. We're drinking. And sharing."

"Just water, I think," Dutch said.

"Well, you're already boring," Gem sneered without much malice, "but whatever. Suit yourself. Tap's back there."

Wordlessly, Dutch went to the bathroom, filled one of the smudgy glasses from the counter from the tap, put it to his lips and drained it in a single go, then did it again. Crossing back to the spare bed, he picked up the VHS tape and turned it over in his hands.

"You figure out what the deal is with this thing yet?"

Anne shook her head as Gem taped another stretch of gauze around her forearm. "Nope. It's dead tech. Useless."

"You know, there's a VCR in that bottom cabinet," Gem offered, nodding to the ancient pressboard console as she tore a strip of medical tape away from the roll with her teeth. "Not sure if it works, but, you know. Worth a shot, at least."

When Gem finished patching up her arm, Anne rose from the bed and went over to the TV, then knelt to slide open the cabinet. Inside, just like Gem had said, sat a creaky, ancient VCR/DVD combo deck. Looked like it was still wired up to the boxy old TV, too.

Experimentally, she pressed the Power button. At first, there was nothing, but then, a second later, the old deck whirred to life, wheezing and clicking as it spooled up.

"Holy shit," Anne coughed. "Okay. Cool. Let's see what's on this thing."

The TV blipped on in front of her face, glowing brightly with a rainbow test screen. She glanced over her shoulder and saw Dutch standing there, remote in one hand, cassette in the other. Gem sat on the bed behind him, face wary but undeniably intrigued. Anne held a hand out, gesturing for him to hand the tape over.

"Here," she said.

Dutch passed it to her without a word, and she laid it on the chipped pressboard beside the deck for a moment, regarding it as she would a wild animal. As if it could reach out and bite her.

It's just a tape. That's all. Some old home movie or a scratchy network-TV recording of Fraggle Rock *or some shit. Nothing more.*

Steeling herself, she took a breath, then slid the cassette into the VCR's waiting mouth. The player thumped and began to whirr inside its cabinet. The TV screen cut first to a static snowstorm, then to fuzzy, glitched-out black, and then the tape began to play.

20

There's singing in the darkness.

Through inky shadow so much more complete than night, a chorus of voices rise together in a beautiful, practiced harmony, intoning the first verses of an old-time hymn:

> *O little flock, fear not the foe who madly seeks your overthrow;*
> *Dread not his rage and pow'r;*
> *and though your courage sometimes faints,*
> *his seeming triumph o'er God's saints lasts but one little hour.*

The darkness shivers with movement, just a faint flicker of something within—here, there, then gone again. The song shifts with the rustle of bodies, and the flicker comes again, carried on a light growing in the distance, far below, briefly illuminating a slow march of human shapes in faint silhouette. There are dozens of them going down, descending a tight stone corridor in single file—a mine shaft.

The ceilings are low, so low that some of the bodies have to duck to avoid hitting their heads on the jagged outcroppings above. It's cramped in here, and based on how the parade breathes as it marches down—shallow, labored—hot, too. Stifling, even. Some of them look sick to their stomachs, while others weep and clutch at their ears as if listening to some terrible roar inside their heads. But still they sing, still they soldier on, farther and farther into the earth and all its darkness, following that feeble light, a delicate beacon beneath churning, oil-black waves. They press against themselves as they go, carrying one another with arms and shoulders and voices that have sung this song together so many times before.

Before long, the crowd finds itself in a shadowy cavern burrowed out of the rock, no bigger than a large bedroom. In this chamber, they squeeze forward for position, trying to get closer to the front to behold the thing that sits in the center of the little cavern:

The icon.

It stands like an enormous tombstone, so perfectly, flawlessly white that it nearly glows. Smooth and powdery like unpolished marble, it's almost entirely featureless but for the deep cleft in its crown, giving it the overall effect of a massive, broken tooth. There's no sign of where it came from, no obvious marks of it having been brought here from somewhere else; it's as if the icon had simply sprouted here fully formed, or else had always been here buried under the ground, waiting eons to be discovered.

Small light blooms into many as vigil candles are lit and passed around, filling the room with a warm, orange glow that flickers against the icon's stone face like waves upon a beach. The camera turns in a slow circle, taking in the entirety of the group. In the candlelight, their dozens multiply into more as they crowd around the stone and resolve into something beyond mere silhouette: shaggy, aging flower children and hale, pink-cheeked families stand shoulder to shoulder with white-haired retirees and sleepless young professionals, all their faces etched with wonder and worry. The camera eye searches their features before catching on a little girl with bright red hair, no older than five or six, darting in between the legs of the adults, circling the icon and laughing to herself, playing some private game. There are other children here, watching her play, but, held tight by their parents, none of them join her.

"Be careful, Annie," a woman's voice warns the redhead from behind the camera.

As if on cue, the girl—Annie—turns toward the camera and trips, flying toward the rocky floor like she's spring-loaded. She barely has time to get her arms out in front of her, palms outstretched to catch the brunt of the fall, and hits the ground hard, but she's back on her feet in an instant as if she were made of rubber in that special way that some six-year-olds are. Shaking off the tumble, she totters unsteadily toward the camera, her eyes wide and curious as she approaches.

"Oh my god, are you okay, sweetie?" the woman behind the camera asks.

"I hurt my hands," Annie replies, as if confused. She turns her palms outward to show the camera: they're marred with deep, messy cuts where jagged rock split tender skin. Thin rivulets of blood sluice over the heels of Annie's hands, down her wrists and forearms to drip-drip-drip onto the stone floor. "See?"

From somewhere deeper in the mine, the stone shifts, and the icon begins to grumble from within, a grim precursor of what's yet to come.

The woman behind the camera keeps the lens trained on Annie's hands and asks again, "You okay, honey?"

The little girl nods. "I think so. It hurts."

"I know. I'm sorry," the woman tells her. "We'll get those patched up once we're done down here, okay?"

Annie nods again. "When is that?"

"Soon. I promise."

"Okay," Annie replies. "Thank you, Aunt Lisa."

A tattooed, ring-heavy hand with turquoise-painted nails floats into the frame and gently cups the little girl's face. Annie closes her eyes for a moment and nuzzles into the woman's palm.

"Of course. I love you, sweetheart."

"Love you, too." Annie wipes her bloody hands on her jeans, then turns and dashes off through the adults, toward the front of the crowd. The camera follows, weaving through bodies until it comes to rest on a single man, tall and burly, standing before the group with his arms raised high like a circus ringmaster announcing a long-awaited showtime. Beside him stands a slender, serious-eyed woman, nearly a foot shorter, with crow-black hair and a sharp, bladelike face.

"Thank y'all for coming down here," the man says. His voice is warm, bright, Southern-accented at the corners. He has shoulder-length brown hair that falls around his face in picture-perfect ringlets. His eyes are green and knowing above a clever grin framed by a well-trimmed goatee. "I know it's late, and cold, but it really

couldn't wait any longer, it really couldn't. I know y'all are confused as to why we called you down here. I'll explain, I swear. But
first I want to thank you."

The crowd falls silent, reverent in their attention.

"We all came up here and built this place together because we
were looking for something to make it all make sense. I know you
know what I'm talking about. There's something missing in each
and every one of us, isn't there? Been there forever, long as I can
remember, at least. Some folks call it the God-shaped hole, but I
don't know, I've never really cottoned to that term. Gives people
no credit for being strong on their own. Because God made us
strong. Built us that way so we can keep searching for something
more, some piece of Him that can touch us and flow through our
words, our deeds. I don't know about y'all, but I've spent years
searching for that something more." He pauses, and a smile, wide
and white like a newscaster's, bisects his head. "But now? I think
we mighta found it."

A murmur cycles through the gathered crowd as the people turn
to one another, asking in hushed voices, *What is he saying? What
is he talking about?* Standing before the icon, the big man raises
his hands again, silencing the whispers, drawing every eye in the
chamber back to him.

"I'm sorry for keeping this from y'all," he says, "but you have
to understand that at first, we didn't know what we'd found. We
didn't understand." He gestures to the dark-haired woman beside him. "Darlene"—except he pronounces her name like he's
calling her *darlin'*—"and I, we've been praying on it. Trying to
divine just what to do about it. I mean, how could we tell anyone, any of you, about this when we didn't even understand it?
How can you begin to try and explain the unexplainable? But,
end of the day, we knew for damn sure that we had to share it, hell
with the consequences. No good ever came from keeping a miracle a secret."

With a flourish of his long, ropy arms, he steps aside, standing
away from the icon at his back. That's when the camera gets its
first glimpse:

There's a crack in the stone, maybe two feet long, shaped like a torn, branching lightning bolt. For a so-called miracle, it seems decidedly unremarkable at first. But the more the camera focuses on that scar, the more it seems to change and shift in place, twisting and quivering in the stone as if it's not a crack at all but something more. Something living. A faint, stained-pale light emanates from the strange fissure, making it seem as if the white rock surrounding it isn't solid stone but a mere façade, the illusion of solidity. The camera lingers on that dirty light, throbbing in time with the odd, pulsating shifts in the fissure's lineation.

"We found it when we came down here some weeks ago, and since then, we've been trying to see the truth. It ain't exactly what I'd call a burning bush, but it speaks to you all the same, if you care to listen properly. Me and Darlene, we've both looked inside, and we've both heard its voice now. Like I told you, we prayed on it I can't tell you how much since we found it. And the more we prayed, the more it spoke to us. The more we could see inside. It was left here for us, I truly believe that. Them that were digging down here all those years ago, they found it. But it wasn't meant for them. It was meant for the true believers. The faithful."

The crowd stays silent as they listen to his words. He presses his hands together as if giving thanks, and looks around at his people, meeting their eyes two by two.

"I'd like us all to pray on it, if you please," he says. "I want you to see for yourselves that prayer can change things for the better. It can show us the way, if we let it. We here, all of us, we're called the Passage of Divinity for a reason. I believe that this? This is that Passage we've been seeking for so long."

Quietly, he turns to Darlene and touches her lovingly on the arm. She looks at him with an expression of purest beneficence, then steps forward, toward the icon and its glowing fissure. Lowering herself before its strange pale light, she clasps her hands together atop her heart and begins to pray, her voice barely a whisper in the silence of the cavern. The big man's eyes search the crowd for volunteers, his eyes wide and expectant, but none step forward. They're all too scared, too confused. His eyes fall on the little girl then, on Annie, standing quietly at the front of the crowd. He raises a hand to her, beckoning her forward.

"Annie, come here. Come on."

Dutiful and sweet, Annie breaks from the crowd to stand next to the big man. He beams down at her, his smile the very portrait of benevolence. On the far side of the crowd, a woman wearing a silver pendant, with red hair to match Annie's, starts forward, her face twisted with worry.

"*Win*," she says, a warning tone in her voice, but the big man waves her off.

"She's fine, Bev." There's a chilly edge to the big man's voice as he shuts her down. Gone is the magnanimous preacher, or maybe he was never there in the first place. Maybe his good nature was all an act, a mask to fool the sheep. The smile returns to his face as he looks at Annie again. "Do you want to pray with her?" He nods toward Darlene, then to the rest of the gathered grown-ups. "Show them all how it's done?"

Annie beams and nods excitedly, like she'd like nothing more in the world. The girl's mother stays silent, but the look on her face telegraphs anxiety.

"Good," the big man tells Annie. "That's real good. I'm so proud of you. Here, go set next to her, okay?"

The girl does as she's told and goes over to kneel beside Darlene, twining her small, bloody hands together in front of her throat. Her eyes slide shut, and she begins to pray with the woman, lips moving in some silent invocation as trickles of blood run down her wrists. The camera zooms in to follow, focusing solely on the two of them as they pray together in silent exhortation.

But then something strange happens.

The sickly light radiating from the fissure grows brighter, building to rival the soft orange glow of the vigil candles, and the blood starts floating from Annie's hands, pulling away from her palms in long, elastic cords like taffy. The blood hangs there before Annie's closed eyes for just a moment, then it starts to drift toward the fissure. The camera pulls back and follows the red strands as they bob and waft through the air, drawn inexplicably toward that wretched light. Nobody else in the chamber seems to notice what's happening, or if they do, they don't say anything, every last one of them—including the girl's mother—as transfixed by this strange turn of events as the woman behind the camera.

Every last one, that is, except for the big man at the center of this spectacle.

In the farthest corner of the frame, his face widens with awe, his eyes going dinner-plate wide with realization. He doesn't speak. He doesn't have to. He didn't plan this, didn't expect it, but nonetheless, he sees as clear as day what's going to happen, and he doesn't do anything to stop it.

Unmoored from gravity, Annie's blood slips through the fissure, silently spinning through into the nauseating light before disappearing altogether.

For a moment, there's nothing. And then everything starts to go wrong.

In the middle of the crowd, the icon rumbles—not an earthquake, but not too far off, either; a tremor, an aftershock, or something else entirely. It's as if the ground itself is awakening, shaking off the dust. Jolted from their trancelike state, the congregation worriedly looks to one another for some kind of explanation or reassurance, but none of them have any to offer. None dare break the spell that's been cast upon them. Not yet, at least.

On the powdery face of the icon, the last of Annie's blood is devoured by the light.

And then the fissure splits open.

What was once a thin scar in the rock is now a gaping, devouring void that bleeds headache-inducing black-white light. The white rock surrounding the scar doesn't crumble or fall away—no detritus falls to the ground, no chunks of stone calve away from the void. It's as if the fissure simply opens itself wide, like a yawning mouth. The camera fixes on that void in its center, zooming in closer and closer as the color washes out and then that ugly sour-milk glow is everywhere, everything, forever. The footage hitches and shudders as it tries to autofocus on the light, aliasing itself to shreds. But between the glitches, there's a shape, something coiling and colossal that pulses and undulates in time with the putrid radiance cascading out of the rock.

Something's moving underneath the light.

Something's waiting on the other side.

Then the sound hits—a deep, almost sub-aural rumble that grows and swells to a gut-churning drone, more a crush of physical force than simple noise. It shakes the cavern, startling the crowd from their frightened reverie—as one, they gasp and scream and scatter, retreating from the chamber and clambering back up the mine shaft. Whatever the big man's miracle has become, they're not sticking around for the rest. Miracles are only miracles when they're small—Jesus on a piece of toast, crying statues, faith healing—but past a certain point of magnitude, they turn into nightmares. It all becomes too much for the mind to cope with, to comprehend. Better to run away screaming than stick around and shatter to pieces.

On the ground before the gaping hole, Annie screams and scrambles away, dashing back toward her mother, clutching on to the red-haired woman's leg with bloody hands, leaving red prints in the denim. Her mom holds her close and stares at the void before her with wide, wet eyes.

But Darlene? Darlene stays put despite it all, hands still knitted tightly over her heart as she prays louder and louder, shouting a plea that's nearly impossible to hear over the unearthly roar of the impossibility before her, but for three words:

"—behold the Revelation—"

Then Darlene starts to rise into the air, floating like Annie's blood before her, drawn bodily toward that shining maw. She doesn't seem to recognize that it's happening at first, even as her dark hair fans out in a black halo around her head. But then, after a moment, her eyes snap open and she starts to scream. This wasn't part of the plan. This wasn't supposed to happen. Her frantic gaze darts from side to side, then falls on the big man, and she reaches out for him with both hands, grasping wildly.

"Win!" she shrieks. "Winston, help me, please! *Please!*"

But Winston isn't helping. He's fallen to his knees before the icon, arms wide as he bathes in the glow, his face naked with selfish awe, mouth hanging slack. Above the roar of the void and Darlene's panicked screams, a sound rises from Win's lips, a kind of exultant laughter. In this moment, his joy and elation are nothing short of obscene.

Floating in midair, Darlene flails, searching for something—anything—to grab on to, to stop herself from being inhaled into that endless, colorless void. Her hands slash uselessly at the stony floor below, clawing desperately, trying to find purchase as her fingernails bend back and tear away, leaving long red streaks across the ground. She's already going through.

The hole devours her, pulling her body into its terrible radius: first her legs, then her torso and an arm, then all that's left of her is a shrieking, terrified face and a single outstretched hand. It happens so fast.

But then, as Darlene's about to slip the rest of the way into whatever ravenous infinity waits beyond, a pair of small, bloody hands close around her outstretched wrist and start to heave her back.

Annie.

Boldly, the little girl has thrown herself forward to pull Darlene back from the brink. Single-mindedly, Annie hauls on Darlene's wrist, bracing both sneakered feet against the lip of the maw. She's silent in her efforts, coldly focused on the task at hand, pulling for all she's worth as more blood rises from her scraped-up palms to drift into the void. For a moment, Annie and Darlene are locked there together, caught between this world and whatever lies beyond, and it seems as if the little girl, with all her gumption and wide-eyed bravery, might actually be able to save the woman—but then something unseen like an electric charge rocks Annie's tiny form, and she starts to scream, too, shaking and shrieking as if she's being tortured.

Annie's mother finally comes to her senses and breaks forward, wrapping her arms around the little girl, holding her tight as she tries to drag her daughter—and Darlene with her—away from the icon. A second later, the camera shakes, and trembles, and falls to the floor with a *CLACK*, but it keeps recording as a tall, solidly built woman with a long shock of silver-white hair rushes into frame and grabs on to the redhead with silver-ringed hands, forming a kind of daisy chain of human bodies, all of them trying to pull Darlene from that wretched, glimmering nothing.

But Darlene isn't Darlene anymore. Trapped in that infinite, ravenous white-black, she's an object, meat that screams as its form starts to warp and disintegrate in the light's corrosion. It rends her apart, tearing the skin from her body in ragged sheets as bloody pustules and tumors bloom on the red musculature underneath and burst open in lumpy gouts of pus. In the force of that bottomless gravity well, Darlene's other limbs are stretched and bent beyond all reason, and the sound of her bones breaking is the sound of the world as she knew it shattering into a million irreparable shards.

Annie screams again, and Darlene screams with her, spearing through the basso drone of the void like a stiletto piercing a bare throat. The footage glitches and warps, and trapped in the light, Darlene thrashes against Annie's grip. Her eyes start to bulge and burn like lanterns in her crumbling skull.

Staring into the heart of that annihilating void, Winston cackles and laughs, lost to his own revelation, eyes glassy and drunken and blank.

Then the screen goes black.

21

For a minute, they all just sat there, staring unblinkingly at the blank screen, trying to process what the hell they'd just watched. Anne's head spun and whipped like an amusement park teacup ride, except if all the teacups were on fire. The scars on her palms throbbed in time with her heart like they were being torn open, and for a second, she was sure that they were going to split apart in twin bursts of blood.

That had been her. She couldn't have been older than six then, and with the fresh cuts on her hands . . . it meant that whatever they'd just seen couldn't have happened long before everything fell apart at the cabin. Before the night her mom died.

Why didn't she remember any of this?

Her stomach pitched and flipped. The sound of that woman's wails as she came apart in the light, braided with the desperate shrieks of that little girl—with no memory of that night, Anne couldn't think of little Annie as *herself*—filled her head, nauseating. She felt like she was going to puke, but Dutch beat her to the punch. He bolted to his feet and went running for the bathroom, hands clasped tightly over his mouth. A moment later, the tell-tale sound of vomiting filled the little motel room.

Abruptly, Gemma stood.

"Yeah, no, I'm out," she said.

"Wait, what—?" Anne stammered. The words were clumsy and alien in her mouth. "What do you mean, *out*? You can't—"

"Yeah, I think I can," Gemma said, cutting across her. Her tone was icy and uneven, a piece of an iceberg calving off and drifting loose in some churning arctic floe. She looked Anne in the eyes just once, then turned and walked out of the motel room, leaving the door hanging wide open behind her.

Another throaty heave from the bathroom shook the motel walls. Anne took a deep breath, trying to still her own stomach, then rose and followed Gemma outside.

22

"Gem, wait up. *Gem.*"

"Nah. Fuck off."

Gemma crossed the motel's lot toward the road at a furious clip, stomping her feet hard into the gravel. Behind her, she could hear Anne quickening her stride to catch up, but Gem didn't slow her pace. Out in front of the liquor store, a small crowd watched her storm away, eyes wide and unabashed. One of them wolf-whistled, mocking. Gem resisted the urge to go over there and smash all the teeth out of their fool heads. There wasn't any time. She had to get the hell out of here.

"Gem, just stop!" Anne called after her.

"*What?!*"

Planting a boot in the gravel, Gem whirled around to face her. A couple of the lingering day drunks hooted and hollered. Gem kept her eyes on Anne, unblinking.

"Don't do this," Anne said, holding her hands out. The expression on her face was a mask of confusion and fear that Gem had never seen before. "Okay? Please, just don't."

"Don't what? Huh? What *exactly* d'you think I'm doing, Anne?" Gem's voice was garrote-tight, as if she could strangle back the scream that was boiling inside her chest, desperate to break free.

"I think you're bolting. I think you want to put as much space between yourself and that tape as you possibly can."

"Give the woman a prize, she got it in one," Gem replied, her words laced with bitter poison.

"Just—wait. Please. A couple of minutes. That's all. Okay? Then you can get the fuck out of here, go as far as you like. I won't stop you, I promise."

Gem pointed a finger in the direction of the motel room, and the TV, and the tape.

"Explain that shit," she said. "Make it make sense."

Anne shook her head and let her shoulders drop, exhausted, hopeless.

"I can't. I can't explain any of it."

"Oh, good," Gemma snapped. "Great. Wonderful. Real glad we had this talk."

She turned to walk away, but as she did, she felt Anne's hand close around her wrist, holding her back. Rage erupted in Gem's chest like lava seething from a fractured tectonic plate. How fucking dare she? She met Anne's eyes, daring her to blink first.

"Take your goddamn hand off me," she growled.

"Or what?" Anne challenged. There was a tremor in her voice that left her sounding shaky and small. Gem had never heard Anne Heller sound like that before, but that didn't really matter right now; there was no tone of voice or imploring look from those sad blue eyes that would make Gem willingly face down whatever nightmare she'd just witnessed.

"You really want to find out?" Gem asked.

She honestly didn't know if she could take Anne in a fight, but at this point, she was prepared to do what had to be done in order to get the entire hell away from here. Even if that meant going through someone she loved. But after a second, Anne released Gem's wrist and took a step back.

"Five minutes, okay? Just give me five minutes so we can talk. Please, Gem. I wouldn't ask if it wasn't important."

Gemma's eyes narrowed, but she didn't move, either. After everything she and Anne had been through, she probably owed her that, at least.

"You've got three," Gem told her. "The hell did I just watch, Anne?"

"I don't know. Like I said. I wish I could explain it, but I can't. If you want, I can tell you what I do know. We can start there and figure the rest out after. All right?"

Gem jerked her head back in the direction of the motel room, already regretting every part of this conversation. "That was you in the video, right? The little girl with the scraped hands?"

Anne raised her scarred-up palms so Gem could see the purple-bubble-gum keloids etched there. "Yeah, pretty sure."

"Do you remember any of that shit happening? At all?"

Anne shook her head.

"No. I remember . . ." Anne screwed her face up in a pantomime of thought. "I think I remember living somewhere in the woods with my mom before the cabin, but that's it. I don't remember anything like we saw in that video. None of it. It's all just gone."

Gem shook her head and sighed, aggravated.

"How is something like that even possible? How is any of that possible? The way you screamed, and whatever happened to that woman . . ."

Anne's face fell. "I said I don't know, okay? People block out trauma all the time."

"That's a shitty excuse, and you know it," Gem said, meaning for it to come out less barbed than it did. Still, in for a penny, in for a pound. "That wasn't just *trauma*, Anne. That was a fucking nightmare come to life. No part of that was normal. So I'm out, all right? Done. I didn't sign up for this crap."

"You think I did?" Anne snapped back, fresh anger reddening her face. "I didn't want any of this, Gem. You don't think I'd nope the fuck out if I felt like I could?"

"Except you *can*," Gem pressed her. "You can walk away. Same as me. You can, and you should, and you fuckin' know it, too."

"Of course I know it!" Anne roared. "But this isn't just some botched job anymore. It's my life. It's me. You say walk away; I say that sounds fucking great. You have any idea how I should do that, seeing what you just saw?"

She had a point. Whatever nausea-inducing dread Gem was feeling in this moment, it hadn't been her in that video. She couldn't imagine the world of shit that had to have been going through Anne's head right now. The way that woman, Darlene, had started to scream, was the worst sound Gemma had ever heard in her life, and even standing here now, under a wide-open sky, she could still feel it clawing at her insides, dragging her back into its naked agony.

She hooked the pads of her thumbs against her eyes and pressed hard as if trying to urge away a stubborn monster of a headache.

"I thought you were crazy," she finally said, her voice a grave whisper. She let her arms drop. "When you told us what happened to your mom, I thought . . . I mean, there's no way, right? But then with what happened to you up at the cabin, and back in Pecos . . . Things like that . . . They can't be real, Anne. That's not how the world works."

"I don't think I know how the world works anymore," Anne said. "I'm not sure I ever did. But I know that whatever we've stumbled on to here, whatever it all means . . . I don't think I can walk away from it, Gem. Not when I have a chance to maybe actually find out what happened to my mom."

Gem's stomach dropped at that. "You're sure?"

It was a dumb question, and she knew it. Of anyone in the entire world, Anne Heller wouldn't have said it if she wasn't sure. Standing there, Anne cast her eyes down at her shoes, and when she looked up again, what Gem saw in her face was a heartbreaking mix of fear and resolve. She was going to see this through to the end, because that was who she was. If this was just some bank job gone bad, Anne would have been gone in an instant, same as Gem, but it wasn't just that anymore.

"You're going to get yourself killed. You know that, right?" Gemma showed Anne a lopsided smirk that she knew was doing a shit job of covering up her worry.

"Not if I have any say in the matter," Anne said. "I'm not planning on doing this careless. Run, hide, or fight, remember?"

"Yeah, in that order, I know," Gem said, rolling her eyes to the bright blue sky above. "Chrissakes." Gem nodded back at the motel room again. "What about him? The cop. He sticking around?"

Anne shrugged. "I don't know. Maybe. Probably. Cops are looking for him, too. Probably going to come down on him like the hammer of god if they nab him again."

"Yeah, he's not the only one," Gem spat. As if she didn't have so much more to lose than some fucking white guy if the cops managed to get their hands on them.

"I know, Gem. The stakes are different for you, I understand. And I'm not going to ask you to do the same as him, but I'm not going to lie to you, either. I don't want you to go. But if you have to, I get it. Really. We can go back and split the money right now and you can get the hell out of here. Free and clear, no strings attached. Promise."

Gem almost took her up on it, too. For a single second, she saw herself burning hell out of Colorado as fast as the Tahoe would take her while the dust settled in her wake, all this shit dead and forgotten. A clean getaway. It was right there, begging to be taken. She could just leave it all behind and start new, become some other person in some other life somewhere. They had the money, after all, and with Travis and Iris not breathing down their necks just yet, the getting was good if she was going to get gone. Except.

Except, except, except.

I don't want you to go.

Goddammit.

Gem had never fancied herself a good person exactly, doing what she did for a living, but walking away from Anne in this moment would have made her a really bad one. Anne would get herself killed chasing this, Gemma was certain of that much. She'd follow it to the bitter, bloody end, because Anne didn't know how to be any different. And as much as Gem needed to get the hell away from all the bloodshed and the nightmares and everything else, she needed Anne Heller alive a lot more.

I don't want you to go.

God fucking *dammit.*

Gem hung her head, not wanting to ask but knowing she was going to, anyway.

"So what happens if I don't?" she asked.

Anne's expression curled into something curious. "What do you mean, don't?"

"You know what I mean. Don't make me say it. Please."

Anne blew out a heavy sigh. "I don't know. We try and get some answers. Try and make it make sense, like you said. Don't get dead."

"What about after that?"

Anne showed Gem the weakest of smiles, like the flame of a candle bending and snapping under the force of a gale wind.

"I don't know. New York?" she said.

Despite herself, Gem felt that little flame light a tiny match of hope inside her chest. They'd talked about lighting out for New York so many times by now that she'd written it off as little more than a pipe dream. But with the money from the bank in hand . . . maybe it was more in reach than she thought. They just had to see the rest of it through first. As if it was going to be that easy.

"Christ," she heard herself saying. "*Christ.*"

"That mean you're sticking around?"

Gem opened her mouth, then closed it again twice as fast, making her teeth click audibly inside her head. Turned her face toward the ground.

"Yeah," she said, closing her eyes and keeping them that way. "For now. Sure."

"Thank you," Anne said, her voice welling with relief. "Really."

On the far side of the gravel lot, Gem heard a door bang open. She looked over Anne's shoulder to see the cop standing in the doorway of the motel room, a wan, bloodless expression on his face.

"What?" Gem said, her voice turning chilly again.

"N-nothing," he said, stammering. "It's just that—"

"Just that *what*?"

"Your phone's ringing," he said.

23

Together, the three of them stood around the little motel room table, staring down at the iPhone's darkened screen, holding their collective breath.

"It won't do it again," Gemma said, regarding the phone as she would a live viper.

"You don't know that," Anne told her.

"Yeah, well. A girl can hope."

Then, as if summoned by some eldritch rite, the phone lit up and started to trill once more, somehow louder than it had been only a minute ago. The caller ID display read, *Unavailable.*

Gemma crossed her arms tight over her chest. "You know who that is, right?"

"I do."

Forgoing the possibility of abnormally insistent telemarketers, there were only a handful of people in the world who had Gem's phone number, and more than half of them were either dead or standing in this motel room. That left a pretty short list of possibilities.

"I'm not going to answer it," Gem said. "He can sit and rot for all I care."

"He's going to keep calling back until we pick up. You know how he is."

"Let him. I don't give a shit. We have the money; he doesn't. End of story."

"It's not that simple anymore," Anne said, her thoughts returning to the men who'd paid her a visit up at the cabin, Norris and John. There was no doubt in her mind that they were Trav's, a couple of low-rent mooks paid to go and take a look around and report back on what they'd found. He was never going to stop hunting them. Not as long as they had the money and he didn't.

On the tabletop, the phone stopped ringing, then started up once again.

"Please don't," Gem said. "I'm telling you, shit is going to go fully sideways if you do."

Anne sighed and shook her head. Shit had already gone fully sideways. Worse, it had gone fully fucking Godzilla, and yet here they stood in the big lizard's path, waiting to get stomped flat. No running away now. The only way out at this point was through. She took the phone from the table, flicked her thumb across the screen, and tapped the Speaker button.

"Hi, Travis," she said.

On the other end of the line, Travis laughed, reedy and nasal.

"Hell's Bells," he said, audibly beaming. "Why am I not surprised? Pretty sure this isn't your phone, but here you are anyway. You're a bad penny. Anyone ever tell you that? Is Jessup James there with you, too?"

"What do you want, Trav?" Anne asked, pointedly not taking the bait.

"What do you think I want, Heller? Shit, what does anybody want? I want what's coming to me."

"Oh, I think we can manage that just fine," Anne said.

"Very fucking funny. You want me to spell it out for you? Fine. The money. I want the fucking money. It's mine. Mine and Iris's."

"Sorry, don't know what you're talking about."

"Don't be a fucking asshole right now."

"You know, you're right, you've already got that market cornered," Anne told him.

"Don't get cute or pretend like you're suddenly fucking smart," Travis seethed. "Trust me, you're not. You and Gem just got lucky, is all. Shit at the bank would have gone off without a hitch otherwise. Speaking of, where the fuck is Poe, huh? Since I called her and not you."

Anne shot Gemma an imploring look. Gem threw her hands up

in the air and shook her head, mouthing, *No way*, but Anne kept looking.

Please, she mouthed at her.

Gem sighed. "Hi, Travis," she said, her voice steady and measured, a thin lid over a pressure cooker of fury.

"Where's my fucking money?" he barked.

Gem's face wrinkled up in a mask of contempt. "Yeah, not ringing a bell," she said. "But hypothetically speaking, if there was any money, far as I'm concerned, you guys gave up any claim you had on it the second you burned everything down back in Durango. Again, just hypothetically speaking here."

On the other end of the line, Travis made a furious, strangled noise in the pit of his throat. "That's pretty big talk from someone who's hiding like a scared little bunny rabbit, you venomous fucking bitch," he snapped. "Trust, the second I find out where the fuck you two are, I'm going to come paint the walls with your brains. Both of you."

"I'm sorry, is this how you convince people to do things?" Anne sneered. "Insults and threats? No wonder you fucked it all up back at the bank, just like you fuck everything else up. It's kind of pathetic, honestly. So, what, you going to try and pull an ambush or something? Crew up and come heavy? You want to know how that's going to go, Trav? Remember the end of *The Wild Bunch*? Yeah, kind of like that."

The line went quiet. They listened to Travis breathing on the other end.

"You're going to drop your guard sometime," he finally said. "You're going to get lazy and slip, just like everybody does. Just like Jessup James. So sure, hang up, walk away, pretend you're safe, I don't care. But sooner or later, you're going to stop looking over your shoulder, and when you do, I'll be there. I don't care how long it takes, how far you go. You've got something that belongs to me, and I'm going to get it back. I promise you that. I'll make you my fucking life's work if I have to."

On the other side of the table, Gem fixed Anne with a piercing

I-told-you-so look, and not for the first time, Anne wished Jess were here. He would have seen a way out of this, some middle path that didn't involve getting everyone dead. Anne had never been good at the strategy part of the job, the pieces that didn't involve going where she was told, looking scary as fuck and shooting people. She wasn't a tactician; she was a gun. Jess was always so much better at managing the toxic ego crap that came factory-standard in their line of work. It was like they said in that one movie: *Everybody wants to be Mr. Black.*

Then Gemma's face brightened, and Anne could almost see the lightbulb clicking on over her head.

"Hold, please," Gem said, a little too sweetly. She plucked the phone from Anne's hand and laid it down on the counter, then pressed the Mute button.

"What? What's going on?" Anne asked.

"Let's just split it with him," Gemma said. Anne could see a clever, nimble spark dancing in her beautiful brown eyes. "The money. Let's just give them half and let them blast off into the wild blue yonder for the rest of their short, miserable lives. No fuss, no muss."

For a second, Anne couldn't believe what she was hearing. Split the money with those traitors, after what they did? No, fuck that. Fuck all of that. The only thing that Travis was going to get out of her at this point was a bullet in the head.

But then again . . . they already had the cops on their tail, didn't they? And they were all over the news. That was to say nothing about the goddamn shape-shifter. The last thing they needed right now was another reason to keep looking over their shoulders.

Yeah, okay. This wasn't a terrible idea. It wasn't great, but it was a lot better than any of the other bad moves they had left.

"You're sure about this?" she asked her.

Gem shook her head. "I mean, no. But it's the only way out of this that I can see that doesn't involve a bloodbath. You got anything better?"

She didn't, and they both knew it.

"Hello? What the fuck am I holding on here for?" Travis said, his voice tinny on the phone's weak speaker. "If you assholes hung up on me, I swear to Christ . . ."

"All right, do it," Anne said.

Gem tapped the Mute button again. "Hey, yeah, we're here."

"The hell are you keeping me waiting for, Poe? The fuck is this?"

"This is us negotiating terms," Gem said.

"Hold up, what?" Travis's voice was incredulous. "You're kidding, right?"

Anne bugged her eyes out at her: *I hope to hell you know what you're doing.* Gem shrugged. It wasn't exactly reassuring, but then, it probably wasn't supposed to be.

"Not kidding, not bullshitting you. You want what's yours, so do we. So let's drop the dick-measuring contest for one second and talk about what kind of split it's going to take for all of us to walk away living," Gem said.

There was a pause on the other end of the line. "Seriously?"

"Seriously," Gem echoed.

"And Heller's good with this, too?"

Gem gave Anne an imploring look, mouthed the word *please.*

"Yep, I'm good," Anne said.

Travis paused. "Okay. All right. Okay. Fuck. What kind of split are we talking about here? What's fair?" It was weird and deeply unnatural to hear him playing reasonable, like watching a dog try to ride a bike.

Anne looked over at Gemma with eyebrows raised, questioning, deferential. She wasn't about to be the one who set terms. This was Gem's rodeo now; she was just along for the ride.

"Fifty-fifty," Gem said. "Way I see it, before everything went to shit, we were going to split the take eight ways, right? So we make it easy and split it straight down the middle, four and four."

"Nuh-uh, no way, fuck that. That's not enough. Not even close."

Anne had rarely heard Trav so indignant. It would have been funny if it wasn't so irritating.

"You'd be shocked at how little I care," Gem told him. "Call it the cost of doing business. Call it a backstabber tax. Call it whatever the hell you want; I don't really give a shit. You wanted more, you should have thought about having fewer members in your little conspiracy of assholes. Fifty-fifty. That's our first, last, and only offer. I was you, I'd take it."

Travis went quiet again for a second. "I'll have to talk it over with Iris."

"Nope," Anne cut in, her voice stony. "Absolutely not. No deal."

"Are you fucking kidding—"

"Yeah, no, gotta go with Anne on this one, Trav. Sorry, but Iris doesn't get a say," Gem said. "We're dealing with you and you alone, right now. You don't like it, that's fine by me. Deal expires in ten seconds. But it was real nice talking to you again. Truly. I hope you assholes have just the worst lives. I'll be sure to stop by and see you in the ninth circle of hell. Four, three, two—"

"Wait, wait!" Travis barked, his practiced calm giving way to a sizzling panic. "Just wait, okay? Fuck. Fine."

Gem smiled at Anne, and Anne smiled back. Gem had him over a barrel, and they all knew it.

"You sure about that, Trav? Like, really sure?" Gem didn't even bother masking the grin in her voice. She was just twisting the knife now. Hurting him because she could. It was petty, but Anne couldn't really blame her. Travis had blown up all their lives, and here they were, still letting him and Iris and Joanie walk away with cash in hand. Far as Anne was concerned, they were already doing them a fucking favor by not hunting them down one by one and killing them slow. So let Gemma have her fun.

"I'm sure," Travis said after another painfully long moment. "There's a little diner in Alamosa called the Pink Flamingo. We'll meet there. All right? Sunset. And fuck you both forever while I'm at it."

Then the line went dead.

24

The bell over the door rang softly as the three of them stepped into the diner. Beyond the big picture windows, the sun was setting slowly over Alamosa, lighting the town up in a kind of iridescent bloom, giving the landscape a dazzling, *Land-of-Oz-in-glorious-Technicolor* look.

The inside of the Pink Flamingo was almost exactly like every other diner Anne had ever set foot in: red vinyl booth seats along a wall of gallery windows, creaky wooden chairs arranged around fleck-topped tables with chrome (or, at least, *chrome-ish*) trim, painted ceiling lights hanging from single wires, old framed photos mounted on the walls, a long countertop running the length of the dining room. True to the place's name, flamingo décor filled the place—rendered in headache-inducing pastel pink between flickering neon palm trees in the windows, printed on the menus and the paper place mats, even a collection of little ceramic flamingo figurines arranged *just so* on a shelf behind the register. It was like a Jimmy Buffett fever dream come to life in here, but at least it was quiet.

Standing by the door, Anne scanned the place from end to end—near the back of the dining room, Travis sat on the opposite side of a long six-top, Iris and Joanie on either side of him. Travis was smiling. Iris and Joanie weren't.

Posted in the corners of the room stood a handful of mismatched white guys, all dressed in upmarket work gear—black canvas jackets and cargo pants and expensive-looking boots, complete with alt-right douchebag-chic wraparound Oakleys mounted high on their foreheads. Of course Travis had brought friends. All of them looked itchy, on edge. None of them sat, none of them ate, none of them even had so much as a cup of coffee within reach. Too concerned with playing scary hard-asses and, frankly, doing a shit job of it. These blockheads didn't have a clue what real scary looked like.

Beside Anne, Gemma shifted back and forth on the balls of her feet.

"*Woooow*," she said. "Look at this trap we've got right here."

"Hey, don't look at me. This was your plan," Anne shot back.

"And wouldn't you know, I'm already starting to regret it," Gem said.

Next to the register, one of Travis's jackboots—a short, stout man with beet-red skin and the words *WARDOG* and *DEIMOS* tattooed down his forearms in flaming Gothic script—peeled himself off the wall and took a step forward to block their path.

"Fuck you think you're going? Huh?" Wardog demanded.

He stepped in close, deliberately crowding their space. Refusing to be moved, Anne showed him a thin, violent smile, like a razor gash carved into her face.

"Careful there," she said. "Don't want to do something you can't take back."

Wardog's eyes narrowed beneath his sweaty brow. He took another step closer. "The fuck you just say to me?"

Anne stood her ground. "I think you heard."

Rage bubbled in the man's face. Anne didn't blink.

"They're fine, Caff," Iris called from the other end of the dining room. "You can let them through."

Wardog—*Caff*, apparently—looked over his shoulder at Iris, then back to Anne. She met his dark, beady stare and made a show of looking him up and down. She didn't know this guy, but she knew his type. Just like every other merc south of Colorado Springs, he was almost certainly a vet of some kind, with at least a couple of tours under his belt. Probably got his first taste of violence early on and never looked back. Worst-case scenario, he was some PMC psychopath whose skills matched his appetite for mayhem, but Anne was willing to bet money that wasn't the case. Private military contractors almost never went the kind of merc that Travis and Iris could afford. Those guys were polo-shirt-wearing motherfuckers who took cushy salary jobs as corporate heads of security, shit like that. No, Caff and his buddies were almost certainly frontline grunts to a man, Dollar General hired guns working on a shoestring budget and the promise of a big fat payday once the job was done. Didn't mean they weren't dangerous, far from it—just that their brand of dangerous was a bit more *boot camp basic training* and a lot less *black site torture technician*.

After a second, the guy stood aside with a huffed *Go on ahead*. Like he was doing them a favor. What a joke.

"Gee, thanks, *Caff*," Gem said, her voice dripping with sickly-sweet venom.

Travis's face twitched as they crossed the dining room to the six-top, his eyes flicking first to Anne, then Gem, then confusedly, nervously, over to Dutch.

"I didn't know you were bringing company," Trav said, jerking his chin at Dutch, eyes narrowing above his plastic smile. "Who the fuck is this?"

"No one," Anne said, and glanced to the muscle posted around the diner. "Who are all your friends?"

Travis's smile grew long and oily. "No one."

Travis had always been a slick fuck; his entire personality was game-show-host-rehearsed, but inside, he was a vicious little shit, the kind of guy who floored the gas when he saw stray dogs crossing the street. Tall and loose-skinned in a way that suggested considerable weight loss at some point in the past, he had an overlong shock of limp, thinning dishwater hair above big, watery cow eyes, a mouthful of blunt yellow Tic Tac teeth, and a chin so recessed that it made his neck and head look like an oversized thumb wearing a cheap wig.

Beside him, Iris met Anne's eyes, her expression cold, business-like. She was a slight woman, almost waifish, with dark, watchful eyes and patchy, bleached-blond hair cut into a moppish pixie cut above a severe, oval visage. Like Travis, she was nearly ten years older than Anne, but unlike her husband, she didn't look it.

"Sit down," Iris said.

"Nice to see you too, Iris," Gemma said, taking the seat on the left, directly across from Joanie. Anne took the chair in the center, and Dutch sat down across from Iris. "This place got anybody on staff? I could really use a cup of coffee or something."

Travis smirked. "Sorry. Sent them all home early. Figured we could use the privacy."

"Where's the money?" Iris demanded, impatient.

Anne met her black-glass eyes, studied them.

"You mean your half?" Gem prodded. "It's safe. Waiting for you."

Before leaving the motel, they'd counted the cash out into two halves—$715,000 apiece, give or take a couple of hundred dollars—and stowed one under the spare tire in the Ninety-Eight's trunk. Their plan, such as it was, was pretty simple: leave Murph in the car while they checked out things in the diner and made sure that Trav and company were actually going to play ball, then Dutch would go out and fetch their cash for them. The other half they'd left wrapped in a plastic grocery bag, tucked in the heat vent back in Gem's room at the Happy Trails Motel. That way, even if things did go all the way wrong here, Travis and Iris and Joanie would only be walking away with their piece, rather than the whole pie.

"Yeah, and what about your half?" Travis's voice was a reptile slither. "Where'd you stash it?"

"A couple miles east of none of your fucking business," Anne said.

Travis showed them his dull little Tic Tac teeth again. "And what if we decide to make it our business?"

Anne wanted to say she was surprised by the threat, but she really, really wasn't. Travis had already proven himself capable of far dumber feats than Anne had previously given him credit for; worse, he was high on his own supply now. The ringleader of his own shithead circus. The second he got impatient or caught a whiff of something he didn't like, he'd probably just pull the rip cord on the whole deal and turn the Pink Flamingo into a killing jar. Just like before.

Beside Anne, Gemma's smile turned stony, but the bright tone in her voice was resolute, unflinching. "Look, we all get to make choices and live with the consequences, Trav. We're trying to give everyone an out that doesn't end with us painting this lovely Cabo

Wabo nightmare with each other's blood, but if you'd rather go that way, we can make that happen," she said.

Across the table, Joanie cleared her throat. "Can we please just drop all of this useless posturing crap and get out of here?" she said, looking at Anne and Gem. "We'll take the money and go. Okay? I'm done with this. All of it. I just want to go home."

Joanie Perez was always easy to miss in a crowd; tall, thin, and reserved, she wasn't anyone's Platonic ideal of an experienced getaway driver, but that was one of the things that made her so good at it. She was quiet, which a lot of people tended to mistake for timidity, but that couldn't have been further from the truth. Joanie was one of those people who was completely internal, every feeling buried well beneath the surface, and she drove the same way, all intuition and split-second decision-making. She never let the cracks show. Anne had no doubt that Joanie'd had her reasons to throw in with Travis and Iris, but looking at her now, there was really only one that mattered: above all, Joanie was a survivor. She was always going to make the choice that she thought would keep her alive the longest. Anne certainly couldn't begrudge her that. Plenty of other shit, sure. But on the list of people Anne felt a profound desire to kill right now, Joanie ranked surprisingly low.

"You should listen to her," Anne said, speaking to Trav and Iris but keeping her eyes locked square on Joanie. "She clearly knows how to save her own ass."

Joanie's glare burned behind the long black curtain of her hair. Anne stared back until Joanie pushed her chair away from the table and rose to her feet.

"Fuck are you doing?" Travis demanded, incredulous.

"I'm sick of this shit. I'm going to go wait in the car. I'll be out there when you're done," Joanie said.

"The fuck you are," Travis started, twisting around as if to get in her way or grab her by the wrist, but Iris stayed him with a freezing glare like a polar wind. He stayed where he was, and together, they all watched Joanie cross the dining room to the front door where one of the pay-goons—not Wardog or Caff or whatever the fuck his name was, but one of the other guys—stood guard, looking nervous and twitchy.

"Move," Joanie said.

The guy's stood aside, and Joanie walked out so fast she nearly left a woman-shaped cloud in her wake.

Gem whistled. "*Dang*. You guys dealing with some dissent in the ranks? Really isn't any honor among thieves, I guess," she needled, smirking.

"Eat shit. You're both just pissed we brought her into the plan and not you," Iris said.

Gemma's eyes narrowed to slits, and she leaned forward in her seat. "Yeah? You really think we'd stoop that low, Iris? Honestly?"

Iris rolled her eyes and crossed her arms, pantomiming how over all of this she was. Gem and Iris had never really gotten on, and that went double for Anne; as far as she was concerned, Iris had always been too precious, too pushy. She never got her hands dirty unless she absolutely had to. Her strengths lay on the far opposite end of the spectrum, all plans and strategies, wheels within wheels. Iris's fingerprints were all over the double cross at the bank, but Anne was absolutely certain that Travis had been the one who'd fucked it all to hell.

Trav studied them above his shitty little smile. "Saw you three roll up in that big old blue boat, by the way. No Jessup James, though, huh? Guess he didn't make it. Sad."

Rage blew through Anne's body like a sonic boom; she bunched her hands into tight fists at her sides until the bones stood out through the skin, but she forced her expression to stay equanimous. This was what Travis did. She had to remember that.

"Yeah, turns out somebody shot him," Anne said. "And a bunch of cops, too."

Travis laughed. "What, like you're suddenly sympathetic to the plight of the fucking fascists in blue, Heller? Come on now, don't sit there and act like you give a fuck. But that does remind me of my favorite joke, actually. Tell me if you've heard this one before: What do you call a million dead cops? *A good start*."

Anne felt Dutch ruffle. Travis wasn't exactly wrong: She didn't have any love for the police, but over the past couple of days, Dutch had proven himself to be a lot more than just some cop. He'd helped her bury Jess. He'd come back when he didn't have to. He kept his word and didn't even seem remotely interested in the money from the bank job. Whatever Louis "Dutch" Greene III was now—hostage, outlaw, collaborator, all of the above—he'd moved well past the badge. But Travis didn't know any of that. He was just being a piece of shit like always.

"What I give a fuck about," Anne said, keeping her voice low, "is the heat you killing cops like a stupid fucking asshole brings down on all of us. If you were going to fuck us over, you could have at least done it a little more privately. Or at least not as fucking dumb."

Iris glared at Travis out of the corners of her eyes. Gemma blasted her with a finger gun, clucking her tongue.

"*Ohhh*, so *that* was the plan. I get it now. Let the bank job go off without a hitch, and then zero everybody who wasn't in on your little side play once we made the getaway. I'm guessing execution-style, right? Bullets in the back of the head, shallow graves in the desert, the whole song and dance. That about the long and short of it?"

"You don't know a fucking thing about a fucking thing," Iris muttered, crossing her arms.

Gemma laughed. "Right. That's why you look like someone shit in your cereal bowl. Not because Prince Dumbfuck over here got impatient and went on a killing spree instead of sticking to the plan. Not at all."

Across the table, Travis smirked and shook his head like this was the silliest conversation he'd ever heard.

"Fuck that," he said. "And fuck those dead cops. You're talking about heat like it's something we gotta worry about. The FBI stopped investigating bank robberies after 9/11, assholes. Nobody's looking for us because nobody cares. The planet's dying, and civilization's falling apart in slow motion. In thirty years, New York City's going to be underwater, and you know what? Nobody cares about that shit, either. They don't give a fuck. They just want a good show before the lights go off, and we sure as hell gave 'em that. Something to pay attention to until the next big-headline so-cial outrage bubbles its way to the top of their bullshit machine. It's all spectacle, fifteen minutes of fame, whatever the fuck you want to call it. If anyone's still paying attention to us in a week, they'll be cheering us on for actually doing the shit they've only ever dreamed of doing, and getting away with it, too. You say *dead cops*, I say *good news*. People fucking hate cops. Us? We'll go down as goddamn folk heroes. Myths. Bigger than life. Robin Hoods with nine millimeters. After that, we'll just get to fade away. It's fucking beautiful. The only person standing in the way of that shit is you, Heller. You and your fucking temper. What's done is done, okay? So get over it already and *give us what we're owed.*"

Another sermon from the clown prince of bullshit mountain. Anne had heard a million of them by now, and they were all the same: nihilism, nihilism, bitch, bitch, bitch. Across the table, Tra-vis kept jabbering, but Anne wasn't listening anymore. She let her attention drift outside—past the big gallery windows, the sun had slipped almost entirely below the horizon, bathing the city and the valley beyond in a rich, shimmering blue-purple-black.

Out on the sidewalks, people trickled by on foot, going about their lives, lost in their own worlds. Anne studied their faces, hunt-ing their eyes for some dead glimmer, any sign that they weren't who they seemed to be, but there was nothing. No white eyes. No flurries of flies and maggots. No grotesque, Pez-dispenser maws filled with mismatched brown teeth. Everything outside was ex-actly as—

Wait.

Across the street, walking past a derelict check-cashing place, Anne spotted a familiar figure—tall, rail thin, bald, bespectacled. Where had she seen that guy before?

Then it hit her: it was one of those poachers, the ones who had shown up out of nowhere. John, that was what he said his name was.

Back at the cabin, Jessup had pegged him and his buddy for Travis and Iris's goons, but if that were true, he'd be in here with the rest of the troops. She'd already seen his face, heard his voice. If he were part of some shitty, ill-conceived ambush, they'd given up the element of surprise by leaving him out there. Maybe Trav was that arrogant, but Iris sure as shit wasn't. No, there was something else going on here. A second later, Anne realized that Travis was snapping his fingers at her.

"Hey, earth to Heller. You with us? I'm talking to you here."

"Sorry, I wasn't listening," she said, smiling sweetly enough to give him diabetes. "Were you finished with your little speech yet, or . . . ?"

That shitty smile crept back toward Travis's ears, but his eyes stayed icy hard. "Oh, fuck you. Play above-it-all as much as you want, but you're not fooling anybody. We all know you're a fucking rattlesnake just like the rest of us. You wanna know what happens to motherfuckers who pretend to be better than they are? Ask dear ol' Jessup James. Wait, shit, *you can't.*"

That phosphorescent fury pulsed behind Anne's face again. She knew better than to let him get to her with a cheap shot like that, but she hadn't been expecting it. Left herself wide open for Travis to jam a shiv into her ribs.

She pushed her chair back from the table slowly, wooden legs honking against the tile, and stood. Travis watched, a sick, satisfied little smile on his dopey face, proud as hell of pushing her buttons yet again.

"What's'a matter? I touch a nerve or something? My bad." He play-slapped his own wrist. "Bad Travis. No cookie." Beside him, Iris was wary. Watchful. Nervous.

Anne met Travis's eyes, then shook her head, fighting with all her strength to keep her cool.

"Just gotta see a man about a dog," she said.

Trav rolled his eyes. "Sure, whatever you say. I don't give a shit. Don't fall in."

Without another word, Anne turned and stepped away from the

table, beelining past the community corkboard filled with Missing Persons flyers toward the hallway near the front of the diner and the bathrooms beyond. Nobody moved to stop her. Nobody dared.

The bathroom door flew open with a *BANG* and swung shut behind her just as hard. With numb fingers, Anne snapped the cheap little slide bolt into place and fell back against the cool concrete wall, craning her face toward the ceiling as she worked to catch her breath.

Standing there, doing her best to quell her own rage, Anne tried to map out all the possible paths the next few minutes could take. There weren't many. Jessup would have told her that there were smarter ways out of this, some combination of carefully chosen words to make Travis and Iris shut their mouths and take the money and fuck off forever. But guys like Travis Cade only understood one language. He'd made that much abundantly clear.

You wanna know what happens to motherfuckers who pretend to be better than they are?

She slipped the comfortable weight of the Glock from her jeans and eased the slide back, checking the load. Seventeen plus one, full up. Same as she'd left it. She tucked the pistol into one jacket pocket, then checked the other to make sure her spare mags were still there. Pulling her wild red locks out of their loose ponytail, Anne ran her scarred-up hands under the faucet, then used wet fingers to tame her hair back and fix it in place again.

If Travis wanted to see a fucking rattlesnake, she'd be more than happy to oblige him.

She left the tap running for a minute longer, then two, letting the steady *whoosh*ing sound of the water swell until it was the only thing she could hear. She blew all the air out of her lungs. Shut her eyes. Let both hands fall on either side of the sink in front of her, feeling the cool porcelain underneath her keloids. Going very still, she let the fury swell in her chest, a flicker growing into a bonfire growing into a conflagration. A house on fire. A city burning to the ground. Anne let the flames build, let them churn and roll through her like a wave until the heat inside her chest felt like it would consume her. Until it had nowhere else to go but out.

Running hadn't worked, and hiding certainly hadn't done her any favors. Only one move left now.

Anne shut the faucet off, then threw the slide bolt on the bathroom door and walked into the hallway.

25

None of this was going the way it was supposed to.

For a single brief, shining moment, Iris had allowed herself to believe that maybe—just *maybe*—Anne wasn't going to be a complete asshole about this. But of course, she had no such luck.

Iris had known the second news broke that Anne had gotten out of the Savings and Loan alive that she was going to be trouble. She always was. Out of all of them, Anne being the one to make it out alive was about as bad a hand as she and Travis could have been dealt. The only way it could have been worse would have been if Jessup had survived that bullet Travis had put in him and shown up here tonight. Him and his bullshit code of honor.

That was what had sealed his fate when Iris and Travis had started talking about making a side move all those months back. Jessup had always thought so much more of himself, as if he were anything more than a jumped-up thug playing noble highwayman. As if any of them were. Jessup had a brain, that much was inarguable, but at the end of the day, he wasn't Butch Cassidy, and he didn't do the shit he did for any reason other than the money of it all. They were crooks. They stole shit and shot people for a living. That was the whole deal. None of them were any better than anybody else on this dumb, doomed rock. Life became a lot easier to deal with once you got honest with yourself and accepted that fact. But Jessup, he'd always had airs—about himself, about the work. It was that shit that made him dangerous, because you couldn't reason with someone like that. You couldn't cut them in, make them see sense. Anne was no better; she was just as stubborn and intractable as Jess, but unlike him, she lacked vision and ambition. Behind all her so-called professionalism, she was a weapon, blunt-force trauma in the shape of a person.

Iris was under no illusions; showing up here, now, like this, was always going to be a risk. With Jess dead and Anne no doubt hell-bent on revenge, sitting down like this was a pressure cooker. But Iris had to believe that despite all her bluster and violence, Heller was a pragmatist at heart, willing to drop the goddamn blood feud for a chance to disappear with her cut of the profits. She could have been wrong. She hoped she wasn't. She'd been wrong more than she'd have liked recently.

Jessup wasn't supposed to get shot at the bank. Nobody was. Gem had been right on the money. The idea—her *plan*—had been for them to pull the job off clean, after which Joanie would drive them all out to the far reaches of the county and leave Jess, Anne, Gem, and Merrill in an empty hole for the coyotes and turkey vultures. Maybe Joanie, too, if she ended up expressing any last-minute moral misgivings. Iris and Travis had brought her in by dint of necessity rather than any real want, and if she proved to be more trouble than she was worth? Well, Iris was ready to do what needed to be done.

But then Travis got *bored*. Decided that he knew better. Just like always. And now here he was, doing it again, sticking the knife in a little deeper just because he could, or because he liked it, or maybe both. It had been fine at first, but now it was making Iris nervous. She needed Anne and Gem distracted, not so pissed off that they decided to do something about it.

Across the table, Gem and the new guy whose name Iris still hadn't caught sat silently, arms crossed, watching, waiting, faces serious as a graveyard. After a second, Iris met Gemma's eyes and nodded toward the bathroom.

"So," she said. "Does she speak for all of you or just herself?"

Gemma's eyes narrowed. "What's that supposed to mean?"

"What do you think it means, Gem?" Iris asked, her voice laced with false friendliness. "Just because you showed up here together doesn't mean you agree on everything, does it?"

Beside her, Travis smirked and leaned forward.

"Yeah, I mean, real nasty temper on that one, huh? You sure you want to take orders from someone like that?" he teased.

"We don't take orders," the new guy said. "Not from her or anyone."

"I don't remember fucking asking you," Travis snapped.

Across the table, the new guy deflated. Iris kept her eyes on Gemma.

"You know what I mean," Iris said. "You know how she is. Goddamn hard-liner."

Gemma sucked her teeth and cast a sidelong glance in Trav's direction.

"Yeah, I don't think she's the one making this harder than it needs to be, Iris."

"Look, we came here to make the deal, Gem," Iris said. "Let's get it done. After that, we'll drop all the rest of it if you—and her—can do the same."

Gemma rolled her eyes. "Bullshit."

"No, really. Everybody gets paid, everybody goes their separate ways. No need to turn this place into another bloodbath. We can just go. Simple as that."

The lie came as easy as breathing. She almost felt bad, lying to her like this, but at the end of the day, half of the take wasn't ever going to do. Especially not now that they had Caff and his guys to cut in. No, in order for this to work, they had to walk away with the whole pie. It was as simple as that. She just had to get Gemma to play ball, because Gem was their only hope in hell of calming Anne down enough to drop her guard. After that, Caff and his guys would do what they did. As for where they'd stashed the rest of the money? Well, Iris was confident that Caff could get whoever was left breathing to squeal.

On the other side of the fleck-topped table, Gem sighed and laid her hands flat atop the shabby old Formica.

"After the shit you pulled? I don't know. Maybe I could see my way past that, for the sake of dying of old age, but Anne?" She nodded in Travis's direction. "She wants his head on a fucking plate. Frankly, I'm kind of amazed she didn't shoot you the second she walked in."

"Hey, fuck you, and fuck her," Travis sneered. "If you expect me to sit here like an asshole and beg for your fucking forgiveness, or hers—"

Iris held up a hand, silencing him. "Don't," she said icily.

Travis stared knives at her.

"You're not helping," she told him, pretending not to notice the shitty, self-important indignation flaring in his eyes. Him and his tantrums. She knew by now that he'd never grow out of them.

"So, what's it going to be?" Iris asked, turning back to Gem. "You going to help us make sure everybody gets to walk away breathing?"

Near the front of the diner, Iris heard the bathroom door bang open as Anne emerged from the little hallway, eyes fixed squarely on Travis. She didn't say anything. She didn't need to. Iris saw what was going to happen a second before it did, and she knew in her heart that she couldn't stop it. She didn't have a hope in hell.

Without a word, Anne walked up to the table, pulled her Glock, and shot Travis in the face.

26

BOOM.

Travis's head snapped back hard as the bullet punched through his face, his skull geysering blood from both sides. He flopped backward and kicked the table with a *BANG*, then toppled over in his chair and hit the floor in a heap.

Iris screamed. Gemma screamed. Everything went to shit.

Anne threw herself across the table just as Travis's pay-goons drew their pistols and started shooting, painting the inside of the diner with gunfire. Chunks of pressboard and plastic flew all around her as she thudded to the floor beside Travis's body. His face was an unholy mess of torn skin hanging off his skull in red, ragged flaps. Blood waterfalled out of his forehead, his nose, his eyes, curtaining up toward his thin, receding hairline. Anne felt a sudden urge to spit in his dead face, but managed to resist it. She had bigger concerns right now.

Another flurry of gunshots burst from the far side of the diner, and for half a second, maybe less, time crawled. Twisting away, she scanned the dining room—near the front of the building, Wardog and another one of his merc buddies had grabbed cover in the bathroom hallway. There was no sign of the other two.

Underneath the big gallery windows, Gemma was curled up in one of the red-vinyl booths with her High Power in both hands, squeezing off shots at Wardog and the other guy, keeping them in place. Dutch had gone the opposite direction and pressed himself against the place where the diner counter bent and curved back toward the kitchen doors. She couldn't see where Iris had gone. That was definitely going to be a problem.

More gunshots burst from the far side of the diner, the bullets smacking into the floor around her. With one shoulder, Anne shoved the long table up onto its side with a great crash. The press-board and laminate wouldn't do much to stop anything bigger than a .22, but maybe it would slow the bullets down, if it came to that.

Glancing to the side, Anne caught sight of one of the mercs, standing in the kitchen doorway with a pistol-grip Mossberg in his hands, eyes crazed and fixed on her. The guy had gone tunnel-vision; he didn't see Dutch kneeling there, only feet in front of his knees. Bad luck for him.

The pay-goon swung the Mossberg up just as Dutch hit him with a picture-perfect football spear, driving a shoulder hard into the soft of his belly, shoving him awkwardly into the doorjamb. Balling one hand into a fist, the goon shoved back and punched Dutch in the face, hard—one, twice, three times. There was a sick, hollow *POP* and Dutch's nose started spewing blood, but Dutch kept pushing, bracing shotgun guy against the jamb. Keeping her aim high, Anne wheeled her Glock around and squeezed the trigger twice—*POP! POP!*

The first bullet caught shotgun guy in the cheek, shredding the side of his face to ground beef; the second blew the cap of his skull back like it was on a hinge. The guy dropped in a messy spray of red and Dutch stumbled past him into the kitchen, scrambling for cover, one hand cupped over his shattered nose. Moving fast and staying low, Anne clambered from the table to the doorway and swept the Mossberg out of the dead guy's hands.

On the other side of the dining room, the pistol snapped empty in Gemma's hands. She cast it aside and dropped flat in the padded bench as another barrage of bullets tore into the booth, blowing white puffs of polyester stuffing out of the red vinyl.

"Gem!" Anne screamed.

When Gemma glanced her way, Anne threw her the shotgun. Gem plucked it out of the air with ease, then kicked both legs against the booth wall, somersaulting backward onto the floor as she lined up her next shot. The Mossberg roared in her hands. Near the front door, Anne heard glass explode. But she didn't hear Iris until it was too late.

"*You!*"

Anne turned. The woman was crouched five feet behind her, a pistol, some compact little ankle-strapper no bigger than a child's toy, clutched tightly in both hands, eyes burning with perfect hatred.

"You fucking killed him, you fucking *fuck!*"

Iris made a screeching noise in her throat, and Anne saw her finger tightening around the trigger. She flopped to the side just as the shot went off.

She felt the heat of the muzzle flare on her face as the bullet droned past her head, a hairsbreadth from the crest of her ear. The shot was deafening at point-blank range, little toy gun or not. Anne felt the round smack into the counter at her back, and she sucked air. Tried to scan her body to make sure she hadn't gotten hit. As Iris rose to stand over her, her wild stare jumped from Anne to the pistol in her own hands, looking amazed that she'd actually pulled the trigger.

That single moment was all Anne needed.

She threw herself forward and drove the flat of her elbow into Iris's solar plexus. Iris made a sound like *CHOOF!* as all the air left her body and she stumbled back, clutching at her midsection. Not wanting to waste her momentum, Anne inverted the Glock in her hand and came up swinging.

She snapped the pistol at Iris's head like she was swinging a hammer, and her arm shook as she felt the butt of the Glock's grip connect, hard. Iris wailed and recoiled, clutching at her temple. Anne heard the little ankle-strapper hit the floor and swung again, hammering the Glock into the side of Iris's face as hard as she could.

Then someone clobbered her from behind.

The pistol flew out of her hand, and she went tumbling to the floor, blindly kicking and thrashing at the body dragging her down. Twisting under the bulk of whoever it was, she saw Iris spinning her wheels and running away, both hands pressed to the side of her head, blood trickling out from between her fingers. Good. Anne hoped it hurt.

Face pressed to the filthy tile floor, she watched Gemma move in close to one of the mercs, then feint to the side and jam the

Mossberg tight against the guy's chest. *BOOM*. The guy flew back and Gem ducked away, racking the slide as a fresh volley of bullets tore into the booth seats behind her.

Anne's unseen assailant threw a fist, drilling her square in the back, then threw another, and another. The pain was astonishing and immediate, bright red solar flares erupting up her spinal cord with each successive impact. Crying out, Anne blindly snapped her elbow back and felt it connect with soft tissue in a soft, damp *crunch*.

Whoever it was yelped and flopped awkwardly off her, uttering a string of curse words. Rolling over, Anne looked and saw Wardog, or Caff, or whatever his dumb name was, glaring at her over the top of what was very clearly a broken nose. *You're welcome, fuckhead*.

Glowering, he drew a stubby fixed-blade push knife from the sheath on his nylon tac belt.

Oh, fuck shit.

The blade flashed in Wardog's hand, and pain erupted in Anne's side as the steel bit into her flesh, freezing cold and scorching hot at the same time. She screamed—she was sure she screamed—and recoiled, thrashing away as the shitty little meat-brick of a man yanked the point from her side with a burst of blood. Grinning, Wardog punched the knife at her again, aiming for her temple this time. A killing shot.

The world contracted around her, time slowing itself down to a matter of endless microseconds. Anne didn't have her gun, couldn't get her own knife out in time, and she couldn't shove him away; the prick outweighed her by seventy-five pounds or more. So left with no other move to make, Anne gritted her teeth tight enough that she thought they might crack and headbutted the smug asshole in his shattered nose as hard as she fucking could.

Fresh blood spouted from Wardog's face and he recoiled as his arm fell to his side, momentarily useless. Anne threw a fist into his nose. Blood splattered her knuckles, and she punched him again, dazing him, then used both hands to wrench the knife out of the man's thick, hairy fist.

Snarling, Anne righted the knife in her hand, then jammed the blade into his throat and twisted until she felt a wet, cartilaginous *crunch*. Wardog's eyes went wide as a heavy jet of bright arterial blood exploded from the wound, fountaining everywhere in an uncontrolled spray. Jesus fuck, she must have hit a major vessel or something. The smell of it was hot and coppery foul. Anne felt sick. She'd never been some shrinking violet; she knew intimately the kind of atrocious mess a human body made when it died, but it had been a long damn time since she'd had to knife someone like this.

Blood pulsed steadily around the blade, spurting from the wound and painting Anne's whole arm red. Wardog whined through his nose like a kicked dog, and he pawed uselessly at the knife, as if he could dislodge it with numb fingertips and a little bit of hope. With one last damp, spluttering cough, he slumped back onto the floor and went still.

More gunshots exploded from somewhere else in the diner; pressing a hand to the fresh hole in her side in an attempt to slow her own bleeding, Anne turned—and saw a slight, bottle-blond figure with a moppish pixie cut ducking through the kitchen, doubtlessly heading for the back door.

Iris was making a break for it.

Bleeding, bellowing, limping, Anne scooped up her Glock and followed.

27

Through the serving hatch in the kitchen wall, Dutch watched Gemma somersault out of the bench seat and onto the linoleum, clearing a path to the front door with one well-placed blast from the shotgun. Travis's guys dove out of the path of the buckshot just in time; one of the front windows disintegrated in a spray of pebbled glass behind them. Popping up like groundhogs, they returned fire, peppering the back wall of the diner with stray shots. The shotgun in Gemma's hands roared again, and then she was on her feet, moving.

Not for the first time in the last ninety seconds, Dutch wished to hell that he'd taken Anne up on it when she'd offered him a gun back at the car. Stupid, stupid, stupid. At this point, he just needed something to defend himself with. With the hand not currently trying to stanch the blood from his broken nose, he swiped a long, shopworn carving knife off the counter, clutching it with his taped-up fingers as best he could. A flurry of gunshots followed by another shotgun blast boomed through the diner. Dutch stumbled back, barking the small of his back painfully against the edge of the diner's ancient stovetop. He heard someone scream,

"You fucking killed him, you fucking fuck!"

as more glass shattered near the front of the building. Pushing off the stove, Dutch limped through the kitchen and burst through the swinging door behind the cash register.

In the short hallway that led to the bathrooms, one of Travis's hired guns had Gemma up against the wall, the pistol-grip shotgun barred across her throat, cutting her air as he pressed down hard with both arms. Gemma gasped and spat as she flailed against the big man's weight, trying to get loose, but it was a losing battle. There was no fighting physics. Not unless you had help.

Without a second thought, Dutch threw himself forward and buried the carving knife right between the guy's shoulder blades. There was a sickening *click* as he felt steel connect with bone. The guy screamed and whirled around on Dutch, eyes wild with fury, Gemma—and the shotgun—momentarily forgotten. His mistake.

Gemma righted the Mossberg in her hands and pressed the muzzle against the base of the guy's skull with a throaty growl. Dutch dropped to the floor just as Gem pulled the trigger.

There was a blast of heat in the tiny space, and the guy's head exploded in a shower of blood and shattered bone, filling the hallway with a revolting pink mist. The headless body dropped to the ground, and then it was just Dutch and Gemma, staring at each other.

Bunching a hand in the front of his gore-caked shirt, Gemma hauled Dutch to his feet and said something that he couldn't hear over the terrible ringing in his ears.

"*What?*" he shouted, without meaning to.

"We gotta go!" she shouted back, her muffled words only barely cutting through the twelve-gauge drone.

Dutch nodded as he picked up the dead guy's pistol in his injured hand and followed Gemma out of the hallway. He shook his head over and over like he had water caught in his ears, trying to clear the noise. Beyond the little hallway, the dining room was a mess of broken glass and dead bodies, painted end to end with blood. Anne was gone—where the hell did she go?

"How many of them are left?" Dutch asked, still only barely able to hear the sound of his own voice.

"Just the one, I think?" Gemma racked the shotgun's pump, ejecting the spent shell from the breach. "But fuck him if he ran. I'm not out here trying to run anyone down. We just need to—"

"Freeze," someone said from behind them.

Dutch and Gemma froze. Moving very, very slowly, Dutch hazarded a glance over his shoulder—the last merc stood in the middle of the dining room, a compact submachine gun trained confidently on their backs. The gun was a nasty piece of work, the kind of expensive machinery that would cut both of them in half with the slightest squeeze of the trigger.

"Drop 'em," the guy said. "Your guns. Now."

Gemma dropped her shotgun to the ground. Dutch held on to his pistol.

"Fucko, you didn't hear me?" the merc snarled at him, his voice choked with rage. "I said—"

More gunfire erupted from outside the diner, around back. The merc faltered at the sound. It was all the chance Dutch was going to get. Holding his breath and forcing his eyes to stay wide open, he twisted on his heel, threw himself to the side, and started shooting at the same time the merc did. Bullets buzzed out of the guy's weapon in a flurry, stitching along the floor, the wall, the ceiling. The noise of it was terrible.

Dutch managed to get three shots off before he hit the ground; two of them hit home, tearing away chunks of flesh from the merc's chest and throat. Blood belched from the guy's wounds, and he toppled to the ground in a clatter of broken glass.

Everything went quiet and stayed that way. Sprawled on the floor, Dutch looked back at Gemma, who was watching him with an expression of wide-eyed astonishment.

"You okay?" he asked, panting.

"Yeah," Gemma said. "I think so. Yeah."

Dutch stood, feeling his body groan and protest from hitting the floor as hard as he had.

"Good," he said. "That's good." Pain flared in his shoulder as he rose, and the gun clattered from his hand. He couldn't keep a grip on it; his bandaged fingers wouldn't obey. What the hell?

"Jesus *fuck*," Gemma choked, staring at him with wide eyes.

Dutch looked down.

Oh.

Underneath his shirt, his arm was a bog of gore. Blood pissed out of a bullet hole high up in his shoulder and another in his upper arm, soaking the fabric and drenching his skin. The feel of it was warm and oily as it sluiced down toward his wrist.

"F-fff-fuck," he gasped. A cold thread snaked through his guts as panic and the pain started to set in. "Oh god, oh god Jesus," he moaned.

Then Gemma was there, pressing a wadded-up souvenir Pink Flamingo T-shirt to the wounds and holding it tight. The hurt was sharp and immediate, and it brought Dutch back to the present.

"Hey, hey, it's okay," Gemma said. "Look at me, okay? Look at my eyes."

He did.

"You're going to be okay," she said. "You're not going to die. These are flesh wounds. Just keep pressure on them, like this." She pressed down on the T-shirt again, gesturing for him to take over. He did, holding the shirt over the wounds, feeling hot blood fill the stiff, starchy cloth. He nodded at her, and she took her hand away. "We'll get you patched up. I promise. You're going to be okay. We just have to get out of here first, all right?"

"Okay," Dutch said, still trying to catch his breath, still trying not to cry. "Okay."

"Okay, come on," Gemma said. "Let's go. Now."

"Yeah," he echoed numbly, trying to ignore the wall of pain radiating up from his arm as he followed Gemma out the front door.

Together, they shambled down the sidewalk, trying to put as much space between themselves and the Pink Flamingo Diner as humanly possible. The street had emptied out in the past few minutes, everyone around no doubt running for cover the second all the shooting started. Dutch didn't know what had happened to Anne, but she was smart, and she was tough. He had to believe that she'd be okay. Just like he had to believe that he himself was going to be okay.

Up ahead, Gemma was silent as she led him past a place called El Super Taco, her head rotoring back and forth like an owl's, scanning the streets for any potential threats. They just had to get back to the car. Then they could get him patched up and he'd be okay. Picking up speed, Gemma disappeared around a corner into a side alley, and Dutch followed, only to find her standing stock-still five feet in, hands raised high above her head.

At first, in his muzzy, blood-loss panic, he wasn't sure why she'd stopped. But then he saw where she was looking, at the gun peeking out at them from the shadows, and understood perfectly.

28

"Iris! *IRIS!*"

Anne's voice scraped and tore as she stumbled out of the diner and into the alley, Glock dangling from one hand. She didn't know exactly what she was going to do when she caught up to her, but she was pretty sure it was going to be fucking horrible. All the pains of the world were coming for Iris Bulauer. All the suffering Anne could muster and then some. It didn't matter how far Anne had to go to deliver it. She'd come this far. She could go a little further.

Outside, the sun had slipped the rest of the way past the horizon, and the streetlights were finally starting to click on, drenching the streets in washed-out electric light. Anne looked around—there was no sign of Iris, but at the end of the alley, past the dumpsters, two more of her mercs stood staring wide-eyed at her, guns hanging useless at their sides.

"*Uh—*" one started.

Anne didn't let him finish.

Raising her Glock, she drunkenly unloaded the magazine into both men, blasting bloody holes in their chests, their arms, their throats, their faces. They shuddered in place, then dropped like cut-string marionettes. Anne didn't stop pulling the trigger until the Glock clacked empty in her hand. Behind her, more gunshots roared inside the Pink Flamingo, followed by a great, wretched silence.

"*IRIS!*" she screamed again, ears ringing as she snapped her remaining magazine into the grip of her pistol. Iris had been here only moments ago—but she wasn't anymore.

She'd gotten away.

Anne stumbled to the side and felt her shoulder hit brick. Leaning against the wall, she pulled her blood-soaked hand away to examine the wound Caff had left in her side: through the hole in her shirt, she could see a gaping black gash just underneath her ribs, jetting blood down the curve of her hip. That wasn't good. She hung her head and tried to catch her breath. Her lungs burned, her limbs rattled and shook with adrenaline, her head rang like a bell. There was blood in her eyes, blood on her hands, blood all over everything.

Anne closed her eyes. Her brain and body were humming something terrible, buzzing with nerves and fear, pure survival instinct. She spat and tried to breathe, tried to figure out what came next.

There were footsteps behind her. She spun, but she was too hurt, too gassed. She lost her balance and hit the ground, hard. Reality flickered in and out around the corners of her eyes. Blinking back oncoming unconsciousness, Anne saw two men materialize over her, both holding shotguns—both familiar. The one on the left was older, in his seventies maybe, his face handsome and smile-worn, framed with long white hair and a matching beard. As for the other guy? Anne knew him plenty well by now. She had seen him at the cabin, then again just minutes ago, across the street from the Pink Flamingo, just outside the check-cashing place. John. That was his name. Nervously, John looked up and down the alley like his head was on a swivel, hands tight around the gun in his hands, but his friend, the one who kind of looked like the guy from *The Big Lebowski*, seemed perfectly at ease.

She heard them talking, but couldn't make out the words. Her ears felt like someone had stuffed them with cotton batting. On instinct, she tried to raise her Glock to threaten her way out of this, to get some answers, anything, but someone plucked the pistol from her hand. She felt her arm fall and her eyes slide shut, resigned to sleep or some greater oblivion beyond. It didn't matter anymore. Nothing mattered. Not these assholes, not dead Travis Cade or shitty, vanished Iris Bulauer, not Gemma or Dutch or all the dead people they'd piled up, not the money, not Jessup, not that hideous dead-eyed monstrosity hunting her with all its stolen fucking faces. Whatever was going to happen now was going to happen, whether she kicked against it or not. She saw that now.

And she'd been kicking for so, so long, hadn't she? She'd kicked until every scrap of fight had gone out of her, for all the good it had done. What a luxury, what an unbelievable indulgence it would be, here at the end, to finally just . . . let go. Everything she had to give was given and gone. All that she had left now was lying here and letting whatever was going to happen, happen. Death didn't sound so bad, after everything she'd already lived through.

The darkness behind her eyes swarmed her and pulled her deeper. She let it. For a moment, she had a vague sense of hands under her back, of floating through the air.

Then, thankfully, the world went away.

III

Darling

29

She woke up alone, covered in sunlight.

Consciousness, such as it was, returned to her in slips and shards as she surfaced from whatever sleep had dragged her under. She didn't remember anything at first, didn't know what had happened to her or when, didn't remember the noise or the pain or the stained smells of gunpowder and blood filling her nostrils. She barely knew her own name. Still half-asleep, she numbly searched her fragmented memories for anything that could tell her where she was, what had happened, anything, anything, but all she could latch on to were the memories of sleep itself, of surfacing just enough to roll over or catch her breath as she broke free from some feverish nightmare that she had no chance of remembering. The rest was a haze.

She turned over and over underneath the thin, pilled sheets and pressed both hands to her eyes, trying to block out the sunlight. She worked her head back and forth, slowly popping the tension from the place where her spine met her skull. She stretched her shoulders and arched her back. And that was when she felt it.

Pain, sudden and cruel, snapped at her side like a stray dog trying to take a bite out of her ribs. Her eyes swept instantly shut as she groaned behind clenched teeth. One hand floated to her side, pulling up her shirt to find a thick patch of gauze taped loosely over a tender spot in her flesh. A wound. She peeled the gauze back: the gash underneath was only a couple of inches long, but it had been punched awkwardly into her side at a bad angle. Someone had stitched the wound tight while she slept, though; she let her fingertips explore the sutures, rolling across their surface from end to end like she was reading braille.

How . . . ?

Now her memories came back to her. The diner. Travis's head whipping back as the bullet blew through his brain. The gunfight. Wardog and his knife and the jet of hot, dark blood that had come fountaining out of his throat. Chasing Iris out the back. Dutch. Gemma. Murph.

Anne's body recoiled instinctively at the images, setting the wound in her side alight once more, like a flare gun fired point-blank into her ribs.

Easy. Easy, now.

As delicately as she could, she curled a hand around the top of the headboard and pulled herself up from her prone position, rolling forward to swing her legs over the side of the mattress. She was in a small, modestly appointed room with a single window above the bed and a door in the opposite wall. Wooden floors, wooden walls, wooden ceiling. This was a cabin.

Automatically, her hand went to her hip, hunting for her gun, but it wasn't there. Shit, she wasn't even wearing pants. She looked around again: next to the bed sat a little rustic-style table with a single lamp sitting atop it; in the corner there was an old wicker-bottomed chair with her busted old jeans draped over the back. Cool. Great. Moving slowly, Anne eased the bottom of her T-shirt up to get a better look at the hole Wardog's blade had left in her. It wasn't pretty, and it would leave an ugly scar, but whoever had stitched her up had done a decent job of it. Probably saved her life. With a little more time to fester, a shot to the ribs like that would have killed her. She just wished she knew who to thank for the rescue.

Sitting on the edge of the bed, she laid her hands palms up on her bare thighs, opening and closing her fingers over the purple scars again and again, trying to get used to the feeling of being inside her body once more. The wounds the shape-shifter had ripped into her forearm had been stitched up just the same as the hole in her ribs, the sutures small and careful. She rolled her hand on the pivot of her wrist, testing—the wounds ached and pulled, but she hadn't lost any mobility. Small miracles, she supposed.

Bracing herself against the little bed's headboard again, clutching tight enough to turn her fingers white, Anne gritted her teeth, counted to three, and pushed. Agony screamed from her side as she rose; she ignored it and slowly hauled herself the rest of the way up until she was on her feet.

Okay. That was done. Next thing.

She pulled on her jeans inch by painful inch, then her shoes, then limped over to the window at the back of the cabin and pushed the old blotter-green gingham curtains back to look outside.

Mountain peaks, jagged and chipped like the burred edge of an old serrated knife, rose up to greet her. She was in the Sangre de Cristos. How the fuck had she ended up here? The sun shone down from high above, lighting up the leaves and pine needles on the trees like rolling green fire. There were so many of them out there—pines and firs, aspens and oaks. Farther back, Anne could see a sheer rock wall jutting out of the ground like a gravestone, terminating a few hundred feet up in a bald, narrow ridge that over-looked . . . well, *wherever* she was.

Leaning back from the little window, she hunted for a latch or a hinge or anything that would let her ease it open and slip out of here unnoticed, but the pane was fixed in place. Numbly, she padded across the bedroom to the door and pulled on the knob, but it wouldn't budge. She was locked in here. Because why wouldn't she be? She pressed her ear to the cool wood and strained to listen. Outside, she thought she could hear footsteps on dirt and distant voices—not just a couple or three but dozens. Wherever she was, she wasn't alone. Not by a long shot.

She took a breath. Held it. Balled one hand into a fist and pounded it against the door, *BAM-BAM-BAM*. Outside, there was a groaning of wood as someone shifted their weight, followed by a mechanical clicking as a key slid into the dead bolt and disengaged it. The door swung open to reveal a kid in his early twenties, if he was out of his teens at all, standing on the little cabin's porch. He was blond and slender, with fine features and big serious eyes set far back in his skull. He wore a faded shearling jacket over farm clothes and mud-flecked work boots that had seen better days. There was a Leatherman multitool on his belt and a range rifle—it looked like a knockoff Mini-14—slung over his back, and as he stood there, she couldn't help but notice how he seemed to regard her with a strange mix of caution and awe.

"You're awake," he marveled. "That's . . . wow, yeah, that's great. I, um. He's up in the barn. Said he wants to talk to you as soon as you woke up. C'mon."

Anne didn't move, didn't take her eyes off the blond, or his rifle. She didn't know who the fuck this *he* was or why he wanted to talk to her, but she had zero intention of going anywhere with this kid, especially not with that gun on his back. Seeming to get the message, he raised both his hands in response.

"I'm not going to hurt you, okay?" he said.

Anne resisted the urge to reassure him that *No, you're really not*.

"I'll go first, lead the way. You follow me as far back as you like. We're cool. Promise."

There was no part of this that seemed even remotely *cool* to Anne, but the more she thought about it, the more she realized that this kid, and whoever else he was talking about, were holding all the cards. And they'd patched her up, after all. With no clue as to where they were and no way to fight back if it came to that, Anne figured the best thing she could do right now was shut the fuck up until she got the lay of the land. So after another second, Anne nodded, once. The kid, apparently satisfied, turned and stepped off the porch, looking back over his shoulder at her with that same weird confusion of reverence and awe. She didn't know what his problem was, but the sooner she could be done with him, the better.

Outside, the morning air was chilly, verging on cold, the bare ground hard under her shoes as she found herself standing on the main drag of a tiny little town, a jagged one-road burg that hooked up the curve of the hill like it was built along the blade of a scythe. The buildings were all mismatched, as if they'd been plucked out of different eras and tossed together like a handful of thrown dice. If Anne squinted, she could see the town's original layout past the newer buildings, a cluster of slouched, barely preserved, single-story clapboard structures that looked like they'd been weathering the elements up here for a long, long time. The newer buildings—

small, propane-heated houses and single-room cabins like the one she'd woken up in, animal pens, a squat structure that looked like it might have been a granary—had been built into the town's existing layout as additions rather than replacements, which gave Anne a weird little shiver at the base of her skull. This place was familiar. She just didn't know how. The slumped, ramshackle little buildings, the bowed dirt road slashing up the hill toward the town's lone church, the bald ridge overlooking it all from high above . . . she knew it, somehow.

That was when Anne realized just how many people there were here. And they were all staring. There were easily a hundred of them, all watching her with that same wide-eyed expression of awe and reverence that she'd seen on the kid's face minutes before. Like she'd just stepped off a flying saucer or something. There was a weird singularity to all of them, a shared body language of crossed arms and rigid backs that seemed to hold her at a removal so they could examine her from a safe distance, a sample in a jar, a specimen under a microscope. They all seemed to know something she didn't, men and women and children all whispering behind their hands as she passed them by, averting their eyes and hunching their shoulders. Shit was fucking eerie.

The kid led her up the dusty road under the wary gaze of all toward the big faded barn that sat opposite the church. Anne could just make out the ghost of an old German hex sign painted on its side, a many-pointed star atop a flower. Anne thought it might have once been a tulip, abutted by a pair of yellow birds. In the field around back, she could see people setting up long folding tables end to end in a kind of horseshoe shape around a pyramid of logs—a bonfire. Anne watched them for a minute, until one of the workers, a man in his forties, looked back at her. His gaze, unlike the others, was prying, nosy, unashamed. There was something in that gaze that unsettled her.

Turning away, she glanced back down the hill, examining the town and the feral wilderness that lay beyond. Past the town's edge, the dirt road wended through the trees and disappeared around the foot of that tall, blank ridge, presumably heading down toward civilization. Anne couldn't see a highway from here, couldn't see anything at all past the pines and hills, but she knew that it had to be there, somewhere. She just had to find it. Breathing out, then in, calming her heart, she turned and followed the kid the rest of the way up to the barn.

Its big double doors hung wide open, giving way to thick shadows beyond. Inside, just beyond the reach of the sun, Jessup's Ninety-Eight sat on an old hydraulic lift, exactly as she'd left it a few blocks down from the Pink Flamingo. Her heart lurched, seeing it here now. She held a hand out as she walked its length, running her fingertips across the cool metal, assuring herself that it was really here. When she got to the nose of the big old beast, she saw that someone had left a bucket filled with old tools on the hood, screwdrivers and pliers and wire strippers and socket wrenches, even a rubber mallet.

Anne let her attention drift away from the car and across the interior of the barn, taking it all in. Ropes hung from the rafters above rough-hewn two-by-four ladders leading to the barn's loft. On the ground floor, the walls were all pegboard and the ground was poured cement, obviously not original. They'd turned the place into a makeshift garage, but the smell in here was all farm, rich and old like animals and hay and sawdust.

"She's a real nice ride," someone said from somewhere Anne couldn't pinpoint. "She's in great condition. Hard to believe she's over fifty years old, and nearly all original, too. You've done a great job taking care of her."

Anne looked around for the source of the voice—softly Southern-accented, it was like old leather, worn and gentle. A second later, there was a burr of plastic wheels gliding across cement as an older man on a roller board slid out from underneath the nose of the Oldsmobile and stood, knees popping like firecrackers.

He was tall, with shaggy, gray-white hair and a beard to match framing wicked, pale eyes. He wore battered jeans, a threadbare Grateful Dead TOUR '74 T-shirt, and a pair of well-worn tennis shoes that looked like he'd been sporting them since Jimmy Carter had been in office. He'd thinned out plenty since the time the video had been shot, but take away thirty years, add fifty or seventy-five pounds, and yeah, she recognized him. She'd watched him stand next to that white stone icon on the tape she'd found at the cabin, eyes brimming with religious fervor as reality tore itself open like a wound and tried to devour everything in its path.

"Winston," she heard herself saying, voice creaky from disuse. How long had she been asleep for?

The old man smiled at her, that same effortlessly charismatic preacher's grin, now partially obscured by the untrimmed shag of his beard, and wiped oil-stained hands on the knees of his jeans.

"That's right," he said. "Winston Mayr Hofmann. But everyone 'round here just calls me Win." He held a hand out to shake. She didn't take it. He let his hand drop as he regarded Anne for another moment, then smiled at the kid.

"Thank you, Tobias. I'll let you know when we're finished here."

The kid turned and walked around the Ninety-Eight toward the open barn doors. Standing just outside, he lit a cigarette and pitched a shoulder against the side of the planks to wait. When she looked back at Win, the old man was still smiling at her, his glittery eyes dreamy and faraway.

"Sorry," he said as if coming back to himself. "It's just, you really do look like her, you know? Beverly. It's kind of amazing."

Anne didn't say anything to that. What could she say? That she knew exactly how much she looked like her mom? That one of the last times she'd seen her Grandma alive, the old woman had told her how much Anne reminded her of her dead, wayward daughter, and not exactly in a complimentary way?

Instead, she nodded to the car. "What were you doing to it?"

Win's smile didn't falter an inch. "Just an oil change. Tune-up. Like I said, she's in really fantastic condition. You've done an amazing job keeping her nice."

"It's not my car," Anne said.

Win raised an eyebrow. "No?"

She shook her head. "Belonged to a friend."

"Belonged? As in past tense?"

"Mm-hmm," she grunted. The last thing she was going to talk about with this asshole was what had happened to Jessup.

"Well, that makes it your car, far as I'm concerned," Win said. "I wasn't trying to overstep; it's just that it's been a long time since I've worked on basically anything but farming equipment and our old trucks. Long damn time. I was in the motor pool, back when I was in the corps. Vietnam. Hell of a thing." He paused, shifting his head from side to side as if he were examining Anne under different angles. "How are you feeling, by the way? That was a nasty wound in your side you had. I'm afraid that patch-up we gave you ain't exactly pretty, but since you're standing here, I figure it musta did the job. We don't exactly have ourselves a clinic up here, but Mike Flores—you'll meet him—he used to be a doctor. You know. Before." His eyes twinkled like stars set in his head, full of wonder. "It's real good to see you, Annie."

Anne narrowed her eyes at the man, studying his face as her last, fleeting moments of consciousness outside the Pink Flamingo returned to her, rising to the surface and bursting open like bubbles. He'd been there, standing over her with John, saying things she couldn't hear before she'd been taken by that vast, comfortable nothingness.

"You came and got me," she said hesitantly.

The old man popped his tongue against his palate. "We did. Real mess y'all made out there. Had to work fast to get you out before the pigs showed up and ruined everything. Brought you back here, got you patched up best we could, like I said."

"Could have dropped me off at a hospital," Anne said. "Would have been fine."

Win smirked at that. "Come on now, I think you and I both know that's not true. You're all over the news, girl. People are on the lookout for you. We took you to a hospital, you'd've woken up behind bars. Never would have seen the light of day again. Plus, you might not realize, but you're plenty special around these parts, Annie. More special than you know."

"*These parts?* What the fuck are you talking about? What is this place?"

Win's face pulled into a look of gentle disbelief, as if he were stunned she was really asking him that.

"This is Cabot," he said. "It's our home. This is *your* home, Annie. This is the Passage of Divinity. Don't you remember?"

Anne's heart skipped a beat, then skipped two as the disparate pieces started to pull themselves together in her head. Norris and John. The VHS tape her mom had left behind, and all the horrible things they'd seen on it. That last line from Aunt Lisa's letter: *The Passage is everywhere.* This was not a good place for her to be.

"So what, you want me to thank you or something?" she asked, hoping she sounded calmer than she suddenly felt.

Win shrugged. "I mean, I certainly wouldn't say *no*, but that can probably wait for now. I'm sure you've got plenty of questions that need answering first. Here, d'you want to have a set-down? That hole in your ribs can't exactly be comfortable, I 'magine."

"I'm fine, thanks," Anne said, her voice clipped.

The old man socked his tongue into a cheek and studied her.

"Suit yourself. Just figured I'd ask."

Moving slowly, Win crossed over to the back of the barn, where he wheeled a creaky old shop stool from under one of the benches and eased himself down into it. He looked so small like this, so much less imposing than the big, burly man she'd seen in the video, but the core of him, that visible spark of something wild just beneath the surface, hadn't changed at all. If anything, it had only grown brighter and more ferocious since then.

"So how'd you find me?" Anne asked, crossing her arms over her chest.

Win grinned, and as he did, his mask of placidity melted and gave way to something else, something infinitely cleverer and far more knowing. Like a magician eagerly awaiting someone to ask him to explain the trick. It was condescending, and it made Anne want to never stop punching him in his fucked-up old face.

"That one's easy," he said. "You called me, remember?"

"I didn't—" Anne started, but caught herself when she realized: the phone number on the bottom of the tape. That had been his voice saying *Annie* on the other end of the line.

The old man glanced at the kid beyond the barn doors. "Tobias out there, he's clever with computers. Once we got your number, he

214

figured out where your cell was pinging. After we got to Alamosa, we just had to follow the gunshots. Didn't exactly make yourselves hard to find, Annie."

"Anne," she corrected him.

"What?"

"My name's Anne. Nobody calls me *Annie* anymore."

"Oh, well, I just thought that since your mom—"

"Don't do that," Anne said, cutting across him, sudden anger bridling in her chest. "Whatever you're about to say, don't. Just because you knew her doesn't mean that you know me, okay? You don't."

Win raised his hands in a cutesy little mock surrender. Condescension, it seemed, was this asshole's default setting.

"Hey, fine by me," he said. "Anne it is. Anyway, point is, y'all made a hell of a mess at that diner. Same as out in Durango, if'n I'm honest. That bank robbery, all those dead people?" He whistled. "Hell of a mess."

Anne rubbed at her eyes. "Wasn't mine. Just something that got handed to me, needed dealing with. That's all. Anyway, I'd worry about yourself, if I were you. I'm not the one harboring a wanted fugitive."

That same easy smile split the old man's face again.

"Oh, I wouldn't worry about that. Nobody's gonna come looking for you up here. We tend to keep to ourselves. Just safer that way. Never known something that couldn't get completely fucked up by government involvement. You understand."

Anne was sure she did—just not in the way the old man meant. Whatever he and his weird hippie cult were up to all the way out here in the back of beyond, they were perfectly happy getting away with it for as long as possible. Best guess, they'd been doing so successfully for thirty years or more. They clearly weren't looking to have it all come crumbling down around them now. But Anne wasn't new to moving underground—she'd spent more than her fair share of time flying under the authorities' radar. Keeping their heads down for that long only meant that whatever the Passage of Divinity was doing up here, they had something to hide.

"So how'd you know about the cabin?"

Now Win's smile faltered, if only by a hair. "Sorry, what?"

"My mom's cabin. Your buddies, John and Norris, I think it was? Came calling a few days ago. Didn't start putting it together until I saw John outside the diner, just before everything went to shit. You sent them up there, right?"

Win rubbed at his beard with one cracked hand as if rolling the question around in his head. "I did. We've been keeping tabs on your mom's place ever since we got word that she died," he explained. "Tried to keep track of you, too, but you fell off the map pretty quick after . . . yeah. Probably for the best. You were pretty little back then. Deserved to have a normal life. Anyway, when you and your crew made the news, I kind of figured, why the hell not? Send a couple of guys out that way to see if you maybe went to ground up there. No harm in taking a look around."

"And they needed guns to do that?"

Win's smile sharpened. "Lot of wild animals out that way. You can never be too safe."

"Is that what you're doing up here, Win? Staying safe?"

"I suppose you could say that, yeah," Win said. His practiced easy demeanor was starting to grate on Anne's nerves more than a little. "As best we can, like I said. They told me about you, you know. John and Norris."

Frustration crackled in Anne's temples at that. She wasn't naive, she knew that people liked to talk, and of course they were going to do it, whether you wanted them to or not, but the idea of those two old shits coming back here and reporting on the whole thing to King Shit himself made her skin crawl. Nobody liked finding themselves under a microscope.

"That so?" she asked.

"That's so."

"And what'd they say? Because I gotta be honest with you, it wasn't much of a conversation from where I was standing."

Win shrugged noncommittally. "Oh, you know, just stuff. How much you look like your mom. What a hell of a shot you are. Hear them tell it, you're a regular Quick Draw McGraw. Blasting a head-light out like that, it sends a message. Sure I don't have to tell you that, though."

"Wouldn't have happened if they hadn't made me."

Win chuckled. "Yeah, I get that. Norris is a good man, but he's got a nasty temper on him. It can get the better of him at the best of times. I hope you know that they wouldn't have hurt you if it had come to that, though."

Anne couldn't exactly say she believed him or that the feeling was mutual.

"Where are my things?" she asked. "My backpack and my gun. My cat. The tape."

"All safe," Win told her. "Put away for safekeeping while you rested up. Nobody's messing with any of it without your say-so. Though, to be fair, the tape's mine. I'm the one that bought it back in the day, so far as I'm concerned, you're just returning stolen property to its rightful owner." He turned his long, knobby fingers in knots, and his face darkened as in thought. "Did you watch it?"

Anne's eyes narrowed, and she offered him the slightest nod she could muster.

Win's expression grew grave. "All of it?"

"Start to finish, static to static. It was a nice sermon you gave, but I think the ending could have used some work."

Win sighed and pressed his hands together, as if in prayer or thought. Anne didn't take her eyes off him for a second.

"I didn't mean for it to happen like that," he said. "Truly. Darlene . . . she was always devout. A true believer." Exactly like he had on the video, he pronounced it *Darlin'*. "She and I were the ones that found the stone in the first place and that tiny little crack in the rock, bleeding light from somewhere else. Just as you saw on the tape. We were convinced we found something holy. Proof that we're not alone in this world. After so many years of doubt, of blind faith taken on nothing, we had something real to clutch on to. Do you even know the kind of power in something like that? It's incredible." He paused. "Were you raised a believer, Annie?"

Anne shook her head. Grandma had never been much of a

churchgoing type, and despite her flaws, she hadn't raised Anne to do anything but think for herself and make her own decisions. The golden rule in Grandma's house was: *Ask an honest question, get an honest answer.* So when Anne had asked her flat out if God was real, Grandma had simply smiled and told her no. There were plenty of things in the universe that we couldn't explain, but none of them were an old man with a long white beard hiding in the sky, secretly watching humanity's every action in some cosmic morality play that ended in either heaven or hell, with no in-between.

"I didn't think so. Though I guess I'm still a little surprised to hear it. Especially after what you saw, what you lived through," he said.

"I don't have any memory of it," Anne told him. "What's on the tape. None of it. It's all gone. So whatever you're talking about, it doesn't mean much in the grand scheme of me, I'm sorry to say."

Win met her gaze, his deadly green eyes glittering like radiant sea glass on a craggy shore.

"See, that's where you're wrong. It has everything to do with, how'd you put it? *The grand scheme of you.* Just because you can't see how doesn't make it not true. Listen, faith is about as powerful a tool as I believe we have on this earth. You were little, but you were a believer, once. Same as your momma. Same as Lisa and everybody else. They were all searching for something, and that search brought them all here."

The name *Lisa* tripped something in Anne's head, some underground wire distantly connected to a faraway routing station.

"Who is Lisa? Like, really," she heard herself asking.

Win's smile fell by degrees, tinged with old sadness. "You really don't remember any of it, do you? Lisa Ray Bonny was one of your momma's best friends, back in the day. Time was, her and Darlene and Beverly were thick as thieves. I remember you running around here all the time asking where you could find your aunt Lisa. It was sweet. She meant well. She helped you and your momma try and pull Darlene back from the brink."

The woman in the video with the bright white hair. Lisa Ray

Bonny, the same Aunt Lisa who'd left that letter for her up at the cabin.

"Where is she now? Lisa, I mean."

Win shrugged. "No clue. She fell off the map not long after she left us. Lost track of her pretty quick. I gather that's kind of what she wanted, though."

"She left?"

"Same night as your mom and you," the old man said. "A few others, too. Just up and disappeared. Didn't say a word to me or anyone else. One day, we woke up and, poof, y'all were gone. Not hide nor hair, as the saying goes. I was worried sick, of course, but I had my own problems needed tending by then. None of us knew what had happened to any of you until we heard about the crash up at the cabin. Broke my heart, hearing that. Doubly so for your loss."

"It wasn't the crash that killed her. It was something else. The crash just slowed us down enough for it to catch up," Anne explained, her voice drawn tight as piano wire.

Win's eyes went razor-slit. "Something like what?"

"Something with teeth. Something that wears all sorts of different faces."

"Sounds horrible," Win said.

"It is. It's still out there, too. I've been trying to outrun it for days now, but it keeps coming. So I appreciate the rescue and everything, but I can't stay here, Win. Not if you and your people want to stay safe."

Win shook his head. "Don't you worry about that right now," he said. "We're safe here. Or at least, as safe as we can be. Whatever it is, it ain't gonna hurt you here."

"How do you know?"

That knowing smile crept into his face again, and Anne knew what he was thinking before he said it.

"Faith."

Of course. The standard refrain from sanctimonious, delusional assholes who chose to believe the world operated in a certain way just because they wanted it to. Anne rolled her eyes.

"Right. Is that what I saw on everybody's faces out there?" she asked. "Faith? Because from where I was standing, they all looked like they'd seen a fucking ghost."

Win's eyes drifted to the side and he chuckled softly to himself. "I suppose I'm not exactly surprised. I'd ask you to forgive them for staring—they mean well, they really do—but we don't get a lot of visitors up here."

"It was more than that," Anne said.

Win nodded, more to himself than to her. "Yeah. I suppose maybe it could have been."

Anne jerked her head toward the open barn doors. "So what the fuck?"

Win shrugged, then rose from his stool. Sitting, it was easy to forget just how tall the old man was, but fully upright once more, he loomed effortlessly.

"We can talk about it later, if you like. I'll explain as much as I can, I promise I will."

Anne shook her head. "Later? Yeah, no, sorry. I appreciate the tune-up and oil change and whatever, the stitches, but I'm not sticking around, okay? I gotta get going."

Win's face first softened into a look of—what was it, pity?—and then sharpened itself like flint. That starlight twinkle was still in his eyes, but it had turned cold and distant and strange.

"I'm sorry," he said. "I don't think I made myself clear. You leaving is just, it's not possible right now. With things pretty hot for you out there, it's just gonna be best if you stay here, rest up, let us take care of everything else."

Anne thought about arguing, but there was something in his tone that made it clear this wasn't really a discussion. After all, Win was very clearly the man in charge around here, not to be fucked with if you didn't want trouble.

"And anyway, we're having kind of a family dinner tonight, in your honor. Despite their . . . awkwardness, folks are plenty excited to get to meet you. You're sort of famous 'round here, I'm sorry to say." He proffered a self-satisfied little half laugh, but Anne wasn't sure what the joke was. "I'll come and get you when it's time, but for now, I'm sure you probably want to see your people, huh?" He held his ropy arms out wide, urging Anne back toward the barn doors.

"Wait—my people?" she asked.

"Yeah, your friends, I assume. Them that we managed to spirit away from that shit show in Alamosa. You weren't the only one we pulled out of that mess, Annie. Sorry—*Anne*."

Anne let the old man's *accidentally on-purpose* slip of the tongue pass without remark.

"There were three of them, the young man with the square jaw, the woman with the braids, and the other one, quiet. Wouldn't stop crying."

Dutch, Gem, and Joanie. Shame burned hot under Anne's skin at the fact that she hadn't thought of them since she'd awoken in the cabin, but now her heart lurched at the idea that they were close by.

Win started toward the barn doors, beckoning her to follow. Hanging back a few steps, Anne reached over and snaked a Phillips-head screwdriver from the bucket of tools. It was old and flecked with rust, but the point was sharp enough to pierce skin if it came to that. It wasn't exactly her Glock, but it would do in a pinch. She slipped it into the back of her waistband and let her shirt fall over the top a second before Win glanced back at her, that clever little smile fixed between his cheeks.

"Well, come on, then," he said.

"Where are they? My friends."

"Just down the hill," he said. "Tobias can show you."

30

The kid led Anne down the curved road to a cabin three doors up from the one she'd woken up in. Like hers, it was one of Cabot's newer buildings, plain and sturdy, like it had been cobbled together from a set of oversize Lincoln Logs. There were windows on either side of the front door, curtains drawn over both. The porch creaked as they stepped up onto it, and Anne heard someone rustling around inside.

From his jacket pocket, Tobias produced an overstuffed key ring and thumbed one away from the rest, fitting it into the doorknob and turning it with an oiled, mechanical *click*. The door swung open slowly to reveal a large space that reminded Anne of summer camp. Wasn't like she'd ever been to camp as a kid; Grandma never had the money, and Anne never had the interest, but she'd seen enough movies and TV shows over the years to recognize a camp cabin when she was looking at it: a pair of twin-size bunk beds, wooden floors, a couple of thrift-store steamer trunks for storage. Gem sat on the bunk on the right side of the cabin, while Dutch sat opposite her with one arm in a sling and Murph in his lap; on the top bunk above him lay Joanie, curled up fetal under thin, starched sheets.

Gemma bolted to her feet when she saw Anne standing there, pushing past the kid to pull her into a big hug that she accepted wholeheartedly, no matter how much it hurt. That shame of caring, of needing her and having somehow abandoned her, even if only mentally, ignited in Anne's belly again, and she felt her cheeks burning hot.

"Jesus Christ, I thought you'd died or something," Gem said, pressing both of her hands flat against Anne's back. "They weren't telling us anything."

Over Gem's shoulder, Anne watched Murph hop off Dutch's lap and come padding over to rub himself against her ankles, tail high like a sand flag on a dune buggy. Gem and Murphy seemed okay, but Dutch wasn't exactly in great shape. There was a distant, despondent look on his face, like he hadn't slept in days. His eyes were ringed with dark circles above his crooked, broken nose; his skin was pallid and sickly. And that sling, what the hell was that about?

Gem squeezed her tighter, and the pressure made the breath catch in Anne's chest, hitching hard against the wound in her side.

"Easy," Anne coughed. "Still hurts."

"Yeah. Sorry. Just . . ." A nervous, vulnerable look danced across Gem's face as she let her go. "Glad to see you, is all. What happened to you?"

Anne screwed her face up in an expression of confusion. "They didn't tell you?"

"No, nothing," Gem said, shaking her head.

"Wardog, or whatever the fuck his name was, Iris's guy? Pulled a push knife, stuck me in the ribs."

"Wait, *what*?!"

Before Anne knew what was happening, Gem's hands were fiddling at the bottom of her T-shirt, lifting it up to inspect the stitches that had been sewn into her side. She froze and felt herself blushing hard as nerves arced down her neck and into her chest, raising apple-red blotches that she desperately hoped weren't too obvious. Of all the ways she'd imagined Gemma Poe pulling her shirt up over the years, this had not made the list. Over by the door, Tobias flushed and cast his eyes down to the floor, bashful and uncomfortable.

"Well, at least they did a decent job of it," Gem said, scrutinizing the sutures close enough that Anne could feel her breath on her skin. *Oh god. Keep it together.*

"You really are a lot tougher than you look, huh?" Dutch mused idly.

Anne resisted the urge to laugh. "Thanks, I think?"

"No, I mean . . ." He trailed off. "I don't know what I mean. Never mind. I'm sorry."

Gem let Anne's shirt drop and weaved her fingers into Anne's for a moment as she looked into her eyes.

"You really scared the shit out of me, you know. Can't go vanishing on me like that again, Heller."

"I know. I didn't mean to. Really. I just—" Anne said, still blushing.

"S'okay. I get it," Gem softly told her, then cast her eyes toward the door, at the rest of the town. "When did you . . . ?"

"Little while ago. Tobias here took me up to the barn to meet the boss."

Gem's eyebrows went up, and she glanced over at Tobias—his eyes still down to the ground—then back to Anne. Her expression was careful, measured. "And how was that?"

"Yeah, it was good. He's . . . he's a nice guy," Anne said evenly, meeting Gem's gaze in a calm, unblinking look: *Not in front of the cultist.*

"That's great," Gem said, seeming to understand. "You doing okay, though? I mean like, generally?"

Down on the floor, Murph sat and stared up at Anne, his big green coin eyes bright in the morning light as he *mrrow*'ed at her, just once. Anne got the message loud and clear. Wincing against the pain in her side, Anne bent and scooped him up into a ginger two-armed embrace as he started to purr against her chest.

"I mean, I guess. Could be worse, but could be better. I still got fucking stabbed, so."

In the corner, Tobias winced at the expletive. Anne pretended to not notice. Rifle or not, the kid was more than a little bit tender. That was good to know.

"How about you guys? You holding up all right?"

"I guess. I mean, given the circumstances." Gem's eyes darted over to Tobias again, but Anne didn't think the kid noticed.

"Sure, I get that," Anne said.

She set Murph down again, then turned to the kid, showing him the winningest smile she could muster.

"Hey, listen, would you mind giving us a couple of minutes?"

Worry arced across the kid's face. "Uh, I mean. Win . . . he said I'm not supposed to—"

Anne held up a hand. "I know," she said, keeping her voice low, friendly, perfectly compliant. "I get it, I do. But, come on, there's one door in this place. We're not going anywhere, okay? Just a few minutes. It's not much. We'll even leave the door open, if that makes you feel better about it. That way, you're not really leaving us alone at all. Right?"

Tobias furrowed his brow in thought. "I mean, I suppose that's fine. But just for a couple minutes, okay? I don't, I mean, I'm really not supposed to, is all."

"Just for a couple minutes," Anne reassured him. "Thank you."

The kid looked from Anne to Gem to Dutch and back again, then turned and hesitantly stepped out onto the front porch, his boots creaking heavily on the floorboards. He hadn't gone far, but it was probably far enough, provided they kept their voices down.

Anne glanced over to the nearest bunk. "Mind if I sit?"

Gemma led her over to the nearest bed and held her hands out to steady her as Anne eased herself down onto the edge of the mattress. A second later, Murph trotted over to the bed, then hopped up next to her and lay down, pressing himself snugly against the side of her thigh. She rested one hand on his back, along the narrow pinch of his shoulder blades, and stroked the top of his head with her fingertips as she threw a glance at Dutch's sling. "So what happened there?"

Dutch blushed and moved a hand briefly to his wounded shoulder.

"One of the guys at the diner. Submachine gun. Tagged me a couple of times."

Anne felt her own eyebrows go up. "A couple?"

Dutch waved her off. "It's not as bad as it sounds. The guy they have doing medicine up here, Mike, he patched me up okay. Says I'll probably get full range of motion back once it heals."

"Jesus," Anne marveled, then looked over at Gem. "How about you? Any new gunshot wounds I should be aware of?"

Gem shook her head. "Nah, I'm cool," she said, jerking her head at Dutch. "He got the worst of it. Well, and you." A tiny, knowing smile danced across her face. "Still glad we stuck around after things went all Godzilla on us?"

"I dunno," Anne said, letting the ghost of a smirk creep into the corners of her mouth. "If nothing else, the company could be a lot worse." A thought occurred to her then. "Pretty sure Iris got out."

"I mean, if that's the case, she's the only one." Gem gestured vaguely with one hand, like a lazy magician trying to summon a new trick out of thin air. "She's got next to no money, no backup, nothing. She's in the wind. Hell with her. We've got bigger problems, and frankly, I don't really care how pissed off she might be about poor dead Travis."

Unbidden, Anne's memory flashed back to the shocked look on Travis's face the second after she shot him, like he couldn't believe it had happened. As if a smug prick like him would live forever. She wouldn't blame Iris for being furious, but Gem was right. They had plenty of other shit to deal with right now. Anne stole another look at the top bunk and the still, dark-haired woman curled up atop the mattress. Joanie hadn't given any indication that she was listening or even conscious.

"What about her? How long has she been like that?"

"Since we got here," Dutch said. "I think the Passage probably grabbed her when she excused herself back at the diner. She eats, sleeps, cries. Isn't really talking much. Probably asleep again."

"Just because I don't want to talk to any of you doesn't mean I'm not awake," came a voice from the top bunk.

Anne watched the woman roll over. Dutch wasn't wrong—Joanie looked like she'd been crying for days, but her eyes were clear now. Clear and numb.

"Hey, Joan," Anne said. "You all right?"

Joanie shook her head. "No."

"Yeah, I didn't think so. Me either," Anne said. Beside her, Gem and Dutch were watchful and still.

"I didn't ask," Joanie sniped. "What the hell have you've dragged me into, Anne? What is this place?"

"It's kind of hard to explain."

"Oh. Great. Thanks for that. Fuck you, too." Joanie's voice was frosty and stiletto-sharp. Without another word, she rolled over and buried her head under her pillow.

Anne didn't blame her for being angry or for shutting down. Joanie had kids, which meant that somewhere out there, there was a whole little family who didn't know where the hell their mom had disappeared to. Joanie hadn't signed up for any of this shit; the Passage had just snatched her off the street and made all of this her problem. Anne would have been pissed, too.

Anne turned back to Gem and Dutch. "So, you guys meet him yet? Win."

"Once," Gem said. "Came and paid us a visit the morning after we got here; told us you were hurt, but they were taking care of you. Hasn't been by since. Mostly it's just been us and Tobias. Been pretty boring, which I guess is kind of a nice change, given, you know, everything."

"When was this? When he stopped by."

"A couple days ago," Dutch said.

"They been locking your door, too?"

Dutch glanced up at Joanie one last time. "Yeah. He—Win, I mean—told us that they're keeping us here for our own safety while you get back on your feet."

"Sounds like a rich line of bullshit to me."

"You got that feeling, too, huh?" Gem said, voice dripping with sarcasm. "What about your talk with the big man? He give you any sense of what the deal is?"

Anne shook her head. "Nothing. Whatever he's playing at, he's keeping it hid. For now."

"Fits. They took your stuff, I'm guessing?"

"Yeah. 'For safekeeping.' Yours, too?"

Gem rolled her eyes. "As soon as we got here. Everything but the clothes on our backs and the laces in our shoes. Not sure where he stashed it all, but smart money's on him keeping it all real close. Best guess, his place; probably somewhere close by if not."

"You know which one's his?"

"Big one, halfway up the hill," Dutch said. "Heard Tobias and Mike talking about it yesterday."

Anne thought she knew the one he was talking about; she'd seen it on her way up to meet the old man.

"Okay. Probably not a bad place to start, when we get a chance. They've got the Ninety-Eight in the barn, too."

"Yeah, they used it to drive us and the furball up here. Tobias can't drive for shit, but at least he managed not to crash," Gem said.

"You think they found, you know, the thing under the spare?" she asked, meaning the bank bag with Iris and Travis's half inside, stashed in place before she'd turned the diner into a war zone.

Gem rolled her head back and forth, as if in thought. "Doubt it. If they had, I think we'd probably be having a way different conversation right now. Whatever these freaks are after, I don't think it's cash, but . . . dunno. This is America. Nobody's better than money."

"What about our friend with all the faces? Any sign? Win told me it's safe up here, but I can't exactly say I'm taking his word on that."

Dutch shook his head. "Nothing. Which means it's probably just a matter of time until it shows up again," he said, failing to disguise the nerves in his voice. Anne couldn't help but notice that all the color had gone out of his cheeks at mention of the shape-shifter.

"So we should probably plan on getting the fuck out of here before that happens. You guys hear anything about this dinner tonight?" she asked.

Gem's face furrowed into a frown. "No, nothing. What dinner?"

"Just something Win was talking about," Anne said. "He said it was *in my honor*, whatever that means. I saw some people setting tables up by the barn. Looked like a bonfire, too."

"How many tables?"

Anne shrugged and thought about it for a second. "Enough to seat a hundred, if I had to guess. Maybe closer to one twenty-five, but could be more. I didn't exactly get a chance to count them all. How many people live up here?"

"About that many, I think," Dutch said.

Gem sighed. "I mean, if they're all planning on attending this dinner, could be a good chance to get some answers, go left while they're looking right. If we're not invited, I can maybe break out of here, get into Win's place, take a look around and figure out what the hell he's planning. Get the hell out of Dodge after that. I mean, no guns, thirty of them to every one of us, probably a good idea to stick to the shadows and keep quiet, rather than playing it loud and stupid, anyway."

Anne pretended to not be a little hurt by that. *Loud and stupid* wasn't the first way she'd have elected to describe her personal problem-solving style, but then again, she was the one who'd shot Travis in the face.

"All right, so, I'll go to dinner with the old man, and you two keep an eye out tonight, okay? The second it's quiet, you guys make your move and see what you can find. That work?"

Gem gave her a questioning look. "Both of us?"

"That's the idea," Anne told her. "That work for you?"

"Works for me," Dutch said. Beside him, Gem didn't exactly look convinced, but after a second, she nodded.

"Yeah, no problem," she said.

Anne showed her a faint smile of thanks. "You going to have any issue getting out or in?"

In an instant, Gem's look of skepticism morphed into a wicked grin. Wordlessly, she kicked off her right sneaker and removed the insole, then held the shoe out for Anne to see: pressed deep into the foam rubber underneath were a bent silver pick and matching torque wrench. Guess Win's people hadn't quite managed to confiscate everything, after all. "Trust me, I'll be fine. You just keep them all looking at you," Gem told her.

"Yeah, I don't think that'll be a problem," Anne said, remembering with a shiver that spooky way everybody in town had stared at her when she'd first emerged from her cabin.

Outside, on the front porch, they heard boards creak and shift as Tobias moved to fill up the doorway. Time was up.

"I should get you back," the kid said, nervously eyeing Anne.

"Sure," she said, then stood, giving Murph one final scritch behind the ears. She looked back at Dutch and Gem, meeting their
eyes.

"I'll see you guys later," she said.

"Yeah," Gem said, with a secret little smile that made Anne's
breath catch in her throat. "See you."

"Take care of yourself," Dutch said. Anne let herself be led out
of the cabin, back into a world she didn't understand and wasn't
sure she ever really had.

31

The rest of the day crept by. Without anything on hand to pass the time, Anne lay on the bed, locked in her little hand-built cabin, and watched the sunlight glide glacially across the ceiling, going over everything in her head, trying to fit it all together, as if seeing the whole picture would somehow make it all make sense. Except she didn't have the whole picture. Not even close. She'd seen frames of it, snapshots, blurry outlines, but with every fresh glimpse, more questions arose, none with easy answers.

This is your home, Annie.

Don't you remember?

She didn't. She didn't remember any of it. Life before that night at the cabin was all shadow and suggestion, more the idea of memories than memories themselves. She knew in her heart that she'd had a childhood, with a mom who she loved, and who loved her in return. She'd died protecting her, after all. But it was all just missing.

Growing up, Anne had managed to push the dead spots aside, telling herself that nobody remembered their childhoods with perfect clarity. Live long enough, and the brain starts making space for other things. Who remembered that much of their lives before age six, anyway? But there was an ocean of difference between memories slipping away to get shredded in the tide and having them burned whole-cloth from your head, with only scorch marks left behind to show that there was ever anything there in the first place. There was real trauma associated with something like that.

More than most people, Anne understood trauma. It latched on to you like a plague or a curse and stayed with you for years, if not your whole life. Trauma left marks, inside and out. She didn't remember this place, or Win, or the night she got the scars on her hands, but she'd watched it—watched herself—on that video all the same, and seeing what she'd seen on that motel room TV, she wasn't surprised that her memories had turned to ash and blown away. The pain and trauma from something like that were far too big to get her arms around, too incomprehensible to internalize. Especially at six years old.

Pain was the default setting for being alive. It was a realization that Anne had stumbled upon early on in life, walking away from the pop-canned Jeep that night with a gun in her hands. Either you made your peace with that fact, or you let it eat you. For the longest time, Anne thought she had made her peace with not getting to know the woman her mom really was, of having half of her childhood seared out of her skull, of the nightmares that chased her for years after the fact. But sitting here, now, in a place she didn't remember where everyone seemed to know her, she started to think that maybe the remembering really would have been worse.

There was a knock at the door. Anne looked up with a start and realized that at some point, the sun had set, slipping gently beyond the trees. How long had she been staring at the ceiling? Had she fallen asleep?

The knock came again. Her first impulse was to go and open the door for whoever was standing on the other side, but then she remembered that the cabin door didn't unlock from the inside.

"Come on in," she said, delicately rolling forward to sit up on the narrow cot. She twisted to the side and braced her back against the wall so her feet dangled off the side of the mattress. The annoyance in her voice was obvious, but why bother hiding it at this point? She was annoyed. Fuck that, she was furious. She was a prisoner here in this weird little cult town, but she was still somehow expected to play nice and invite people into her cell? Fuck all the way off.

A key rattled in the lock, and a second later, the door swung open to reveal none other than Win standing there on the front porch. He'd traded his vintage tee and jeans for narrow khakis and a well-ironed oxford, but he still somehow looked as rumpled as ever.

"Hey there. You hungry?" he asked, stubbornly wearing that bulletproof smile. "I mean, I sure hope so. Folks have been cooking all day for this. Family dinners are kind of a big deal around here, even when we don't have a guest of honor. Come on, get your shoes on, I'll walk you up."

Anne studied him from her little cot, the mechanic's scars on his hands and the lines in his face, the crow's-feet at the outside corners of his bright green eyes, trying to square the old man before her with the laughing zealot she'd seen in the video. Win wore his charm and easy good looks like a kindly, easygoing grandpa; he didn't strike her as a cult leader type, but that was probably the point. Probably made it easy to wriggle his way under people's skin and coil himself around their hearts like a strangling worm. Good looks had that effect. Folks just naturally trusted beautiful people. Handed them everything and more without even being asked to. Most beautiful people didn't even realize it was happening; they just thought that that was how the world was built, that they were somehow entitled to what was being offered to them on a daily basis. By and large, they were harmless, but it was the ones who were acutely aware of their own beauty that you had to look out for, the gorgeous monsters. Like Ted Bundy or Gwyneth Paltrow.

Standing in the doorway, Win cleared his throat expectantly.

"Yeah, sure, just give me a second," Anne said, leaning forward to haul herself off the bed.

Win's smile was warm and bright, perfectly practiced. "Course. Take your time. I'll be out here," he said.

Once she was out of his sight line, Anne slid her feet into her shoes, then took the screwdriver from under her pillow and quickly tucked it inside of one of her socks. Pulling her pantleg over the yellow resin grip, she turned this way and that, making sure that it wasn't too obvious or wouldn't come falling out as she walked. She doubted that she was going to have to stab anybody at this so-called family dinner, but she didn't know these people, and she sure as shit didn't trust them. Better to have it and not need it and all that.

Win led her up the hill to where she'd seen the people setting up the tables before. Anne was honestly taken a little aback; where it had previously just been tables arranged end to end, now it was a scene fit for any feast. Crisp white linens covered every table, stacked high with platters of food: meat and vegetables, home-baked bread, butter and dressings and sides, and more. There was a full goblet of red wine in front of nearly every seat. The bonfire blazed brightly in the middle of the horseshoe, bathing the wintry space in warmth and light, bolstered by tall lawn torches arranged *just so* around the edges of the tables. From the looks of it, the en-tire town was here, dressed in their Sunday best, expectant smiles plastered across their faces as they sat in silence and watched her approach. Her. Not the old man, but her. Having all those eyes on her like that made Anne want to peel her own skin off. Not for the first time, and certainly not for the last, it occurred to her how ter-ribly unsafe she was up here in Win's weird little kingdom.

The old man raised a hand to greet the gathered Passage of Divinity as he led Anne to the two open seats at the horseshoe's vertex. Not bothering to mask her own apprehension, Anne took another look around at the Passage, the feast, the night beyond the glow of the fire. The goblets in front of her and Win's place settings were yet empty, with a full bottle of wine sitting between them. For a moment, everything was silent. All around her, the members of the Passage watched expectantly, as if they were waiting for her to do a trick or grow a second head or some shit. Off to the left, she saw two familiar faces in the crowd: John and Norris. They'd cleaned themselves up since the last time Anne had seen them to-gether, both dressed in white oxfords kept unbuttoned at the col-lars. John had combed his barely-there hair straight back from his brow and sat with his hands folded on the table. In the next seat, Norris glared unblinkingly at Anne from under his black cater-pillar eyebrows, his bushy mustache curled back from his yellow teeth in an expression that could have been a bitter smile or a pissy little scowl, depending on the angle. Probably still smarting about their tiff up at the cabin. He didn't seem like the kind of guy who'd get over being outgunned by a girl. Probably why it was John that Win had brought to Alamosa to help collect them after everything went to shit. Good. Fuck around and find out, asshole. Anne met his eyes and showed him a wide, shit-eating grin while she thought about how good it would feel to bury the point of the screwdriver in his chest. Beside her, Win pulled Anne's chair out from the table for her, indicating that she should sit. She sat.

Still standing, Win raised both of his hands, palms upturned, drawing all the attention in the space onto himself. Expectant silence crashed over the congregation like a tidal wave, and then he started to speak.

"I'm so glad you're all here," Win said, projecting his voice loudly enough that it boomed in Anne's ear. "I'm honored by you all." He clasped his hands together in front of his heart, almost like he was praying. Maybe he was. "Sometimes, the Lord deals you a hand that you weren't expecting, that you wouldn't have chosen for yourself had you been given the choice. That's what happened to us, to all of us, the day we lost Beverly and her daughter."

A freezing bolt blasted through Anne's chest at Win's mention of her mom's name. She bit down on the inside of her cheek and dug her fingertips into her knees, willing herself to stay still. All around her, the parishioners—the *cultists*—were rapt, some of them nodding reverently to themselves as if they'd heard this particular sermon before.

"Not all of you were lucky enough to know Beverly. In fact, I think most of you came long after her time. But I'm sure that you've heard us talk about her before, me and John and Norris and the rest of us old-timers."

He cracked a humble half-smile then, as practiced and pitch-perfect as any other part of him, and a gentle susurrus of laughter circled through the congregation. Anne looked over at John and Norris again—John nodded deferentially, as if basking in his own memories of Anne's mother, while beside him, the menacing expression had fallen away from Norris's face like the shell off a hard-boiled egg, revealing something infinitely softer and more vulnerable underneath. Anne had a hard time believing that her mom had ever had the time of day for that asshole, but sitting here, now, she had to admit, even if only to herself, that she could just about squeeze the sum total of what she knew for sure about Beverly Heller into a fucking thimble. All she had were her memories and the stories Grandma had told her—but sitting here was proof positive that there were people out there who knew the woman far better than Anne ever could.

"Bev left us too early," Win continued somberly. A few voices in the crowd muttered among themselves with dissatisfaction, but Win held his hands out, silencing them. "I know, I know. The exodus, it hurt us. Left us weak. Left us lacking strength when we needed it most. But we cannot begrudge paths for diverging from ours, because we know in our hearts that those paths were authored by a power far greater than us. So I choose to look back on our time with Beverly with fondness, and I recommend y'all do the same. Beverly . . . she came to us in a time of great personal turmoil, searching for something else, something new, something *real*. But what she found was so much more than real, it was family. It was love. Most important thing in the whole damn world. I knew her, and I came to love her, just as everyone else did. Beverly was great friends with my Darlene, almost like sisters. Bev was there the night of the revelation—y'all know that. And I know there's not a one among you that doesn't know what she and her daughter did that night. The bravery it took to stand in the light of the infinite and try and save someone . . . Well, we should all be humbled by that. Doubly so now that Annie's been returned to us."

Wait, the *revelation*? Was that what he was calling that living fucking nightmare that had come crawling out of solid stone down in that mine shaft? Unbidden, Win's hand fell on Anne's shoulder. Trying not to shudder or slap it away, she shrugged it off, and if the old man was offended by that, he gave no indication.

"We're all so glad you've come home," he told her. "We've been waiting for this, for you, for a long, long time." He turned to the crowd again. "Annie opened the path for us. Gave us a way forward, a direct line to commune with our God, that great, good Other to whom all paths lead, eventually. Showed us what strength meant. What selfless sacrifice truly calls for. And for that, we are all in her debt. Hers, and her mother's." The old man filled both goblets in front of them from the wine bottle, then plucked one off the table and raised it high. "To Beverly. To Annie."

With that, Win drank deep. So did everyone else. Everyone except for Anne. She'd seen enough true-crime documentaries about Jonestown to know that was a bad idea. So she just sat there in silence, watching the gathered congregation drink their wine, waiting for any potential cyanide convulsions to start.

Anne felt her face grow hot under the pressure of the crowd's scrutiny. Usually when everyone in a given space was looking at her, somebody was about to get hurt, and grievously so. Down at the corner of the horseshoe, John beamed at her. Beside him, Norris just glared.

Win set his goblet aside and beamed at the gathered crowd. "Our true passage is upon us, friends," he announced. "It's almost here. Our time is finally at hand. We are expected, and there is no price too high for entry into the Kingdom of Heaven. Nothing can stop us now that we're all here, all whole once again. Our weary days are almost over. The path ahead is not without sacrifice, of course"—the crowd's faces turned solemn—"but we know a little bit about sacrifice, don't we? All thanks to Annie here.

"I promise you, it's not in vain. Those of us allowed entry will be granted all the gifts of the infinite, my friends. The power to breathe life where there was none before, to raise those who fell. It is ours to pave our passage with great sacrifice—those we lost, those we have yet to lose—so that all among us may live eternally in the embrace of the endless."

For the second time in as many minutes, Anne suppressed the urge to smell her wine for bitter almonds. Beside her, Win brightened.

"But tonight? Well, tonight is for celebrating, and family, and honoring the short path we have yet to walk. So enjoy it, please. The food's not going to stay warm forever, so please, eat! Eat! This is a family dinner, and one that's certainly worth celebrating. I love you all. Thank you so much for being here with me."

All around them, the crowd erupted in applause, then dug in, draining their wine and piling their plates high from the platters laid out in front of them. The night filled up with the clink and clatter of flatware against china as Win lowered himself into his seat and looked over at Anne.

"So how'd I do?" he asked with a genial wink. "Think they liked it?"

Anne was pretty sure that he could have said or done anything in front of these fucking lunatics and they would have lapped it up. She recognized that look on all those faces, that naked awe and complete devotion. Win played humble, acted like he was just a shepherd, nonthreatening and unassuming, but she'd already caught a glimpse of what waited underneath his carefully-curated surface. She'd seen that flicker in his eyes back in the barn, the raw, wolfish hunger that the people around here either didn't recognize or simply chose not to.

"Yeah," she said. "I think they liked it."

Win sipped his wine. "I'm glad. What about you, though?"

"What about me?"

"Did you like it?"

Was he serious right now? What the hell did he care if she liked it?

"I don't know. I don't really have an opinion, I guess," Anne said.

"Oh, come on now," Win chided playfully. "You must have thought something. You're your mother's daughter, after all, and she had plenty of opinions about plenty of things. Used to be a time she and Darlene were the only ones who'd call me out when she thought I was being an idiot." He took another deep quaff from his goblet, sighed contentedly, then turned his gaze back on her. "So, what do you think, Annie? You think I'm an idiot?"

A sharp chill danced along Anne's arms, stiffly raising the fine hairs there to attention. She kept her expression impassive as she studied his face. That cold, twinkling light had returned to his eyes, another peek of the laughing, exultant madman that still lurked underneath his friendly-grandpa exterior. How much did he know? Had Tobias heard and gone tattling to Daddy? They'd kept their voices low, but it wasn't unrealistic to imagine the kid might have overheard something, and even the littlest bit of information in the kid's hands might have been enough to sink them. Still, the old man hadn't cut her throat yet, and there was no sense in blowing it all up unless she absolutely had to. Better to play the game to its end than flip the board.

"No, Win. I don't think you're an idiot. Far from it."

Win's smile spread. "That so?"

Anne's back teeth ground against each other without her telling them to. She truly couldn't tell if he was interrogating her here, in front of all these poor people who he'd fooled into buying his particular line of bullshit, these lunatics who looked at him like they'd throw themselves in front of a truck or a bullet if it meant saving him—or if he was just looking to have his ego stroked. Either way, she hated it.

"That's so," she said. "Look at this place. These people. You wouldn't have been able to make all this happen, let alone keep it going, if you didn't know what you were doing." The words were battery acid on her tongue, foul and chemical.

The cold, maniac light in his eyes dimmed, then disappeared, replaced in an instant by that same practiced, artificial warmth, like Old Hollywood sunlight on a fuzzy cathode-ray TV. It might have looked passable from a distance, but once you got up close enough to see, it was obvious that it had never been the real thing. It was just yellow paint on a canvas backdrop. Another imperfect mask covering the rotten, fucked-up reality, just like the shape-shifter with all its stolen faces.

"Well," he said, using his fork to stab a bit of food off his plate, "I do hope you'll let me know if your opinion changes."

"Will do," she said, trying to hide her frustration.

She scanned the horseshoe again, marking the faces of the congregation as they ravenously tucked into their meals. Slowly, she picked her own goblet up off the table and took an experimental sip. It tasted like cherries and bitter chocolate. She didn't know much about wine, but maybe this stuff wasn't half-bad. She took another sip and cleared her throat, keeping her eyes on the crowd.

"So what did you mean, when you said *Our true passage is upon us*? And what does it have to do with me? What does any of this have to do with me, Win?"

The old man sopped up a dab of gravy on his plate with a heel of bread. "All in good time," he said. "I promise, I'll explain everything to you soon. You're owed that much, I know."

"I thought that was why I was coming to dinner. So you could explain. That's what you said," Anne told him, tamping back a fresh cloudburst of anger.

Win cracked a smile and chuckled as crumbs stumbled out of his mouth and bounced off the plate in front of him. "You came to dinner because you're home again. You're a member of our family, Annie. Always have been, always will be."

Again with the *Annie* shit. He was just fucking with her now, testing boundaries, seeing how much he could get away with. Same as every other egomaniacal asshole she'd ever met. She'd corrected him once already, and he clearly didn't give a shit, so whatever; let him call her what he wanted. She wasn't about to give him the satisfaction of knowing he'd gotten to her.

"Like it or not, you're one of us," he said. "Me, them, all of us? We're your people. We're you're family. And if you don't mind my saying, it kind of seems like family's something you're a little light on these days. You need people if you're going to survive living in this dying world of ours. That's just the way of it. Nobody's an island. Anybody says otherwise is fooling themselves or selling something. Trust me, I've been around enough to know."

Brittle, wounded anger screwed itself tight into the base of Anne's skull. *Nobody's an island*, fuck you. The old man didn't know her. Just because him and his followers had been part of her and her mom's life twenty-fucking-something years ago didn't mean that they were even remotely Anne's people. Ever since Grandma had died, Anne didn't have *people*. She'd kept her life solitary by design. It was a choice, one she'd made to mitigate unnecessary risk and avoid collateral damage. The closest she'd managed was Jessup and Gemma and the rest of the gang, and look how that had turned out.

Win nodded to the piles of food in front of them. "You should really have something to eat. You gotta get your strength back up. Can't go starving yourself, certainly not after the way you've been running yourself ragged." He scooped a forkful of mashed potatoes up off the plate, twirled it in the gravy, then popped it in his mouth. "Eat," he said as he chewed. "Please. It's a sin to waste food. You eat some, and then after we're done here, we'll go and talk. I'll explain everything. Promise. Scout's honor."

She considered the old man for another moment, then set her wine down and started to fill her own plate from the same platters she'd seen Win serve himself from. She figured that meant they weren't poisoned. Probably.

32

Gem stood by the window beside the door and watched the town's denizens march up the hill, carefully balancing plates and platters and bottles of wine in a silent, solemn parade as the sun went down behind the trees, leaving the tiny town bathed in flickering half-dark. There were more of them than she'd originally thought, maybe a hundred and fifty all told. Far more than she'd have liked. A hundred and fifty people meant three hundred eyes, give or take, watching for any sign of trouble. They'd have to be triply careful if they wanted this to work.

Behind her, the cop shifted on his cot to look at her. On the top bunk, Joanie shifted in place, shrugging the thin blankets higher up her shoulders.

"What's the deal?" the cop asked.

"Looks like they're heading up now," Gem said, turning back to watch the town through the little window. At some point, someone had lined Cabot's single road with lawn torches; the light from their fluttering little oil flames wasn't much, but it was enough to see by.

"Any sign of Anne or Win?"

Gem shook her head. "No, not yet," she said.

After a little while, the parade of bodies carrying food thinned out, winnowing down to a few stragglers. The rest of the town had surrendered to the solemn silence of absence, all the buildings and cabins left empty and dark. Gem shifted in place and looked down the hill to see two figures approaching at a steady pace: one tall and gaunt, the other smaller and more compact with a tangle of red hair.

"There they are," she said to no one in particular.

There was a scuffling of feet, and then the cop was beside her. Together, they watched Anne and Win pass their cabin by, following the crowd up toward the old barn and the shabby little church and whatever lay beyond.

"So should we go?" Dutch's voice was impatient, nervous.

"Let's give them a few more minutes," Gem told him. "Make sure that's everybody. Then we'll get moving."

Turning away to the window, she went to the far bunk bed and stood on the lower cot to get in close to Joanie on the top bunk.

"Hey. Hey," she said. "Joanie."

"What," Joanie replied without turning over, her voice brittle and bored.

"Am I going to have to worry about you?" Gemma asked.

"I don't know what you mean," Joanie said.

"I mean, are you going to make this shit any harder than it has to be?"

Joanie pulled the blankets tighter around on her shoulders, drawing herself into a little ball.

"I'm not going to squeal, if that's what you think," she said.

"You sure about that?"

Now Joanie rolled over to face Gem, her expression exhausted and miserable. "I'm sure, Gem. It wouldn't do me any good, anyway. I just want to get home, okay? That's it. I don't care what you're do-ing, just don't get caught. I have kids."

As if she was the only one with a life to get back to. Maybe Gemma wasn't a parent, and ever since her divorce, her social life had admittedly started to slowly but steadily dry up, but what life she had managed to cobble together was hers. She'd worked hard for it, and she wasn't about to bail on it if she could help it. But of course, that hardly mattered to Joanie. Why would it? Why would she think of anything other than saving her own skin? If nothing else, at least she was consistent. Gemma glared at the woman until Joanie rolled back over to face the wall. Gem hopped off the bunk and started stretching out. They had work to do.

Outside, the chill breeze slicked along Gem's bare arms and neck like dread given form. Together, she and the cop stole through the shadows toward Win's cabin, staying low, keeping their footsteps as quiet as they could. Farther on, Gem could see a bright glow beyond the barn, probably where the Passage was hosting their weird little family dinner. Anne had mentioned something about a bonfire, hadn't she?

As they approached Win's place, Gem scanned the little wooden building, casing it for any obvious entry points. It happened automatically, without her thinking about it or even realizing that she was doing it. It was just a reflex at this point. She'd started off her career pulling small-time B&Es, back when she was just a dumb teenager, training her instincts to search for weak spots, potential advantages, problems, whatever. She'd done the same exact thing when she'd woken up inside their cabin—getting in clean was crucial, but getting out even more so. You always had an exit strategy. That was the way you stayed alive and a step ahead of the wolves.

Getting out of their little cabin wasn't hard. The lock on the door was a cheap, factory-standard thing, and Win's people hadn't bothered padlocking the other side. A little pressure here, the right turn there, and pop went the weasel. Getting into the old man's place, though? She figured that might be a touch more challenging. She kind of doubted that Win had bothered installing a state-of-the-art alarm system on this little shitbox—he had everyone in this crapshack town wrapped around his little finger, hanging off his every word. Still, her overall impression of the guy was that he was way more cautious than not. If his place wasn't shut up tight, she'd be shocked.

Stepping onto the creaky front porch, she tried the doorknob first—locked. It seemed like an elementary thing, but people would be stunned how many B&Es went off without a hitch just because folks forgot or otherwise neglected to lock their front doors. That was why you always tried the front door first. Her eyes traced the edge where the door met the jamb, noting the three heavy-duty dead bolts Win had installed above the knob. She could get through them easily enough, but it would take time that they didn't have. They'd have to turn around and hightail it out of there as soon as they got through.

Turning back, Gem caught the cop's eyes and pointed toward a shadowy spot along the side of the cabin. Wordlessly, he followed, stepping into the shadows and nearly disappearing.

"Stay here. Keep an eye out," she told him brusquely.

His eyes were wide and nervous. "Why? What are you going to do?"

Gem smiled at him without joy or kindness. "I'm going to find us a way in." She could feel him nearly vibrating with anxiety as he stood there in the shadows.

"What do I do if someone comes?"

Annoyed, Gem made a face. With one mangled hand and two fresh bullet holes in him, the cop definitely wasn't going to be able to do much running or fighting if it came to that.

"You *hide*," she said as if it were the most obvious thing in the world. Then she turned and circled around to the back of the cabin.

There wasn't a back door to the place, but there were a couple of windows. The first was locked tight, of course, but around the far corner, she found a small sliding job that looked like it might work. It was too small for the cop to fit, but if she twisted and held her breath, Gem thought she might be able to squeeze through. If it was unlocked. Uttering a silent plea to whatever higher power was listening tonight, she braced both hands firmly against the bottom pane and pushed.

At first, nothing. Shit. Shit, shit, shit.

But then, slowly, the window started to give way, sliding open inch by grinding inch. It didn't squeak or squeal in its track, which was a mercy, but Christ, this thing was most of the way to stuck. Gem kept the pressure on the glass, sliding it slowly upward until she'd opened a gap large enough to slip through. Using both hands to grasp the window's frame, she glanced around again, making triple sure she wasn't being watched, then blindly pulled herself up and in, and then she was falling.

She hit the ground in a heap, landing awkwardly on cold linoleum, barking her knees and elbows against the ground hard enough that she had to bite down on her lower lip to keep from crying out. Rolling over, she pressed herself against the wall below the window and rubbed frantically at her bruised joints, willing the stubborn ache to fade as her vision adjusted to the dark.

She was sitting in a bathroom, nothing fancy, just a shower and a toilet, but it was a hell of a lot better than the facilities that she and Dutch and Joanie had had to share over the past few days. Whenever they had to go, they had to bang on the front door of their cabin, and whoever was keeping watch, usually that kid, Tobias, would escort them out to the communal showers. They weren't terrible, but they weren't exactly private, either.

Rising to her feet, Gem moved quickly through the cabin to the front door, throwing each dead bolt in sequence, and poked her head out. Dutch was nowhere to be seen. She propped the door open and cast a quick glance up the hill toward the gentle glow of family dinner. There was still no one on the dirt road, but Gem was sure that wouldn't last long. They had to move fast.

"*Psst! Psssst*," she whispered to the cop, the sound like air escaping out of a jackknifed tire.

A half second later, the guy's face appeared from around the corner, coalescing from out of the shadows like a phantom apparition. Wordlessly, Gem beckoned him inside and shut the door after him.

"So what exactly are we looking for in here?" he whispered to her as she threw the dead bolts back in place.

"Our stuff," Gem said. "Our bags, guns, whatever. Any of it. All of it. Beyond that, I don't know, man. Something. Whatever tells us what the old man's angle is in all of this, I guess. Maybe we'll know it when we see it; maybe we won't. Anything out of place. Anything that seems weird."

"This all seems weird to me," Dutch said.

"Anything weird*er*, then."

"Oh, good. Very helpful, thanks."

Gem rolled her eyes at the cop's cheap sarcasm. As if he was doing any better right now. As if he hadn't spent the last few days shaking like a leaf in their cabin, tending to his wounds and flinching at any too-loud noise. Paper tiger prick. Whatever. She turned away from him and started poking around.

Win's place wasn't huge, maybe a room or two bigger than the sparse summer-camp-style cabin that they'd been stuck in for days now, but something about the way that the inside had been outfitted made it seem a whole lot bigger than that. This place was well lived in and had been for years, bearing all the telltale hallmarks of a real home: bookshelves lining the walls of the living room, half-empty coffee cups discarded on end tables and countertops, dishes unwashed in the kitchen sink. There was a desk in the corner, piled high with clutter underneath photos and art prints and yellowing concert posters framed behind glass. Gem got in close and inspected the show posters in the low light: the Grateful Dead, Creedence Clearwater Revival, Junior Kimbrough, Ash Ra Tempel, Akira Ishikawa & Count Buffaloes. Some of them were even signed.

On the other side of the room, there was a turntable and a stereo rig atop a couple of densely packed shelves of vinyl opposite the sofa that took up most of the far wall; the cop knelt in front of it, silently thumbing through Win's collection. Gem left him to it. She knew enough by now to know that musical taste wasn't a reliable barometer for the relative quality of a person; she'd known plenty of horrible people who listened to nothing but Miles Davis, and she'd known some decent folks who were—inexplicably—really into the Osmonds. It didn't matter at the end of the day. Your taste in music was only that: your taste in music.

But books? Well now, that was a different ball game; shit, it was a different sport altogether. What books a person read (and kept around long after they were done with them) could tell you damn near everything you needed to about their overall quality.

Running one long, lithe pointer finger from spine to spine, Gem inspected Win's bookshelves, counting off Tolkien, Feynman, Child, Márquez, Hawking, Tolle. It was all in a jumble, no order to them that Gem could see beyond *This fits here, I guess.* Fiction and nonfiction commingled with metaphysics and cookbooks, philosophy and political theory, lacking any comprehensible cadence, intent, organization. Maybe Win knew where he'd put everything, but to an outsider, it just seemed like chaos.

Her eyes fell on a small photo standing on one of the shelves, a four-by-six in a thrift-store frame, the glass caked in dust. She picked it up and used a thumb to wipe away some of the grime, then held it up to the light to get a better look: six people standing arm in arm in the sunlight, all of them beaming at the camera, shiny and happy and perfect and young and immortal. In the picture, they stood before a tall ranch gate, twelve, maybe fifteen feet high, with a wrought iron sign at the top that read, THREE-STAR CATTLE RANCH, and a matching logo underneath. Gemma picked out Win right away; he stood on the far left-hand side of the group, decades younger, his beard only just starting to grow in along a jawline that could have cut glass. Beside Win stood that woman with the burning eyes and the raven-black hair Gem had seen in the video. Darlene, that was her name. She'd been Win's wife back then. Before she died.

Beside Darlene was John, the tall, skinny guy that Gemma had come to think of as Win's right hand. He'd been the one to pull her and the cop off the street after everything fell apart at the diner, snapping a couple of potato sacks over their heads at gunpoint and dragging them off to pile in the back of the Oldsmobile. Gem was kind of surprised to see that he actually had hair once. Wonders never ceased. Beside John stood a woman with long white hair and tattooed hands heavy with silver rings, wearing a *cut-the-shit* smirk. She was familiar, but Gem didn't remember how.

Then there was Beverly Heller, her red hair and big, bright smile unmistakable. Gem had to marvel, looking at the woman. She looked so much like her daughter. There were some key differences, sure, but Anne had grown up to look so much like Beverly, it was honestly a little freaky. In the photo, Beverly wore a big floppy sun hat and a floral-print dress that offset the scatter of freckles that danced across her chest and shoulders underneath a silver necklace, rising up her throat to her cheeks and nose. In Beverly's arms, leaning against her mother and beaming with laughter, was little Annie. She looked so happy in this photo. They all did.

On the other side of the room, the cop rose from the turntable and looked over at her. "What do you got there?"

"A picture," Gemma said.

"Of what?"

Without looking, she tossed the frame over to him, just a little bit harder than she really needed to. Out of the corner of her eye, she watched the frame ricochet off his unwary hand, bumbling back and forth in his palm until he finally snatched it out of the air and righted it.

"It's them," he said. "The, the—"

"Yeah, all the old-timers," Gem finished.

The cop shifted in place to get a better look at the photo. "Not many of them left these days, huh?"

"Doesn't seem like it, no," Gem replied, her voice flat and inflectionless to mask the irritation thrumming in her temples.

Turning to the cluttered desk, she started to rifle through its contents, sifting through the junk stacked on top, pulling open drawers and thumbing through files. There really didn't seem to be much here, but then again, what had she been expecting, exactly? Tax returns? W-2s? Birth certificates and Social Security checks? People who joined up with fringe religious groups, hippie communes, cults, whatever you wanted to call them, didn't go in for shit like that. They dropped off the map as soon as they could and spent the rest of their lives flying under the radar. They didn't keep paperwork lying around to be seized in some government raid or some shit. The whole point of a place like this was to live free, or at least as free as Win let them be.

Gem heard the cop cross the small living room area to stand directly behind her, peering at the desk clutter over her shoulder. Crowding her. Waiting for her to tell him what to do. Looking confused and out of place, like a little kid lost in the supermarket. Jesus Christ, this guy.

"Help you with something?" she asked, even though she wasn't really asking.

"No, no," he stuttered. "No, I-I'm . . . just looking, I guess. Why?"

"You're hovering."

"I didn't mean to."

"Yeah, well, do me a favor and go do it somewhere else, okay? Not like we have a lot of time right now. We're supposed to be searching the place, remember?"

"I mean . . . where else should I look? It's not like it's a huge place."

Irritation streaked through Gem's temples again, brighter now than it had been a moment before. "Anywhere. I don't care. Check the bathroom for all I care. Just *back off.*"

The cop didn't move. Didn't say anything, awkward. The silence that passed between them was a nervous, frail thing, a rocky ridge one out-of-place pebble away from a disastrous landslide. Gem chided herself inwardly for going along with this play. When Anne suggested it, she should have told her that she could pull it off on her own, that it was going to be easier for her to handle it alone. It would have been a whole lot better than having to babysit Danny Butterman over here.

"I'm not going to say it again," Gem said, tempting the landslide.

A second passed, then another, and then she heard the cop finally take a step back. Good boy. Gem pulled the desk's center drawer open and ran both hands through the contents: pens and pencils and crumpled sticky notes, pushpins and loose change and rubber bands. Near the back of the drawer, she found a cinch-top cloth bag. She picked it up, pulled the strings open and looked inside to find—

Driver's licenses. Dozens of them. Some dating back twenty years or more, stacked like a deck of cards. Gem shuffled through them, scanning the pictures and the names. *Erika Steleck. Dean Garritsen. Timothy Gant. Cherie Sbila.* None of the names meant anything to Gem, but they sure seemed to be special to Win, for whatever reason. Did they belong to his people? Was he taking their driver's licenses to make sure they stayed up here or some shit? Everything else in the cabin had the undeniable feeling of having accumulated without plan or intent over the course of decades, but the licenses were . . . deliberate. Hidden away from view, but not too far. Weird. She slipped the stack into her pocket, then cinched the empty bag shut and returned it to the drawer. Working quickly, she put the rest of the desk back in a reasonable facsimile of how she'd found it, then stood straight and turned around to find the cop standing right behind her, looming. Again. If it had been anyone else, any other cop especially, she would have called it some kind of twisted power play, but that wasn't him. He was an overgrown boy, awkward and insecure, and his *aw shucks* act was wearing plenty thin.

"What?" she asked flatly.

"What did I do to you?" he asked.

The question took her off guard. After three days locked up together, the two of them had, Gemma thought, found their way to a kind of comfortable silence. They hadn't talked much that first day, both of them too busy nursing wounds and bruises and trying to figure out what the hell had happened. After that, they'd fallen into a kind of rhythm that Gem had personally thought was working well enough. Not least of all because it didn't involve discussing her feelings with a fucking cop.

"Nothing," she said. "You didn't do a damn thing, but it's not really about that. It's about trust. And I do not trust you at all."

"Why not?"

"Because you wear a badge for a living. You really need me to explain it more than that?"

The cop's expression darkened. "After everything we've been through? Kind of, yeah. I do. Back at the diner, you were done, Gem. That guy had the shotgun on your throat, remember? He would have crushed your windpipe if I hadn't stuck him with that butcher knife. I mean, come on, I got shot for you. Twice. So when are you going to drop the cold shoulder act and just let me in already? I'm not my job any more than you are. So why are you treating me like I'm going to turn on you the second you take your eyes off me?"

Gem fixed him with an icy look, driving it as hard as she could into the center of his face. It wasn't her job to explain this shit to him. But there was nobody else here.

"You really want to do this? Fine. People who do what you do for a living are told in no uncertain terms that people who look like me are a threat. No two ways about it. Shit, you can draw a direct line from American policing as it stands today to slave patrols in the Carolinas in the seventeen goddamn hundreds. The system is unapologetically built to endanger the lives of people of color. Has been from the start. And you chose to play ball with it. You want a better reputation? Pick better friends, because the ones you've got kind of have a way of killing innocent people. Don't believe me? Watch the news once in a while—you'll see what I'm talking about. Promise."

"Oh, come on," Dutch said, taking a step back. "I'm not like that. I never—"

"Nuh-uh, no. I've heard that crap before. *Not all cops,* fuck you. It is. It's *all. Of. You.* The whole brotherhood. The bad cops, the ones doing the killing and the stomping and the choke holds and whatever else, they're scary enough, but the so-called *good ones*? The ones like you who sit quietly by while your coworkers murder people like me for daring to be born a different color? You're the real poison. You're the reason this shit never gets any better. People like you make me sick. And while I'm at it, the constant insistence that it's *just a few bad apples* is missing the entire point. The phrase is *one bad apple spoils the whole barrel.* You're *all* complicit. Or did your superiors not explain the finer points when they handed you your official police department talking points, *Dutch*?"

The words came out of Gemma's mouth in a venomous hiss, and for a second, Dutch looked like she'd slapped him.

He stared at the ground like a chastised kid. Down at his sides, his hands closed and opened at irregular intervals. He shook his head, just a little bit, as if trying to keep up with some charged internal dispute. Gem let the silence hang there between them for a long moment, then two, then three, and when Dutch looked back up at her again, his eyes were watery, his expression slack and ashamed.

"I never thought about it like that," he said. "I just wanted to help, you know? All my life, I just wanted to help people, and I thought that, you know, in the movies, police officers, they . . . but we don't. Not always. I'm sorry. I was just . . . I was thinking of myself, and not the whole picture, and then with everything that happened back at the diner, I thought . . ."

He trailed off. Gem didn't want to admit it, but he had a little bit of a point. He'd saved her twice at the Pink Flamingo, put himself in the line of fire for her when he didn't have to. Whether she liked it or not, that made him a lot more than some run-of-the-mill racist storm trooper. All cops were bastards, that much was undeniable and would remain so in perpetuity until the heat death of the entire goddamn universe, but it was pretty clear that Dutch wasn't exactly a cop anymore. At least he seemed like he was listening. That wasn't nothing.

"I'm really sorry, Gem," Dutch said. "Truly. And I'm not asking you to make me a full-fledged member of the team or anything like that. I just don't want to keep being treated like I might flip and burn you or whatever at a moment's notice. I won't. I promise. I'm just trying to help."

Gem rubbed at one clenched eye with the heel of her hand. On the list of things she'd expected to come out of his mouth, an apology was not. Maybe there was some hope for people after all.

"Yeah, okay, fine," she said.

Dutch's face brightened, and Gem held up a hand.

"Don't say thank you, okay? Please. Don't make it weirder than it already is."

"Okay." He jerked his chin at the desk behind her. "Did you . . . did you find anything?"

Gem shook her head. "No. Not really. Some IDs, that was about it."

Dutch's face pulled itself into an expression of confusion, as if he hadn't heard her right. "IDs?"

"Yeah, like driver's licenses. A whole stack of 'em. Probably belong to his people, but I have no idea why or for what."

"Anything else?"

"Nothing that points to us or Anne or anything. Shit's a bust. Come on, let's get out of here. They're probably nearly done by now. You go out the front, I'll lock up behind you and then I'll go out the back."

Dutch nodded, then started for the door. Gem followed him and paused as she threw the dead bolts.

"Wait for me where you were before. I'll only be a minute. If you see anybody—and I mean anybody at all—just split, okay? Run for the cabin. Don't look back. Stick to the shadows, stay low, stay quiet. Don't worry about me. I'll catch up."

Worry furrowed Dutch's brow. "You sure?"

"Pretty sure, yeah."

"All right. Okay. Here."

Standing at the door, he passed the photo of the Passage back to her and walked out. Gem closed the door behind him and threw the dead bolts, then looked down at the framed picture, at all those smiling faces that had no idea what was coming for them. She supposed that was how life was sometimes—one second everything was fine, and the next, everything was falling apart around your ears. No way to anticipate it. Best you could do was roll with the punches and hope that was enough.

Flipping the frame over in her hands, Gem pulled the backing off and slipped the photo out, stashing it in her pocket. Win or not, it wasn't a bad picture of Beverly. Anne might want it. Moving back to the bookcase, she put the empty frame face down in the clutter where she'd found it.

Cocking her head by the open bathroom window, Gem listened to the night beyond the walls of the old man's cabin. She could just barely make out voices on the breeze. Guess dinner was over. Quickly, she slithered through the small opening and eased the pane down into place, hoping Win wouldn't notice the smeary finger smudges she'd left on the glass. Too late to do anything about it now.

Around the side, she found Dutch waiting for her in a pocket of shadow no bigger than a coffin. He pointed up the hill, toward the voices coming closer. Gem beckoned him on, and together, they left the cabin behind. They had to get back.

33

After dinner, Win led Anne up the hill, past the church toward the tree line beyond. From below, the church looked a whole lot more imposing than it really was close up; the angle it sat at over the town made it seem huge. That was probably the point, if she had to guess. The building itself was old, small, almost chapel-like in its modesty, with few windows and a wide, uncovered porch leading to a single wooden door. It was almost certainly one of the original town buildings, back when this had just been a mining outpost deep in the Sangre de Cristos. Anne figured that the porch was probably where Win gave his sermons from, when he wasn't preaching over family dinners. No way there was room inside enough for the whole town.

All around them, the night had gone from chilly to frosty; it was that kind of sharp, indifferent bitter cold that you only got in the mountains. Most of the valley was only a couple of thousand feet higher in elevation than Denver, but wherever on the map that Cabot fell, it had to have been a bit higher than that. Anne turned her head up toward the sky and that infinite, icy blackness and watched the stars fade in and out, smudged off the firmament by the low-hanging clouds as they floated by. There was snow coming. A few early flakes drifted down around her, but this was Colorado. A few flakes were always just prelude. The storm would hit in earnest sometime tomorrow and would probably keep going for a long time after that. Winter was here, leaching into the air and the ground, hanging on like grim death, refusing to be burned away by the sun. Soon, the cold would be everywhere. The cold would take everything. Just like it always did.

Up ahead of her, past the church, Win disappeared into the

trees, slipping into the shadows like he was pulling a blanket around his shoulders.

"Come on," he said from nowhere, voice warbling through the darkness. "It's just up here. I need you to see this."

Reluctantly, Anne followed, arms crossed tight against the chill. Holding her breath, she stepped into the shadows between the trees and followed the sounds of Win's footsteps until she came out on the other side and found herself standing at the edge of a rocky clearing at the bottom of a steep slope. Overhead, the moon had slipped free of the clouds' grasp, illuminating the whole of the hillside in a soft blue glow.

Standing there beside the old man, Anne paused for a moment, catching her breath, then followed his attention up the slope, watching Win soldier on ahead toward a shabby wooden adit cut in the side of the hill, long boarded up and chained over.

It was a mine.

Shit, it was *the* mine.

Ballmer's Hope, that's what they'd called it, back before Cabot had died. It had been an explosion that had done it, killing the mine and the town with it, along with nearly a hundred unlucky miners that got caught in the blast or trapped underground. Anne's mind flashed to the few photos she'd seen of this place, of the two men that had made it out, one burned nearly beyond recognition, the other with an arm torn straight from the socket, blood gushing out of the hole. Her skin crawled, standing here now, staring at it.

"You heard about what happened here, right?" Win asked without looking over. "A hundred years back. Why this place ended up abandoned, way back when."

Anne tightened her arms around her chest. "I heard. Accident in the mine. People died. Money dried up, and the company took its interests elsewhere."

"That's about the long and short of it. Lotta folks died up here," he said. "Whole damn lot of them."

"Darlene included, right?"

Win paused. His head fell with a soft, sad sigh. "That was different. We were looking for a home," he said. "Someplace we could make our own. We were in Crestone for a little while, had a place out in the Baca, but it started to get . . . too crowded for my liking. I always found it hard to pray proper with a whole lot of strangers around. It's an intimate thing, prayer. Better to do it when it's just you and the powers that be. Not so many looky-loos. We wanted to believe that there was a place for us in this world, a place all our own, just waiting for our arrival. Somewhere given unto us by the Lord. Lo and behold, here we are."

Anne stood in place, waiting for him to get to his point, however long that took. She could wait all night, if she had to. Gem and Dutch were counting on her. She wasn't used to this part of the job—handling people, drawing their attention and keeping it laser-focused; that had always been Jessup's purview. He was the talker, the charmer, the social creature. His was a rare talent, the preternatural ability to instantly take the temperature of any room he stepped into. That, more than anything else, was how he always kept things from spiraling out, letting them walk away from so many jobs without a single shot fired or a drop of blood shed. Anne had no idea how he was able to do that. But there wasn't any Jessup here to do the talking for her now. Like it or not, she was on her own, and she had to play the old man's game until further notice.

Win blew a thin plume of steam in the winter air. "We were up here for a few weeks before I found it. I guess I knew there'd been an old, closed-up mine up here, way back when, but I never really gave much thought to it. We were too preoccupied with getting a toehold in Cabot proper, making it our own, trying to make sure it was the kind of place we could stay forever. I promised my people, *our* people, a home, and I meant to deliver. But building a home, it's hard work, Annie. So I started taking walks, just to blow off some steam, maybe get to know this land that we'd been given. Back and forth, all over, but I'd never gone up the hill until that day. Then I did, and found it here. Waiting for me. It was boarded up, but there was something special about it. You can feel it in the air, can't you?"

Anne looked over at him, ready to tell him that she didn't know what the hell he was talking about—but then she stopped. Because he wasn't wrong. There was a faint charge in the air up here, a kind of wispy, amorphous energy surrounding them, like the rising electricity before a thunderstorm. She could feel it along the edges of her arms, dancing across her scalp, prickling at the backs of her eyes. What the fuck was that?

"Wasn't long after that I started hearing it in my sleep," Win said. "See, the mine . . . well, it speaks to you, if you can figure out how to listen. It whispers to you, from underground. You know what I'm talking about, don't you? You saw it. In the video."

Electricity sputtered along Anne's brain stem as her mind flashed to the grainy footage of that white slab in the guts of the mine. The way it had rumbled as it devoured her blood and spread itself open; the yawning, dead void beyond.

Beside her, Win was still talking.

"It spoke to me, you see. Showed me the true path. Taught me that the Lord wasn't something you could find in books and Bible verses or churches or any of that shit. We'd been looking in the wrong places for so long. But . . . the truth will out, as the saying goes. Heard the voice and, well. Wasn't long after that that I came up here, pulled the boards and chains back and took a look inside for myself. Far as I could tell, nobody'd been down there since the mining company boarded it up and left all those years ago. Place was a tomb, but it wasn't exactly empty, either.

"The whispers got louder the deeper I went. Not loud as in hearing 'em, but loud inside my head. Started off as a tiny little ringing in my ears, but before too long it was like listening to a dead TV channel blasting inside my skull. Static. Noise. Made me sick to my stomach, but I kept going anyway. You see, the Lord tests us, Annie. Never forget that. Most people, they just shrink away or recoil from it. They're not strong enough to be given the gifts intended for them. But I forced myself to be. We're told from childhood, *Be not afraid*, but fear is natural. It's the most natural thing in the world, next to pain. To fear is to be human. But you know what they say, right? True courage is being scared out of your mind and then doing it anyway. That's what the Lord teaches us. So I kept going. Puking, crying, each step worse than the last. But when I finally got near the bottom, it all just went quiet again. Perfectly quiet. No static. No noise. Just that whispering inside my head again. That was when I realized that what I found down there, it's what I'd been searching for all my life. Something greater than myself. Something holy. Something left here by God Himself.

"I brought Darlene down the next night to witness it. My—*our*—miracle. After so many years spent hoping, searching, praying, we finally had it. I couldn't not share. So after a few days spent praying on it, we took the rest of y'all down to see, suffering the pain of passage for a chance to glimpse the eternal. Such a small price to pay, in the long run. Darlene was the most devout of all of us, even more so than me. You saw the way she prayed, nearly pressing her face to the stone. She knew from the first moment how special it was. She saw how blessed we were. Then you split your hands open, and . . . welp, something in the miracle opened up before us all. You saw what happened next. That night, I glimpsed the truth for a moment—just for a moment. And then it took my Darlene away from me. From all of us. Wisdom, knowledge, they always come at a cost. No revelation is ever free."

Somewhere beyond the clearing, deep in the tangle of trees that surrounded them, a branch snapped, sharp and sudden as a gunshot. Anne twisted in place, searching the hillside for the source of the noise, but there was nothing there but shadows and field and forest.

"Did you hear . . . ?"

Win glanced over at her, nonplussed. "Hear what?" he asked.

Anne studied his face, searching for any trace of bullshit. Had he really not heard that? There was no way, right? She looked back at the trees and the darkness that flowed between them like water. Farther down the hill, she could just make out the soft glitter of Cabot's lights through the trees, and for the first time, it struck her how far afield they'd really wandered. It hadn't felt like that much of a hike, but standing here now, she wondered if anyone in Cabot would be able to hear her if she screamed. She looked back at Win. His expression was still and stony, unchanging.

"Nothing," she said. "Nothing. Never mind."

"It broke us. Broke me. What happened to Darlene down there . . . I blamed myself, you know. Of course I did. I was the one that led us all down there, I was the one that wanted them to see what I saw. If I hadn't brought you all down there that night . . . I don't know, Annie. I'm not sure we'd be having this conversation right now," Win said, his voice stained with regret and sorrow.

The old man rubbed his eyes as if clearing away tears, but Anne wasn't exactly convinced by the performance. She nodded toward the chained-up mine entrance up the hill from them.

"What happened down there, Win? That night, after the tape ended."

Win's shoulders fell. He blew a sharp, thin jet of air between pursed lips.

"Rock sealed itself up tight again," he said. "Not even a scar left in the stone to show what had been there before. You saw what happened to Darlene. After that . . . your momma took you and left. Didn't even bother waiting 'til dawn. The Keoghs did the same, so did Lis. A few others, too. More'n I'd like. All of you, just . . . scattered to the wind. I tried to stop it, but with what happened to my Darlene, I was in no shape. So I let them go. Live and let live. I had my own house to set in order. I couldn't worry about the unfaithful anymore."

That must have been the *exodus* he'd mentioned at dinner. Anne's mind went to the screaming faces she'd seen in the video. All those horrified people, staring into the dead white-black eye of something they had no chance of understanding. She didn't blame anyone for leaving after that, after seeing what the vortex of Win's so-called miracle had done to Darlene. Not for the first time, she found herself trying to remember the details of that night, attempting to travel back along the thread of her own memory to that little girl she'd seen on the video, but it was all still just rubble. The memories that she was looking for just weren't there, or if they were, they were so buried that the result was the same.

"You never saw us again after that?"

The old man shook his head. "Not your momma. Not the Keoghs.

Not Lis. Ken Andrews and his family, you knew them, they came back to us for a time, but it didn't last. See, there are doors in this world, Annie. Doors that shouldn't be here, doors that can't possibly exist, and yet, they somehow do. Doors to another place, another time. Call it a higher plane of reality. Somewhere beyond this cruel, cold place we call home. The Cabot miners discovered it, all those years ago, and they were found unworthy. That's the only explanation I can make fit. I don't know how many there are, but the one that we—that *I*—found waiting for us at the bottom of that hole, what the mining company unburied all those years ago, it's mine. It's ours. All of ours. And the Lord, He's waiting on the other side for us to step through and be welcomed into paradise."

That rustling came from the trees again, closer now than it had been before. Anne's skin flashed cold, and her brain went to the Phillips-head in her sock. There was definitely something there, only feet behind them. She whirled in place, forcing her hands to stay still, to not go for the screwdriver just yet. She stared into the unblinking darkness between the trees as her heart thundered in her chest, sending blood screaming through her temples.

"Win . . . ?"

But the old man was silent. He stood still among the rocks, face turned serenely toward the night sky as if he were waiting for something. A second later, Anne heard a sound like the fluttering of dry wings on the breeze. She turned, expecting to see a bird breaking free from the trees, some raven or owl, but there was nothing. The sound was only a sound.

A whisper.

"*—suSsSsUsSssUusSuSSsu—*"

It floated through the night as if on powdery moth's wings, somehow soft and sharp at the same time. Its faint buzzing rose to replace the silence that preceded it, creeping through the branches and between the black trunks like an oil slick, and as it swelled to fill the forest, Anne realized she could hear a single word trapped within its hum, repeated over and over and over like a curse or an incantation:

"*Annie . . . Annie . . . Annie . . .*"

As Anne peered into the darkness that lay beyond, she saw something separate itself from the shadows, gliding between the trees like a phantom. A human shape. There was someone else here. Anne took a step away from the tree line, then another, backing up and up the rocks, feeling her heart jackhammering against her rib cage, her pulse singing wildly in her throat and her wrists. Suddenly, the air around her tasted stale and foul, as if she were trying to breathe through a mouthful of grave soil.

"Win . . . ?"

"It's okay," he said. "I promise."

A moment later, a body drifted out from the shadows, a woman, slight and slender, almost bladelike, with a long shock of midnight-black hair. The whisper returned then, a faint hum scraping at the very outermost edges of Anne's perception—it took her too long to recognize it as the buzzing of flies. Bitter cold rippled up Anne's spine. Finally, the woman stepped free of the shadows of the trees and moved fully into the moonlight.

It was Darlene Hofmann. Unchanged, unaged. As if she'd been frozen in time that night she'd come apart in the light of the icon. This wasn't possible. None of this was possible.

"She didn't die that night, Annie. When that door opened, she wasn't killed. She was *chosen*," Win said. "She looked into the eye of the infinite, and it looked back into her. Touched her. Blessed her. It saw something in her, my Darlene. Something devout, something pure. And it changed her. Rewarded her. Made her new."

As Anne stood there watching her, the woman's eyes flashed a bright, terrible white. Anne knew those eyes. She'd had nightmares about those eyes ever since she'd been six years old. She wanted to scream, but the sound caught in her esophagus like a rock.

The woman smiled, and then her face split apart along that smile and peeled back into a new configuration, ringed in mismatched teeth and torn, sinewy meat: a lantern-jawed police officer, a little girl, then Jessup Lees before folding back and giving way to Darlene's face. The same face that Anne had seen in the video, the one she'd watched get pulled apart inside the icon as Anne's younger self struggled with all her might to drag her back from the edge of that mutilating unknown.

Anne gasped for air that wouldn't come. She was suffocating. Her head swam as her vision grew fuzzy. There was no way. Darlene Hofmann was dead. No one could survive the horror that she'd been subjected to in the light of that burning dead hole in reality. All the food in Anne's stomach flopped over and over, threatening to eject itself from her system.

"She wasn't trying to hurt you," Win said, his voice barely a whisper now. "I keep telling you, Annie. Nobody here wants to hurt you. You're one of us. You'll always be one of us."

Then he said the next thing, the thing that made Anne feel like he'd reached into her chest and clasped her heart in a freezing, iron grip.

"Darlene was just trying to bring you home."

34

Anne felt her legs go numb a second before they went out from under her. Her vision went black, even though she knew her eyes were still open. For a moment, it was as if she'd left her body entirely, separated without her even noticing the excision. Faintly, she felt her back hit the rocky ground below, and then there was nothing.

Consciousness came back to her inch by bloody inch. She opened her eyes and studied the dull wood-slat ceiling over her head, and the log walls in the low, orange lamplight. This had happened before, waking up in this room with no clue as to how she'd gotten here. She didn't like it any more the second time around—if anything, she liked it less now, because she already knew exactly where she was.

Raising her hands to her face, she rubbed at her eyes with her scarred palms until she saw starbursts, trying to clear the fuzziness and attendant ache from her head. Drawing a slow, deep breath, she felt her stomach do another somersault. She could still feel the dull tension in her chest from her heart jacking itself up to a million miles an hour the second she'd laid eyes on Darlene.

Jesus fuck, *Darlene*. The shape-shifter had been Darlene Hofmann all along. What the hell had Anne been dragged into?

Down at the foot of her bed, she felt someone shift their weight. Anne's brain flew to attention, and she recoiled like a scared kid, shoving herself back to curl against the little cot's headboard, knees pressed to her chest. It was Win. Of course it was Win.

He sat perched on the foot of the bed, hands folded together in his lap, looking at her with gentle concern.

"Hey there," he said, his voice soft. "You okay? Gave me a scare. Had to carry you all the way back down the mountain in the dark."

Her first impulse was to pull the screwdriver from her sock and jam it into his mottled old neck, but she held back. For all she knew, Tobias—or worse, Darlene—was posted on the other side of the cabin door, waiting for the first sign of trouble.

"You look like you managed okay," she said, her voice broken and craggy.

Win's smile spread. "I suppose. Guess these old bones have more life in 'em than they might look like. How are you feeling?"

"How do you think I'm feeling, Win? Honestly."

The old man nodded to himself and re-laced his fingers together on his lap. "Seeing her for the first time can be a lot, I know," he said. "Though it's hardly your first time, is it? Far from it, in fact."

"You say that like it's a good thing."

He shrugged. "As far as I'm concerned, it is. It's a blessing. Most folks are lucky to get a glimpse of the sublime underneath all her faces, if they get one at all. But you, you've seen it what, three times now? Four?"

Anne nearly laughed in his face. She probably would have, if the thought didn't make her want to puke all over the bedsheets. There was nothing *sublime* about Darlene. Not in the least.

"What the hell is she, Win?"

"She's my wife," Win said, sounding genuinely hurt by the question.

"You know what I mean," Anne said, feeling fear and fury shake her voice. "What the fuck happened to her to make her that way?"

"You know what happened," Win said, a conspiratorial glimmer in his eyes. "You opened the door, you held her hand as she was ushered across the doorway. She was called home, Annie. But you kept her here. You, and your momma, and Lis. You held her astride the threshold. And then you returned her to us, so much holier than she'd been."

Anne's stomach churned and threatened to empty itself again.

"I didn't make her into that. None of that is my fault. I was just a kid. I fell. You're the one who was fucking around with something you didn't understand. You led those people down into the lion's mouth. You're lucky nobody else died down there."

"Nobody died. You saw what happened as well as I did. Darlene was remade," Win said. There was a thread of steel in his voice that hadn't been there before.

Explosive rage roiled in Anne's chest, blasting up from her heart like a volcano. *Nobody died*. Where the fuck did this piece of shit get off, saying something like that to her of all people? Now more than ever, she wanted to stab the point of the screwdriver through his eye and deep into his brain. If it hadn't been for him and that hideous, shape-shifting freak that he called by his wife's name, Anne's life would have been completely different. Her mom wouldn't be dead. Every part of her would have been something else, someone else entirely. He'd stolen her whole life away from her, all in the name of his own want.

"People died, Win. A lot of people. Darlene, whatever the fuck that thing is, it killed my mom. It tried to kill me, more than once. Did you tell it to do that? Was that your plan? Send that fucking thing to kill my mom, kill me, kill anybody who got in your way?" The wrath was a living thing inside her chest, a city-leveling explosion just itching to be unleashed.

"I told you this already, Annie," Win said, his tone like an exasperated schoolteacher explaining something to a particularly slow student. "*She* was just trying to bring you home. What happened up at that cabin back then, what happened to you up there a few days ago and everything else since, it was just a big misunderstanding. I sent Darlene up there that night to fetch you two. Your momma's the one that had to make it personal." Win hung his head. "All I ever wanted was to bring you back home. To protect you. To help you. You and her. But Bev made her choices, just like always. That was her, though. Right up until the end. All action, no thought. Does that sound at all familiar to you, Annie?"

Underneath the thin cabin blanket, Anne curled her fists against the sides of her thighs and thought about how Travis had looked the second that bullet had cleaned out the shit between his ears. Win would get no better, if it was left up to her. She was going to kill this fuck if it was the last thing she ever did in this world. But it wasn't going to happen now. Making a move now wouldn't just get her dead, it would kill Gem and Dutch, too. She couldn't let that happen. If nothing else, they deserved better.

"That fucking thing—*Darlene*—" she said, spitting the name out like a mouthful of rotten food, "attacked me, Win. *Hurt* me. Look." She pulled her stitched-up arm out from under the blanket, raising it for the old man to see. "I mean, you guys stitched me up, but it still happened. It killed my friend, too. Up at the cabin. Did you know about that? You say you want to help me, how in the fuck did any of that shit help? Did you tell it to do that, or did it just go rogue on you? Huh?"

"That was . . . unfortunate," Win said, playacting remorse. "And I am so sorry that losing him hurt you like it did. But it had to happen. Your friend was wounded, holding you back. He was dying, Annie. Surely you understand that. Wasn't like you could go your own ways at that point. He was keeping you chained to a path that wasn't yours to walk. Darlene freed you."

The fury inside her fired brighter. Where the fuck did the old man get off, presuming to know whatever path was or wasn't hers? As if he were the sole authority as to who deserved to live and who deserved to die.

"I need you to listen to me on this, Annie, and really hear me, okay? Everything that you've been through, everything you've survived up until this point, it brought you back to us. To your home."

"Stop saying that. This place isn't my home," Anne snapped. "And you dragged me here. I didn't choose this."

"Home is where you're loved best," the old man said, shrugging. "It's where you can go no matter what, no matter how bad you screw up. It's where there's always a place for you. By my estimation, Cabot's the only place you've ever been that fits that bill, Annie. Doesn't matter how far you run, you'll always end up back here. You should know that by now. Darlene, she can find you wherever you go. She's got your scent burned into her. I believe she has since that night. You bled into the door, bled into *her*. I believe that connected you in ways you don't even realize. The only two that ever touched the other side and lived to tell the tale."

Except they hadn't. Not both of them, anyway. Anne remembered what she saw on the tape. She remembered the blood floating from her own hands and into that deadbright gullet, feeding it, splitting it open. She remembered the blurry writhing that lurked on the far side of that abyss, and she remembered Darlene Hofmann hanging in the jaws of oblivion, screaming bloody murder as her body was pulled apart and corrupted into a garden of cysts and tumors. Whatever the hell else Win's door had done to Darlene, it hadn't left her alive. The woman that had gone down into the mine that night was dead and gone, and even if the monster that had taken her place had spawned from her cancer-bloomed rot, it wasn't the real Darlene, and it never would be, no matter what line Win had somehow managed to sell himself.

"What are you telling me right now, Win? What the fuck am I here for? Why are you keeping us here? No more bullshit, okay? Just tell me."

The light crept back into the old man's eyes—just a small flicker at first, a tiny pilot light that quickly grew into a blaze.

"You're going to help us open up the door again," he said. "Just like before. And then all of us—including you—are going to walk the path of our divinity to be with the Lord in the next world. To claim our true salvation."

A wave of revulsion crashed through Anne then, as if her body were physically rejecting the crazy shit that was coming out of his mouth. She didn't want his reward, and she wasn't interested in his salvation. Not if it meant going down into that mine and staring into that dead eye in the rock again. She wouldn't. There was no fucking way.

"And what if I say no?"

His well-practiced magnanimity slipped at that, a hairline crack slicing through porcelain. As if he hadn't even considered the possibility of her not going along with his psychotic plan.

"I'm sorry, I don't think I follow," he hissed, his voice all oil and menace.

"I think you do," Anne said, clenching against the roiling in her stomach. "I'm not going to do it. Find someone else to open your door. Find anyone else."

"There is no one else. There's only you."

"How the fuck do you know?"

"You have no idea the lengths I've gone to, girl," he said. "Door sealed itself shut again after that night. Trust me when I tell you that we've tried to open it again. So many times, so many different ways. But none of it ever worked. None of it. Nobody. But then I saw you on the news, and I realized that we've been going about it all wrong. It's you. You did it before, you can do it again. No one else can."

His glittery eyes darted down to her hands, and the thick purple keloids carved into both palms. She caught his meaning almost instantly. It was the blood. Her blood. The crazy old fuck wanted to use her blood to try to open the door again.

"That sucks for you, then."

She knew she shouldn't have said it. But she couldn't help herself, either. She was so sick of the old man's crap, all his wheedling and rationalizing. He might have had everybody else up here fooled, but she wasn't fucking buying.

Win's expression buckled like a crushed beer can, and he stood abruptly, raising his hands to the sides of his head in an uncharacteristic show of frustration. His comfortable old mask of geniality, drooping just a bit too far down again.

She remembered how Win's younger self had looked at the end of the tape, the way he'd stood by exultant as his wife was consumed. The way he'd stared into that horrible hole in reality as if he'd never seen anything so beautiful. That was the real Winston Hofmann, she realized now. The zealot. The selfish maniac. He'd seen something on the other side of that door, and there wasn't anything in the world that was going to stop him from getting to it again. There was no reason to be found here, no rationale, no patience. Just the frenzied, desperate need of a fanatic.

"You don't know what it's like, seeing everything you've ever prayed for unfold itself before you and then having it ripped away

from you. You can't possibly understand the pain of having everything you've ever dreamed of within your grasp and then slipping
through your fingers," he said, his voice a furious whisper.

The anger inside Anne was like living quicksilver. Smeary images of her mom's face rose up from the roiling depths of her brain.
"Fuck you, Win. You don't have a patent on loss."

"And you're not the only one willing to do what has to be done
to set the scales to balance, *Annie*. You want to make this harder on
yourself, on your friends, that's fine by me," he said. "Just remember that you chose this."

He threw one last livid glare at her, then turned toward the door.

"Tobias'll be by in the morning to fetch you."

Then, without another word, he walked out and slammed the
door behind him. A second later, Anne heard the heavy clicks and
snaps of locks being fastened on the other side. Silently, she fished
the screwdriver out of her sock and swung her legs over the edge
of the thin mattress.

She'd hit a brick wall. No going around it. So she'd have to make
a hole and go through. But that was fine. She was good at that kind
of thing.

35

Anne was already up and waiting by the time she heard the thin rattle of keys on the other side of the door. She'd risen early, wanting to give herself as much time to get ready as she needed. Win had said that Tobias would be coming to get her, but he didn't say when. Standing in the middle of the little cabin space as the sun rose over the ridge, she stretched, starting with her wrists, then moving onto her elbows, shoulders, back, her midsection and the stitched hole in her side down to her hips, her knees, then her ankles. Seeking a sense of calm. A center. However this day turned out, it wasn't going to go like anybody—least of all Winston fucking Hofmann—had planned. Not if she had anything to say about it.

The door swung open to reveal Tobias standing on the porch, dressed in a fresh set of farm clothes under his shearling. The Leatherman was still on his belt, but he'd swapped the ranch rifle for a compact little pistol that sat on his opposite hip in a Velcro-strap nylon holster that probably cost all of twelve bucks at Walmart. Beyond his slight frame, Anne could see that the snowfall was really starting to pile up. It was going to be a full-on winter wonderland out there before too long.

"Good morning," Tobias said bashfully, stepping into her cabin as he brushed stray flakes from his sleeves and shoulders. She'd half expected him to come in here and try to play hard case so she'd stay in line or some shit, but there wasn't a trace of intimidation in him. He'd been told to come and fetch her, and like a loyal puppy, he'd followed orders. He carried a gun, but odds were good he never thought he'd actually have to use it. Anne almost felt bad for what was going to happen next.

"Ready to go?" he asked, face pulled into a polite—if tense—smile.

"Almost," Anne said. "Just gotta get my shoes on."

"Oh yeah. That's a good idea. It's really starting to come down out there. Luckily, I don't think the ceremony'll take too long."

Ceremony? What the fuck ceremony was he talking about? It didn't matter right now; she was sure she was going to find out before too long whether she liked it or not.

"Sure, whatever," she said. She met his eyes, then gestured to the far corner of the room behind the kid's back. "You mind handing me my shoes? Over there in the corner."

Tobias's smile grew, happy to help. "Oh. Sure. Of course."

The kid was sweet, but Christ, was he dim. He didn't even look down at her feet to see that Anne's sneakers were already on.

She was moving by the time he turned his back. She crossed the cabin in three long strides and threw her left forearm around his neck, yanking him back as she drew the screwdriver from her jeans. Both his hands went to her arm, trying to pull it away from his throat—until she planted the point of the Phillips-head at the corner of his eyelid and pressed it tight enough to hurt, but not enough to break skin. His hands froze. For a moment, the fight went out of him, and he went still in her arms, though she could still feel the tension and fear vibrating just underneath his clothes.

"Tobias, listen to me, okay? I need you to nod if you're listening. Now."

The kid nodded carefully, so to not lance his own eyeball on the screwdriver.

"Good. I'm not going with you. Understand? I'm leaving. Me and my friends, we're leaving. Now, there's an easy way to do this, and there's a hard way. The easy way is you shut the fuck up and play nice, okay? You get locked in here and you sit tight until we're long gone. The hard way is you make me use this screwdriver. Do you under—"

"No—no—!" the kid whined through gritted teeth, sounding as if he were on the edge of tears. His body went rigid for a moment as panic set in, and then he started to thrash. He wasn't exactly a big guy, but he was solidly built and outweighed Anne by fifty pounds or more. If he decided to hulk out, she wasn't going to have much choice in what happened next. But she still wanted to avoid that.

"Listen, okay? Just *listen*," she snarled in his ear. "I don't want to hurt you, okay? I don't. But you have to *hold still*—"

The kid wasn't holding still. He was windmilling against her, trying to pull away, wrest himself free from her grasp. Tobias threw himself forward, then back—too hard. They hit the floor in a painful, bone-raw heap, and all the air burst from Anne's lungs in a single, torturous gust as she was sandwiched between the kid and the hardwood.

A cold breeze blew in from the open door, raising sheets of gooseflesh across Anne's bare arms. Tobias was flailing like an upturned turtle. Kicking both legs forward, she locked her ankles around the kid's hips as she tightened her forearm across his throat. She didn't want to choke the kid out, didn't want to hurt him at all, she just wanted to hold him still.

"Tobias, *please*," she implored. *"Don't—"*

Then Tobias's hand went for the gun on his hip.

Mistake. Stupid fucking mistake.

Using her forearm to lever the kid's head back, Anne pistoned her arm and plunged the point of the screwdriver into the hollow of his neck, feeling metal pierce skin, muscle, and the tough sinew of his throat in a hard, rubbery *snap*. Blood burst from the wound, and the kid went rigid in Anne's arms as he started to make a wet spluttering noise like he was trying to scream but couldn't force it out. Gritting her teeth against the horrible sound of the kid's impending death, Anne yanked the Phillips-head from his neck and stabbed him again, punching the point in deeper than before.

Blood welled from Tobias's mouth and from the ragged holes in his larynx, pumping out in thick aortic throbs that spilled down over Anne's arms and onto the floor beneath them. The kid twisted and writhed in her arms, but Anne held him fast and brought the screwdriver down again, and again, and again. A thin, silvery whine rose in Tobias's chest, a frightened nasal warble that shimmered and trembled before dissolving into nothing as the kid shook and convulsed in her arms.

Please, please just die already.

She held on to him until the last muddy breath escaped his lips and he finally went limp. Unceremoniously, Anne shoved his dead bulk off her and rose, using her bare hands to squeegee the kid's blood from her forearms. Anne stared down at him as she bent at the waist and rested her red-smeared hands on her jeans, leaving bloody squid shapes on her knees. She kept her breath steady until her heartbeat returned to normal. Square breathing, *in one-two-three-four, hold one-two-three-four, out one-two-three-four, hold one-two-three-four.* She wasn't sure now where she'd learned that particular trick. Maybe Jessup had taught it to her once upon a time, back when she was still just a kid with little more than a gun and a whole-ass dinner plate on her shoulder, before she'd gotten her shit together and learned how to focus. She couldn't be sure now.

Another chill blew in through the door, and for a second, Anne could see little wisps of steam rising off the pool of blood underneath the dead kid. Tobias's visage was a mask of horror and rage and fear and confusion all mixed into one, his painful last moment of life frozen on his face. *Sorry, kid.* Kneeling down, she slipped the Leatherman and the pistol, a matte little Kimber Micro 9, from his belt, and left him there on the floor, screwdriver still lodged in his torn-up throat.

Outside, the morning was beautiful and blue-white and so unbelievably bright it was nearly blinding. Fat white flakes drifted down from the sky above. Holding one bloody hand above her eyes, Anne stepped out onto the cabin's front porch and looked up and down Cabot's single road, waiting for the sound of shouting, for Win's people to come running, armed to the teeth. But there was no one.

This could work. But she had to move, now.

Pulling the cabin door shut behind her, Anne scurried across the snow-laden ground, her footsteps crunching against the packed-flat snow as she stole through the silent little town toward the cabin where they were keeping Gem and Dutch and Murph and Joanie. She didn't know what Win had planned at this point, didn't know what fucking ceremony he had lined up or how he was intending to open that magic door of his, but she knew that none of them deserved whatever was coming next. Not even Joanie. There was no question in Anne's mind that she'd square up with her for turning backstabber eventually. They just had to get the fuck out of Cabot first.

Keeping low, both hands tight around Tobias's pistol, she dashed through the cold brightness, up the snowy road toward their cabin— and stopped dead in her tracks. The door was hanging open, letting heavy flurries of snow bluster in through the gap. It was dark inside, no signs of life.

A cold serpent of dread writhed awake in Anne's belly. That old familiar sense of impending danger, sharpened to a wicked edge over so many years. The key to making it in her line of work had always lain in knowing when to cut bait and walk away. If something felt off, it was off. If something felt wrong, it was wrong. And something felt very fucking wrong here.

Feeling her heart hum in her throat, she stepped up onto the creaky wooden porch and pitched her shoulder against the door-jamb to look inside. She didn't have to look too hard to see that things had gone wrong. The bunk-beds had been dragged away from the walls, the sheets snarled and discarded, the mattresses thrown across the little room. The thrift-store steamer trunks were in shambles: one was upside down while the other had been tossed haphazardly into the far corner of the cabin, its lid caved in, scattering the ground with jagged splinters of pressboard.

She pushed the door the rest of the way open and stepped through into the shadowy little space, trying to make sense of the chaos that she was seeing. There was a heavy spray of red decorating the edge of the nearest mattress and the floor beneath it. More blood on the inside doorknob, plus a few crimson finger-swipes on the wood next to most of a handprint. There'd been a fight in here. A bad one. The message was clear enough: Win had taken them.

In the center of the room, there was, inexplicably, a deck of plas-tic playing cards strewn across the floor, their faces glinting in the bright winter light. Anne knelt and saw that they weren't playing cards at all; they were driver's licenses. There had to be close to thirty of them here, maybe more. What the hell? Where did these even come from?

She gathered up as many of them as she could find and stuffed them into her pocket. Softly, a terrified mewling came from the far corner of the room. Murph. Anne's heart lurched behind her ribs and she tucked the pistol into her waistband, then got down on her hands and knees to search underneath the rubble for her cat.

She found him in the corner behind the upturned steamer trunk, curled up into a tight little ball, his green eyes huge and wide, the hair on his back standing straight like a ridge of pine trees. He yowled when he saw her, a pathetic little noise that telegraphed pure fear.

"Hey. Hey, it's okay. It's me, all right? Just me," she whispered to the tabby. She held out a hand in his direction, curled into a loose fist, their longtime signal for *no threat*, and waited. Cautiously, he rose to his feet and slunk over to her, first sniffing at her knuckles, then rubbing his whiskered cheek along the blade of her hand. She gently petted his face, reassuring him until he came closer, pressing the length of his body against her thigh, purring cautiously. She scooped him up and stroked his back until she felt him finally relent and relax, even if only a little.

Holding Murphy close, she rose to her feet again and looked around the tossed cabin for his carrier, finding it discarded underneath one of the bunk mattresses. She got Murph into the bag with one of the discarded blankets from the floor and zipped it shut. She slung its nylon strap over one shoulder, letting it hang crosswise around her chest, the carrier braced against one hip. That way, she could use both hands if she needed them. She sure as shit wasn't going to let Murph out of her sight again if she could help it.

She cupped her hands in front of her face and blew hotly into them before furiously rubbing them together, trying to return some heat into her thin digits. Behind her eyes, a quick to-do list pulled itself together:

Get Gem and Dutch and Joanie. Get your shit; get the Ninety-Eight. Get the fuck out of here.

It sounded a lot easier than it was going to be. But she really didn't have any other option at this point. It was that or nothing. So, squaring her shoulders, she checked the load on Tobias's pistol, then stepped out of the ransacked cabin and started up the snowy slope toward the church, and Win, toward his ceremony and whatever fresh hell lay in wait for her there.

36

The town had gathered outside the little chapel at the top of the hill and stood wrapped up in their winter warmest, arm in arm and deathly silent as they watched Win orate from the uncovered church porch. As she approached, Anne couldn't catch more than a few scant words, carried on the wind: *family, burden, sacrifice,* and *trespassers* were about all she could make out. On the old man's hip hung a long, curved knife that hadn't been there the night before. John and Norris stood behind him, faithful guard dogs, long guns slung over their shoulders. Darlene stood beside Win, wearing the same face that Anne had seen in the woods last night, the face that the icon had ripped apart as it made her into a fucking monster. On their knees on the edge of the porch, hands bound behind their backs and gags in their mouths, were Dutch and Gem and Joanie. Between the state of them and that fuck-off blade on Win's hip, Anne figured she could guess what came next.

Darlene saw her coming first, eyes brilliant in her dead mask of a face. She stirred hungrily as Anne stalked toward the crowd, but she didn't raise an alarm or say anything; shit, at this point, Anne wasn't sure if the hideous woman-thing could speak even if she wanted to, at least not with any kind of appreciable coherence. She knew how to say *Annie,* but the sound of it was so ragged and ugly that Anne had to guess that it caused a considerable amount of pain to do so. Whatever the reason, the shape-shifter was staying silent. For now.

Up on the porch—Anne was already starting to think of it as Win's *stage*—the old man was still performing, stomping back and forth behind his bound captives, waving his hands like some revival preacher. As she drew close, Anne could hear his words a bit better:

"—been waiting for this day for years, I know you have. I have, too. Decades, for some of us. We've struggled, fought, given so much in pursuit of this day. I know your hearts, make no mistake, and He does, too. You've all given so damn much of yourselves, because we know that sacrifice here, in this place, will be rewarded a hundredfold in the next world. We know that we are awaited, expected, and we will be reborn and remade into our true forms once we cross that threshold, just as my Darlene was. So rejoice, my friends. My *family*. I love you all so much. All your suffering is over. Our time is now. Your ascension is at hand."

At the back of the crowd, nearest Anne, someone gasped as they caught sight of her standing there, gun in hand, drenched head to toe in fresh blood. In a wave, every head in the crowd turned to stare at her, mouths agape, expressions unguarded and guileless. None of them dared speak too loud, but all of them whispered. They muttered prayers to themselves, buzzing softly behind the hands they clapped to their mouths, breathing pleas for protection and salvation as if they were anything more than wishful thinking. Nothing failed like prayer. Anne stood still before them, watching in case anybody decided to make a move. But no one did. These people were sheep, and they parted like the Red Sea, forming a perfectly straight path from Anne to the stage. Kneeling on the wood, Gem and Dutch thrashed and tried to scream out as the face of the old man looming above them pulled itself into a mask of confusion and unabashed rage.

"Annie Heller," Win called out, sounding so much calmer than he looked. Still orating, still performing. "Just what in the hell do you think you're doing?"

Behind him, John and Norris started forward, unslinging their long guns as if to intercept her, but Win stayed them with a raised hand. Beside them, Darlene was statue-still—except for her eyes. They pulsed and twitched in her face, predatory and all-seeing.

"I asked you a question, girl," the old man growled.

Anne nodded to the three people bound before him. "Let them go," she said. "We're leaving."

Win laughed—actually laughed—at that. "No, you're not. No. Absolutely not."

Anne blew out a thin stream of air.

"You don't think so?" she asked.

The old man shook his head. His eyes were cold slate as he studied her, the blood in her clothes, the gun in her hands.

"What happened to Tobias?" he asked.

Anne wasn't about to take the bait. "Let them go, Win. I'm not going to tell you again."

"You don't tell me *shit*," he hissed. "This is my town. My home. My people. Who the hell do you think you are, to march up here and order me around like some proud cunt?"

Anne raised Tobias's pistol, aiming it dead at Win's brain. She didn't say anything. She didn't have to. All around her, the crowd recoiled with a collective gasp, frozen in place.

"Transcendence requires sacrifice," Win said softly, daring. "There's not a man, woman, or child around you that thinks otherwise. We're all of us prepared to do exactly what we have to in order to ascend. Our consciences are clean. How about yours, Annie?"

"Stop calling me that," Anne growled.

"That's who you are, though. Whether you want to admit it or not. I *know you*, girl. Now put the gun down and let go of this ridiculous melodrama. It ain't gonna help you. There are so many more of us than there is of you. All you're going to do is get yourself hurt. These people, these sinners?" He jerked his head at the captives before him. His hand went to the knife on his belt. "You. Can't. Save. Them. They're dead, just like you. So what are you going to do, Annie? What choice do you really have in this moment?"

Anne ground the inside of her cheek between her molars and looked at the old man, remembering the way he'd cackled and reveled in that chaos in the bottom of the mine. The way he'd let his own wife get dragged into that void and how he'd let a little girl risk her life without lifting a finger to help. She didn't remember Win, but she knew him damn well. She'd known assholes like him her whole life. He was the kind of person who would let the world

burn down as long as it got him what he wanted. These poor cultists that he'd pulled into his orbit, his true believers, he'd let them
all suffer and die before risking his own neck. He was a coward
who used bodies and faith to insulate himself from any risk, any
harm.

And the thing was, he was probably right, too. The second she
tried to pull the trigger, everyone here would seize on her like a
swarm of rats. Not out of a sense of innate violence or some great
urge toward self-preservation, but out of obedience. Blind fealty
to their herdsman. They'd followed him this far, after all. They
all saw the bound captives on the stage same as she did, and not a
single one of them had spoken out against it. Broken, brainwashed
or both, it didn't really matter at this point. Win would command,
and the crowd would obey. They'd press her to the ground, rip the
gun from her hands, and then drag her down to the bottom of the
mine and bleed her dry to try to force the door open again. The old
man wasn't wrong. She was almost out of moves.

Almost.

Dropping her arm, she let the pistol hang down by her thigh,
still cradled lightly in one hand.

"That's better," Win said. "No need for this to be any more painful than it has to be."

She watched the snow fall onto the old man's head and shoulders, mossing them in white. The storm was going to keep going
for a while yet. Without looking, she dipped her free hand into her
pocket and slipped Tobias's Leatherman free, thumbing the short
pocketknife from the handle. There was no part of this that wasn't
going to suck, but she didn't see any other way out. Not now. Up
on the stage, Win's face scrunched up into an expression of amused
confusion.

"Now, just what are you planning on doing with that?" he asked.
"You gonna whittle me to death, Annie?" Still so superior. Still not
fucking getting it.

Anne threw an obvious glance over toward Darlene.

"Not exactly," she said.

Horrified understanding bloomed in Win's face as it finally connected inside his head. "Wait, no—!" he screamed.

But it was too late.

Inverting the Leatherman in her left hand, Anne slipped the blade underneath the stitches above her other wrist and jerked it upward, splitting the sutures with a spray of fresh, red blood. A trembling ribbon of pain shivered up her arm as the wound parted, the threads popping apart one by one by one, and as she yelped, she saw Darlene's eyes bulge, a wet, snarling growl rising in her trembling, monstrous chest.

And then all hell broke loose.

37

It happened in milliseconds, but it felt like an eternity.

Darlene's posture snapped and tightened, her back arching like a hungry wolf's as the rest of her body warped itself into impossible angles, sickening geometries, the monster underneath her dead mask forced to the surface by the scent of Anne's blood. Her head split apart along the corners of her mouth and folded back onto itself, revealing rows and rows of brown teeth and the bloodred gullet underneath. Her hands spread and distended, as if the bones were stretching and shattering under the skin. Her body was already starting to lose definition, the Darlene costume sloughing away, the wreckage of a ghost ship rent apart and dragged under violent waves. Darlene's eyes—milky blue before, Anne had been sure of that—turned pure white, so white that they glowed. How many times had Anne seen those eyes, in real life and in her nightmares? Too many to count now. Too many for any one lifetime.

Drawing breath, the shape-shifter turned its heinous no-face to the snow-filled sky and let out an ear-splitting shriek that made Anne's skull pound, the acid inside her stomach churn and froth. That sound, clamorous and cruel, shook a memory loose inside Anne's head—she'd heard it before, long, long ago, when she'd been that little girl she'd seen on the tape, desperately trying to pull Darlene from the mouth of oblivion with small, bloody hands. Inside his carrier, Murph yowled and hissed, scratching at the nylon mesh, trying to get away.

Beside Darlene, Win recoiled from the sound, arms raised as if to protect himself. As if he could. Fleetingly, Anne wondered how long it had been since Win had truly seen the thing that his wife had become, the atrocity that he'd let her be turned into all those years ago. She doubted he'd ever truly acknowledged what lay in wait underneath all her faces—if he had, he wouldn't have turned her into his pet hunter, after all. Changing from form to form and face to face, she was useful to him, a dagger hidden up his sleeve. But Anne had seen enough to know by now that beholding Darlene for what she truly was up close didn't square with his version of the story, the one that said that Win and all his people (but mostly Win) had been chosen by some higher power for some higher purpose. He didn't want to see how the sausage got made, he just wanted to eat until he was full.

Still standing in the middle of the stage, the old man, desperate to keep control of the situation, did the dumbest thing he could have possibly done in that moment—he got in Darlene's way.

Spreading his arms in a shaky Christ-pose, he darted forward into the thing's path. Anne heard him bark, *"No!"* at the slavering shape-shifter, but of course it didn't work. All Win's curated delusions of perfect control had flown to shreds the second Anne's blood had tasted fresh air. Effortlessly, Darlene swatted the old man aside as she charged blindly ahead, tearing past Gemma and Joanie, thrashing her claws in a vicious frenzy. Gem ducked out of the way just in time. Joanie wasn't so lucky—one of Darlene's claws glanced against the side of her face, and she hit the floor.

Darlene dropped to the snowy ground nimbly, like a gymnast, and surged through the gathered crowd, throwing bodies to the side, jabbering and snapping her hundreds of teeth, raking at the flesh that stood in her way with outstretched claws. Then, somewhere above the crowd, a gunshot punched through the air. The impact jolted Darlene's tumorous brute form forward as a baseball-size chunk of flesh was blown from high up on her shoulder. For a moment, everything went still. Up on the stage, Norris stood tall, or at least as tall as an angry bowling ball like him could be, rifle socked into the soft of his shoulder, smoke rising from the muzzle.

Darlene spun in place to face the little man, drawn from her frenzy for just a moment. The rifle kicked in Norris's hands, and another shot rang out, and then a third, rocking Darlene in place as blood and tissue flew off her deformed mass in gory sprays. It was all the time Anne needed. Pressing her bare hand to the bleeding hole she'd opened up in her own arm, she shambled back from the panicking crowd to the side of the road where the trees grew thick and pressed herself into the nearest shadow. Darlene whipsawed both arms out in a bloody blur and roared again as all around her the crowd screamed and scattered, bumbling back from the grotesque woman-thing, trying to make a break for safety. But it didn't help them. It wouldn't save them.

Confused, blood-frenzied, ravenous, Darlene tore into the wailing, thrashing bodies around her like a slaughterhouse chainsaw whirring through a side of beef, painting the snowy ground with sprays of bright crimson as ripped-off limbs and shreds of skin flew every which way, bodies torn apart in wild red flurries. Some sprinted uphill toward the trees, but most went the other way, careening through the snow down Cabot's single road, either straight on or weaving between the buildings and cabins. It didn't seem to matter much to Darlene. She followed the rolling wave of bodies at top speed, snarling and snapping, so light on her feet she barely touched the fallen snow at all.

Down the hill, deep in the town proper, there were more gunshots. More screaming. Darlene was a rabid wolf locked inside a double-wide chicken coop. It wouldn't be long before all that was left was a lot of blood and a few tattered feathers. For now, chaos reigned, but it wouldn't last. Eventually, Darlene would run out of bodies to tear apart and feed on, and then she'd catch the scent of Anne's blood again. Then she'd come running. Best thing to do about that was get hell and gone by the time it happened.

Unfolding herself from the shadows, Anne ran back up toward the church, past the ripped-apart bodies and the red-smeared snow. Win was missing. So were John and Norris. At the front of the stage, Dutch and Gemma were still on their knees, bound in place, screaming bloody murder behind their gags. It was only when Anne stepped up onto the wooden platform that she saw what they were seeing—what had become of Joanie.

She lay still on her side, unseeing eyes turned upward at the gray-white storm sky above, jaw wide around the knot of cloth in her mouth, frozen in a silent scream as she gasped for breath that wouldn't come. Her face was a mangled snarl of flesh, the skin and meat torn back from bone in a gruesome zigzag pattern. Anne had seen Darlene tag her as she tore past, had seen Joanie hit the stage out of the corner of her eye, but it hadn't clicked then how bad the damage really was. Joanie was still alive, but she wouldn't be for long, and judging from her wounds, whatever time she had left was certain to be pure agony.

Fuck.

Using the Leatherman, Anne cut Gem and Dutch loose and hauled them up to their feet, looking up toward the barn.

"Car's in there," she said.

Gem rubbed at her wrists. "Yeah. Probably our stuff, too. Wasn't anything in the old man's cabin."

"Okay, go," Anne told her. "I'll catch up. You all right?"

"No," Gem said. "But I'll live. You good?"

"No," Anne told her honestly.

Gem took her hand and gave it a reassuring squeeze, just once. Anne squeezed back, silently wishing she never had to let go of Gemma's lithe fingers, and proffered the best smile she could. Off to the side, Dutch was kneeling over Joanie's shriveled form, a frightened and heartbroken look on his face.

"She's not okay," he started, his voice timid and tremulous. "She's, I mean. What . . . what should we do about her?"

"I'll take care of her," Anne replied. "You guys go on ahead. Get to the barn, find our shit, and let's get the fuck out of here while we still can. I'll be along in a second. Promise." She held Murph's carrier out to Gem.

Gem took the carrier from her, understanding. "Yeah. Got it. See you in a minute."

She took Dutch by the elbow and pulled him off of the church porch. Anne watched them set off, then knelt next to Joanie. Her dark hair was fanned out around her head, soaking up her blood as it crept along the old boards. Anne wanted to hate her in this moment, but found she just didn't have the energy for it anymore. It didn't matter that Joanie had turned traitor and thrown in with Travis and Iris; it didn't matter that she'd burned them, tried to kill them over something as paltry as stupid fucking money. Nobody deserved to die slow like this, with their face half torn off, bleeding to death in the cold. Maybe there was a little mercy that Anne could spare her yet.

"Close your eyes, Joan. It's okay, I promise," Anne whispered to her, hearing the ragged panic staining the edges of her own voice. Darlene would be back any second, but there was no reason to be cruel. Not now. Not in this moment. With her free hand, she cupped the unwounded side of Joanie's face and held her gently. "Just close your eyes, okay? You're with your kids, and everything's okay. It's going to be all right now, I promise."

Slowly, Joanie's unseeing eyes slid shut. Her rib cage rose and fell unsteadily, her breaths coming in arrhythmic hitches and shudders. Softly, Anne brushed the blood-matted hair way from her forehead with one hand, then pressed the muzzle of Tobias's pistol against her temple. On the ground, Joanie moaned, just once, a pathetic, mewling noise. Anne bit back a sob of her own and mouthed a silent *I'm sorry*.

Then it was done.

Inside the barn, Anne's breath hung in front of her face in thick, steamy clouds as she rushed through, calling back and forth to Gem and Dutch as they searched for their things. Nearly ten feet off the ground, the Ninety-Eight loomed above it all on the old hydraulic lift, exactly as it had been before. Near the back, Gem and Dutch were ransacking Win's little workshop, breaking open cabinets and pulling out drawers, looking for any sign of their stuff.

More terrified wails floated in through the barn doors. She couldn't make out any of the words, but she didn't need to. She understood well enough. A moment later, a fusillade of gunshots pierced the screams, fading quickly in the moments before an explosion rocked the town, like a pipe bomb going off. Jesus Christ, somebody had shot one of the propane tanks.

Glancing over her shoulder, Anne saw a black finger of smoke rising from farther down the hill, lit with a sick orange glow from underneath. The smoke grew into two fingers, then three. The cabins had caught fire. Cabot was burning. Everything was going to hell. This was the kind of mess that even shitty, dead Travis would have been impressed by. They couldn't afford to waste it.

Moving quickly, Anne circled around the lift to the control knobs and pressed the big red button on the panel. With a gaseous *THUMP*, the hydraulics juddered and hissed, and the Ninety-Eight slowly began sinking toward the ground.

On the far side of the barn, Gemma used a rusty old tire iron to lever open another cabinet.

"Bingo!" she shouted.

Anne looked over and saw her hold Anne's backpack aloft, grinning victoriously. She set the pack on the smooth concrete and used her foot to slide it over to Anne, then pulled her own bag from the same cabinet.

Kneeling down over the pack, Anne unzipped it and went digging through its contents—cash, fake ID, burner, her Glock and spare magazines, it was all still here. Well, except for the VHS tape, but that was probably for the best. She could spend the rest of her life living happily if she never had to watch that video ever again. At any other time in her life, she would have jumped at the chance to have actual footage of her mom, exactly as she had been back in the day. But now? Knowing what she knew? No. She couldn't have all the pain and horror of the abominable things that happened down in the bottom of Ballmer's Hope poisoning the few good memories she still had of Beverly. So let Win keep it. Her mom was so much more than a few minutes on an old cassette, anyway.

Her hand found the grip of her Glock and snapped one of the mags home, then thumbed off the slide lock. The pistol's slide snapped forward with a wicked *clack*, and Anne slipped it into the waistband of her jeans at the small of her back. If they actually got out of here alive, she was really going to have to get a holster for the thing. She punched in the safety on Tobias's pistol and dropped it in the bag on top of everything else.

"Got the keys!" Dutch shouted from the opposite corner of the barn. "Here!"

With his good arm, he threw Jessup's key ring over to Anne in an underhanded toss—she stood and plucked them out of the air like she was catching a fly ball, then turned back around to find herself staring down the barrel of a gun.

"Don't you *fucking* move," Norris snarled at her, standing in the barn's double doorway, blocking the Ninety-Eight's path. His face was apple red against the gray, snowy day, his hair plastered to his face with sweat and blood. There was a pistol clutched tightly in both of his sausagey hands, a blocky, silver-and-black revolver. Steam billowed out of his mouth as his chest swelled and deflated in rapid time, in and out, in and out. He looked like he was about to have a coronary or a stroke or something. For a second, all Anne could hear was the thunder of her own heartbeat and the steady *drip-drip-drip* of the blood rolling over her fingers to dribble onto the concrete.

"Norris, what are you doing?" Anne asked, loudly enough to alert Gem and Dutch to his presence.

He gestured to the keys in her fist.

"Drop 'em," he wheezed. "Fucking *now*, I said."

Anne opened her fingers and let the car keys fall to the concrete floor with a silvery clatter.

"I knew you were trouble the first time I laid eyes on you, you vicious little *bitch*," Norris said, spitting the last word at her as he stepped into the barn. "I always knew, but Win . . . he wouldn't listen. Said you were *special*. Well, look what special gets you. Huh? Huh?!"

"We just want to leave. That's all," Anne said.

"That's not how it works!" he snarled. "You saw what happened out there! You know what you did!"

A cold wind blew through the barn, ruffling Norris's jacket in a swirl of flakes, but he hardly seemed to notice. His hands were shaking around the gun—from the cold, from the adrenaline dump, Anne wasn't sure, but it didn't really matter, either. This close up, he could have strapped his wrists to a paint shaker and still not miss.

"Now, back up," he said, gesturing with the revolver. "Slow."

Anne did as she was told, taking a step back, then another,

keeping her hands out to either side. Where the hell were Gem and Dutch?

"Norris . . ." she started.

"Sh-shut up," he spluttered. "Just shut the fuck up, okay? You don't get to talk. You . . . you don't get to do this to us. You don't get to take all this away from us, not like this, not now. It's ours, and we built it, without you, or your bitch mom, or that Bonny twat. It's fucking ours, and *you ruined it!*"

Anne hazarded a half step forward, moving slowly. In response, Norris took a step back—but he didn't shoot. Ever the fucking lapdog, faithful to his master's voice. Whatever Win was planning for her down in the bottom of that mine, it didn't include her getting her head blown off up here, no matter how much hell she'd managed to wreak in the past ten minutes, and Norris knew it. She'd clocked him for the asshole he truly was back at her mom's cabin, but he wasn't a fool. She had a feeling that if he really pulled that trigger, Win would flense the skin from his bones while he was still breathing.

"It's not yours, though," she said, forcing her voice to sound a lot calmer than she felt. "It's not yours, or John's, or anyone else's. Just like it wasn't my mom's. You knew her, right? Back in the day?"

Norris's big, watery cow eyes twitched with anger.

"Don't fucking try and talk your way out of this," he said. "You can't."

"And if you were going to shoot me, you would have done it already," Anne said, pressing her luck. "You've got me dead to rights here, Norris. I'm not going anywhere. It's a simple question. Did you know her, back then?"

He offered her the smallest possible nod of confirmation, a tiny jerk of his chin down toward his collarbone. "A little," he said.

"And you know what happened to her, right? What really happened to her?"

"Yeah. Maybe. Why? What's it matter?"

Anne took another step forward, spreading her fingers wide at her sides: *Nothing up my sleeves.* Norris took another step back, then a third, until he was standing even with the barn's big double doorway.

"It matters because she thought all this was hers, too. Because that's what Win told her. Just like he tells everyone." She was just guessing now, but they weren't exactly blind guesses. She'd heard enough of Win's bullshit by now to hit close to home, to make it count. "But it's not yours. It's not anybody else's. It's just his. Only his. All of this, all of you, he thinks it all belongs to him. He's no good at sharing. But I think you probably know that already. Don't you, Norris?"

The man swallowed, his Adam's apple bobbing and working in the center of his meaty, stubble-bristled throat. "It's not like that," he said. "He's not like that. You don't know him. He takes care of us. He watches out for all of us."

"He watches out for himself. And he lets all of you think he's doing you a favor. He sent you up here, didn't he? Just like before. Up at the cabin. Remember? That's what he does. He sends you and John to do his dirty work while he reaps all the rewards. Just like always. Doesn't sound like any of this belongs to you at all to me. Sounds like you belong to him."

"You don't understand," Norris said, taking one final step back, beyond the edge of the doorway. "You don't—"

To Norris's left, Anne saw a flash of motion from the other side of the barn doors—Gemma swinging the rust-flecked tire iron at the guy's head with both hands. She must have snuck out the back and circled around to get the drop on him.

Norris caught Anne's expression and twisted back at the last possible second. The tire iron went wide, missing his skull by a country mile as it whistled through the air—and came down on both his forearms with a hard, bone-ringing CRACK. The man screeched and recoiled, pressing one arm to his belly as if to protect it. Anne could see from the way it was hanging that Gemma had almost certainly shattered his wrist.

With his good hand, Norris snapped the butt of the revolver into Gemma's solar plexus. Gem gave a pained wheeze and dropped the tire iron as she stumbled back, clutching at her middle, all the wind knocked clean out of her. Norris raised the gun to shoot her—Anne started forward to stop him. The blocky little man wheeled around and stuck the gun in her face, eyes wild and furious.

"Fucking *don't*," he growled, his voice ragged with pain.

Anne froze in her tracks. Behind her, the thin hydraulic hissing ceased as the Ninety-Eight's tires finally came to rest on the barn floor, giving way to the sound of footsteps pounding on concrete. Anne didn't dare turn to look. Norris's eyes flashed over her shoulder and widened, delirious with pure, freezing hatred. His finger tightened on the trigger. Anne knew what was going to happen next.

Then someone grabbed her from behind and threw her to the side.

Somewhere far above her, she thought she heard Dutch scream, "*No—!*"

The sound of the gunshot punched her in the chest, and she crumpled up as she pinwheeled backward, thinking, *I'm dead, I'm dead, oh my god, I'm really dead—*

But as she fell, she saw Dutch there, frozen in midair above her, arms outstretched as if he were trying to catch a touchdown pass. She didn't realize what was happening until it had already happened.

The bullet caught Dutch high up on the forehead, and his body recoiled like he'd been hit by a car. He didn't make any noise, didn't scream or cry out; he just shuddered and fell to the ground like a popped parade balloon, boneless and rubbery as blood and flecks of brain fountained from the blown-open back of his skull.

They hit the ground together in a heap, a tangle of bent limbs and bad angles, Dutch splayed limply across the top of her, pinning her to the floor, blood pouring out of his ruined head. Over the ridge of his shoulder, Anne saw Norris standing in the barn door-way, revolver trembling in his hands. He took a step forward, then another, closing in to finish the job. Anne twisted under Dutch's deadweight, desperately grasping for the gun at the small of her back. Her fingers brushed the grip—almost . . . almost . . .

Then Norris was standing over them, glowering down at her.

"Fucking . . . fucking *bitch*," he groaned. "Gonna make you fucking pay . . . See if I don't . . ."

With his free hand, he took hold of Dutch's wrist and yanked him off the top of Anne, dragging him to the side. Dutch's dead-weight gone, Anne's hand found the grip of her Glock, and when Norris looked back at her, he was met by the dead-empty eye of the boxlike nine mil. He started, baffled, and a single word escaped his lips:

"Wait—"

Then Anne pulled the trigger.

The bullet erased half his face in a blur of red, ripping it apart from jawline to hairline. Reeling from the impact, Norris swayed in place, trying numbly to regain his footing, pawing at the mess with one hand, lowing like a cow. Tiny droplets of gore spattered across Anne's face and hands like gentle rain. Still supine, she shot him again, this time through the brain. Norris's head snapped like a speed bag. A cloud of blood coughed out of the far side of his head. Then he fell.

Anne let her arms drop and felt the back of her head *thwock* against the concrete. She stared up at the barn ceiling, heart drumming wildly in her chest as she huffed and puffed and tried to get her brain back under control. Then Gemma was there, kneeling over her with wide, concerned eyes. She said something that Anne couldn't hear; the words were muddled to blank static by the ringing in Anne's ears.

She heard herself asking, "What?"

This time, Gemma's words came through clearly.

"Are you hit, I said. Did he tag you?" Gemma's voice was calm and surgically direct.

Anne searched her own body for any pain, any new wounds, but there were none that hadn't been there a minute before. Dutch had taken the bullet, not her.

"No," she said breathlessly. "No, I don't think so."

Uneasily, Anne rose to her hands and knees and crawled over to where Dutch lay, hoping against hope that she hadn't really seen what she did, that the bullet had somehow done less damage than she thought. That his head would still somehow be intact.

But of course she was wrong. Dutch lay face up in a pool of his own blood and brains, limbs bent at awkward, unnatural angles, eyes wide and unseeing. The back of his head had been ripped away like the lid of a can, leaving only a gaping black hole behind. His skin had gone gray and pale in death, his eyes bulged out of their sockets, looking like rotting hard-boiled eggs. He didn't even really look like himself anymore—the essential topography of his face had been bluntly reshaped underneath his skin by the impact of the bullet. He was more like a Halloween mask version of himself now than the man she'd known.

"Anne, we gotta go," Gem said, pulling on her free arm. "Anne, *please*—"

Anne let herself be pulled away, but never once did she take her eyes off her fallen friend. The whole world had gone tumbling out of order. This shouldn't have happened. It wasn't fair. None of this was fair.

Inside the Oldsmobile, Gemma tossed Anne's backpack into her lap as she slid behind the wheel. Fitting the key into the ignition, she started the engine up, then, letting it idle, turned to Anne.

"Hey," she said. "Hey, look at me." Her words were muted and faraway, a distant radio broadcast from some far-off planet. "Anne. *Anne.*"

Gemma's hand flashed out and she slapped Anne hard across the face, just once. But once was enough. The pain was sharp and immediate, and it knocked the static clean from between Anne's ears.

"What the *fuck*?!" she roared, recoiling.

Gemma was unfazed.

"I know, okay? I know. I get it, I really do, but I need you cool," she said, her voice that same kind of lethal cold as before. "I need you here with me, and I need you cool. Can you do that or not?"

Anne felt the heat in the corners of her eyes threatening tears. Blinked them away. "I'm cool," she said.

"Are you sure?"

"No," Anne spat. "But I'm here. Good enough?"

Gemma studied her face for a moment longer. "Good enough," she said.

Gem dropped the Oldsmobile into drive and gunned it—the big sedan tore out of the barn, engine roaring, tires bouncing over something lumpy that Anne was distantly aware had to have been Norris's body. Good. Fuck him. He deserved that and so much worse.

Outside, the town of Cabot had descended into total pandemonium. Those black fingers of smoke from before had grown into a full-blown hand as the cabins burned and raged against the falling snow, the fire jumping excitedly from building to building. Underneath the smoke and flames, it was all bodies and blood. Everywhere she looked, she saw people stumbling between the buildings and along the side of the road, painted with soot and gore, clutching for limbs that were no longer there, trying and failing to hold in their insides with mangled, blood-slick hands. Parents cast their shrieking, red-faced children away to save themselves. Maimed bodies spilled from broken windows and fiery doorways.

Against one of the burning cabins, she saw a man sitting on the ground, head buried in his palms as if he were crying. But when he pulled his hands away from his face, his face came with them, the skin peeling off and hanging from his fingers in rubbery rags as he numbly tried—and failed—to press it back into place. Underneath the stripped skin, the man's skull was a mess of red, punctuated only by the white of his teeth and his wide, lidless eyes. His jaw worked open and closed at a staccato pace, and Anne could see the fat pink worm of his tongue hunting behind his teeth as he screamed or laughed or both. Anne's gorge rose.

The Ninety-Eight hurtled down the hill at the very furthest edge of control, bucking and weaving along the snowy road between the burning cabins and outbuildings. Gemma yanked the steering wheel this way and that, keeping the car from spinning out or leaving the road as desperate members of the Passage raced toward them, screaming to be rescued, to be carried out of this living nightmare.

"They're dead already," Gemma said, eyes fixed straight ahead on the road. "Either they'll get out or they won't. I don't really care."

For a brief second, Anne gawped at the lack of emotion in Gem's voice, the cold indifference to the suffering surrounding them, but it had only been minutes before that these fucking cultists had been standing silently by to watch her and Dutch and Joanie get executed. If these people wanted sympathy, they were barking up the way wrong tree.

Gem cranked the wheel and pumped the brake, fishtailing the Oldsmobile around a wide turn near the bottom of the town, then stood on the accelerator as the road straightened out again. The Ninety-Eight took off like a shot, charging ahead like a Sherman tank on meth as the fire on both sides of the road started to spread to the trees. The snowfall was keeping it at bay, but unless the storm got a lot heavier soon, the whole mountainside would be up in flames before too long.

Good.

Anne's skin hurt. Her eyes burned. The scars on her palms throbbed like they were threatening to burst apart into horrible, gaping wounds. Ignoring them, she twisted around in the seat to look out the Ninety-Eight's big back window for any sign of Darlene, watching the little town recede into the distance—

And suddenly, she was six years old again, buckled tight into the passenger seat of her mom's old Jeep as they fled the safety of the cabin, running from shadows in the middle of the night. Except now she knew what they were running from. Missus Darlene, her mom's friend that she'd known for years, was gone. They'd lost her for good in that sick, empty light burning on the other side of the stone. She had gone through and touched the other side, and the light had taken away everything that made her *Darlene* and replaced it with itself. A tiny piece of the ravenous, hateful infinity that lay beyond, grafted forcibly onto whatever was left of Darlene Hofmann.

And Annie was connected to it, too—by blood, by trauma, by the nightmare that they'd endured together. Darlene Hofmann was dead, and the thing that had taken her place would never stop eating. It would never stop killing. It would never stop hunting her.

She could have screamed. She might have screamed. And as Gemma barreled the Oldsmobile down the mountain, away from Cabot, back and forth through trees and rocks and drifts of snow, it was all Anne could do to hug her knees to her chest and cry.

38

She sat at the shadowy end of the musty old bar, nursing her fourth vodka tonic, pretending to not watch the news coverage on the streaky old TV mounted high up in the corner of the barroom. They'd been airing the story—the parts they knew, anyway—pretty much nonstop since that first day, when everything fell apart at the bank. Since then, the story had taken on a life of its own, somehow proving itself immune to the twenty-four-hour news cycle, with all its fresh outrages and bullshit social media gaffes. Maybe it was all the mayhem and dead people that did it, or the fact that by some minor miracle, none of the so-called perpetrators had yet to be brought in alive.

The dead ones, though? Oh yeah, everybody knew about the dead ones. In the span of less than a week, Cathy, Jessup, Merrill, and Travis had become prime topics of conversation among all the usual talking heads. Especially Travis. And they wouldn't stop showing his face.

It was an old mug shot, taken when he had a bit more hair and that dumb handlebar mustache he'd tried to make work for a year or so. Iris had hated that mustache. Trav had gotten pinched on a minor beef back then, a routine traffic stop that some asshole cop had decided to make into a whole thing, hauling him in on suspicion of drunk driving or some similar jumped-up charge. Trav had refused a roadside sobriety test, naturally, and the booking photo certainly hadn't helped his case any: unshaven, eyes bloodshot to glowing, skin pasty and swollen in the harsh white flash. There were a million better pictures of him out there, but of course they'd picked the worst one. It suited their narrative. Still, seeing his picture made her heart hurt, made her feel like crying until she screamed up a lung.

Raising her eyes to signal the bartender, Iris twirled a finger in a tight little circle: *Another round, if you please.* Screw it. She didn't have anything else to do today, so getting absolutely shit-faced seemed like a pretty great option. Iris knocked back the dregs of number four and slid the glass to the far side of the pine.

The TV cut to a commercial break. A last-known photo of some girl played across the screen while the words *MISSING WOMAN, ERIKA STELECK, REWARD FOR ANY INFORMATION* scrolled along the bottom. A second later, the news came back, now recounting the official report of the gunfight at the Pink Flamingo. Iris sighed and nodded her thanks as the bartender passed her vodka tonic number five. She really didn't need to hear any more guest-contributor analysis about what had happened at the diner. She'd lived through it. But just like the rest of their so-called expert coverage, these news assholes only knew part of what had happened that night.

She'd been halfway down the block when she'd seen those hippies roll up in their ratty old trucks, descending on the Pink Flamingo like flies on shit. She didn't know what they were doing there or what their angle was in all of this, but a few days after the fact, she was pretty sure they had something to do with Anne making it out of the diner alive. All the talking heads said the authorities were still on the lookout for Heller and Gemma both, as well as that guy they'd brought along with them, Greene, they said his name was. According to the headlines, the guy was apparently a cop, but . . . Iris wasn't so sure. He certainly didn't seem like a cop back at the diner. Maybe there was something she wasn't seeing.

Still. The fact remained that Anne was still out there, upright and walking around, which was a reality Iris Bulauer simply could not tolerate. Not after what she'd done to Travis. She hadn't even given the guy a chance. She'd just strolled up and blown his head off, no preamble, no warning. Iris couldn't let that go.

She took a long sip off the top of number five and kept watching the news until it switched over to another piece of the story, a report on the lonely old cabin where they'd finally found Jessup's body. Iris had seen this segment enough times on enough channels to figure that was where Anne had gone to ground after skating out of Durango. The reporters had been purposefully vague as to what the cops had found when they'd dug Jess up out of the dirt, but Iris could read between the lines. Whatever had happened to him, it had been way worse than the slug Trav had put in the man's belly. There was something else going on here.

The segment switched over again, now focusing on the lead-up to the bank job and the precious little the cops had found after scouring her and Trav's apartment. Anger boiled in her stomach, souring the vodka. Every time these news assholes told the story, they were shuffling the deck, telling it out of order, and every time they did, it somehow became a little bit less *hers*. Another piece of her life torn away from her. First the money, then Travis, now her own life story. It wasn't right, and it certainly wasn't fair.

Maybe she should go check out this cabin of Anne's, see what all the fuss was about. She might even get lucky and find something that pointed her in the woman's direction. No doubt the cops had been through the place three times over already, but they didn't know her like Iris did. Could be she'd hit on something they'd missed.

On the TV overhead, the screen cut to another mug shot: Iris's, and a spectacularly unflattering photo at that. The chyron on the bottom of the screen read, *WOMAN WANTED IN CONNECTION WITH BANK ROBBERY IN DURANGO.* She figured that was her cue to leave. So far, the barman hadn't once looked at her funny, hadn't even met her eyes in any kind of lasting way. Better she get out of here while that was still true than run the risk of him making the connection. Rising from the rickety old stool, she tossed a twenty and a ten on the bar top, drained the rest of number five, and walked out into the chilly daylight beyond. The bartender didn't look up as she went, and that was just as well.

IV

*Our Lady
of
Perpetual
Destruction*

39

They drove until the orange needle on the Ninety-Eight's fuel gauge buried itself firmly on E, then drove some more until it sagged past the bottom line. They were well and truly running on fumes now.

They'd burned down the slick mountain trail that led in and out of Cabot at top speed, slipping and sliding across the snow-caked dirt. The second they hit asphalt, Gemma had floored the gas and cut south as south could go, wrestling with the big blue sedan's wild forward momentum while Anne rewrapped her wounded arm and slumped in the passenger seat, trying to slow her racing thoughts. Every time she closed her eyes, she saw Dutch's face— not as it had been when he was alive, but in death: forehead caved in from the impact of the bullet, the back of his skull ripped clean off like the top of a soft-boiled egg, blood everywhere, getting on everything. One shot. That prick Norris had managed to squeeze off one shot before Anne had deleted him from the world, and Dutch, for whatever insane reason, had jumped in front of it.

Some part of her hated him for it. A bigger part of her was ashamed.

She hadn't asked him to do it, and she wouldn't have, given the choice. She was a big girl, and she'd learned a long time ago how to live with the consequences of her actions. Sometimes that meant making someone dead, sometimes that meant taking the hit she'd well and truly earned, without getting anyone else involved. Collateral damage was unavoidable, but if you were smart enough, you could at least try to minimize it. That was the reason—or at least part of the reason—that she'd so endeavored to keep her life small. Modest. Manageable. Other people did stupid things all the time. That was part of their whole deal. Expecting them to do otherwise was at best foolish, at worst blatantly fucking suicidal.

As far as Anne was concerned, the math was pretty simple: you didn't have to deal with people gumming up the works when there weren't any people around.

Norris had gotten the drop on her, outdrawn her, outshot her. The only reason she wasn't the one dead on the ground collecting snow in her brain-hole was that Dutch had made a choice. With Cabot burning and people dying all around them, he chose to take the bullet for her without thinking, without hesitating.

Anne hated him for that part of it more than just about any other.

Thinking back, she remembered how he'd looked, standing in her spartan little apartment, with that sad, disappointed expression on his face like, *Is this it?* It had pissed her off then—*How the fuck dare you judge how I live, cop*—but now, sitting in the passenger seat of the Ninety-Eight—*Jessup's Ninety-Eight*, she reminded herself, another dead friend to add to her collection—she saw that anger for the cover-up that it truly was. She'd never felt ashamed of the life she led before dragging Dutch into it, not once. But seeing it as he must have? Yeah, she understood a little why he looked disappointed. Pitying the smallness of her life. Shit, back at the cabin, he'd told her that he had family, didn't he? His sister and his niece. Kinsey, that was the girl's name. Some eight-year-old kid out there who'd never see her uncle Dutch ever again because he decided to jump in front of a bullet for someone who unquestionably did not deserve it. Kinsey'd be shattered into a million tiny pieces when she finally realized that he was never coming back. Another little girl growing up scared and confused and so much more alone than she'd ever been before. Anne's heart crumpled like a torn-out page thrown into a fire barrel at the thought.

She'd never bought into the two-point-five kids and a dog, white-picket-fence Americana bullshit fantasy this country still tried to sell its people. As far as she was concerned, shit was a myth of a myth, pure, undiluted vanity. But there was something there, some undeniable element that she hadn't ever really allowed herself to consider until now: the people. For years, she'd thought of others as a burden to bear, but maybe in reality, people were what built your life out, connected you to the world you lived in. Maybe people were what made a place to sleep and store your stuff into a real, actual home. Even if they pissed you off sometimes and did stupid shit that broke your heart.

She wasn't sure precisely when Dutch had gone from *hostage* to *accomplice* to *friend*, though she knew that it must have happened at some point. She just hadn't been looking for it—what reason did she have to look? In a moment of panic, she'd dragged the man—a cop, no less—off the street at gunpoint and thrown him into the deepest end of the crazy pool without a second thought. She'd blown his whole life up, burned him with the cops, forced him to abandon the people that loved him and the life that he'd built brick by brick. But against all odds, he'd kept up somehow, even held his own. Helped when he didn't have to. Which meant that he must have seen something in her worth helping. Worth saving.

And it had gotten him killed.

She had gotten him killed.

Underneath the hood, the Ninety-Eight's big V-8 engine chugged and coughed, rumbling against itself. Sounded like even the fumes were running out now, too.

"Look."

Anne followed Gem's gaze out the windshield. Through the swirling squalls of snow, maybe half a mile down the road, she could see a lonely little two-pump filling station on the mountain side of the blacktop. Out front, a single streetlamp lit the white-blanketed lot up in a weak yellow cone. There was only one car in the lot, probably the proprietor's—nobody else was fool enough to be out driving around in this shit.

"Think they're open?" Anne was amazed at how bone-tired her own voice sounded.

"I mean, if they're not, we're screwed," Gem said, and popped on the turn signal.

Carefully, Gem steered the Oldsmobile into the station's modest little lot, gently toeing the brake pedal down until the sedan rolled to a stop next to the pumps with only minimal ice-skid. Throwing it in park, she twisted the key out of the ignition and turned in her seat to look over at Anne. Staring out the glass at the snow falling steadily all around them, Anne pretended not to notice.

"Hey," Gem said. "Hey. Heller."

Finally, Anne looked over at her. "What?"

Gem's eyes were wide and worried in the reflective glare of the snowfall. She reached a hand out for Anne's, braiding their fingers together and squeezing.

"You holding up okay?"

Anne scoffed, letting the question hang in the air. Gem should have known better than to ask her that shit right now. But she didn't let go of her hand, either.

"No, really not. Are you?"

"I mean, no," Gem replied. "But here we are anyway, right? Nothing to do but keep moving. Just gotta gas up first. You have any cash that's not in the trunk?"

Anne jerked her head toward the back seat, where her backpack sat beside Murph's carrier.

"In my bag," she said. "Envelope in the front pocket with the burner. Take whatever you need."

Gem released Anne's hand and arched her back to lean over the bench seat and grab the backpack. Holding it in her lap, she unzipped the front and pulled out a pair of wadded-up twenties, then set the bag aside.

"Thanks. This won't take long, all right?"

Anne nodded, but didn't say anything else.

"You going to be okay in here?" Gem asked, her tone measured, gentle.

Anne caught her meaning. She wasn't really asking, *Are you going to be okay?* She was asking, *Do I have to worry about you right now?* Anne could hardly blame her for that. She'd have done the same if the tables were turned. Except she probably wouldn't have been nearly as tactful about it.

"Yeah, no, I'm good," she said.

Gem gave her a skeptical look that said in no uncertain terms that she didn't buy it.

"You sure?"

Anne met her eyes and held her gaze for as long as she could. It was harder than she expected, but somehow she managed it without blinking or looking away.

"I'm good, Gem. Promise. I'm all right."

Gemma looked at her for another lingering second.

"All right," she said. "Good. Great." She snapped her fingers. "Shit. Here."

Gem dug in her pocket and held out a folded rectangle for Anne to take.

"Found this in Win's place last night. Figured you might want it."

Carefully, Anne plucked it from Gem's fingers. It was a photo. She set it on the dashboard, then met Gemma's eyes again.

"Thanks," she said, unsure of what else to say.

"Sure. I'll be right back, okay? Couple of minutes."

"I'm not going anywhere," Anne told her. "Promise."

"Okay. Good."

Gem pushed the door open and stepped out into the snowfall, knocking the door shut behind her with a practiced snap of her hips before dissolving into the flurries. A minute later, Anne heard the squeak of the gas cap being removed and the steady *glug-glug-glug* of the tank filling. She unbuckled her lap belt and turned around in her seat, leaning over the bench to get a look at Murph. The big brown-gray tabby was curled up asleep in his carrier, purring softly as if he didn't have a care in the world. This cat was so much tougher than Anne had ever given him credit for. So much more resilient than Anne herself. She unzipped the top of the carrier just enough to slip a hand inside, and scratched at his cheek with her fingertips. Rousing briefly, Murphy pressed his face against her knuckles, then meowed, rolled over, and went back to sleep. Sweet, entitled, perfect little shit that he was. Anne zipped the carrier closed again and turned to face front, looking at the folded photo on the dashboard.

She unfolded it and smoothed it out against her knee, then held it up to examine it in the light. She recognized her mom straight away, grinning in a woven sun hat and a silver necklace, her tanned, freckled arms wrapped lovingly around little Annie; beside them stood Aunt Lisa, a beautiful woman with long silver-white hair and tattooed hands adorned with stacks of rings. Anne recognized her as the same woman who'd been behind the camera in Win's video, who'd tried to help Anne and Beverly pull Darlene back from the maw of oblivion.

Speaking of Darlene, there she was, one place in from the far left-hand side of the photo, beaming arm in arm with Win. It chilled Anne to see her in this picture, after what had happened up in Cabot. John was there, too: younger, with more hair, his body less slumped and hollowed out by worry. Win, Darlene, Beverly, little Annie, Aunt Lisa, and John. All six of them standing in the sun, happy as happy could be. And behind them, a massive gate with a wrought iron sign at the top that read, THREE-STAR CATTLE RANCH. There was a logo below the words, three interlocked stars. Anne turned the picture over and over in her hands, looking on the back for any kind of annotation, but there wasn't any. Just the yellowed, faded photograph.

Some part of her wished she remembered it—some of it, any of it. She'd gotten the occasional flash here and there, a fleeting spark in the shadows, but everything before that night at the cabin was still all fog. She studied the faces in front of her, searching her memories for any trace of this moment. They all looked so happy, perfectly ignorant of the bloody hell that awaited them only a few months in the future. All those nightmares yet to come, still unrealized. Lucky them. Poor them.

Some stubborn part of her had long believed that her mom had just been crazy, and that Beverly's particular brand of insanity had somehow infected her young daughter, corroding Anne's memories of that last night they had together. The dead-white eyes in the dark had to have been a hallucination, some folie à deux or something, right? There was no other explanation. But now, after everything she'd seen and lived through, she knew better. She'd witnessed it firsthand. There was plenty of crazy to go around in-side the Passage of Divinity, but none of it—no more than her fair share, anyway—had belonged to Beverly Heller.

Had Win always been the man she'd seen standing above the crowd, his madness so cold and megalomaniacal? Anne figured that in some way, sure, he probably had been. Maybe it hadn't always burned with the same ruthless intensity, but nobody became some-body, some*thing*, like him on accident. She studied that wild glint in his eyes in the photo, same as it had been standing right in front of her, same as it had been in the video, and it was all the proof that she needed. He'd always been some version of the monster he'd be-come. Everyone else in this photo, up in Cabot—shit, in the whole wide world—they were just grist for the mill of his plans.

There was something about the photo, though. Something in-tensely familiar that Anne still couldn't place. It stuck in her brain like a fishhook. What the fuck was it?

She scanned the faces again, searching for any glimmer of a hint, finding none. So if it wasn't the people, then it had to have been something else. Judging from the telltale vastness of Blanca Peak in the background, the photo had definitely been taken in the valley, probably not too far from here, either. But Anne had grown up in Blanca's shadow—it had haunted every horizon and every dream she'd ever known. What was one more photo? The Passage of Di-vinity was San Luis Valley homegrown, coming up in Crestone, cult central itself, before migrating into the deeper valley hills in search of something greater. It only made sense that whatever pic-tures and relics the Passage left behind would come from the valley, too.

Okay, so not the people, not the mountains. That left . . .

The gate. The stars.

That logo, that ranch brand with its three interlocked stars ren-dered in wrought iron, Anne had seen it before. She was sure of it now. It was familiar, but in a faraway, dreamy way, something no-ticed and immediately set aside for later, only to end up forgotten and collecting dust on a shelf. Where had she seen that star pattern before?

Then, all at once, it came back to her: the letter. Aunt Lisa's letter. The woman had scribbled a rough version of that same emblem at the bottom of the page she'd left behind for Anne at the cabin. In her exhaustion and turmoil that first night, Anne had seen the stars drawn at the bottom of the letter and thought that they were just some doodle. The letter itself hadn't fit with the rest of the day, hadn't made sense or added up to anything then, so why would she have paid attention to a few hastily-drawn scribbles?

Feeling her heart quicken, Anne pawed at her backpack with numb fingers, unzipping the front-most pocket to pull out Lisa's letter. She unfolded it and laid it on her lap beside the creased photo, and read through it again:

> Annie,
>   If you're reading this, you need to get out of here as soon as possible.
>   The cabin isn't safe. Watch your back, and don't trust anyone.
>   The Passage is everywhere.
>
>   — Aunt Lisa

Lisa had been trying to warn her from the start. About Win, about Darlene and the Passage, about everything. The stars at the bottom weren't some doodle—they were directions. They were an invitation.

Stuffing the letter back into the bag, Anne threw the car door open and stepped out onto the asphalt, turning her shoulders against the blowing storm. Outside, the snow was finally starting to let up a little, and from where she stood, she could just make out the soft drab-white swell of the Great Sand Dunes and Blanca's towering blade edge, splitting the low clouds like a dagger. Comparing the Blanca before her to the one in the photo, Anne saw that she'd been right on the money before: the angle wasn't that different at all. Wherever the picture had been taken, it couldn't have been that far from where she currently stood.

Near the back of the car, Gem crossed her arms against the cold as gasoline pumped steadily into the Oldsmobile's tank. She gave Anne a curious look.

"Hey, you okay?" she asked. "Anne?"

Anne jerked her head toward the station's shopette, old neon signs hung in its barred-over windows.

"Anyone in there?" she asked.

"Just the old-timer who runs the place," Gem said. "Why?"

"Give me a minute."

Anne crossed the lot in a few quick strides, kicking blusters of snow into the air with each step. The shop's door rang as she pushed it open, the brass bell mounted high on the jamb a tarnished relic of days gone by, just like the man jockeying the register. Weathered and sun-beaten even in winter, the guy's face was a road map of wrinkles and veins drawn around a weary smile that seemed practiced, if not entirely genuine. Judging from that smile and the oil-stained coveralls that hung off his beanpole frame like a flag on a windless day, he'd been working this place for a long time. Exactly what Anne was hoping for.

"Help you?" the guy asked, giving her a look that was somewhere between *curious* and *freaked out*. Anne didn't blame him; after everything up in Cabot, she was sure she looked a full-on horror show. But she got the sense that way out here in the sticks, this guy had seen plenty worse than her roll through without batting an eye.

She laid the photo down on the tacky old counter between them and turned it around for him to see.

"Yeah, I hope so," she said, and tapped a finger against the star brand in the picture. "You ever see something like this before? This logo?"

With tobacco-stained fingertips, the old-timer slid the photo up off the counter and held it in front of his face to get a closer look, squinting.

"Oh yeah," he said after a second. His voice was rough with age and cigarettes, but not unkind, not guarded. He handed the snap-shot back to Anne. "Sure. That's the brand for the old Three-Star Cattle Ranch, but I'm sure you got that from the words on the gate. Used to be the Three-Star was one of the biggest cattle operations in the valley."

"Used to be?"

"Yup, just as you said. Used to be. Time was, ranch was run by old Ruston Bonny."

A piercing shiver corkscrewed through Anne's chest, hearing that name. Unbidden, Win's voice floated up through her memory: *Lisa Ray Bonny was one of your momma's best friends, back in the day.*

"You said Bonny?"

"Oh, yeah. Place was Ruston's for years before he finally took ill. Daughter of his took over operations for a while after that, until the fire."

"Wait, what fire?"

"*The* fire," the old-timer said. "Whole ranch burned down some twenty-odd years back. Bonnys lost everything, including, I think, something like eight hundred or so head of cattle? A thousand, maybe? It was all over the news back then."

"Where was it? The ranch, I mean."

The old guy shrugged and pointed a single tobacco-stained fin-ger out the musty window.

"About fifteen miles up the highway, I reckon. Maybe twenty. Just keep going the way you were going, then down County 417 a ways. Can't miss it, really. But if you're thinking about heading that way, I wouldn't much bother, if I was you. Nothing left up there. Just dead trees and dead cattle and a lot of bad memories."

Anne folded the photo back up and pocketed it.

"Bad memories don't faze me," she said. Dutch's face—

both sides blown wide open, eyes crossed, scleras soiled with inkblots of blood, mouth agape, jags of broken bone poking through torn skin, a halo of pulped brains spilling out from the underside of his skull

—flashed across the backs of her eyes again, followed closely by Darlene's revolting lotus maw, Jessup's ruined body, Tobias's stabbed-apart throat, and that horrible ghastly light at the bottom of the mine.

"I've got plenty of my own," she finished.

On the other side of the counter, the old-timer gave her—and her blood-crusted clothes—a questioning once-over and shot her a look that was at once understanding and pitying. Almost fatherly.

"Don't we all," he said. "Whatever you end up doing, just be safe out there, okay?"

"I'll do my best," Anne said as she walked back out into the storm.

Once they were on the road again, Anne explained the plan—what little plan there was to speak of—to Gemma.

"This is thin," Gem said, not taking her eyes off of the snowy highway ahead. "Like, real thin. Wafer thin. Paper thin."

"I get how it sounds," Anne told her. "But it's the only solid lead we've got right now. I know it's not much, but she wanted me to go up there. That's why she left the letter." She held it up, displaying the stars at the bottom. "That's why she drew those."

"As compared to just, I dunno, maybe just saying it? Giving you an address, or a map, or something? Literally anything other than this cryptic guessing-game shit? Like, come on." Gem rubbed at her face with one hand, frustrated.

"I don't know," Anne told her. "Maybe she was trying to keep a step ahead of Win, in case somebody from the Passage found the letter first."

"Right, sure, but do we know if she wrote it before or after this ranch of hers burned to the ground?"

Anne laid her hands on her knees and shook her head. "No," she admitted.

"Yeah, that's what I thought. Come on, this is a long shot, and you know it."

Gem wasn't even bothering to mask her irritation or skepticism right now. And Anne had to admit, she had a point: it was thin. If the old-timer was right, the Bonny ranch had burned down a couple of decades back. Whatever her so-called aunt Lisa wanted her to find up there, odds were good that it was long gone by now.

But she still had to try. After Cabot, after Win and Norris and Darlene and Tobias and Dutch, they were fresh out of options, and if Anne were really being honest with herself, she knew none of this was over. Not by a damn sight. Not with Win and his pet monster still running around out there, trying to find a way to break through to that other place. At the very least, the Bonny property was somewhere for them to go to ground while they figured out their next move. Even if it was as abandoned as the old guy had said. Hell, especially if it was abandoned. It was better than all the nothing they had right now, and Anne told her as much, trying to sound a lot more reasonable than she felt.

In the driver's seat, Gemma sighed and curled her grip tighter around the steering wheel, making the knuckles on both her hands stand out like sharp mountain ridges.

"Fine," she said. "But after this, I'm pushing the Godzilla button. Okay? We do this, and then we get the hell out of the valley for good. Agreed?"

Anne nodded. "Yeah. Agreed."

40

The Oldsmobile's grille shredded another snow-heavy tumble-weed, sending dry, grassy scraps and wet flurries flying over the hood and windshield as the sedan slid around another long, winding bend in the road. The storm had let up some by the time they were a few miles out from the filling station, but the cold outside was bitter enough that the accumulation wasn't going anywhere soon. The trip down the highway had been dicey, with the Ninety-Eight threatening to spin out at every barest hint of a slick patch, but once they'd turned onto the wide gravel divot called County Road 417, the drive had turned outright treacherous.

The road started off flat but quickly turned to a steady upward incline, leading into a cluster of rocky foothills that were a whole lot steeper than they looked. Under the Olds's long, heavy frame, it felt like the rough, unpaved road had already frozen over hard, the tires spinning and grinding against the ice and snow in a white-knuckled struggle to maintain forward momentum. Behind the wheel, Gem was handling herself—and the car—admirably, working the steering wheel like a racecar driver, deftly keeping the big four-door on the road no matter what. She kept her foot steady on the gas pedal, goosing it or backing off as necessary, but this boat wasn't ever meant for winter transport, and under the hood, it was clear that the old engine was flagging. They'd been creeping up County 417 for what felt like an hour already, and despite the cold, her lack of waterproof shoes, and the fact that she had no idea how much farther there was to go, Anne was starting to wonder if the smarter move at this point was to just get out and walk.

The sedan skidded around another icy curve, and its quad high beams illuminated an old aluminum sign planted on the side of the road, the words THREE-STAR CATTLE RANCH still visible despite age and wear. Underneath the words, a single arrow urged them forward.

"Well, that's encouraging, right?" Gemma asked, but it was clear she wasn't really interested in an answer. Every ounce of her attention was still trained on the car and the road and on keeping the former safely atop the latter.

"Here, give me your gun," Anne said.

Gem shrugged and removed one hand from the wheel to slip her High Power from her pocket, then passed it over to Anne. Anne took it from her and laid it across her knees, then dug in her backpack for Tobias's compact little Kimber.

With steady, practiced hands, she pulled the pistols apart and put them back together, making sure they'd work as well as possible, if it came to that. Silently, she chided herself for not thinking to grab a cleaning kit or at least a bottle of gun oil or something back at her apartment. She wasn't sure what—if anything—waited for them up at the derelict old ranch, but after everything, she wasn't prepared to take any unnecessary chances. Stealing a look over at Gem, she figured neither of them were.

Satisfied that the guns would work if they needed them, she passed Gem's High Power back to her, then stowed the Kimber back in her bag and turned her attention out the window, studying the landscape as they prowled steadily through it. Rocky hills had given way to more rocky hills as County 417 led them back and forth in a switchback pattern that reminded Anne of the winding approach to her mom's cabin. Formerly one of the biggest cattle operations in the San Luis Valley or not, the Bonny ranch was certainly well isolated from the rest of the world. Maybe that was the point, better suited to keeping your herd together or something. Or maybe not. Anne didn't know shit about cattle ranching, and she kind of doubted that was going to change any time soon.

On either side of the car, scraggly clusters of dead trees dotted the hillsides, their leafless branches scraping idly at the gray sky above. On the ground, tiny tufts of lifeless grass crept through from under the snow's blanket, sickly yellow lesions marring the

otherwise untouched landscape. Everything out here was dead.
Had been for a long time.

"Jesus," Gemma gasped as they rounded the last bend.

Anne followed her gaze and felt her own jaw drop.

Just ahead of the car stood the gate arch from the photo, its tall
post-arms half rotted away by time and weather, the words THREE-
STAR CATTLE RANCH mounted across the top in beaten, rusted
wrought iron. Below the words sat those three interlocked stars,
same as in the photo, same as in Aunt Lisa's letter. But it was what
lay beyond that really took Anne's breath away.

The Bonny ranch was still standing, or at least what was left of
it was. Somehow. Blackened beams and posts rose sharply from
the snowy ground, no longer the buildings that they'd once been
but now only the faintest suggestion of building-shapes, the after-
image of a photo flash burned on the backs of your eyes long after
you'd said *cheese*. Ghosts of ghosts, memories of remembering itself, the details too vague and blurry to make out unless you knew
what you were looking for.

There had been half a dozen buildings up here, once upon a
time. Anne couldn't guess at what they'd all been exactly, but it
was probably a safe bet that there had once stood a house, a barn
or two, a couple of stables, maybe even a silo. Now there was nothing. Just scorched bones poking out of the snow.

As they drew close, Anne felt a wave of alien nostalgia rise up
and crash over her, dragging her down. She'd been in this place before, she knew she had, even if the memories themselves wouldn't
come. It wasn't just her face in that photo from long ago, either.
This place, this ranch, it was familiar to her in a way that reached
all the way down to the bone. But where there had been life before,
purpose, structure, now there was just wasteland.

"Are you seeing this?" Gemma asked breathlessly.

Anne saw. Beyond the blackened remains of the farmhouse and
its outbuildings, the ranch grounds were a ruin—dead, burned
trees like spears planted in the ground commingled with new
growth, a charred forest that reached back and back and back into

the low, rolling hills. For a moment, Anne could see the fire that the old-timer had told her about, an out-of-control blaze tearing its way through the Three-Star Cattle Ranch, churning and devouring.

Gem eased the Ninety-Eight to a halt beside the biggest cluster of scorched posts—Anne immediately and for no reason started to think of it as *the farmhouse*—then threw the transmission in park and killed the engine. With the reassuring rumble of the big-block V-8 gone, the gray afternoon went curiously, uncomfortably silent around them—there were no signs of life up here, not even the gentle rusk of the wind over the ground. They'd wandered into a forsaken place, somewhere no other living thing dared to tread. Even the saplings and shrubs seemed twisted and feeble, as if the fire that had cleared everything out had poisoned the ground, too, turned it sour and salted. The Bonny ranch was a lacuna, a dead spot on the map, a chilly oblivion unto itself. There was no sign of the thousand dead cattle that the old man had mentioned, but maybe that was for the best. Last thing Anne needed right now was to go tromping through a field of bones.

"So what now?" Gem asked, her voice shot through with trepidation.

Anne shrugged. "Get out and take a look around, I guess. See if there's anything left, any sign."

Gemma threw her a look that made it clear how low she set the odds of finding anything, but she didn't argue. Twisting around on the bench seat, Anne leaned over and made sure that Murph was okay in his carrier—they'd been running the Oldsmobile's rattle-trap heater full blast since they'd left the filling station, so no doubt he'd stay warm in here for hours, not that Anne planned on sticking around that long. Searching the ranch grounds at this point was a last-ditch move, and she knew it. Even if Aunt Lisa had left something behind for her once upon a time, that had been twenty-five years and at least one deadly, catastrophic fire ago. Time wore on, just like time always did. Thinking it would do otherwise was just choosing foolishness. Still, they'd come this far. Might as well see it through.

Gem was first out of the car, circling around to the back of the

Oldsmobile and popping the trunk to sling Anne's Remington over her shoulder. Bundling up in her coat, Anne followed her out into the freezing afternoon, and together, they started poking around the ruins of the ranch, running their hands along the burned posts, walking straight lines in the snow, tracking the corners and the imaginary angles of the buildings that used to be there. Nothing of consequence remained, but still Anne searched, telling herself that there had to be something, some sign or indicator, some crucial piece of the puzzle that would make it all fall into place. She searched until the cold stole the breath from her chest, until her fingers and toes went numb. She must have walked the perimeter of the farmhouse five times before moving farther out, to the bones of the barns and the silo and the stables or whatever these buildings once had been, finding them all burned beyond recognition, devoid of detail beyond the char.

The fire had taken everything.

Was this all there was? Really? Feeling the snow creep through her shoes and into her socks, Anne tried not to believe it. There was no way.

But slowly, steadily, hopelessness settled into her chest like a fist squeezing her heart, and nearly an hour after they'd stepped out of the Olds, Anne was ready to go. This place was a dead end, and that was it. Best thing for them to do at this point was to get the fuck out of these hills, head to the Happy Trails Motel for the other half of the cash, then set out for New York and never look back. She could maybe work part-time tending bar somewhere. Gemma could get a job in IT or something. She was so smart, after all. They could get an apartment. Nothing fancy, just something small that would be enough for them and Murph. Anne thought that sounded just about perfect.

But then, standing in the ruins of the old Bonny place, Gemma paused midstep and turned her face toward the sky, taking a long, deep inhale through her nose. She looked over at Anne.

"You smell that?"

Raising her face to the sky, Anne sniffed but didn't detect anything out of the ordinary. Just the same cold winter air they'd been breathing for the last hour. Except—there was something there, wasn't there? A faint, smoky richness that she hadn't noticed before, floating atop the breeze like mist dancing across the surface of a still lake.

"What is that?" Anne wondered aloud.

Gem's face split into a surprised little smile, her eyes brightening. "Food," she said. "Someone's cooking."

They followed the smell deeper into the hills, where the burned-out trees grew thick and dense, their scorched trunks so much closer together than they'd been around the farmhouse and outbuildings. There was no new growth this far back, no saplings or shrubs poking through the snowfall, punctuating the destruction with little flourishes of yellow and pale green. Out here, it was all black and white, and the farther they pushed into the immolated forest, the more it seemed like black was winning.

Still, the farther in they went, the stronger that scent grew, until it seemed as if they were right on top of it. That was when Anne saw it—a hundred yards ahead, parked in the middle of a stand of burned pines as if it had grown there of its own accord, was a Winnebago motor home. The thing was old—easily a couple of decades out of date by Anne's estimation, the windows scudded over with filth, the paint on the sides faded and peeling off in stripes. It might have been the snowfall, but even the tires looked, well, tired, either long deflated or sunken deep into the ground below, as if the thing hadn't moved from its spot in years.

Just beyond the pine stand, Anne could just make out a short, rocky drop-off—not exactly a cliff, but a drop nonetheless. No way of telling what lay beyond, but smart money was on *more burned forest*. It looked like whoever had dragged the big beast out here had taken it as far as it could go without sending it over the edge and down the hill.

A white plume of smoke or steam issued from a vent atop the old RV, floating up and diffusing into the gray sky above. Gem was right—somebody inside was cooking.

Somewhere nearby, she could hear the steady hum of a gas generator puttering against the cold. It was the only noise around. From where they were standing, Anne couldn't see the genny, but from the sounds of it, it was a fair amount smaller than the one up at her mom's cabin. Probably the RV didn't take much juice to run its essential functions, especially if it had been parked out here for as long as it seemed. Nobody blundered their way into living like this, out here in this dead wasteland back of beyond. Nobody who didn't want to be left alone.

The name *Lisa Ray Bonny* pinballed back and forth inside Anne's head, but she did her best to quiet it. Whatever nascent hope she'd assigned to that name and the person who came attached to it was useless until she actually laid eyes on the woman herself.

Soundlessly, she gestured to Gemma with one hand and brought a single finger up to cross her lips: *Shhh*. Gem nodded in assent, and together, they stole silently through the thicket of burned trees, keeping their bodies low, their footsteps silent in the powdery snow as they advanced. Eighty yards, then sixty, forty, thirty-five—

SNAP.

Together, Anne and Gem froze in place and looked down at Gem's feet—and the trip wire she'd stepped on, buried in the snow. Gemma had just enough time to say

"—oh, the *fuck*—!"

And then the whole of the forest erupted in a storm of noise.

41

In an instant, the scorched forest was alive with sound, filled with a deafening cacophony of shrieks and whistles and trills that forced Anne's hands up to cover her ears. It was the loudest thing she'd ever heard in her life; so loud that after a second Anne almost felt like the sound was coming from inside her head, as if someone were taking a power drill to the roof of her mouth at top speed. It was pure agony.

A few feet away, Gem had clapped her hands to her own ears in a futile attempt to keep the noise out. She opened her mouth as if she were screaming, but Anne couldn't hear her. She couldn't even hear her own thoughts. She fell forward, felt the rocks underneath the snow bite into her knees, but she didn't care. The screech pounded against her body, less a noise and more a physical force, and just when Anne thought she couldn't take anymore—

It stopped.

For a second, Anne thought she'd gone deaf from the onslaught, both eardrums blown to hell. But when she pulled her hands away from her ears, there was no blood. Then she heard the footsteps crunching through the snow behind her and the telltale *clack-clack* of someone chambering a round in a lever-action rifle.

"You two must be lost," an oddly familiar voice said, already so much closer than Anne would have expected. "Because I sure as fuck don't remember inviting you up here."

Still kneeling on the ground, Anne raised both hands high over her head, then got one foot under her and rose, turning in place to look at the woman holding them at gunpoint. She looked so much like she did in the picture, same as she had in the video. Her long white hair had only gotten longer in the interim, her face creased with deep lines but still remarkably beautiful behind simple, rimless bifocals. She wore a heavy Carhartt canvas coat and old jeans above heavy work boots; stacks of silver rings adorned her tattooed hands, which held a walnut-stocked Marlin repeater trained squarely on Anne's heart.

The blood went out of the woman's cheeks when she saw Anne's face. "Annie," she gasped.

Anne gave a wave with one of her raised hands.

"Hi, Lisa," Anne said. "Sorry I'm late. Ran into some trouble up in Cabot."

42

The inside of the RV was a lot nicer than the outside made it seem, and for a second, Anne wondered if maybe that was the point. Where the outside of the Winnebago had been faded and grimy and peeling, the inside was warm and cozy and well maintained, if a bit cluttered. It felt like a home.

Opposite the step well and the door, there was a busted little two-seater sofa and laminate table, atop which sat a single white ceramic coffee cup and an old-school brown glass bar ashtray filled with half-smoked joints. On the wall behind the love seat, Lisa had hung a sheet, once baby blue, now long faded to a muted kind of sky-drab. Beside the door, a wooden wind chime hung on a nail, fashioned from cut lengths of bamboo braided together with twine and fishing line like a string of firecrackers. An old fifteen-inch CRT TV sat on a shelf beside the modest kitchenette, which mostly consisted of a stainless steel sink, a silver chef's knife on a cutting board, and an electric hot plate positioned just below a humming vent. Steam rose from the shallow pan atop the hot plate—chicken and beans and rice. It smelled amazing.

Farther down, Anne could see a little shower/toilet combo cubicle, and beyond that, a double bed tucked into the back, piled high with pillows and rumpled sheets. On the shelf above the bed, Lisa had stacked dozens of paperback books beside a little Bluetooth speaker that could probably fill the whole RV with music if she so chose. It wasn't much, but Anne got the sense that for Lisa's purposes, it was more than enough.

"Siddown if you like," Lisa said, shucking off her coat and mounting the Marlin on a woodworked gun rack behind the RV's driver seat. Underneath her jacket, she wore a deep purple sweatshirt with kittens and lilacs printed on the front—a Walmart grandma sweatshirt if Anne had ever seen one. Near the collar, she could just make out a braid of scar tissue on Lisa's neck that stretched from where her jaw met the gutter of her ear down into the sweatshirt.

Anne stayed standing. Gemma did the same.

"All right, whatever, suit yourselves," Lisa said, easing herself down onto the little love seat. With two tattooed fingers, she plucked one of the larger roaches from the ashtray. "Hope you don't mind."

Anne shook her head and glanced over at Gemma, who looked more than a little bit hesitant.

"I mean . . ."

"Wasn't asking, just telling," Lisa said, and sparked the joint with a disposable Bic. The old woman took a deep hit and held it, then raised her face toward the ceiling and blew a thick plume of smoke. A second later, she used one hand to wave the cloud toward the sucking vent above the hot plate. The RV flooded with the skunky smell of good cannabis, soft and earthy and murky-rich. Lisa ashed the roach into the tray, then looked back at her two visitors, the expression in her face no less hard-assed for the addition of weed into her system.

"What was that out there?" Gemma asked, stomping snow off her shoes. "That sound."

Lisa took another deep hit and held it. "Noisemakers," she said, her voice squeaky and breathless. "Made 'em myself." Finally, she exhaled again and gestured to the side of the door and the bamboo-and-twine wind chime hanging there. "Wind 'em up, set 'em to start spinning the second anybody or anything trips the wire. When that happens, whole forest lights up with sound. Think of it like an early-warning system."

"Early-warning system for what?" Gemma asked.

Lisa gave her a look. "Uninvited guests."

Taking a closer look at the wind chime, Anne saw what she was talking about: each length of bamboo was cut on a bias, with a tone-hole notched in both sides. When the bamboo spun, the air blew the whistle. Get enough of them spinning at the same time, shit would be louder than an air-raid siren.

"That's really smart," Anne said.

"Aw, gee, thanks," Lisa said humorlessly. "Lucky you only set off a handful of 'em. When the trip wire actually breaks and they all go off together, well. That's a hell of a thing. Now, if you two wouldn't mind telling me just what in the holy fuck you're doing here, I'd surely appreciate it."

Anne pulled the folded letter from her pocket and tossed it on the table between them.

"That," she said. "You left that letter for me, didn't you? You invited me up here. Well, here I am. Here we are."

Lisa took another hit and smirked at her joylessly. "Right. Of course. Jesus Christ." Smoke fountained out of her mouth and nose as she spoke, her voice rising. "Kid, I left that shit for you, like, twenty-five years ago, okay? Figured that you'd get sick of living with your grandma at some point and come looking for answers. At least I figured you'd come looking a lot sooner than now, and I definitely didn't expect you'd come rolling up here with one of your goddamn partners in crime after the kind of shit show you got yourselves mixed up in, fuck."

"Okay, the hell is your—" Gemma started, outraged.

"Yeah, no, I know who you are, Gemma Poe," Lisa said, shutting her down in an instant. "You've both been all over the news for the better part of the last week. Sorry to have to break it to you like this, but you're both fucking famous. Shit, news said that you even teamed up with some cop. That true?"

Dutch's dead face flitted across Anne's mind again, the spray of his brains, the subtle shift of the architecture of his facial structure from the impact of the bullet. She didn't say anything. She just looked back at Lisa, anger plain on her face—but the old woman only cocked her head and blew smoke.

"Christ. You're crazier than they're giving you credit for, which at this point is kind of a fucking feat. So, not to be rude or anything, but I'm going to go ahead and ask you again: What—*the fuck*—are you two doing here?"

"Didn't you hear what she said?" Gemma asked. "We were up in Cabot. This morning."

That got Lisa's attention.

"What," she said.

It wasn't a question—it was more as if she exhaled it like another hit of smoke, the single syllable riding out of her lungs unbidden. The look on her face hadn't softened, exactly, but it had changed, morphing seamlessly from irritated concern to outright worry in the span of that single word.

Crossing her arms over her chest, Anne nodded solemnly at the old woman. On the love seat, Lisa seemed to deflate a little bit. She set the guttering roach in one of the ashtray's runnels, then slumped back against the cushions.

"Why the fuck would you go up there?" she asked.

"We weren't really given much choice in the matter," Gemma said.

Lisa pursed her lips and narrowed her eyes. "Win?"

"Win," Anne confirmed.

The old woman took another deep breath and let it all out in a long, slow sigh. A second later, her eyes found Anne's wrapped forearm.

"Was that him?"

Anne shook her head. "Darlene."

"Okay. Okay," the old woman said. "Fuck."

Moving deliberately, she rose from the sofa and went over to the little kitchenette. From the topmost cabinet, she drew a half-empty bottle of Stolichnaya and three short, finger-smudged glasses. Setting the glasses on the tabletop, she poured a generous measure of vodka into each and passed one to Anne, another to Gem. The third Lisa drained straight away, knocking it back like a double-tall shot before refilling it.

"All right," she said, her demeanor slightly bolstered. "Catch me up. What the hell happened to you, Annie?"

Together, Anne and Gem walked her through it all, piece by bloody piece. The bank, the cabin, Pecos, the motel and the video, the diner, Cabot. By the time they'd finished, the rest of the vodka was gone, and Lisa, in her desperation, had moved on to the cooking

sherry. Gem joined her for a glass, but Anne abstained. Three double vodkas on an empty stomach was about her limit for one afternoon, even though it wasn't really afternoon anymore.

Outside the Winnebago, the sun had started to edge closer and
closer to the horizon and disappeared behind the low clouds. How
long had they been out here? Two hours? More? Anne's thoughts
turned to Murph—she knew the big cat would be fine in his blanket-
and-shirt-filled carrier, but her heart lurched at the thought of him
being scared and alone. The way she'd found him in the cabin this
morning, all hunched up and terrified, she wasn't eager to put him
through something like that ever again, if she could help it.

Perched on the edge of the sofa, Lisa was watching her, both
hands clasped tightly around her glass. Not for the first time, Anne
studied the old woman, the wrinkles on her face, the guarded way
she held herself, the thick, dark lines and coiling, arcane symbols
etched into her fingers. Lisa's gaze narrowed and turned furtive.

"What?" Anne asked.

"Nothing. It's just. You really do look like her, you know," Lisa
said. "Your mom."

"Yeah, Win told me the same thing."

Lisa scoffed. "Of course he did. He always had a thing for her.
Fucking creep."

"Did they ever . . . ? You know," Anne asked, trying to be delicate.

"Oh, no. God, no," Lisa said with a bitter laugh. "Absolutely not.
Beverly had better sense than that. Even if she thought that he was
onto something, leading us all up into the hills like he did, she
knew better than to get mixed up in whatever weird shit was going
on between him and his *Darlin'*."

Sitting on the floor with her back against the passenger seat,
Gemma tossed back the rest of her sherry with a grimace while
Anne leaned forward, resting her elbows on her knees.

"What happened to you? After that night in the mine, I mean.
After . . ." She turned her hands out toward Lisa, displaying the
banded purple keloids on both palms.

"What do you think happened?" Lisa teased. "I got the fuck out of there and didn't look back. Swore off the Passage of Divinity forever, same as your mom. Figured, live and let live, right? So I came back up here to try and live my damn life in peaceful obscurity. Thought that was the end of it, too. Except, you know, *Win*. He never was any good at taking no for an answer. You two were supposed to be coming up this way the night everything fell apart. You'd been hiding out at the cabin a couple weeks by then, and your mom wanted to get you out of there before Win tracked you down. Lousy fucking timing."

A distant echo shook itself loose from the calcified strata of Anne's memory then, a question posed to her over and over in the days she'd spent up at the cabin with her mom. She didn't even realize at first that the voice inside her head doing the asking wasn't her own, but Beverly's:

What do we do when we're in trouble, Annie?

"We follow the stars," she said softly. In the silence of the RV, she might as well have shouted it. "Jesus, the *stars*, the fucking ranch logo."

Lisa winked and clucked her tongue as she blasted her with a finger-gun. "Got it in one," she said. "Course, I don't have to tell you that it didn't work out that way. After they killed your mom and you disappeared into the night, I was the next stop on their revenge tour, I s'pose. I don't know if they thought you'd somehow made your way up here, or if Win was just looking to keep the flock in line by making an example of the apostate, or what. Result's the same, I guess."

"Meaning what?"

"Meaning you and your mom aren't the only ones they hurt, Annie."

Without another word, Lisa whisked her purple grandma sweatshirt over her head and tossed it aside. Underneath, she wore a plain black tank over skin that was twisted and bunched with terrible scars. The thick, fleshy braid on her throat that Anne had seen before was the least of it—they covered half of the old woman's body from the neck down, knotted and coiled in shades of red and purple and pale, bloodless white.

"The fire," Gemma said. "Christ, that was them?"

Lisa smirked. "Come on, of course it was. You've seen what Win's capable of. You can't exactly tell me you're surprised."

She raised the sherry bottle, a silent question. Gemma held out her glass and let Lisa fill it halfway up.

"I mean, no," Gem said, "but, come on. Even for him, burning a whole ranch and forest to cinders seems like overkill."

Lisa shrugged. "I don't know that it was him that did it. I was in bed when it happened, which is probably why . . ." She gestured broadly to her scars. "But if I had to guess, no. Probably not him. At least, not personally. On his orders? Absolutely. Doubt he even said that it should be a fire, though. More likely, he just sent those sick fucks John and Norris my way, told them to make an example, make it messy, and salt the fucking earth when they were done." Still holding the bottle, she topped off her own drink and sipped. "Anyway. After I got out of the hospital, I made myself real scarce for a long time. I don't know if they thought I was dead or what, but I wasn't about to give Win any cause to come looking for me."

"So why come back at all?" Anne asked. "There's nothing left up here."

"Exactly," Lisa said with an impish smile. "They already burned everything to the ground. Why would they bother coming back to look for me up here?" She picked the letter up off the table. "I headed up to the cabin and left this for you, then came back here, rigged the place nice and good to fuck shit up in case I got any unexpected visitors, and I've basically been out here ever since." She let the letter fall to the table and trained her gaze on Anne. "Look, when you were up there, up in Cabot, did he tell you what he wants?"

Anne sighed. "Yeah. He wants to open the door again. The one that . . ." She trailed off, unsure of why she was trying to explain. Lisa had been there. She'd seen what happened as well as anyone else. "He wants to go through."

Now it was Lisa's turn to sigh. "That tracks," she said. "I think he's probably been trying to do exactly that ever since he saw through to the other side. It's probably why he sent Darlene after you that night."

Darlene was just trying to bring you home, Win had told her. Fuck.

"He thinks my blood's going to do the trick," Anne said. "That it's the key to opening the door again. That nobody else's will do."

A sour smile pulled itself across Lisa's face. "Yeah, well, at this point, he'd know," she said.

On the floor, Gem leaned forward, narrowed her eyes. "What's that supposed to mean?"

Wordlessly, Lisa reached behind her and bunched one ring-laden hand in the sheet that was covering the wall at her back. With a sharp jerk of her arm, she tore it away from the nails holding it in place, and as it fell, Anne finally saw what Lisa had been doing up here on her own for all these years.

43

It was a map.

Hand-drawn on butcher paper in thick black Sharpie lines, it covered most of the wall behind the love seat, nearly six feet end to end, decorated in multicolored pushpins and photos and newspaper clippings and pulled-taut strands of yarn. At first glance, it seemed cluttered and messy, but Anne would have recognized that landscape anywhere. It was the San Luis Valley. None of the places on the map had names, just outsized stars denoting the cities and towns: Alamosa, Monte Vista, Crestone, Fort Garland, even Cabot. They were all here.

Pushing herself off the far wall, Anne crossed over and leaned in to examine the map up close. The photos and news clippings were connected to specific points on the map, each hand-annotated with a different date. There had to have been twenty of them up here or more, the names and dates stretching back decades. Near the southern edge, a length of red yarn connected a pushpin to a crumpled missing poster that Anne realized she'd seen before. Dean Garritsen, gone missing from Alamosa all the way back in June.

Tearing her eyes from the map, Anne glanced over at Lisa, trying to make sense of exactly what she was looking at.

"How long have you . . . ?"

"A while," Lisa said. She jerked her chin at the pan of food on the hot plate underneath the vent. "Come on, dinner's almost ready. Let's eat something, and we can talk some more. I'll answer whatever questions you've got. Sound good?"

Anne's stomach grumbled. She hadn't eaten a bite since last night's meal up in Cabot, and she was feeling it. She stole a glance back at Gem, asking a silent question—Gem shrugged.

"Yeah, sure," Gem said.

Anne turned back to Lisa. "Sounds great," she said. "Thank you."

"Yeah, well, don't thank me yet. Been awhile since I made food for anyone but me, so don't complain if it sucks."

The food didn't suck.

It was simple fare—straight up and down rice and black beans with chicken—but in that simplicity, Lisa had created something kind of marvelous. Anne tasted sweet onion and tomato, rich, nutty garlic, and even a little bit of smoky heat on the back end that might have been dried chipotle. They'd already drained all of Lisa's booze, so the old woman had quickly fixed them a pot of strong coffee, which they all drank from chipped mugs. Anne thought it might have been the best thing she'd ever eaten in her life.

The three of them sat around the small laminate table, eating in total silence for the first few minutes, tucking into their plates like it was their last meal on earth.

Naturally, it was Lisa who finally broke the quiet, smiling not-so-innocuously at Anne over a fresh forkful of food.

"So, when'd you start shooting people for a living, Annie?"

Anne took another bite. Chewed methodically. Thought about her answer.

"Not long after people stopped calling me *Annie*, I guess," she said.

Lisa smiled, not unkindly, and for a moment, Anne caught a glimpse of the woman that she'd seen in the video.

"And that was . . . when, exactly?" she asked.

"After high school," Anne said. "Had a friend who needed some help with this thing. Ex-boyfriend, hanging on to something that wasn't his to keep. I offered to get it back for her."

"What was it? This *something*," Lisa clarified.

"About a hundred Oxys," Anne chuckled.

Gem laughed, bright and guileless. "Jesus, you never told me this story," she said, bumping her shoulder against Anne's, lingering there for a moment longer than she needed to.

Anne couldn't help but smile—and blush. "Yeah, well, you never asked." She laughed softly to herself. "Anyway, I'd been in trouble plenty of times at that point, kind of figured I might as well keep a good thing going, I guess."

"So instead of college, you pursued a career in robbing people," Lisa said.

Anne took another bite of food. "Essentially," she said, mouth full.

"So what happened to the hundred-or-so Oxys?" Gem asked.

"Oh, I got 'em back. Had to break ex-boyfriend's nose and about three of his teeth with a softball trophy to convince him to hand them over, but whatever. Eggs and omelets."

Now it was Lisa's turn to break into laughter. "Jesus, you sound so much like Beverly when you say shit like that."

"Really?"

Lisa smirked. "Really. You're more like her than you think."

"I had no idea," Anne said honestly.

"Yeah, well, why would you, right? Look, you're walking your own path, kid. You know what you're about. Your mom would have been proud of you for that. Even if it did end up leading you straight to *him*."

Out of the corner of her eye, Anne saw Gem watching the old woman with renewed curiosity. She jerked her head toward the map on the wall.

"Speaking of," Gem said. "You're sure those are him? All of them?"

"Yeah, pretty sure. Near as I can figure it, he's been taking people up to Cabot for a while now, probably bleeding them to try and open the door again," Lisa said between bites of dinner. "Mostly folks who won't be missed, drifters and the like, but there's a reason he sticks to the valley. You know how this place is. Just eats people up, sometimes. Makes it easier for shit to slide by under the radar."

"So what makes these different? What's tying them all together?" Gem asked, gesturing at the map with her fork.

"I'unno, common elements, I guess. Most people who go missing, they leave something behind. Some indication. Not so here.

Everybody up there on the wall just . . . disappeared into thin air," Lisa said.

Gem chewed her food. "You got any proof?"

"No, of course not," Lisa scoffed. "And even if I did, fuck am I going to do with it? Go to the cops? Try and explain it all? Come on. The second Win gets a whiff of the law, he's going to turn the Passage into *Jonestown 2: Electric Boogaloo*. Still, it'd be nice to have something that told me I'm not completely crazy."

Anne and Gem shared a look, then Anne slipped a hand into her jeans pocket and pulled out the stack of driver's licenses that Gem had found in Win's cabin.

"Something like these?" she asked, and dropped the licenses onto the table in between their plates like a deck of playing cards.

Lisa's eyes flared as she set her fork down to shuffle through the IDs. Momentarily rising from the love seat, she held the licenses up to the map, matching names to the threaded-together disappearances.

"Erika Steleck. Cherie Sbila. Wayne Hull. Kurt Johnstone. Shit, I missed a few." She threw Anne and Gemma a look as she dropped back into her seat. "Where did you get these?"

Anne nodded at Gem. "She found 'em."

"They were in Win's place. Found them in his desk," Gem explained. "Didn't even really bother hiding them."

Lisa shook her head. "Naturally the sick fuck kept souvenirs. Arrogant, serial-killing prick. And of course none of it worked—not that it kept him from trying, what, like twenty-five times now? He's a fucking sociopath."

"*No price too high for entry into the Kingdom of Heaven,*" Anne said, parroting Win's words from the night previous.

Lisa snorted. "Why am I not surprised he's still saying that shit?" she sneered. "As if that isn't the biggest red flag imaginable. I should have realized the second it came out of his mouth. Your mom sure did. Not that it saved her. Shit—sorry."

Anne winced at Lisa's words, but she shook it off as best she could. For the longest time, she'd selfishly thought that her mom's death had happened in a bubble, that it only affected her and her grandma, but Lisa had lost her, too. She didn't blame the woman for being callous. Living up here alone, she probably had a long time to practice growing scars over that particular wound, along with all her others.

"It's okay," she said. "I mean, it's not, but . . ."

"I get it," Lisa said. "It happened a long time ago, but she was still your mom."

"Yeah, exactly," Anne replied.

Gem spun her fork in her food. "You two were really close, huh? You and Beverly."

"We were," Lisa said with a sad smile. "I mean, as close as Beverly let anyone get. She had a way of holding people at arm's length, whether she meant to or not. She loved hard, but she had a fucking temper on her. She'd been burned enough times that she didn't exactly suffer disappointment lightly. But once you were in with her, really in her heart, you were in there for life. Everybody else on the outside could go and fuck themselves, far as she was concerned, but that was the trade-off. Made her a bit of an acquired taste, I guess."

"Oh yeah, I have no idea what that's like at all," Gem said, her voice laced with playful sarcasm.

"Uh-huh," Lisa said knowingly.

Anne flushed hot and looked down at her own plate. Her heart ached something terrible, and as she sat there, staring at her food, she realized why: Sitting here with Lisa over a home-cooked meal was the closest to her mom she'd been in decades. For the first time in her adult life, she felt taken care of, like she was part of a family again, she and Lisa and Gem against the world.

For a fleeting moment, Anne felt like she could see the future unfolding before her in perfect clarity, one with more meals together like this, catching up and drinking and laughing away the darkness. A future where she wasn't so fucking alone all the time, where her few memories of her mom didn't have to be something she kept locked away out of fear of losing them forever.

Tears prickled at the back of her eyes. She blinked them away. A second later, she felt Gem's steady, cool hand alight on her own, giving it a gentle squeeze.

"I'm going to give you two a couple of minutes to talk, all right?" Gem said. "I'm kinda getting the sense that we've gotten to the none-of-my-business part of this conversation." Her eyes flashed with understanding and kindness.

Anne's heart lurched, and she met Gemma's gaze, holding it for a long, lingering moment. "Yeah, that's, um. Yeah. Thank you, Gem."

"Nothing to thank me for. You two talk. I could use the fresh air, anyway," she said, rising from the table to grab her coat and the Remington. She crossed over to the door, pushing it halfway open, then turned back to look at Anne. "You need anything, you give a shout, okay? I'm right out here if whatever."

Anne showed her her best reassuring look. "Will do."

"Mm-hmm." Gemma smiled and showed herself the rest of the way out, letting the door swing shut behind her with a soft mechanical *click*. Then it was just Anne and Lisa, alone in the Winnebago.

"She's intense," Lisa said, glancing at the door with a clever little smile. "I like her. I can see why you two are together. You make a cute couple."

Anne felt herself flush hot again. "I . . . I mean, we're not . . ." she stammered. "Me and Gemma, we're, we're not together."

Lisa gave her a look. "Could have fooled me. The way she looks at you and all. But no big deal. I'll mind my business. Anyway," she said, pulling her purple grandma-print sweatshirt back on over her scars, "what was it that you wanted to talk about, Annie?"

The look on Lisa's face told her that she already knew, but that she still had to ask if she wanted answers. She was starting to really like her. Aunt Lisa Ray Bonny, from way, way back in the day. Anne didn't remember her, but she couldn't deny the fact that her heart felt somehow connected to the woman. Memories could be buried or burned away, but maybe love wasn't so easy to erase.

"What was she like?" Anne finally asked, screwing up all the courage she could muster. "My mom. What was she like?"

Lisa's eyes drifted up and to the side, remembering.

"Beyond her temper? Intense, kind of like your not-girlfriend," she said with a little smirk. "Other than that, she was smart. Funny.

Complicated. Like I said, she didn't really like a lot of people, but the ones she let in, she loved them with her whole heart. Even when it ended badly. I think Beverly figured out pretty early on that the point of life is to love as much and as hard as you can. She used to tell me that love's a verb. It's a doing-thing, not a being-thing. If you're lucky enough to find love that really matters, you'd better chase it as hard as you can for as long as your legs will carry you. That's what your mom did. We should all be so lucky."

"Did you two know each other before the Passage?"

Lisa shook her head. "Nah. She and you joined up about the same time as I did, few years before everything went down. You were just a tiny baby back then."

"You know, I really don't remember any of it," Anne said.

Lisa raised an eyebrow, questioning. "None?"

Anne shook her head. "Basically nothing before that night at the cabin. All the rest just sort of got wiped away, I guess. It's all blurs and best guesses."

"Jesus. Not exactly a surprise, after something like that, I guess. But it's still a shame, if you don't mind my saying so. For a while there, before everything that happened down in the mine, things were basically good. I mean, thinking back on it now, Win was definitely going crazy, but there was nothing we could do about that. He was quiet about it, until he wasn't. Nobody saw what was happening until it was too late to course correct. But yeah, for a while there, everything else was just kind of status quo, you know? Buncha old hippies trying to live honestly among ourselves, maybe make the world a better place in the process. We had a community, y'know? Friends. People to lean on."

"I'm so glad to hear that," Anne said grimly. "Must have been nice."

"It was," Lisa said, shooting her a look that told Anne in no uncertain terms that she wasn't going to take the bait. Whatever anger and loss were left bubbling underneath Anne's skin, the old woman wanted none of it. She had plenty of her own.

"Do you remember *anything* about her, Annie? I mean, honestly."

Not nearly for the first time in the last week, Anne searched her memory for any sign of Beverly that loomed larger than what had happened the night that she died. Most of the time, her memories of her mom were messy and clouded by those last few terrifying, bloody moments they'd spent together, but right now, sitting in Lisa's presence, she was amazed to find that something actually shone through, bright and clear as day.

"Her laugh," Anne said dreamily. "I remember her laugh. It was so . . . real. So big and loud. I remember how she would throw her head back, like she was laughing at the sky. Like, when she laughed, you knew she really meant it. She never laughed just to make you feel good. She didn't bullshit people like that."

Lisa nodded and lit another roach. "She did have a great laugh, didn't she? Shit, I haven't thought about that in years." She paused, took a hit. From where she sat, Anne could see now that the tattoos on her hands weren't limited to only her fingers; there were fading mandalas inked into each of her palms, almost elegant in their gradual erosion.

The old woman blew a thick cloud and ashed the roach into the brown glass tray, then gestured outwardly with the still-glowing cherry.

"So how'd it feel being up there again? The cabin, I mean. Guessing you hadn't been there since that night, right?"

"Right. It felt . . . I don't know. Weird? Bad, but mostly weird."

"Bad and weird are a good start," Lisa said from behind her curtain of smoke.

Anne set her plate aside. "It was like falling into a dream I had a long time ago. But it was more than that, you know? Not *haunted* exactly, but not that far off, either. It was almost like everything up there had been frozen in amber and left to collect dust. It was all exactly like I remembered, just . . . smaller. Sadder, I guess. I think I probably remember it being a lot nicer than it really was."

"That's just how memory works, I think. Especially when you're a kid. Shit, that's how the farmhouse felt to me when I came back. Before those fucking shitheels burned it down, I mean." She took another hit. "Did you at least find your mom's necklace while you were up there? Or that old deer rifle of hers?"

Anne paused. "Sorry, my mom's what?"

"Her necklace? The silver one? And the, the rifle," Lisa said again. "You know the one, that dusty old semiauto." She studied Anne's face. "You don't have any idea what I'm talking about, do you?"

Anne shook her head. Lisa held up a hand as she rose from the couch once more, her knees popping like bubble wrap.

"Wait right there," she said, brushing past Anne as she made her way to the back of the RV and started rummaging around. Anne did as her aunt told her, listening to the buzz and hum of the vent over the quickly cooling hot plate. After a few seconds, she heard Lisa say *Here the fuck you are* under her breath before returning to the little living room with a small frame in her hands.

"Here," she said, holding the frame out to Anne, giving it a little shake. "Take it."

Anne took it, and turned it over to look at the picture inside: It was the same photo that she had folded up in her pocket. From inside the crenellated edges of the frame, Lisa, Beverly, Darlene, Win, John, and little Annie stared back at her, all bright shiny smiles under the Three-Star gate. Anne gave Lisa a curious look.

"Didn't figure you for the sentimental type," she said.

Lisa fired back her best patronizing smile. "Fuck off," she said, and tapped a single fingernail against Beverly's face. "This is the necklace I'm talking about."

Anne looked closer at the photo and the necklace that hung around her mother's neck: a simple silver chain, a bit on the thicker side, with a circular pendant at the end. Now that she was looking at it, yeah, she had seen it before. Beverly had been wearing it in the video, too.

"She wore it all the time," Lisa said. "I don't know if she had it that last night or not, but I figured that since you'd been up there again, maybe you'd grabbed it. Kind of hoped that you had, I guess. Wouldn't be a bad thing, having a little piece of her to hang on to, right?"

Anne shook her head. "Nope, no sign of it. Sorry," she added, almost as an afterthought. "What was that about a deer rifle?"

"Just what I said, an old hunting rifle that belonged to your mom. Not sure what kind, I never knew shit about shit when it came to guns. I got the lever-action, but I just know how to load and shoot the thing. Anyway, I know your mom's rifle had a scope on it, big old bastard, too. I do remember her saying it was a thirty-aught-six, though. Just like the Tom Waits song."

Anne didn't know the song she was talking about, but didn't feel compelled to ask right now.

"Anyway," Lisa continued, "I remember her telling me she'd stashed the thing up at the cabin for safekeeping. Probably still up there, unless the cops found it, which I kind of fucking doubt. Your mom had a talent for keeping things hid."

Over the hot plate, the rattling buzz of the vent grew louder. The sound of it made something inside Anne's stomach twist and crawl, like there was an animal in there trying to claw its way out.

"Hey, you okay? Annie? You still with me?" Lisa asked.

But Anne wasn't paying attention to the old woman. All her focus had been drawn to a needle's point, blocking out everything that wasn't the rickety old vent or the noise boiling out of it. Anne had heard that buzzing before.

Please, no. Please, please, no.

She held her breath and clenched her fists, silently willing away that sound and the nightmare that it carried with it.

Then, as she watched, a fat, glossy blackfly crawled out of the vent and took flight, buzzing through the air in long, lazy loops. Then there was another.

And another. And another.

44

Outside, the air had gone from cold to bitter freezing in record time, like somebody'd flipped a switch the second the sun had gone down. Bundled up in her heavy coat, Gemma stood a few feet back from Lisa's RV and turned her shoulder against the wind in a futile attempt to keep the chill out. Cupping her hands in front of her face, she blew hot air into her bare palms, trying to return a little precious warmth to her cold-brittled digits as she waded through the snow toward the tree line once more. She'd only been out here for a few minutes, pacing back and forth like a sentry as darkness took hold in the burned-out forest, but the cold had already managed to chew through her outer layers and settle into her skin, into her bones.

She didn't begrudge Anne needing a few minutes alone with the old woman; old Lisa Bonny was the closest thing to family that Anne had left in the world. If it had been Gem in that same position, she'd take all the one-on-one time she could get and wouldn't even think to apologize. The least she could do was read the room like a decent human being and step out for a few minutes. Anne deserved that much.

Never in a million years would Gem have guessed that she'd wind up out here, chasing down a lead at the end of the world, especially not knowing what she now knew and seeing what she'd seen. Guilt needled at her from the deepest pit of her stomach; she'd never admit it to anyone, but she hadn't truly believed everything Anne had told her about the shape-shifter until she'd seen it with her own eyes in Cabot. How could she have? Things like that didn't actually happen in real life, and anyway, she'd had way bigger problems at that point.

In the immediate aftermath of the come-apart at the bank, she was ready to get gone and never look back. As far as shitty, last-minute plans went, she could have done worse: hide out at the Happy Trails Motel with a bottle of gin and her aftermarket police scanner until the worst of the storm blew over, then hit the road and never look back. Full Godzilla protocols.

But then she got that goddamn voicemail from Anne and heard her name crackle across the police band not an hour later, and just like that, all her plans for making a clean getaway went right down the toilet.

For years, Gemma had labored to split the difference between her professional life and her personal, working as hard as she could to draw that wide, dividing line down the middle, as if dividing lines ever really meant anything. She'd bought herself a house in Trinidad—nothing fancy, really, just a two-bedroom ranch-style in some anonymous suburb—but it was still *hers*. She'd married Chris. She'd even joined a weekly book club, for Chrissakes. She built a whole life around her to keep people from looking too close, knowing full well that if push came to shove, she'd walk away from it all in a heartbeat. Things had a way of bleeding through, whether you wanted them to or not. You had to be ready to make sacrifices if you wanted to make it out alive.

And the thing was, for a while, it had actually worked. Some-how, against all odds, Gem had managed to keep the division line in place, untouched and inviolate. Even when Chris up and left after finding $50,000 in cash and a .45 with the serial number Dremeled off in a shoebox in the back of the hallway closet, she managed to keep all the plates spinning.

But then she went and did the dumbest thing possible. She fell for someone on the wrong side of the line.

It was her kindness that did it more than anything else. Gem had long seen a difference between being *nice* and being *kind*—nice was a performance put on by people who cared more about how they were perceived than about doing what was right. Kindness, on the other hand, was a selfless thing, generous and patient when it didn't need to be. Anne Heller wasn't anybody's definition of *nice*, but she was sure as hell kind. Awkward and intense and maybe a little too comfortable with shooting people, but kind nonetheless. It certainly didn't hurt that she was absolutely beautiful and somehow didn't seem to realize it.

She'd been close back at the motel, after seeing the shit show on that tape. But if she were really being honest with herself, there was no version of this world in which Gemma would ever walk away from Anne. Despite—or maybe *because of*—all the shit that they'd been through together over the years and the course of the past week, standing next to her was the only time Gem had ever felt like she really belonged anywhere. Like there was someone else in the world who understood—because there was. The division line had done her no favors; she saw that now. The suburban half-life that she'd built around herself like a barrier wall was just that: a construct. A mask to hide behind, a way for her to pretend that she wasn't what she was. Life had been a flat-out nightmare since Durango, but Gem would have been lying if she'd said there was anyone else she'd rather be going through all this shit with.

So here she was, hunched against the cold in some far-flung, burned-out backwoods, trying to get answers from a woman who, for all her cool, disaffected posturing, was just as terrified and hapless as they were. The way Gemma figured it, if Lisa wasn't scared to death, she probably wouldn't have been living off the grid like this. No way. As for what came next, New York wasn't a bad place to start. They'd figure the rest out after that.

Nearby, something rustled in the trees, crunching the snow. Gem snapped to attention in an instant, her hand immediately finding the grip of the shotgun. Behind her ribs, her heart jacked itself up to a machine-gun pace, but despite that, she managed to stay still as stone, scanning the night for the source of the sound. Probably just birds or squirrels or something. Probably.

Then the rustling came again, closer now than it had been a second ago. But it wasn't a rustling, exactly—it was more like a low humming, a persistent buzz at the base of her skull, insectoid and sibilant. It was nauseating, and as it snaked deeper into her stomach, it made the whole blackened forest feel suddenly airless, as if Gem were standing on the surface of the moon.

She tensed, coiling her body tight like a spring ready to snap, and searched the shadows with slitted eyes. Gasping and breathless, the sound shivered through the wintery cold like a blade slipping between ribs, frantic and yet somehow calm, inviting, almost gentle. Gem strained her ears, trying to listen to the shape of that strange noise, and then it finally hit her: it was a voice.

Someone was whispering to her from the trees.

45

A shotgun blast tore through the silence outside, and then the sound of the noisemakers crashed through the forest, so much louder now than they'd been before. The noise shook the RV like an earthquake, a physical force, cataclysmic in its sheer enormity— the sound was everywhere, the sound was everything. What they'd heard before was only a small taste. Lisa had said it herself: *Lucky you only set off a handful of 'em.* The full effect was so much worse than anything Anne had imagined. It was the loudest thing she'd ever heard in her life, and yet never once did her attention falter or slip from the flood of flies boiling out of the vent.

Beside her, she thought she heard Lisa shout *Fuck!* as she went scrambling for her Marlin. Anne's thoughts immediately went to Gem, and tearing her gaze from the flies, she bolted for the door. The freezing air punched her in the heart as she dashed outside, frantically searching for any sign of Gemma.

"Gem? Gem!" Anne called, but her voice was lost in the screech. As her eyes adjusted to the darkness, she finally saw Gemma standing still at the edge of the burned copse around the RV, her back to Anne.

"Gemma, what the fuck is going on? Did you see anything?!" Anne screamed, still struggling to hear her own voice over the cascading din of Lisa's noisemakers. "Gemma? *Gemma!*"

Ankle-deep in the powdery snow, Gemma finally turned around to look at her and smiled. Her face was crawling with fat, glossy blackflies, their wings shimmering together in the low light in a kind of nauseating wave. Gemma's smile spread, a razor gash slicing itself wider and wider underneath the writhing fur of insects, cold as space, cold as hate, and for a second, Anne couldn't hear the noisemakers anymore. She couldn't hear anything beyond the hammer of her heart in her chest, the hum of the insects, and her own frost-shredded breath.

Behind her mask of flies, Gemma blinked, and her eyes were no longer the deep golden brown that Anne had felt such an ache for but empty white, glowing like ghostly lanterns in the night.

No.

The word spun frantically through Anne's head in a mad litany, *no-no-no-no-no-no-no*, and before she knew what she was doing, her Glock was in her hand, and she was unloading it into Darlene's stolen face, screaming as loud as she could but unable to hear her own voice.

Bullets tore pieces of the shape-shifter away in bloody hanks, messily tattering Gemma's (*Not Gemma's*, Anne told herself, *not Gemma's*) face chunk by chunk. Anne pulled the trigger five, six, seven times, but Darlene stayed standing. Of course she did. Anne had learned this lesson too many times already. She watched in horror as the wounds started to heal themselves over, flesh liquefying and coursing over bone to melt into smooth, scarless skin. Then Darlene started to change again, discarding the Gemma mask as her face and body twisted and contorted into a fresh configuration. Behind her, Anne faintly heard the RV door bang open.

"Jesus fuck!" Lisa screamed.

The shape-shifter's blank eyes gleamed bright, and then she was moving, her body juddering and snapping like an insect's as she skittered through the snow, closing the distance between herself and the RV in a few fleeting seconds. Anne threw herself to the side, sprinting for the back side of the RV. She was midstep when something crashed into her from behind and sent her flying toward the short drop beyond the stand of pines. She felt her feet leave the ground.

For a moment, Anne was floating through the air, free of gravity, free of worry or pain—and then she flew over the edge and hit the ground hard, all knees and elbows as she went tumbling downhill, through the powder and the mud. Her face smacked against something hard and sharp buried in the snow, raising a white blade behind her eyelids as the skin split open. Distantly, Anne heard the *crack-crack-crack* of Lisa's repeater punching holes through the night.

She finally came to rest at the bottom of the hill, caked in mud and snow, every part of her body screaming in pain. Her every bodily impulse told her to stay on the ground, but she knew she couldn't. Any second now, Darlene would come flying over that short little cliff and then she'd be on her, either mauling her to death or dragging her back to Cabot to play her part in Win's twisted psychodrama.

Her head swam drunkenly as she forced herself to rise, her body swaying like a sapling in the wind. Somehow she managed to stay upright, counting her breaths like she was waiting for the crack of a starter pistol. When she got to five, she ran. Until her heart pounded, until her lungs ignited with bitter, icy cold, she sprinted away into the trees, feeling the low, ashy branches whip at her as her sneakers punched messy postholes in the frozen snow.

Another flurry of gunshots erupted from Lisa's repeater far behind her, round after round echoing through the night until they finally fell silent. Anne's stomach turned to think of what had become of Lisa. Another person Anne had unwittingly led to their death, fed to the maw of oblivion like so many others. But unlike the rest of them, at least Lisa had always known that this was a possibility. Maybe not Anne showing up on her doorstep like she had, but Darlene, definitely. She'd trapped the whole of the blackened forest in anticipation of that inevitability. She'd known, and she'd planned for it.

Fat lot of good it had done her in the end, though.

Anne slowed her pace among the thick, gnarled trunks and finally risked a glance over her shoulder, fully expecting to see Darlene there, wearing some new horrible face, jaws hanging open, hungry. Waiting. But Anne was alone. For now. It wouldn't last. It never did. She finally understood that. Darlene—whatever Darlene had become as she was pulled apart and remade by that malignant underground light—would always run her down, no matter what dark corner of the earth Anne fled to. They were connected, had been ever since six-year-old Annie had made the childish decision to try to save a woman who couldn't be saved. She'd kept Darlene from being dragged all the way through to the other side, and in doing so had trapped the remains of the woman in the hell of her own warped, stolen body.

As long as Darlene was out there, as long as Win was pulling the strings, Anne was doomed to spend the rest of her life running.

Gathered in darkness, Anne paused a moment and braced herself against the nearest tree, bending at the hip, trying to catch her breath. Blood streamed off her nose and cheek into the snow between her feet. Biting back a fresh flurry of panic, she probed at her face with her fingers, trying to survey the damage from the fall. Pain lit up electric as one fingertip dipped past the edge of the gash under her eye, and she sucked air between gritted teeth. She drew back and gently tried to trace the wound's outline, moving millimeter by millimeter as her breath fogged the air in front of her eyes.

The gouge reached along the ridge of her cheekbone, from the outside edge of her face to the bridge of her nose. It was bleeding like hell, too—even brushing her fingers against it left them looking like they'd been dipped in a bucket of blood. There'd be a nasty scar there, if she somehow managed to get out of this shit alive. Big fucking if.

And what about Gemma? Had Darlene mutilated her like she'd done to Jessup and so many others? Left her tangled in some barbed wire fence after stealing her face? Anne felt a panicked, heartbroken cry rise in her chest at the thought. Gemma deserved better than that—they all did, but Gemma more than anyone else. She hadn't wanted any part of this shit; she'd tried to leave, after all. The second the video had run to static back at the motel, Gem had been unequivocal: *I'm out.* But Anne hadn't let her go. She'd followed her outside and pleaded with her to stay. Begged her like an asshole. Now look what had happened. Another dead friend. But it wasn't just another dead friend, it was *Gemma.* The pain of that was like someone cutting her chest open and taking an auger to her heart.

All she ever did was get people hurt. Get people killed. With

Gemma gone and Lisa almost certainly the same, Anne had nobody left. She was alone. She'd always been alone, and she'd always be alone.

Now all that was left was for her to get back to the car, get out of
this forest. Get the hell away from Darlene for a little while longer.
Maybe that was all she could hope for from here on out.

Anne slowed her breathing, then held it. Examined the woods
around her, bathed in moonlight, draped in shadow. In the distance, Lisa's wailing army of noisemakers had finally started to
die out. Between the trees, Anne could hear the chitter and thrush
of the forest starting to reassert itself. Standing back up straight,
she looked down at the gun in her hand—empty. She'd dumped
every bullet she'd had into Darlene, and it hadn't even slowed her
down. She glanced back the way she'd come, through the trees
toward the muddy drop-off. She could probably make it back to
the Ninety-Eight and get the fuck out of here, but to do that, she'd
have to get past Lisa's campground—and Darlene—on foot. Injured. Exhausted. Bleeding. With zero bullets in her gun.

Great.

But then again, Lisa's Winnebago had an engine, didn't it? It
had wheels and headlights. Maybe she'd been wrong before and
the busted old hulk still ran just fine. Maybe, with a little luck, she
could get it started up and hightail it out of here, crashing through
the dead forest at top speed back to the Oldsmobile, and Murph,
and the stacks of nine millimeter rounds that waited unspent in
her backpack. It was worth a shot, at least.

Another cold wind blew through the scorched forest, making
it groan like a living thing. Shadows flickered between the blackened trunks, every sound a potential threat. Whatever had happened back at the RV was hell and over. Anne had to go, now, or
she was going to die here or worse. She tucked the empty Glock
in her waistband and started to move, stealing through the forest
like a wraith, dashing from shadow to shadow, all her senses on
high alert.

The forest groaned again as the wind hushed between its
shattered-finger branches like a rumor of death. She broke free of

the trees and moved up the snowy, mud-slick hill behind the RV on all fours, then crested the edge of the drop-off, keeping low. All around the Winnebago, the little campsite was drowned in shadow. The RV was dark, too. With the scream of the noisemakers gone, everything was painfully, horribly silent. Every footstep rumbled like an earthquake; every breath escaping her lungs roared like a gale.

A few feet away from the Winnebago, Lisa lay on the ground, crumpled up like a discarded fast-food wrapper. The hammered-flat snow between her and the RV's front door was painted with blood, as if the old woman had gotten hurt inside and dragged herself away. Her repeater lay beside her, empty, useless. Against her better impulses, Anne dashed over to the fallen woman and rolled her onto her back.

Lisa's face was a curtain of red, beaten and slashed to ground beef. One of her eyes was completely gone, clawed out, the empty socket a black, blood-caked hole in her face. At first, Anne thought she was dead, but then a wicked rattle escaped her lips like the tail of a diamondback. Somehow, the old woman was still breathing. Cradling her in her arms, Anne gave Lisa a tiny little shake.

"Lisa," she whispered. "Hey, Lisa, wake up. It's me. It's Annie. Come on, I need you here with me, okay?"

Uneasily, the old woman's remaining eye slid open, the pupil wide and unfocused.

"Annie . . ." she gasped. "Annie . . . ?"

"We need to get you out of here, okay? We need to go. Does the RV still run?"

One of Lisa's ring-heavy hands floated up out of the snow to stroke the side of Anne's face. Her cold, bloody fingertips sliding from temple to jawline, a loving gesture.

"You need to," Lisa croaked. "It's you . . . You need to . . . It's . . . She's . . ." Her voice devolved into a wet coughing fit. Blood spewed from her lips and ran down her chin. She wasn't going anywhere in this condition.

"Okay," Anne whispered. "I'm going to go get the RV started, all right? I'll be right back."

Lisa's remaining eye drifted shut.

"*Don't . . . I don't . . . you . . .*" she said, the words slurred and messy. "*Go, just go . . . I . . .*"

"I got it," Anne told her. "I'll be right back, okay?"

But Lisa was already unconscious again, dragged under the waves by pain and shock and blood loss. Anne eased her down into the red snow as gently as she could. From somewhere deeper in the woods came a brittle, piercing shriek. Darlene. Anne's head sloshed like a water balloon as she scrambled toward the RV.

Through the darkness inside, all of Win's victims stared at Anne from the wall behind the sofa. All the people he'd fed to his mania. Trying to keep herself from spinning out, Anne started rifling through drawers and cabinets and shoeboxes, searching for the RV's keys. If she could get the thing started and get it moving out of the snow, she might stand a chance. Maybe.

Frantically, she yanked open another drawer, and finally, there, among half rolls of masking tape and mismatched screwdrivers and discarded batteries, sat a ring of keys, threaded together on a smiley-face key chain. Anne snatched them from the drawer and bolted for the driver's seat, jamming the key into the ignition like a knife piercing flesh.

She turned the key. But the motor home wouldn't start. There wasn't even a click from the engine. The battery was dead. This was a fucking pipe dream. She was going to die up here, and there was nothing that she could do about it. Shit. *Shit.* Something screamed inside Anne's skull, and she clenched her teeth hard enough to crack a molar just to keep that scream inside. Fucked. She was so, so fucked.

Outside, another scream ripped through the trees. Anne's breath caught in her throat. It was too late. Darlene was here. Just outside the Winnebago, the shape-shifter was stalking around, waiting for her chance to strike.

Leaving the keys in the ignition, Anne slithered from the driver's seat and crawled down the length of the RV. As she passed the hot plate and cutting board, she raised her arm and closed her hand around the handle of the chef's knife. It wouldn't do a damn thing to slow Darlene down, she knew, but there was no way in hell that Anne was dying empty-handed like an asshole.

Run, hide, or fight. Well, running sure as shit hadn't worked, and taking the fight to Darlene at this point was a clear non-option. Hiding in here felt like a surrender, but at this point, it was the only move she had left. In the darkness, Anne crept back toward the motor home's little shower/bathroom stall and folded herself inside, then pulled the plastic accordion door shut.

She held her breath and willed her heart to slow as she pressed herself against the outside wall, feeling the bitter winter cold seeping into the Winnebago through the cheap aluminum siding. Eyes shut against the darkness, she held the knife vertically across her heart like she was some fringe saint rendered in stained glass mid-prayer. *Anne Heller, Our Lady of Perpetual Destruction.*

Please. Please.

Outside, she could hear Darlene crunching through the snow, drawing closer and closer to the side of the Winnebago. Then she went silent, and all Anne could hear was the blood racing through her temples like swollen water pipes about to burst.

The RV door swung open with a creak.

Heavy footsteps thudded against the RV's floor. First to the front of the Winnebago, the driver's seat, the map, then reversing course and moving slowly toward the back. Toward Anne.

Step. Step. Step. Step.

Something glass clattered to the floor and broke, punching through the silence. Anne bit back a cry, staying still and silent. Her fingers tightened around the handle of the chef's knife, so tight that she could almost hear the skin of her hand stretching like leather.

I'm not here. I'm not here. I'm not—

The footsteps came to a stop on the other side of the accordion door. She was only inches away now, and Anne could smell her, all raw meat and vile, unwashed flesh, fetid and stomach-turning.

Through the thin plastic, she could hear the shape-shifter sniffing the stale indoor air, hunting her. There was a wet slurping noise as it smacked its lips and opened its terrible mouth.

"Annie . . ."

The sound of its voice was horrendous and hideous, rusty metal grinding against brick. It wasn't even recognizable as a human imitation, but then, no part of Darlene was human anymore.

Alone inside the little stall, Anne drew breath to scream.

And then Darlene came through the wall.

46

It was like a bomb had gone off inside the little motor home.

In a brutal, screaming rush, Darlene tore through, shredding the door frame and the wall like a wrecking ball. Wood and plaster splintered under her terrible velocity; metal howled as it bowed and snapped. Anne screamed for her life and thrashed against it, as if thrashing would somehow help—but of course it didn't. She was trapped here in this tiny cell, a paper target in a shooting gallery. She never had a chance.

The impact ripped through the RV like it was made of papier-mâché, all violence and sound and fury, like nothing Anne had ever felt before. Her whole body recoiled, ragdolling like she'd been hit by a speeding semi on the interstate. The agony was everywhere; it was everything.

It all happened in an instant: the crash, the impact, the pain. Trapped between her own body and Darlene's, Anne felt her left forearm bend wrong with a wet *crunch*, and she heard herself scream, the kind of desperate, animal braying that she'd never expected to hear herself make. The sound of it blended with the shriek of tearing metal behind her head, and she felt herself tumbling backward under Darlene's might. Her every nerve howled in pain, but even that word, *pain*, did no justice to the enormity of what she was feeling.

Cold air lapped at her skin, and somewhere outside of her body, she felt her spine collide with the hard, snowy ground. Rocks bit into her spine and shoulder blades. The knife fell from her fingers, lost in the debris, and as she opened her eyes, she realized, distantly, that they were outdoors again. Stray snowflakes spilled between burned trees from the black sky above.

Darlene had ripped a hole clean through the side of the Winnebago.

Lying flat on the ground, Anne blinked, breathed, tried to clear her head. It didn't work. Everything hurt. Her body felt disconnected from itself, as if the impact had severed her sense of touch from her brain. She flexed her toes inside her shoes first, then tried her hands, and choked back a scream. Her right arm seemed to be in working order despite its wounds, but the left one, the one that had gotten wedged between her and Darlene, refused to function. Even the slightest shift of her fingers made the bones inside grind like gears inside a rust-caked machine, driving a bolt of searing agony all the way from her wrist deep into her chest.

It was broken. She knew it was, she'd heard it crunch and snap like driftwood when Darlene had come through the wall. At this point, it was only a question of how bad. A thin sheen of sweat broke out across her forehead as nausea eeled its way through her belly. The pain was astonishing, a crushing weight that sat on her body like a concrete slab and refused to let up. She'd never felt physical pain like this before. Until just a few seconds ago, she would have said that pain like this was impossible to stay conscious through. She was learning a lot today.

Footsteps rusked through the snow, somewhere above and behind. Slow, heavy, deliberate. Anne wanted to scream, wanted to jump to her feet and run for all she was worth, but her body refused to obey. All she could do was lie there, staring up at the dark, snowy sky as Darlene—wearing her own face once again—bent over her, grinning, then curled a fist in her hair and started to drag her away.

Anne felt herself sliding over the snow as if she weighed nothing. Less than nothing. With her good arm, Anne pawed numbly at the shape-shifter's grasp, but it was useless. Her grip was like cold cast iron, perfectly and utterly unyielding. Anne would more readily be able to bend a frying pan with her bare hands.

A realization occurred to her then: She couldn't stop this. There was no escaping. Run, hide, fight—none of it had worked. None of it had helped. After all the bloodshed and suffering and meaningless death, the monster had caught up to her anyway. There was no stopping it. Darlene was inevitability incarnate. Everything that

Anne had tried, every plan and every dodge, it all amounted to nothing in the end. She was going to drag her back to Cabot, and to Ballmer's Hope, and the awful thing that lay in wait in the bottom of that mine shaft. Then Win would hold her down and bleed her dry just to try to get his door open again, and that would be the end of Anne Heller.

It was almost comforting, finally giving up all hope.

Darlene dragged her around what was left of the Winnebago, through the little clearing, toward the burned trees that separated Lisa's home from the rest of the forest. Eyes blurry, head drunken from pain and exhaustion, Anne glanced to the side, searching for the old woman—but her eyes wouldn't focus on anything more than a few feet in front of her.

A gunshot rang out, splitting the chilly silence. Over her head, Anne felt Darlene recoil and shudder. She stopped with a jolt, and Anne stopped with her. Pain erupted up her arm from the suddenness of the movement and she shrieked, her vision blurring white again. When the glare cleared, she looked toward the sound.

Lisa was slumped against one of the blackened trees, legs splayed out in front of her. Her remaining eyelid hung low as she clutched her repeater with one hand, steadying it in her armpit, stock braced against the trunk at her back. Shakily, the old woman racked the rifle's lever, kicking an empty brass shell loose into the snow and jamming a fresh one into place.

"Go," Lisa moaned.

At first, Anne didn't understand.

"Come on," Lisa snarled at Darlene. "Come on, you ugly fuck, I'm right here. *I'm right here!*"

Darlene's grasp slackened, then vanished as she started toward the fallen woman. Anne felt herself dropping, then the back of her skull hit the ground with a hard jolt. Teeth sawed into the tender flesh of her tongue. She tasted blood.

Thirty yards away, the repeater barked again, belching flame. Anne saw a new bloody hole blow through the shape-shifter's back, but of course, it didn't slow her. Anne could see the old woman struggling with the lever, trying to chamber another round. Too slow.

"GO!" Lisa roared.

This time, Anne understood and felt a horrid, burning thing catch and ignite inside the furthest chambers of her heart: hope. This was her chance. She wasn't going to get another one. Lisa wanted her to go, so she needed to go. Now.

Marshaling all her strength, she rolled over, planted her good arm deep into the packed-in snow, and pushed for all she was worth. It only took a few seconds for her to rise, but the pain and exhaustion made it feel like hours. Her left arm hung dead at her side, the broken bones crushed to gravel inside the skin, but she didn't have time to worry about that right now. Swaying unsteadily, she stumbled backward from the RV and Lisa and Darlene on rubber legs, unwilling to turn away or even blink in case the shape-shifter changed course and came after her again.

Darlene was only feet away from Lisa when Anne saw the old woman raise a cell phone, modified with aftermarket components and sprouts of wire, high above her head, its face glowing brightly in the dark. Disconnectedly, Anne thought, *This is what she was talking about when she'd said she'd rigged the place to fuck shit up.*

It had never just been noisemakers.

She felt the heat before she saw the explosion, a brutal, punishing wall of blistering fury that crashed over, under, *through* everything in its path. It was as if the air around her had turned carnivorous, gnashing deep into her whole body in an instant. It was agony. She was dying. This was what death felt like. There was no other reasonable explanation for something this all-encompassing.

The flames rose in a mushroom cloud, swelling upward in a plume of black and orange before erupting outward through the trees in a torrid wave. The force of it blew Anne off her feet, throwing her backward into the snow. Her spine connected with the hard winter ground at a bad angle, bowing like a Slinky. A sharp gasp escaped her lips and she went tumbling through the snow and the rocks, rolling end over end away from the scorching blast. The pain from her crushed arm lit her whole body up in a luminous fireworks show. But the flames inside her body were nothing compared to what had happened to Lisa's RV.

In an instant, the Winnebago—and the land around it—had been reduced to a burning crater. The trees, blackened before, were now splinters and ash, burning match heads planted upright in the snow. Fire and smoke rose from the ground in columns where the earth had blackened and the snow had evaporated. Lisa's RV was gone, blown to rubble in the blast. The only sign that it had ever been there were the black stains on the ground where the tires had melted under the heat of the explosion.

There was no sign of Lisa's body. No sign of Darlene, either. They were both just . . . gone.

Rising once more, Anne struggled to stay upright, but once she'd managed a kind of balance, she was moving. She tore through the burned forest as fast as she could without pitching forward onto her face, good arm crossed tightly over her chest to keep the cold out. It wasn't that far. She had the keys. She just needed to make it back to the car. Then she'd get the fuck out of here. She'd figure it out after that.

She was well past the farmhouse when she found Gem.

She sat slouched in the snow beside the Oldsmobile, chin on her chest, her eyes half-open behind the braids that hung down around her head like a curtain. Her shirt was torn, her stomach a swamp of red. Fuck. Anne limped over to her on shaky baby-giraffe legs and dropped to her knees to lay two fingers across the woman's neck, searching for a pulse. It was there, but it was weak. Uneven. Still, Anne's heart leapt at the fact that Gem was still alive. Still hanging on, despite it all. Up close like this, she could see that Gemma's midsection was a lattice of deep, messy wounds, no doubt Darlene's work.

"Gemma? Gemma, hey, it's me. It's time to wake up, okay?"

Anne shook Gem's shoulder with her good arm, trying to rouse her, but Gemma wouldn't respond. Sitting unconscious, or half-conscious, or whatever, in this cold wasn't doing her any favors. Anne had to get her out of here.

Letting her bad arm dangle down by her side, Anne snaked

the other under Gemma's armpits and lifted her up to her feet to walk her around to the back of the Oldsmobile. Inside the car, Murph yowled unhappily inside his carrier, but he could deal. She laid Gem legs-first across the bench seat, then unzipped Murphy's carrier and pulled out both of the crumpled-up T-shirts from inside. It would have to do. Folding one up, she pressed it against the wounds in Gem's belly, trying to stanch the bleeding. Gemma moaned and recoiled from the pain, eyes fluttering.

"I know, I know," Anne said to her, trying not to cry. "I know it hurts. But you have to keep this here, okay? You have to hold it here tight to stop the bleeding. Please, Gem. *Please.*"

Slowly, Gemma's hands floated up to her belly and closed over Anne's, pressing down, holding the shirt in place. For a moment, Anne could feel Gem's pulse in her fingers, the rise and fall of her uneven breath underneath her scarred palm. She was still alive. She hadn't gone anywhere yet. Anne's eyes slid shut, and her head sank, coming to rest against Gemma's sweat-dappled brow.

"I'm so sorry." Anne's voice was an agonized whisper against the hurt and the panic that were rising up inside of her chest like a tangle of thick, thorned vines. For a moment, she could see a hideous future where Gemma Poe didn't survive opening itself up before her in a bottomless pit of horror and despair, and Anne felt herself plummeting into it, faster and faster toward oblivion. A desperate moan escaped her mouth then, a raw, heartbroken noise that echoed up from the very deepest, most sacred parts of her heart. Tears burned her eyes and went streaking down her cheeks, scorching her skin in the bitter cold. "I love you, Gemma. I'm so fucking sorry. I love you so much."

I love you. The words fell unbidden from her lips in a messy, awkward spill; she hadn't meant to say them, had been holding herself back from saying them for as long as she could remember, but in this moment, confronted with the very real possibility that she'd never get another chance to tell Gem how she truly felt, they were all she had left. On the bench seat, Gemma moaned weakly and shuddered. Anne laced Gem's fingers in her own and squeezed. She didn't want to let go. Not now. Not ever. But they had to get out of here.

Behind the wheel, Anne used the other shirt to fashion a quick and ugly sling for her shattered arm, then reached back and relocated Murphy's carrier to the passenger seat beside her. Behind the mesh, Murph glowered at her with his big green eyes, blinking slowly, clearly offended by the unceremonious loss of his bedding.

"I know, okay? I get it. I'm sorry," she told the cat.

Murph snuffed at her, then lay down and went to sleep.

Anne strapped on her seat belt and angled the rearview mirror down to check on Gemma. She was asleep again, or close to it, but the T-shirt was still in place, stanching the blood. That was good. Anne righted the mirror and slid the key into the ignition.

47

It was well after midnight by the time they pulled into the shabby little town, if the one-road collection of crumbling stucco single-stories really deserved such a distinction. The valley was filled with places like this, wide spots along county highways where a few people still lived, keeping their heads down and shoulders up against the elements. Some of them even had names.

This one didn't. On any map or kind of official paperwork, this place was probably listed as *Unincorporated Conejos County*, comprised of a couple of duplexes, a vet's office, and a boarded-up grange. It would do just fine. Anne parked the Ninety-Eight in the snow-dusted alley behind the vet's office and cut the engine and headlights, but left the heater running. In the back seat, Gemma moaned and stirred, still unconscious. Anne sighed and let her forehead connect with the crest of the steering wheel. Gem wasn't getting any better, but it didn't seem like she was getting any worse, either. They could probably wait a few hours until she had to do the next thing. That was the smarter play, anyway. Alarms in the middle of the night tended to draw more attention than alarms at dawn. One meant that somebody was doing some shit they shouldn't, while the other probably just meant somebody had fucked up while they were opening up shop.

Keeping the volume down, she switched on the radio without looking, still tuned to the same news station as before:

"Reports are still scattered concerning details of the deadly forest fire that broke out late yesterday morning in Colorado's San Luis Valley. The US Forest Service reports that they're starting to get the blaze under control, but ground crews are still struggling to fully search the area. Early reports indicate six dead, with more expected—"

Anne switched it off again. Rubbed at her eyes with her good hand. Only six dead. Guess that meant the Forest Service hadn't made it up to Cabot yet. What an absolute mess she'd made of everything. It was like no matter where she turned, no matter what she did, the end result was fucking anarchy and a mountain of dead bodies, courtesy of Anne Heller, Our Lady of Perpetual Destruction.

She let her tired gaze drift up and out of the windshield. Overhead, the thin thumbnail moon hung low above the earth, as if on the verge of a full-on planetary collision. Most nights when the moon was this clear and big and bright, Anne found herself looking at the crescent, that sharp, glowing scythe suspended in midair as if hung by a wire, but tonight? Tonight, she couldn't help but stare at the dark of it. The shadow of the earth, inking out every trace of the moon save for that razor scythe. No shadow should be that big. Shadows were small things, insubstantial, temporary. Finger-rabbits flickering on bedroom walls. A shadow so big that it could disappear the whole goddamn moon? That was something else entirely, incomprehensible in its enormity. A perfect reminder of how small and fleeting life really was.

Human beings styled themselves the masters of the universe, but that was just self-flattery. The universe, in all its infinite immensity, didn't give a shit about them. Their lives, their problems, all their endless failures, it was all so infinitesimal. They hardly existed at all, on a cosmic scale. A hundred generations born and gone within a single fraction of an instant. None of it mattered. None of it would last.

Sitting there behind the wheel of the Oldsmobile, watching the stars drift slowly through the early morning sky, Anne found a great comfort in that. Meaninglessness had never bothered her. She didn't need the world to be an orderly place to feel all right about it. All the unexplainable shit she'd lived through had only served to underscore the central chaos of existence. It was all just flux and discord. There was no inherent meaning to any of it, and nothing anyone ever did would change anything on a universal scale. This tiny, momentary existence was all anyone ever had. So the only things that meant anything were what you chose to give meaning to. That was all. And right now, the only thing that really mattered in Anne's world was making sure that Gemma didn't bleed out in the back seat of their dead friend's car.

In the faint glow of the dashboard light, she turned the heater up until it started to rattle and screech, then unbuckled herself, leaned over the seat, and checked the bloody T-shirt against Gemma's slashed-up belly. Gem flinched at her touch, but didn't wake, her eyes spalling back and forth underneath sweat-slick lids. Anne peeled the wadded-up fabric away and looked at the mess underneath: the bleeding had slowed, but it wasn't going to stop without stitches. Those gashes needed to be disinfected, too. No telling the kind of nasty shit Darlene had caked under her claws.

She waited until the blue light of dawn started to climb the horizon, then grabbed the lock-out kit from her backpack and left the car. There was no one around to see her go; this place was remote enough that even if there was, the county sheriffs wouldn't arrive on the scene for a half hour or more, and by then, she'd be long gone.

The back door to the vet's office was a battered old metal job, painted over a half dozen times and chipping away in as many different shades. It had probably come with the building way back when, with no security features beyond a single dead bolt set above the handle. Even one-handed, it wouldn't be tough to get through, unless the pieces inside had started to rust out. Anne hadn't pulled a B&E job like this in years—she'd all but given that shit up once she and Jessup had found each other—but picking locks was basically like riding a bike. Once you learned how to do it, you never really unlearned it. Unzipping the lock-out kit, she knelt and went to work. It took her a couple of minutes longer than it normally would have, but with a little elbow grease and a lot of patience, she managed to slide the dead bolt back and slip through the old metal door unnoticed.

Inside, the vet's office was dark, save for a few weak always-ons in the exam rooms. Anne let the old door close behind her with a soft metal click and stood in the hallway, straining her ears to listen—for people, for alarm systems, for guard dogs, whatever. At first, there was nothing, but then—there. Something was definitely beeping in the front of the office. Biting back the waves of pain that flowed out of her shattered arm with every step, Anne stole through the office to the lobby and the hardwired security system mounted to the wall next to the front door. It was an old model, years out of date, but still counting down the fifteen-second grace period before it alerted the authorities. Anne knew the brand. Moving quickly, she lifted the plastic panel covering the keypad and punched in the thirteen-digit manufacturer's override, her own personal Konami Code, never to be forgotten. Up, up, down, down, left, right, left, right, B, A, fuck you. The system beeped once more, then shut itself off. Great. Easing the panel back into place, she limped past the receptionist's desk toward the exam rooms and started hunting for the supply cabinets.

Anne had learned a long time ago that if you needed to cadge medical supplies and buying them outright wasn't an option, you didn't hit doctors' offices or urgent cares, and you definitely didn't go to fucking hospitals. You hit vets' offices. The supplies they used were basically the same as they used on people, and unlike every ER and most urgent cares, they didn't keep cops posted on watch at all hours. Pharmacies weren't a bad choice when you could chance them, but with the flaming shit show she'd been dragging behind her since Durango, she wasn't going to risk another cow-eyed rent-a-cop recognizing her and calling 911, or worse, going all Clint Eastwood on her. Not when Gemma's life hung in the balance.

The supplies were in a metal cabinet in the farthest back of the three exam rooms, its heavy metal doors closed up tight with a combination padlock. Anne's stomach dropped into her shoes. Goddammit. Her lock-out kit wasn't getting past that, and she hadn't exactly thought to pack a pair of fucking bolt cutters. Fuck. Fuck, fuck, fuck, fuck, f—

Overhead, the exam room lights snapped on, momentarily blinding her. Near the doorway, she heard the shuffle of soft shoes on tile.

"Something specific you're looking for?" someone asked.

Anne's shoulders fell like a dilapidated house collapsing under its own weight. Unsteadily, she turned around, feeling her face burn hot. The woman standing in the doorway was short, curvy, with a head of curly dark brown hair above a pair of sleek horn-rimmed glasses. She was wearing rainbow kitty-cat scrubs and pair of busted Converse All-Star high-tops. A stethoscope hung around her neck. An ID card on a lanyard was clipped to the hem of one pocket.

"Jesus *fuck*," the woman said, wide-eyed at Anne's sling-held arm, and all the blood and filth covering her scorched clothes. "The hell happened to you?"

All the fight that was left in Anne went out of her in a heart-beat. Blood loss, shock, sheer exhaustion, she didn't know what else. Maybe all of it. In this moment, it hardly seemed to matter. She felt herself swaying backward without meaning to. Her shoulder blades smacked against the supply cabinet, jolting her crushed arm, and then she was sliding down and down until her ass hit the cold tile floor. A second later, the woman was kneeling next to her, feeling for her pulse with two fingers. Her touch was cool and sure against Anne's flush, filth-streaked skin.

"Hey," the woman said. "Hey, you gotta stay here with me, okay? Tell me what's going on."

The words *no cops* burbled out of Anne's lips, a chewed-up mouthful of raw meat.

"I'm not going to call the cops," the woman told her. "But we gotta get that arm set, all right?"

Drunkenly, Anne rolled her eyes up to look at the woman. Took a deep breath, then another. Felt the wet gauze inside her head start to clear. She worked her jaw again, trying to speak, but the words came out all smeared.

"What was that?" the woman asked her.

Anne swallowed back a mouthful of spit and bile. Tried again.

"It's not just me," she said.

Limping down the alley, Anne braced herself against the brick wall as she led the woman toward the Ninety-Eight.

"She's there," Anne said, gesturing at the big blue sedan. "In the back."

Stepping softly, the vet crossed over to the side of the Olds and bent to look through the window. Anne knew what she'd see inside: Gemma, delirious and blanketed in blood across the back seat, Murph riding shotgun in his carrier. It wasn't what anyone would call *good*.

"Please," Anne groaned. "Please, just help her."

Pulling away from the glass, the woman looked back at Anne, and for a moment, her expression softened.

Together, they wheeled Gemma in from the Ninety-Eight on the biggest stretcher the woman—Dr. Rebecca, she'd said her name was—had. Apparently it was for Great Danes. Murph slung high over her back, Anne helped as much as she could, but with her left arm little more than skin covering splintery pulp, it was a minor miracle that they managed to get Gem on the exam table at all.

Dr. Rebecca pointed to the bench seat on the far side of the exam room as Anne set the carrier down on the floor and unzipped it.

"Sit down over there," the vet said as she went to the locked supply cabinet. She spun a few numbers into the combination padlock and tugged it open with a heavy *CLUNK*, then threw the doors wide and started pulling supplies from shelves.

Anne did as the doctor ordered and sat, sliding herself onto the bench before removing Jessup's squall coat as gingerly as possible. Underneath, her forearm was a smashed-up wreck. Black and red and blue and swollen all over, it looked like raw blood sausage, or like someone had tried to play a Buddy Rich drum solo on it with a ball-peen hammer.

"*Mrrrowl.*"

A soft, insistent pressure brushed against her shins—Murphy. Cradling her destroyed arm against her belly, Anne leaned forward and dangled her other hand down to rub lovingly at the big cat's whiskered cheeks. He nuzzled into her fingers, then hopped up on the bench next to her and padded onto her lap, pressing himself against her. She curled her good arm around him and held him close, resting her face on the soft fur between his narrow shoulders as he started to purr, low and gentle. A second later, Dr. Rebecca was there beside her. Anne watched her fill a sterile hypo from a rubber-capped bottle.

"Do you have any food?"

Quizzically, the vet raised an eyebrow. "What?"

"For him," Anne said, nodding toward the purring cat in her arm. "He likes chicken. If it helps."

"Oh. Uh. Yeah. I'm sure we can wrangle up something here in a little while," Dr. Rebecca said, her tone softer than it had been only a moment before. "Just, let's . . . Here, give me your arm."

Anne shot a questioning look at the needle and bottle in the woman's hands.

"For the pain," Dr. Rebecca explained.

Anne shook her head, trying to stay the woman for a moment.

"Can't be fuzzy," she said.

"You won't be. We still need to get your arm x-rayed and set, and I can't do that if you can't tell me what parts hurt the worst. It's not going to put you under; it's just going to take the teeth out of it. That's all. Okay?"

Anne studied the woman's face, trying to figure out how much shit she was full of. If she'd called the cops already, they'd have shown up by now, and the doc certainly wasn't blind; it wouldn't take much more than a strong breeze to put Anne down and keep her there. She didn't need the needle.

"Fine, yeah, do it," Anne said.

Dr. Rebecca already was. With an easy, practiced movement, she swiped an alcohol swab over the skin just above Anne's elbow, then sank the needle in. The relief was almost immediate, shivering up and down her trashed arm in a cold, slushy wave like an ice floe. Anne sucked air between her teeth. The worst of the pain was already starting to ebb.

"Holy shit," she coughed. "Just, holy shit."

Dr. Rebecca smiled, satisfied. "Yeah, that's what I thought. Now you just sit here and chill for a couple of minutes, okay? Let that

do its job. I'm going to take care of your friend, get her stitched up.
After that, we'll get your arm looked at."

She rose without waiting for a response and crossed over to the
exam table and Gemma. Like magic, a bottle of rubbing alcohol and
a short stack of paper-packeted needle-suture combos appeared on
the prep cart beside her. Unrolling a bundle of steel surgical tools,
Dr. Rebecca looked over at Anne, then nodded at Gem.

"What's her name?"

Anne thought about lying. Decided against it. "Gemma."

Getting in close, the vet peeled Gem's eyelids back one by one,
checking them with a penlight, then snapped on a pair of blue surgical gloves.

"Gemma, I'm a doctor, okay?" she said, her voice stadium-
announcer-loud. The tee stanching the bloody furrows on Gem's
belly went into the trash can as Dr. Rebecca used a pair of bent surgical scissors to flense away the raggy remains of her shirt, exposing
the wounds underneath. "I need you to say something if you can
hear me, okay?"

Face up on the table, Gem's face buckled, and a thin, pained whine
came warbling out of her. That seemed to be enough for the doctor.

"That's good," she said. "That's real good, Gemma." She looked
over at Anne. "Can you stand?"

"I think so?"

"Good. Come here."

"Why?"

"So you can hold her hand. Trust me, she's going to need it."

Still feeling the cool rush of the painkillers coursing through
her veins, Anne set Murph aside, then stood and shuffled over to
the table. Awkwardly, nervously, she slipped her good hand around
Gemma's. Her skin was feverish, hot and clammy. On the other
side of the table, Dr. Rebecca capped the bottle of alcohol and used
the point of her thumb to pierce the foil underneath.

She gave Anne a grave look. "Hold on tight," she said, then raised
her voice: "Gemma, I'm really sorry, but this is going to hurt. A lot."

Then she upturned the bottle of alcohol over Gemma's bloody
midsection and squeezed. A thin stream of clear liquid jetted out

of the mouth of the bottle, and the sharp, acrid tang of isopropyl hit Anne's nostrils like a punch to the face. Gem's fingers clamped down on Anne's hand like a hydraulic press, and she started to scream and thrash while the vet rinsed the worst of the mess from her wounds. Anne sucked air against the sheer force of Gem's grasp and squeezed back as hard as she could, as if she could anchor her to reality, as if her touch could somehow carry her through the worst of the agony.

"Please don't die," she whispered without meaning to. "Please, Gem. Just hang on for me."

A moment later, Gem went still and silent as she mercifully passed out once more. Anne realized with no small amount of wonder that she was on the verge of tears again. Gemma Poe being in this much pain was unacceptable, unfathomable. She didn't deserve this. Gem didn't deserve any of this, but Anne had dragged her into it, headlong toward certain death because of her own selfish fucking curiosity.

This was all her fault. Just like Lisa. Just like Dutch. Just like all of it.

On the other side of the table, Dr. Rebecca ran the stream over the brace of gashes in Gemma's belly again, clearing away as much gore as she could, then set the bottle aside.

"Christ, those are nasty," she said, poking at the wounds with nitrile fingers. "You going to tell me what the hell you two ran into?"

Anne wheezed. Didn't answer. Dr. Rebecca gave her a wary look as her hands worked, tearing open paper packets and laying curved needles threaded with thick purple sutures side by side atop the cart.

"Yeah, okay. No problem." With an elbow, she gestured to a rolling stool between Anne and the bench seat. "Kick that over here, will you? This is going to take a minute."

With one foot, Anne rolled the stool over, then turned her attention back to Gemma, watching the vet work.

"Why aren't you calling the cops?" Anne blurted. The words came out of her mouth in a clumsy surge, the syllables all bunched together like it was all one word, *Whyaren'tyoucallingthecops.*

"Are you really complaining?" Dr. Rebecca didn't look away from the task at hand.

"No," Anne said, shaking her head. "No. It's just. You don't have to do this."

"Trust me, I am acutely aware of what I do and don't have to do, thanks," the vet said as she slid the needle through Gemma's skin once more and pulled the suture taut.

"So what the fuck?" Anne said. "Why?"

"Look, I know who you are," Dr. Rebecca said after another second. Anne bristled, but the vet waved her off. "Relax. At this point, it would be kind of hard not to. You guys are all over the news."

Anne sighed. "Yeah, I've heard that."

"Then you probably know that they're making you out to be these big, bad psychopaths, right? Makes sense, everything they've connected you to the past week or so. The debacle in Durango, that shoot-out in Alamosa. I mean, you know all about it, right? You were there."

She pulled another stitch through Gem's belly and kept talking.

"It's an easy narrative, no doubt supplied by the cops. At this point, I'm kind of amazed they haven't blamed antifa or some shit. And yeah, from far enough away, sure, it might look like the work of a psychopath." She raised a finger. "Except."

"Except what?"

Now Dr. Rebecca looked up at her—just for a second, just long enough for Anne to see the knowing smile that was playing at the corners of her mouth and eyes.

"Psychos don't beg strangers to help their friends, and they don't plead with the people they love to not die," she said.

Anne felt her face flush.

"The other piece of it is, psychopaths definitely don't take as good care of their cats as you clearly do." Dr. Rebecca glanced over at Murphy, asleep on the exam room's bench seat, fat and happy, then went back to work on Gem.

"I don't know what you've been through exactly, Anne Heller," the vet said, "but whatever else they're saying about you? You're not some monster." She kept working.

When it was done, Dr. Rebecca taped the stitched-up gashes over with long strips of white medical gauze, removed her gloves with a snap, and tossed them in the trash. On the table, Gem was still unconscious, but her breathing seemed to have steadied.

"All right," the vet said, turning back to look at Anne. "Your turn. Let's get your face and arm stitched up, then we'll take a look at that wing and see how bad the damage is."

It wasn't good. Anne didn't have much experience reading x-rays, but looking at the screen before her, she didn't need to be an expert to understand how completely fucked her arm was. Above the wrist, the human forearm consisted of two bones running in parallel, the radius and the ulna, and in going through the RV's wall like she had, Darlene had managed to completely demolish both. These weren't hairline fractures or clean breaks; the x-rays showed that both bones in Anne's forearm were fully in pieces, shattered like glass. Beside her, Dr. Rebecca's face was grim as, on the floor between them, Murphy ate from an open tin of cat food, lapping up mouthful after mouthful of shredded chicken, barely even bothering to chew.

"Look, I'm not going to bullshit you; this is bad," the vet said. "Like, really bad. You're sure you can't go to a hospital?"

Anne shook her head. "I'm sure. Why?"

The woman pulled the horn-rims off her face and rubbed at her eyes with the heels of her palms. On her scrubs, the cartoon kitty cats grinned unblinkingly at Anne, a technicolor horror.

"Because I can't fix this," Dr. Rebecca said, replacing her spectacles.

"What do you mean, *can't?*"

"I mean, if you'd just fractured it, sure, yeah, that'd be one thing. I can fix a crack. Even a clean break I could work with. I'd get you in a cast and send you on your merry way, but this . . . isn't that. This is *catastrophic*. No other way to put it. You need surgery to set this right, screws, wire, physical therapy. I'm a backwater vet, okay? I can't do that kind of shit here. Even if I tried, I'd probably just end up doing more damage."

Anne chewed on the inside of her cheek. In the dark parts of the screen, she could see her reflection, a thick black train-track pattern where Dr. Rebecca had stitched up the gash in her face. Her other arm, the one that hadn't been crushed to pulp, the vet had zippered together with three neat rows of surgical staples that seemed to be holding her tattered skin in place all right. All in all, she looked like a ghost of herself, hell frozen over and thawed out in the sun.

"So what are my options?" Anne asked.

"Other than going to a hospital, like, now?"

"Other than that."

Dr. Rebecca widened her eyes and puffed out her cheeks. "I mean. Amputation?"

If she was joking, Anne didn't think it was funny.

"Honestly, there aren't many," the vet said. "I can try and set the fragments in line as best I can, get you in a cast, and give you something for the pain, but I can tell you right now that it ain't gonna help it heal right. You don't get this thing to an actual trauma surgeon in, like, the next day, my guess is the arm stops working altogether. That's at a minimum. More likely, probably end up losing the whole thing anyway. Breaks like this, they can cause nerve damage and shit, go septic. All sorts of nightmares, medically speaking. Can't just rub some dirt on it and walk it off."

So she wasn't joking. Good to know. But lopping her arm off at the elbow wasn't exactly an option right now. Anne jerked her chin toward the hallways and the exam room beyond, where Gem lay sleeping.

"What about her?"

"She'll probably be fine if you can keep those gashes from getting any more infected. I shot her up with enough antibiotics to last her for a couple of days, but after that, she's going to need a full run. 'Til then, keep her hydrated, keep her resting."

"You have any more of those antibiotics around?"

"Sure, but they're for horses. People are a little different."

"But they'll work?"

The glasses came off the vet's face again. "I mean, yeah, I guess, if you cut the doses down to like a third? Maybe less? It's not great, but it'll do the job."

"That's all I need them to do."

Dr. Rebecca looked back at the glowing x-ray images on the computer screen. "So what are we going to do about that?"

Anne tried to smile at her. The doctor didn't return the gesture.

"What cast colors do you have?" Anne asked.

Dr. Rebecca set her up with a racecar-red cast that reached from the ridge of her knuckles to just below the crook of her elbow, then handed her a paper bag filled with prepacked painkiller samples, individually wrapped alcohol swabs, and the promised horse antibiotics in prefilled hypos. Gem was still in and out, so the vet helped Anne walk her and Murphy out to the Oldsmobile and pile her in the back seat. Above, morning had taken full possession of the sky again, lighting the snowy valley up in a panoply of whites and blues and browns. As they wheeled her out, Gem moaned softly and rolled onto her side. Anne and Dr. Rebecca lifted her onto the blood-ruined bench seat, then pushed her feet the rest of the way inside and closed the car door as gently as they could manage.

"She's probably going to be sleeping for the rest of the day," Dr. Rebecca said. "Let her. She needs rest. Honestly, all three of you do."

Anne glanced sideways at Murphy in his carrier, then showed the woman a thin, joyless smile that pulled at the stitches in her face.

"Right," the vet said. Her breath hung in front of her face in thick steam clouds. "Look, I'm not asking you to tell me what happened, because it's not really any of my business. But you came here for a reason. You brought *her* here for a reason. Right?"

Anne felt her face turning hot under the woman's scrutiny. "Your point?"

"Whatever your plan is, whatever happens next . . . just make sure it's the right move, okay? Trust me, I get it. Shit gets complicated when you love someone. That's why I'm telling you, she can't go on like this. She just can't. So take care of her. No matter what. Can you do that?"

Anne ground her teeth, but she didn't say anything. What could she say? That the vet was wrong? She wasn't. She had a point. Shit, she had more than a point, she had Anne's entire number.

"Yeah. I think I can," Anne said.

The vet held out a hand, and Anne took it. Gave it a gentle shake.

"Good. Keep your head down, Anne Heller. Shit's getting crazy out there."

You don't know the half of it, Anne thought. She let go of the vet's hand and got in the car. She was already peeling out of the alley by the time Dr. Rebecca headed back inside to open up for the day.

48

Anne navigated the Ninety-Eight along the cracked, snow-dusted blacktop, heading farther and farther south until she saw the yellow sign rise up on the roadside: WELCOME TO NEW MEXICO, LAND OF ENCHANTMENT. A few miles down the highway, the road forked; Anne went left and rode the winding two-lane to a hilly little town called Vasquez. There were a handful of well-kept houses scattered around, plus a food mart, a derelict Texaco, and a two-story motel that didn't seem to have a name at all. Snow and frost blanketed it all, reaching from the asphalt all the way up to the hilltops and covering everything in between. In the distance, she could see a cell phone tower rising out of the bare trees, surrounded by long, low-hanging lengths of power line sprouting off in every direction.

The Oldsmobile's tires thumped over the raised curb as Anne nosed into the L-shaped motel's small parking lot. Cranking the wheel hard to the right, she parked in the last spot in the lot, then cut the engine. Driving a car with both her hands made her crushed arm ache something wretched underneath the fire-engine cast, but at least she could still drive. That had to count for something.

Cold air chapped at her face and lungs as she crossed the little parking lot to the office situated at the very bottom of the L. Inside, she passed the bored teenager behind the desk a hundred and eighty in cash, the going rate for a three-day stay, plus another hundred for the security deposit, since she wasn't using a credit card. Taking the room key without a word, she showed herself out.

The room was on the first floor, halfway up the far side of the building, facing away from the main road. Anne pulled around and parked in front, then left the car idling and stepped out into the cold once more. Wary of prying eyes, Anne worked the room key—an actual key, rather than a card with a magstripe or an RFID chip inside—into the lock and let the door swing open. The room itself was just like the one Gem had driven her out to after saving their asses back in Pecos: two queens with an end table and lamp between, a TV against the wall, a desk table in the corner, and a bathroom in the back. There was something almost comforting about its familiarity.

Everything inside—the blankets on the beds, the carpet, the drapes, even the fucking wall art—was rendered in the same faded, mass-produced imitation Ganado print that you saw everywhere across the Four Corners. Probably hadn't been replaced since the early '90s. Sure smelled like it hadn't. This place was musty as hell. Chances were good that the kid at the front desk was what passed for cleaning staff here, and if Anne had to guess, he was probably more interested in jerking off and doing on-the-clock bong rips than making sure every room in the motel was perfectly daisy fresh.

Whatever. The room didn't need to be spotless, it just needed to be safe. Locks on the doors, blinds on the windows, heat, and running water. End of list. One by one, Anne flipped on all the lights, then went back outside to get Gem and Murph.

Cold winter wind blustered at her back as she stepped inside the modest little food mart. Comprising three dusty aisles, the shelves were stocked with staples and essentials, with an ancient display fridge humming in the back, a crack in its glass door patched over with a peeling stripe of duct tape. Near the front of the shop, a woman sat behind the 1980s-era cash register, her nose buried in a paperback novel. She barely took notice as Anne stepped inside and lifted one of the black plastic shopping baskets from beside the door.

Standing in the middle aisle, she set the basket between her feet and started filling it with nonperishables: peanut butter and jelly, cans of tuna and SpaghettiOs, beef jerky and granola bars, food for Murph. She didn't know how long they'd be staying in Vasquez, but

she didn't want to take any chances. With Dr. Rebecca confirming
that their faces were still all over the news, the less they had to leave
the room, the better.

Up at the front, Anne emptied her basket onto the counter and
turned her attention to the liquor wall behind the cashier. She
scanned the bottles, the labels. Gin. Gemma liked gin. With her
casted arm, Anne pointed to a large green-glass flask of Tanqueray.

"That, too."

The cashier nodded. "Sure," she said, and added it to the pile on
the counter.

Anne's attention drifted to a small rack of cheap office supplies
next to the bubble gum, pens and markers, and wide-ruled note-
books under a sign that read SCHOOL SUPPLIES!! She passed
one of the spiral-bounds and a four-pack of blue ballpoints to the
cashier.

"And these."

When everything had been rung up, Anne passed the woman
a few twenties and smiled innocuously while she made change.
The bell above the door chimed pleasantly as Anne stepped outside
again, both bags in her good hand, and began the short walk back
to the motel.

Anne ripped another page out of the notebook and started again.
At this point, the pockets of her coat were overflowing with
crumpled-up false starts and failed attempts. Anne had never been
any good with words; she was even worse with feelings. Trying
to combine the two was a recipe for disaster. Still, she had to try.
Gemma deserved that much, and they both knew it.

Can't go vanishing on me like that again, Heller.

Anne put pen to page and gave it another shot.

Under the covers of the nearest bed, Gem moaned and shifted,
curling her knees up to her chest. She'd been in and out (but mostly
out) since they'd left the vet's, though when Anne had gone to
fetch her from the car, she'd actually surfaced for a couple of minutes, leaning on Anne the whole way into the room. After that,

she'd crawled into bed, asking if they were safe now, the question muddled by sleep. Anne told her they were. When Gem then asked Anne if she was okay it just about broke her heart. Not knowing what else to say, Anne told her, *Yeah, I'm good.* It hurt so bad, lying to her like that, but what else could she say?

Murphy ambled out of the bathroom with a soft, grumpy *mrowl* and hopped up on the bed next to Gemma. He kept his big green coin eyes trained on Anne, as if he knew exactly what she was planning to do and clearly didn't approve. She held a hand out to him, curling her fingers into a loose fist, knuckles down. Reluctantly, Murph traipsed across the bed to her and ran a whiskered cheek against her fingers, purring softly.

"I know, okay?" she told him, her voice little more than a whisper. Any louder and she'd risk waking Gemma, or worse, start crying again. "I know. But I've got to."

Murphy fixed her with the look of loving contempt that only cats were capable of, then turned and retreated across the bed to curl up next to Gemma. Anne didn't blame him. She wished she could do the same. Instead, she went back to her notebook.

It would have been easy to say it had happened the second Norris's bullet had obliterated Dutch's brain, or when Anne found Gem mauled and bleeding but miraculously alive in the snow up at the Bonny ranch, or a hundred other single moments she'd lived through in the time since shit went south in Durango, but that wouldn't have been the truth. The truth was, it wasn't any one moment that had made Anne's mind up about what she was going to do next. It was all of them, together. It was everything. Every moment she'd survived, every ounce of pain absorbed and every loss suffered. The continuum of her life had led her here, to this old motel in this tiny little nowhere town, trying and failing to put her feelings into words, and the hell of it all was that maybe for the first time in the entire history of her, she finally felt like the path forward was perfectly clear.

At the end of the day, Anne's life—just like every other life, she supposed—was a story of loss. It was a crooked, winding trail that mapped all the way back to the night her mom had died. No loss she'd ever suffered had ever hurt quite like that first one, because with it came the horrible realization that at any time, for any reason, or no reason at all, the world could pull your card and decide to snatch away the things that were most precious to you. Control was an illusion. It was all just chaos and havoc masquerading as order. What a shitty thing to learn at six years old.

Beverly had been the first, the single stone that had kicked off the landslide that followed. But what a landslide it had been. Grandma, Merrill, Jessup, Joanie, Dutch, Lisa. Shit, even Travis and Iris had broken her heart in their own way. There had been plenty of others she'd lost along the way, but those were the ones that hurt worst.

Anne had never thought of herself as a particularly naive person—she knew that pain and loss were part and parcel of life, just like the beating of your heart or the air in your lungs—but at a certain point, you had to make a choice: accept the hand you were dealt, or punch the dealer in the face as hard as you fucking could.

For the longest time, Anne had been playing the cards she'd been handed, making the best of shitty situation after shitty situation, and what had it netted her? Gemma was the only person she had left, and she wasn't about to let her burn for some shit that should have never been her problem in the first place.

Another page came out of the spiral, wadded up and thrown away. Fuck. She didn't know how to say any of it, and she was getting sick of trying. She already felt like a prize asshole for what she was about to do. If Gem had been in any shape to argue about it, she knew she'd have told her as much—she'd come this far, hadn't she? But look what it had gotten her: a belly full of stitches and a head full of fever, on the run from something neither of them could understand, let alone fight. No way in hell would Gem survive another fight; not in the shape she was in. Anne wasn't prepared to let that happen. Not now, not ever. She was done losing people that she loved.

Left of anything else to say, she scribbled the only words she could think of on the page in front of her. They weren't much, but she hoped like hell they would do. She ripped the sheet out and folded it in half, then pulled back the blankets and tucked it into

Gemma's front pocket. She turned to go, then paused. *Hell with it.* She bent over the bed and, pushing a stray braid away from Gem's face, kissed her—just once, softly, gently, hoping that wherever Gemma was right now, she could feel it. Standing up straight, she scritched Murph behind his ears.

"Keep an eye on her, all right?"

Murphy purred and curled up closer to Gem. Anne figured that was about as much assurance as she was going to get. She took one last look around the little motel room, making sure she hadn't forgotten anything. It was time to go.

The sun hung low over the hills, already well past the halfway point in its slow march across the sky. Night came on early in the winters out west. It was going to be dark soon. In the driver's seat of the Olds, Anne reached across the wheel with her good arm and pulled back the silver knob in the control panel, switching on the headlights. It was only going to take her a few hours to get where she was going, and after that, well, she'd figure it out.

Only a few hours on the road. Even with her busted arm, she could manage that. She turned on the heat, switched on the radio. "Childhood's End" by Pink Floyd started pumping out of the Ninety-Eight's tinny old speakers, its insistent beat almost arterial in her ears. Anne turned it up as she pulled back onto the road out of Vasquez, heading north. Back to Colorado. Back to the valley and all the horrors that waited for her there.

49

Yellow police tape hung off the cabin, snapping and dancing in the wind like streamers off the world's most depressing parade float. Lit in sharp relief by the Ninety-Eight's brights, the place was somehow more of a wreck tonight than it had been only a week ago. Anne shouldn't have been surprised that the cops had found their way up here, because that was what cops did: kept digging until they hit bedrock. But still, it felt like a violation, seeing the cabin draped in crime scene tape like this. Another painful reminder that nothing could be trusted, that nowhere was safe.

For the twentieth time in the last two minutes, Anne checked her mirrors, studying the darkened hillside around her. She figured the cops probably hadn't posted someone up here in case she came back, but the chances weren't exactly zero, either. Still, everything seemed quiet. If there were any badges waiting in the wings for her to show her face, they'd have been on her by now. Cops weren't exactly known for their subtlety. She shifted her toe over to the brake pedal and eased the Oldsmobile to a stop in the frozen mud. Then she got out of the car, leaving the headlamps on to light her way to the front door.

A wave of déjà vu crashed into her—she'd done this same exact thing before, stalking toward the empty cabin in the glow of the Ninety-Eight's headlights. But this felt like a fun-house-mirror version of that night, all the details warped and distorted. Tonight, there was no Jessup, no Dutch, no safe haven, no intent to stay longer than a few scant minutes. She had to get in and get out. There was a plan in place here, and no part of it involved getting herself lost on some misguided nostalgia trip.

With her cast-wrapped hand, she pulled a few lingering belts of yellow tape from the open doorway and stepped inside. The cold from the snowstorm had suffused the cabin in the time she'd been away, but Anne could still make out the unmistakable smell of other people in here. A sour cocktail of old sweat and cheap hand sanitizer and coffee breath hung in the air. Judging by the way it lingered, coupled with all the footprints in the mud and snow outside, there'd been a lot of them. Instinctively, she loosed her Glock from the waistband of her jeans, letting it hang down by her thigh.

"Anybody in here?" she called out, expecting no answer and receiving none.

The living room had been tossed—couch cushions gutted, picture frames knocked off their nails and left in puddles of broken glass on the floor. All the cabinets in the little kitchenette hung wide open, emptied of their meager contents. Opposite the front door, Anne could see a rusty scuff mark on the wall where Darlene had thrown Dutch that night, tossing him out of the way as if he weighed nothing. Bemusedly, Anne wondered what the cops had made of that shit, if they'd even noticed it at all.

The bedrooms were in similar shape as the living room, tossed top to bottom as the cops excavated the place looking for clues and evidence. In the big bedroom, they'd taken the mattress—soaked as it was in Jessup's blood—out entirely, leaving only the empty wooden frame behind. Anne knelt beside it and slid the false panel in the floor back, then lay down to feel around inside. Nothing. Naturally. Not that she'd expected her mom to hide a hunting rifle in there or that she herself had somehow missed it the first time around. But that didn't stop it from being a little disappointing.

Still, she needed to find that rifle. The whole plan, such as it was, hinged on it. Without it, she'd have to pivot, and at this point, with one busted arm and running on two days without sleep, that seemed more than a little suicidal.

Anne searched the cabin from top to bottom with no luck. Despite all her hopes, despite the plan, the rifle wasn't here. Could be the cops had found it first and taken it with them, logged it as evidence, in which case it was basically lost forever. Might as well have thrown it down a bottomless pit. It was a worst-case scenario, sure, but one that was seeming more and more likely with every

passing second. Bending at the hip, she picked up one of the disem-
boweled couch cushions off the floor, tossed it back onto the sofa,
and sat down.

Had Lisa been wrong? Whatever rifle she'd been talking about,
could be Beverly never even brought it up here in the first place.
She might have ditched it or sold it or something long before she'd
dragged Anne away from the Passage to hide out up here. All
Anne had to go off of was the cannabis-smeared memory of one
paranoid old woman in the woods, and at the end of the day, that
wasn't going to go as far as Anne had hoped.

She sat forward on the couch, letting her eyes relax as she owled
her head around the living room one last time: the kitchenette,
the empty cabinets, the broken-down little coffee table, the stone
hearth with its stopped-up chimney—

Wait.

Wait just the fuck a minute.

Rising from the couch, Anne crossed the living room in a few
quick steps. The hearth was cold to the touch, a stack of smooth,
cinder-block-sized stones mortared together long ago, built to
withstand the punishing Colorado winters. Her hand found the
wrought iron flue handle and pulled—jammed. Last time she'd
been up here, she'd thought it had been bird's nests or something
stopping up the chimney, holding the flue in place . . . but now she
wasn't so sure.

She pulled on the handle again, harder this time. It still wouldn't
slide all the way back, but it gave, just a little. Anne wished she had
both hands for this shit. Bracing one foot against the stone, she
gritted her teeth and pulled as hard as her bruised, broken body
would allow, until she felt her arm strain and wail in its socket.

This time, it worked.

Metal ground against metal as the handle slid outward along
its track. A gray surge of ash gasped out of the fireplace's mouth,
blanketing the floor. Anne kept pulling, forcing the flue open inch
by rickety inch until something solid came tumbling out. Long
and heavy and wrapped tightly in a filthy old blanket, it thudded to
the ground from the chimney above, scattering ash across Anne's

shoes. Anne laid it atop the broken coffee table and set about unwrapping it.

She could feel her heartbeat in her fingertips as she peeled back
the duct tape and layers of sodden fabric. This was it. This had to
be it. There was nothing else it could be.

And the thing was, the rifle that waited for her inside the blanket was beautiful. Long and sleek and deadly with a rich walnut
stock and blue-black finish on the steel, it was exactly what Anne
had hoped it would be. Better, even: it was a semiautomatic, which
was good news for her, since the odds of her working a bolt-action
with any measure of dexterity with one arm were close to none.

There was a monster of a scope mounted on the thing, too—on
a clear day, you could probably just about draw a bead on someone
two states over, looking through that. The words *Browning BAR
Mk. II* stood out on the rifle, etched deep into the metal. This was
one hell of a gun that her mom had owned.

That was when she saw it: Wrapped around the Browning's barrel, just behind the notched foresight, was a thin silver chain. A
matching disk pendant hung from its length, glinting in the low
light. Just like Lisa had said. Anne could see that it had been engraved with a looping letter *B*.

With shaking fingers, she lifted the necklace from the rifle's
barrel and wrapped the chain around her fingers, pressing the little pendant into her palm, the metal cool against her skin. So few
times in her life had she felt like she was actually connected to her
mother—most of the time, Beverly was a memory of a memory,
a fuzzy recording of a decades-gone shadow play. Every piece of
her that Anne had was second- or thirdhand, passed down to her
through various intermediaries—Grandma, Lisa, even Win.

But not this. Not the pendant, not the rifle. Beverly had hidden
these away herself, and they'd sat here undisturbed until Anne
came to lay hands on them. These things were a direct line from
Beverly to her daughter, and for a brief moment, Anne felt as if her
mom were there beside her, pointing her in the right direction.

Then the moment passed. Anne was alone again. But maybe—
just maybe—that was okay.

The chain went around her neck. The rifle went back into the blanket, and the blanket went into the trunk of the car. She left the cabin door hanging open, just like she'd found it, wreathed in yellow tape. Starting the engine up, she waited for the heater to get warm, then pulled her burner from her pocket. She thumbed through the call log until she found the number she was looking for. He answered on the first ring.

"I swear to god, I thought your ass woulda been in the ground by now. I shoulda known it was too good to be true. Serves me fuckin' right, I s'pose."

All the genteel lilt had gone clean out of Win's voice, leaving his Southern accent a lot more *hill country* than *high society*. Him and all his airs.

"Can't kill what's already dead, Win," Anne said, her tone as calm and still as a mountain lake.

"You got a lotta balls, calling me after what the fuck you did."

There was a trembling vein of fury buried just beneath his voice. He was keeping it under control for now, but Anne knew that it wouldn't last. Shit like that never did, and especially not with men like him. Win's anger was destined to be everybody else's problem. The trick was getting him to hear her out before that fury came up for air.

"I'm aware," she said.

On the other end of the line, she heard the old man take a steadying breath.

"So what the hell d'you want? Can't imagine this is a social call."

"I want this over, Win. Done with."

"You had your chance," he hissed. "Kinda fucked that one up, didn't you?"

A wire of rage shivered inside Anne's chest. He'd been the one to kick the hornet's nest, not her. He'd dragged her up there to Cabot, he'd hurt her friends, he'd forced her hand. She wanted to shove his face into it, but pissing him off would only fuck things up worse for her in the long run.

Stick to the plan.

"I'm not going to die for your bullshit, Win."

On the other end of the line, the old man made a strangled noise.

"Now you just wait the fuck a minute—" he snarled.

"But if you want to, I'm not going to stand in your way."

Silence flooded the line. For a second, Anne thought he'd hung up on her, but then realized that she could still hear him breathing.

"Meaning what?" he asked, suspicious but suddenly calm.

"Meaning that if it's going to take me opening up your door so you and Darlene and whoever the hell else can march through like good little lemmings and leave me the fuck alone? So be it. I'll do it. Just don't expect me to go with you."

"You wouldn't," he said, his voice barely a whisper now. "You wouldn't really."

"I would, though."

"Why?"

"Way I see it, it's this or you and Darlene spend the rest of your lives trying to run me down. Shit, you'll probably make it happen eventually. Let's just cut the knot and get it over with."

There were muffled voices on the other end of the line. Win was conferring with someone—probably John—with his hand over the phone.

"Fine," he said a second later. "When?"

"Let's say dawn. I'll meet you in Cabot. We'll head up together, then you and yours can walk hand in hand into the waiting jaws of oblivion. I truly don't give a shit. As long as I never see you again."

"You won't," he said. "My word on that. Dawn?"

"Dawn. And, Win?"

"Mm?"

"No bullshit, okay? No tricks, no games, none of that. You're getting exactly what you want here. Don't try and fuck me over on this."

"I wouldn't dream of it," he told her. "I'll see you in the morning, Annie."

She killed the call without saying anything else. There was nothing left to say. If he actually showed, he was a dead man, and that was all there was to it. Sliding the back of the burner off with her thumb, she pulled out the battery and the SIM card. The battery she tossed out the window. The SIM card she snapped against the dash.

Dropping the transmission into drive, she wheeled the Oldsmobile around and, for the very last time in her life, drove away from the ramshackle little cabin that she and her mom—for a little while at least—had called home. She had a long way to go and not much time to get there, and as her taillights faded into darkness, the shadows rose up around the cabin and welcomed it, abandoned again, into their loving embrace. Before too long, it was like no one had ever been there at all.

50

She watched the big blue sedan sweep off the dirt road and back onto the two-lane blacktop about fifteen minutes after it had first shown up, materializing out of the darkness and distance like a robin's-egg wraith. Her first thought had been to follow her up and do it here, but she'd held off. No good ever came from jumping the gun. Travis was proof positive of that. So she sat silently in the dark of her stolen Toyota on the side of the road and waited. Whatever Heller was looking for up there, it was a safe bet she wasn't staying long. Iris had already gone up to check it out, see what the big deal was, and she hadn't exactly come away impressed. It was just a pile of old bones half-buried in the snow, another shitty abandoned cabin in a state full of shitty abandoned cabins. A couple of crappy bedrooms, a kitchenette on the verge of falling apart, a few framed pictures on the walls that Iris had taken great pleasure in smashing on the floor. Trash everywhere.

But it meant something to Anne. Maybe that was how she knew she'd be back eventually. It was only a matter of being here when it finally happened. The waiting didn't bother her, really. Finding the place had been the hardest part. As long as no extra-curious cops came back to poke around, she'd be fine up here for as long as she needed. And she was. A few hours after she'd pulled her boosted Corolla off to the shoulder a half mile down the road, here came Heller, just like clockwork. Without looking, she reached over and picked up the newsprint-wrapped bundle from the passenger seat, feeling its comfortable weight in her hand.

On her way up, she'd stopped off at an army-navy surplus in one of the valley's innumerable little shitball towns. The place was a white supremacist fuckhead's wet dream, the kind of place with more flags on its front than windows: *Don't tread on me, POW*

MIA, the American flag, the Confederate stars and bars. Inside, a camo-clad guy wearing a name tag that identified him as *Reff* had helpfully informed her that they didn't sell guns there, not even antiques, because of the *fed'ral govurmint*, and no, he didn't know where she could source one extra-legally, either. But he could sell her a nice blade or two if she thought that might do the trick.

Of course she took him up on it. Her contacts had started changing their numbers once the assholes on the news started connecting her name with the Durango job; after the blowup at the Pink Flamingo, they'd all miraculously dried up and blown away.

She'd walked out of the army-navy with a pair of high-powered binoculars and a couple of new knives wrapped up in the previous day's *Colorado Sun*: a nasty little folder that she could open with a flick of her wrist, and a big mean fixed-blade that the January 6 insurrectionist behind the counter had called a KA-BAR. Obviously, Iris would have preferred a .45 or a shotgun, but any port in a storm. She'd just have to be smarter about how she went about this, that was all.

Far up ahead, the big old sedan's lights vanished over the crest of a hill. Iris started the Toyota and pulled off the shoulder, tires spluttering gravel. She had to keep her distance. With a little bit of luck, Anne wouldn't notice her on her tail until it was too late. With a little bit more, she wouldn't see her coming at all.

51

Anne got to the foot of the mountain an hour and a half before sunrise. Everything was still dark, drowned in the kind of obliterating void that made it seem like the whole of reality had somehow been deleted from existence. It only ever got dark like that out here, away from the city lights and the people. Used to be that kind of darkness scared her, but this morning, it was a comfort. A cloak to hide herself in. Exactly what she needed.

Outside of the Oldsmobile, the air was cold and rich and sweet from the fire. The smell of burned pine hung thick in the air; it stuck to the back of Anne's throat when she breathed in, forcing her to suppress the urge to vomit. Seemed like the Forest Service had finally gotten everything under control up here, but in the early-morning dark, there was no way to tell the extent of the devastation. She guessed it wasn't inconsiderable. Fires burned hard in Colorado. Probably something to do with the elevation. A mile and a half above sea level, the sun just baked everything dry. All it took anymore was one loose spark to send the whole countryside up in flames. Seemed like every year there was some blaze chewing up the hills and mountains, displacing people from their homes, causing untold damage. Time was, it mostly happened over the summer months, but lately, it was starting to seem like Colorado fire season lasted all year round.

Anne had retraced her steps back to the dirt road that she and Gem had come screaming down only two mornings ago and ridden it until the switchbacks and narrows got too much for her to navigate in the dark. She knew it was possible to get the Ninety-Eight the rest of the way to Cabot—the Passage had driven it up there before, after all—but she wasn't going to Cabot. At least, not the way that Win thought she was. She was going up high, and that meant going on foot.

The cold was vicious this morning, though. The hike up was going to be a real bitch, even bundled up tight as she was. Best thing for it was to keep moving. In the low glow of the single trunk bulb, she checked her backpack to make sure she had everything she'd need, then tossed her Glock in on top and set about unwrapping her mom's rifle from the blanket. There hadn't been any spare ammunition in the chimney, which meant that she only had the four shots in the Browning's magazine, plus one in the pipe. That was okay. If everything went according to plan, she wasn't going to need more than five shots, anyway. And if it didn't? Well, that was what the Glock was for.

With no small amount of effort, she slung the backpack over her shoulders, then one-handedly slid the Browning through the pack's straps so it hung crosswise against the small of her back. Getting it loose in a pinch wouldn't be easy, but that was why you showed up early. You could never totally avoid pinches, but with a bit of forethought, you could at least minimize them. Jessup would have been so proud.

The trunk lid thumped shut underneath her hand. Time to get this show on the road. Anne turned toward the slope and started hiking. She didn't think it was going to be that far, but doing it uphill, in the dark, was definitely going to drag it out. In the distance, she could already see faint orange light starting to bleed past the edge of the horizon. She still had time, but not much to waste.

Overhead, a few stars had slipped free of the clouds and hung high in the sky, cold and twinkling-bright. Anne followed them up the mountain, huffing and puffing and feeling every second of no rest she'd gotten over the past few days. But still she forged ahead, over rocks and fallen branches, rotting logs and blankets made of dead leaves and pine needles. The slope grew steeper, then stole her breath entirely. Her head swam. But she didn't stop. She couldn't.

I wouldn't dream of it. What a fucking joke. No matter what ludicrous promises he made, Win was never going to let her just walk away. His ego wouldn't allow it. Not after everything that happened. If she took him at his word and walked her ass into Cabot like it was no big deal, he'd cut her off at the knees faster than she could draw breath. It wasn't that so many of his people were dead, though she didn't doubt that was what he told himself—it was that she'd embarrassed him. She'd pulled his pants down in front of everybody that he'd spent years conditioning to regard him as high pontiff. To someone like Win, shit like that couldn't go unanswered. Better to hit him before he even saw her coming.

She'd seen the ridge from the window of her cabin that first morning in Cabot, a high, narrow bald patch at the peak of a towering rock wall that sat just east of the little ghost town. It had seemed imposing at first, yet another obstacle trapping her in Cabot with Win and his cadre of lunatics, but the more she thought about it, the more she realized that with the right timing, a little patience, and a powerful enough rifle, you could do some real damage from up there if you wanted to.

And she really, really wanted to.

The only problem was how bald the ridge itself was. No rocks, no trees, no cover. Just a smooth, empty stretch of stone, perfectly exposed for anyone on the ground to shoot back at if they were so inclined. But that was why she'd told Win dawn: The ridge sat on the eastern side of Cabot, meaning that for a little while at least, she'd have the sun at her back. Anyone on the ground looking her way would be blind, forget about them returning fire with any kind of accuracy. And anyway, by the time any of Win's remaining faithful got their shit together enough to try to shoot back, it would already be too late.

One bullet. That was all she needed. One bullet to delete Winston Mayr Fucking Hofmann from the world and scatter the rest of his true believers to the goddamn wind. Darlene would still be a problem, but without her dear husband to point her at his problems like a body-horror cruise missile, she was all violence and hunger and chaos. No thought. Anne had seen enough to know that shit for sure. She'd deal with Darlene later. Win was the linchpin. Knock him off the board and watch the whole rotten game crumble to pieces.

The sun was already crawling up past the horizon by the time she settled down on the cool stone to set up and wait. The light had been bleeding in from beyond for a while now, growing steadily like some great and terrible fire in the distance, but it was nothing like the full blaze of the sun. The brightness this high up was as absolute as the darkness that had come before it, illuminating everything, warming her as she set her backpack aside and lay there on the ridge, studying the whole of the ruined little town through the Browning's scope. There wasn't much of it left.

Up and down Cabot's single dirt road, the buildings that hadn't burned to the ground stood in blackened shambles, charred ghosts of what had been there before. The cabins had been shredded by the fire, same as the old outbuildings and the church. The only structure that seemed relatively untouched was the barn, its faded red glory set far enough back from the rest that the fire hadn't had a chance to spread its way. But the rest? A ruin, a total loss. She was pretty sure that Aunt Lisa would have called that poetic justice.

It hit her with a twinge of pain that Dutch's body was probably still down there inside the barn, exactly as they'd left it. His certainly wasn't the only one: Corpses dotted the whole landscape between the piles of wreckage, abandoned where they'd fallen and left to burn. There were dozens of them down there, crumpled up and scorched to crisping, fed to the monster by a man who didn't give a single solitary shit about them beyond what they could do to serve his twisted interests. What was it he had said, that night at family dinner? *It is ours to pave our passage with great sacrifice.* Funny how he'd neglected to mention whose.

Balancing the forestock of the rifle atop her cast, Anne swept the Browning back and forth over the smoldering hole that used to be a town, watching the tree lines for any flicker of movement. Just because the place looked empty didn't mean it was, but the sun was well and truly up at this point. Win should have shown his face by now.

Something was wrong. Something had to have—

Out of the corner of her eye, she caught a flicker of movement among the trees near the top of the town, just past the pile of black bones that used to be the old church. Anne shifted her weight and repositioned, drawing a bead on it with the Browning. Took a long, slow breath in, then blew it all out, stilling her hand. Waited. Watched.

One bullet. That was all it would take. One single bullet.

A tall, gaunt figure emerged from the forest above the town, his pate reflecting the morning sun under a limp wash of thinning hair. John. With him was a blond woman Anne didn't recognize, another cultist from family dinner or the gathered crowd before everything went to hell or both. She watched them step fully from the tree line, noting the gun in John's hands: the same semiautomatic range rifle Tobias had been wearing over his shoulder that first day. Somebody had been expecting trouble. He wasn't wrong to.

More movement from the trees behind them: two more Passage faithful stepped free of the trunks and joined John and the blonde, eyes wide and alert, each carrying pistols. No Win, though. She wasn't exactly shocked. Why would the old man bother keeping his word when he could just send a death squad of true believers up here to do his dirty work? Not like Anne hadn't seen this as a strong possibility, anyway—this shit was a Hail Mary, and she knew it. And it wasn't like she had any room to talk about playing it fair.

Either he'd known that she was feeding him a line, or he'd decided to make a play of his own. Result was the same either way. She took another long, slow breath and sized up her options as she watched the cultists spread out and snake through the wreckage of their annihilated town, searching. Maybe it was best to just pack it in, pull back to the Ninety-Eight, and try to come up with a new plan. She could head down into Cabot and take the fight to these assholes proper, but then what would she do? Grab John or one of his friends and hurt them until they gave the old man up? Maybe that shit would have been a viable approach when she had a body that wasn't like 80 percent broken glass, but now? Forget about it.

Through the scope, Anne watched one of John's troops—the blonde he'd emerged from the woods with—weave between a pair of torched cabins. Anne followed her with the rifle, tracing her every step. She couldn't have been older than eighteen if she was a day, with dirty-blond hair tied back into a ponytail and a faceful of painful-looking acne. The old man really must have been scraping the bottom of the barrel for gunfighters at this point, or else he was betting that Anne wouldn't hurt a kid. Maybe he'd already forgotten what had happened to Tobias. Fucking psychopath. Anne really didn't want to shoot the girl, but if it came down to that—

She heard the footsteps a second too late.

Just in time to get kicked in the head.

52

Her finger slipped as she recoiled from the sudden pain in her skull. The Browning bucked in her hand, but she barely felt it. A gunshot clapped at the air. Stars swam in front of her eyes. Whoever it was kicked her again, this time catching her in the ribs. Anne flipped onto her back and groaned, grasping frantically at her side. Someone ripped the rifle out of her hand and she heard it clatter to the stone.

When she opened her eyes again, she found herself staring up into the glowering visage of Iris Bulauer.

"Surprise," Iris hissed.

Anne didn't think. She didn't need to know how Iris was standing here right now. She didn't even draw breath, because she couldn't afford the half-second it would take. She just reared a leg up and kicked Iris in the stomach as hard as she could.

The air belted out of the woman in a single, heaving gust, and she stumbled back, clutching at her midsection. That was when Anne saw the knife in Iris's hand, a big, wicked hunting job with a serrated spine and a nastily-curved point. Jesus. Rising as quickly as she could, Anne backed up toward the edge of the bald ridge, keeping distance between them. Iris looked like shit. Her bleached-blond hair, a patchy, grocery-store-box job on the best of days, hung greasy and limp above the dark, sleepless circles ringing her eyes. *Road-worn*, that was the word. Too much running, too little sleep. She could have—*should* have—gone to ground anywhere else in the world, taken the L and limped away with her life. But instead, she was here, looking to settle up.

And the hell of it was, Anne didn't blame her. She would have done the same thing in her position. Shit, she kind of had, in her own way. But there was so much more on the line right now than Iris Bulauer getting her revenge.

Far below, in the shambles of the town, Anne could hear John and his people shouting to each other. Coordinating. So much for the element of surprise.

"Iris," Anne coughed, trying to catch her breath. "Don't fuck-ing—"

But Iris wasn't really interested in talking. She leapt at Anne in a mad balestra, slashing wildly with the knife. It was all Anne could do to duck out of the way as she felt the tip of the blade part the air an inch in front of her nose. Her mind went to her Glock, but it was well out of reach, inside her backpack and set aside when she'd first reached the ridge's summit. Going for it now would be suicidal. Iris would skewer her through the second she showed her back.

The smaller woman lunged again, thrusting the knife at Anne's stomach with both hands, eyes glassy and feral. Feinting left, Anne went right and clapped her good hand around both of Iris's wrists, digging her heels into the ground, trying to shove her off course. Iris course corrected faster than Anne would have guessed and redoubled her efforts, driving the blade at her midsection. Anne pushed back as hard as she could. The curved tip of the knife hovered an inch away from Anne's stomach, spinning in frantic little circles as Iris tried and tried again to force it the rest of the way forward.

"*Fuck you, fuck you, fuck you, fuck you,*" Iris snarled, spraying strings of saliva with every spat syllable.

"Iris, stop—" Anne grunted, throwing all her remaining strength into holding the woman off.

It wasn't working. Iris was smaller and older than she was, but she wasn't hurt, and what was more, she was fucking pissed. The tip of the blade sank a half-inch closer, plucking at the fabric of Anne's shirt.

"Iris, please—"

But Iris wasn't listening. That much was obvious from the frenzy in her eyes, the way the cords stood out on her neck. There was no reasoning with someone like that. One more good push and the woman would belly her.

So Anne did the only thing she could think of: she clubbed her in the face with the broadside of her cast.

Pain exploded up Anne's arm, pulling a bright white curtain over her eyes. She heard herself scream as she fell back, and for a second, the knife moved with her like a cart on a rail. Then it reversed course, sliding through her bare hand as Iris stumbled away. Anne didn't even realize she'd been cut until her vision cleared and she saw the blood. The hunting knife had filleted her hand, slashing the thick purple scar open in a deep red arc. It didn't hurt, though—why didn't it hurt? Maybe crunching her ruined arm against Iris's chops had maxed out her body's ability to feel any more pain right now.

Blood welled out of the gash in a sick wave, rolling down her wrist and forearm to splatter on the ridge's smooth stone. Only a few feet away, Iris rocked back on her heels, rubbing at her face with her free hand. Her nose was bleeding, and one of her eyes was already starting to swell shut.

"Asshole," Iris wheezed. "Oh, you unbelievable asshole . . ."

Inverting the knife in her hand, she darted forward again, stabbing at Anne in a vicious overhead swing like a tiny little Michael Myers. This time, Anne lunged forward to meet her, pushing off the rock and dropping her shoulder to drive her full body weight into Iris's stomach. She felt the knife split the fabric of her shirt, but didn't think Iris had stuck her for real. Anne shoved Iris back once more, took another step closer to the cliff's edge—and her backpack.

More shouting from below. Then a scream—piercing, cruel, inhuman, and loud enough to shake the whole mountain.

Oh, fuck.

"Iris, you need to get out of here, right now," Anne said.

The older woman spat a mouthful of blood and snot as she glared at her.

"Fuck you," Iris snarled. With her other hand, she pulled a second knife from her pocket, a stubby little folding job. "You don't get to walk away from this. Not again. Not after what you did."

Anne took another step to the side, swallowing back a fresh jolt of pain-nausea as she scanned the ground for her bag or the Browning. They both lay at the edge of the rock, still a good ten feet away. Well out of reach.

"No, you don't understand, it's not about that—"

"I don't care what it's about! This shit ends here!" Iris's voice was working itself toward crescendo, louder and louder until she was full-on screaming at her, punctuating every word with a thrust of the knife. "Everything you did. Everyone you hurt. What gives you the right, huh?! You *took everything from me*, you fucking asshole! My *whole life*! What makes you think I'm just going to—"

Blood burst from Iris's mouth as a small, slender shadow rose up behind her. The blonde from the bottom of the mountain. But of course, the blonde wasn't the blonde. She never had been. The skin hung too loose off her bones, the smile on her face was too vacant, too carnivorous. Her eyes were too white.

The blonde opened her mouth wide—too wide—revealing row after row of foul, jagged teeth, then chomped down hard on the place where Iris's shoulder met her neck. The woman thrashed, and the knives flew from her hands. Gore belched from Iris's face as Darlene tore through her, ripping away skin and muscle and splinters of bone in a frantic, carmine spray.

Anne watched it happen in slow motion, though it couldn't have taken more than a second or two: Darlene burrowed into Iris, *through* her, digging out everything inside the skin with those hideous, bestial claws. Torn loops of intestine and tatters of organs spilled out of the hollow trunk of Iris's body in a waterfall of blood, and then, all of a sudden, there was no more Iris. Just a pile of shredded flesh on the ground.

Standing over the ruins of the woman that no longer was, Darlene shivered and shook herself like a dog trying to get dry. The bottom half of her stolen face was a beard of blood. Anne suppressed a gag and snatched up Iris's little folding knife from where it had skittered to a stop near her feet, then backed up closer to the cliff's far edge. Rocks slid out from under her heels and went skittering over. She hazarded a momentary look over her shoulder—the slope wasn't that steep on this side of the ridge. It wasn't great, but it was a far cry from the sheer rock face that overlooked the majority of the town. She took another step along the edge, then another. The rifle and her pack were almost in reach now. Just a little farther . . .

The shape-shifter spread her ropy, blood-streaked arms in a beneficent pose, like a biblical saint bathing in the warm morning light, and then she started to change. Her skin rippled like liquid, then tore away in rags. Her mouth opened wide and wider, splitting at the corners and folding back, giving way to all those awful fucking teeth and the new face hiding in the depths of that mutilated gullet. New eyes peered out from the maw as yellow tumors bloomed on the red flesh rising to the surface, bursting open to reveal fresh, unblemished skin underneath.

The folds of Darlene's mouth peeled back and back, wrapping around her skull like a caul as the new face emerged, pulled and stretched in only wrong ways. A wet tearing noise violated the morning silence as Darlene bent and warped herself into a fresh configuration.

At first, Anne didn't recognize this new mask. Her body was too deformed and misshapen to even read as human anymore—too many eyes, too many teeth, too many open wounds gushing too much blood. But when Anne saw a tuft of red hair burst from one of those swollen sarcomas, she dove for the rifle and started shooting. She knew what face the shape-shifter was going to show her next. The same face she'd dreaded seeing ever since she found herself in this mess, rendered in grim, gory parody.

Not her. Anyone but her.

The Browning kicked and jumped in her hand with every pull of the trigger, the big .30–06 bullets blowing messy holes in Darlene's mutating form, exposing pale, bloody twists of half-grown bone underneath the flesh. Anne pulled the trigger one last time, and the rifle snapped empty in her hand. Darlene swayed, then fell. It wouldn't last. It never did. So without thinking much about what an unbelievably stupid decision she was making, Anne tossed the Browning aside, grabbed her pack, and threw herself over the shallow side of the ridge.

The ground rose up to meet her too fast, and Anne felt herself bounce against it like a rubber ball. Then she started spinning. The world melted to a smear of brightly colored paint as she tumbled end over end down the snowy slope. Her face connected with rock, then she felt her cast smack against the stone ground, and she screamed—at least she thought she did. She really couldn't hear anything beyond the heavy deadweight crunch of her body caroming down the side of the ridge. An hour to climb up; all of fifteen seconds to fall back down. It was almost funny.

She finally slid to a stop at the bottom of the hill. Her head rang like a bell, and her nose was pouring blood. The staples on her right forearm seemed to be mostly intact—only one or two had come loose in the fall, and threads of bright red blood trickled out from where metal had torn away from skin. Experimentally, she flexed her hand, making sure she'd still be able to shoot. Seemed good enough. On her other arm, the cast was cracked into pieces where she'd belted it against the ground, but it would probably hold for a little while longer. More than anything, she was just amazed that the cast (and probably her nose) was all she'd broken on the way down. Just as amazing was the fact that she'd somehow managed to hang on to her backpack.

Moving fast, she unzipped the biggest pocket, searching frantically for her Glock. Some part of her expected to find the pistol in pieces, shattered irreparably in the fall. She'd seen that movie before. But somehow, the streamlined nine mil was intact, cradled safely among her fresh burner and her contact book, Lisa's letter, and the boxes of bullets. Glory be to Austrian engineering. With the gash in her good hand, she wasn't going to be winning any marksmanship competitions anytime soon, but she could still shoot. She found the pistol's grip and drew a bead on the top of the ridge, waiting for Darlene to come spilling over after her like a landslide made of teeth and hate.

But Darlene didn't come. Inside her head, Anne counted to ten, then to fifteen and twenty, but the ridge stayed still and silent. Good. She rose to her feet again and slung the backpack over one shoulder. Some part of her wanted to be glad that Iris was gone, happy even. But she'd meant it when she'd told her to run—Iris was a double-crossing, murdering asshole, but getting ripped to literal shreds by Darlene wasn't a fate Anne would wish on anyone.

The fall down the ridge had deposited her just outside of town, in a patch of pines that the fire had left relatively untouched. From where she stood, she could make out a handful of outbuildings just beyond—Cabot's main drag. Pausing for a moment, Anne tore a strip of fabric from her own shirtsleeve and wound it tight around her slashed-open hand. It wasn't going to do much, but it was better than nothing.

Farther into town, Anne kept low and strained her ears, listening to the morning around her, hearing voices whispering back and forth:

"—shouldn't be out here, we should be with him—"

"—you heard the gunshots. That was her, you—"

"—just keep looking. We're going to—"

Slipping from shadow to shadow, Anne made her way up the hill as she listened to them chatter, counting the voices against what she'd seen through the scope of the Browning. Unless she was way off, with Darlene out of the picture for the moment, that left John with his rifle and the two others. She was pretty sure it was a safe bet that neither of John's sidekicks had any experience using a gun when shit got heavy, but that didn't make them not dangerous. Pretty much the opposite, really. Experience meant control. Cooler heads prevailing. Inexperience made you panic, made you do dumb shit because you didn't want to die. Amateur-hour assholes got people killed for no reason, every single time.

Near the top of the town, the remains of the cabins thinned out near the church, spacing themselves apart in direct contrast to the packed-tight barracks-style housing farther down. Win's cabin used to be around here somewhere. Folding herself deep into the nearest shadow, Anne stood still and waited, watching. John and the others were already heading her way, spreading out as they swept the town for any sign of her. She stayed frozen until one of them—an older guy, freckled, sallow, slow—drew close, then she stepped free of the darkness and stuck the muzzle of her Glock in his face.

The guy came up short and stopped in place. His eyes bulged in his sockets as his Adam's apple bobbed up and down. His mouth fell open an inch, then two. He was going to scream.

"Don't," Anne warned. Her voice was dry and craggy, her tongue like brittle old sandpaper. "Please."

But then the guy did it anyway.

"*JOHN!*" he howled, his voice high and reedy. Anne winced at the sound, then saw the guy's hands twitch around his pistol.

She pulled the trigger.

A little red poke-hole appeared high up in the guy's cheek as his skull snapped backward in a fog of aerosol red. The gunshot swallowed his scream, ricocheting off the ridge and disappearing into the clear blue sky.

The guy fell to the ground as another gunshot barked from farther down the hill. Beside her head, one of the blackened posts belched splinters. Flinching back, Anne wheeled around and saw John standing in the middle of Cabot's one road, still some forty yards away, range rifle nocked firmly into his shoulder.

He fired again. Anne felt the bullet drone past her ear, heard it smack into the dirt somewhere behind her. Then she was moving.

Chased by bullets, she sprinted through the rubble, arms up around her head. The rifle shots were getting louder—John was advancing, marching straight up the hill to close the distance as he squeezed off shot after shot like the fucking Terminator. Stupid, John. Really fucking stupid. Anne juked right, then went left as the skinny old prick fired in the way wrong direction.

Anne heard the rifle click dry as it fired on an empty chamber, magazine spent. Jamming one leg into the ground, Anne changed

direction and rushed the old man full-tilt, screaming like a ban-
shee. He never had a chance. She crashed into him with her full
weight and buried the Glock in his belly. The gun kicked twice in
her hand. John went silent and dropped like a stone, gasping and
pawing numbly at his gut.

"Sweet God, oh God Jesus," he gasped.

Blood, thick and dark, brimmed out of the holes in his belly like
an oil strike, bubbling and chuckling as it rolled over his sides to
soak into the snowy ground beneath him. Anne stood over him,
watching him bleed. She kicked the range rifle away.

"Oh, you bitch," he wheezed. "Oh, you rotten little *bitch* . . ."

Anne pointed the Glock at his face. "Where is he, John?"

"Fffffffuck you," he groaned. Blood frothed out of his mouth,
staining his chin stringy red.

Anne kicked him in the ribs, hard enough that she heard something inside crack like dry firewood. John screeched and rolled over,
clawing at the ground like he was trying to drag himself away. Anne
kicked him again. He yelped and went still.

"Tell me," she said. "It doesn't get any better for you after this, I
promise. So you might as well—"

A scream exploded from the wreckage behind her, a sharp wail
of panic and fury. Anne turned and saw the last Passage member
charging her, a silver revolver clutched in both of her hands. Her
voice jumped an octave and the little six-shooter started barking
flame. Anne felt something punch into her side like someone had
thrown a fastball into her ribs.

Two more shots from the Glock—*pow, pow*, in quick succession—
and then the girl was on the ground, too. But unlike John, she didn't
stop screaming. Anne limped over to her and saw that her bullets had
punched a hole below the girl's navel and torn away part of her neck.
The scream finally died in her throat when she saw Anne standing
over her, the grim reaper herself. The girl raised her revolver—but
she didn't point it at Anne. She just smiled and placidly tucked the
muzzle under her own chin. Anne saw her mouth moving, but she
couldn't hear the girl's words over the wet gurgle of her breathing.

"What'd you say?"

The girl's smile widened. *"It is ours . . . pave our passage . . . with great sacrifice,"* she wheezed. Then she pulled the trigger. The revolver popped against her chin, just once, and for a second, Anne swore she could see the girl's eyes light up like flashbulbs. Then she was gone.

What the fuck?

Anne took a step back, a stabbing pain buzzing from deep in her ribs. With sore digits, she probed at the place she'd been hit. Her fingertips came away wet with blood. Shit. Crazy little cultist had tagged her good. But if she moved fast enough, she probably wouldn't have to worry about it for long. Holding her cast-wrapped hand over the fresh hole, she trudged back over to John. Kicked him onto his back with a sharp toe to the ribs. Sprawled there, his eyes rolled in his head and he started sucking air like a fish drowning on dry land, drawing breath in pathetic little half-sips.

"Where, John?"

"Below," he mewled between clenched teeth. "He's below . . . with . . . with . . . please, you, please . . . Annie—"

Whatever he was going to say next, the Glock stole the words right out of his mouth.

53

She knew something was wrong the second she stepped into the dark of the mine. Maybe it was something in the air, the stifling underground warmth of it, or maybe it was the crushing, horrible silence that rose up to greet her as she passed through the wooden adit that marked the way.

Maybe it was the smell. Nothing else in the world smelled like that.

As she moved farther into the shadows, she felt her foot brush against something on the ground. Something heavy. Something made of meat and bone. She didn't have to get the flashlight out of her bag to know what it was, but she did it anyway.

The body lay slumped against the stone wall with his chin on his chest, eyes half-open and dull as pencil erasers. A dark carpet of blood waterfalled from his nose and mouth, plastering his shirt to his chest. The look on his face was calm, even tranquil; peaceful in death in a way that Anne had never seen on anyone. She didn't recognize him, didn't know who he used to be, but that didn't make him special. He wasn't the only one.

Bodies littered the ground all the way down the mine tunnel, men and women and kids, marking the way. Each of their chests were blanketed in blood just like the first, their faces showing that same tranquil composure. These people had welcomed what had happened to them. Embraced it. Anne didn't get close enough to really understand how they'd died, because it didn't matter. Whatever had plucked the life from their bodies, they'd done it to themselves or sat there smiling while it was done to them.

Now Anne understood. *It is ours to pave our passage with great sacrifice.* Jesus fuck.

Down and down and down the mine they went, lining the path,

filling the cramped corridor with that telltale sour-milk stench. But Anne hardly registered it.

It had started as a faint tremble at the base of her skull, the place where her spine met her brain stem: a nervous thrum that quickly built to a cascade of images and feelings, sights and smells and sounds that came from everywhere and nowhere at once, from within as if *within* had been waiting all along to spin across the surface of her brain. At first, Anne didn't understand what was happening to her, but then something inside her broke like soft yolk and it all made sense:

She was remembering.

She knew this place. She'd been here, a long time ago.

Surrounded by muttering bodies, grown-ups who had barely acknowledged her existence, she'd gone down this hole in the world before, unsure what she'd find waiting at the bottom. The mine had been bigger then, or Anne had been smaller. Back then, it felt like Ballmer's Hope had gone down into forever, the march downward into the dark so long and so steep that they must have walked past the earth's core.

They were following Win. They were following the noise, that whispering inside their heads, the same one Anne was hearing now, trembling in the darkest corners of her skull, urging her on, turning her stomach. And then . . . And then . . .

Her memories fell into place—every crack and gash in the stone, every hitch in the stone floor and low point in the ceiling. Her fingertips knew the feel of the rock, her skin the stale warmth of the air. If she closed her eyes, she could almost see the VHS glitching behind her eyelids, hear the drone of the void against Darlene's last scream.

The memories. The video. The memories. The video. They spun around and around, bleeding into each other like watercolors. It didn't matter where one ended and the other began, because they were one and the same. Every corner she turned ignited another dusty synapse in Anne's brain, firing another memory she didn't know she had, the gap between *Anne* and *Annie* growing shorter with every step until it finally faded from view and disappeared completely.

Ahead of her, the corridor took a sharp turn downward. The corpses on the ground went from propped against the walls to prone on the rock. Anne had to steady herself against the stone to keep from pitching forward and falling the rest of the way down. She wasn't going to risk breaking her neck now. Not when she was so close.

A hard, throat-splitting scream shook the mine from far above. Anne's skin went cold. Darlene had finally caught up. Anne pressed forward, anyway. There was no other way for her to go now. No turning back. No way to end it but to do what needed to be done.

Anne had known since Lisa's that she was marked for death. She would've had to be blind to miss it. Win and Darlene were never going to let her get away, no matter how hard she fought, how far she ran, how well she hid. As long as they drew breath, Anne would never be safe, and neither would anyone around her. They'd kill the whole world if they thought it would get them what they wanted. The fact that the last remnants of their people were lying dead in this hole was proof enough of that. *No price too high for entry into the Kingdom of Heaven.*

Darlene above, Win—and the icon—waiting below. One way or another, Anne was going to die down here. But she wasn't dead yet.

Farther down the corridor, deep in the darkness, past the bodies and the blood and all the things she'd never done and would never do, she could finally see a light.

The chamber at the bottom of the mine was lit with torches, small handcrafted things that flickered and danced despite the lack of breeze. They cast bent, warped shadows over everything, stretching the light like warm taffy as it lit the icon from below.

Jesus fuck, the icon. Twenty feet tall and dull white, it dominated the little space, a massive tombstone planted in the center of the chamber. Smooth and perfectly featureless but for the deep cleft in its crown, it was exactly as it had been in the video and in Anne's memories.

Oh yes, she remembered this place, too. The memories of the last time she'd stood here came back to her not in a flood but in an instant. Like a switch had been thrown, returning to her as if they'd never been gone at all. An entire wing of her memory restored in less time than it took to blink. She remembered the light and the screaming, the crush of fleeing bodies and the pain in her hands. She remembered Darlene coming apart in the light, the way her skin ran like hot wax around her bones as tumors bloomed and burst from what was left.

She remembered the way that Darlene's eyes had burned like lanterns in their sockets, trapped in that uncolor void.

Win knelt before the stone, hands folded in his lap, head bent forward as if in prayer. He'd swapped out his standard faded T-shirt and jeans for a moth-eaten, embroidered baptismal robe. Anne couldn't see his face from where she stood, but she could hear him whispering, a faint susurrus threaded through the silence of the chamber:

"—deliver us from the evils of this world that we may be reborn in the light of creation and behold all the glories that—"

Anne's shoes crunched atop the rocks that blanketed the floor near the mouth of the chamber. Win stopped praying and turned his head halfway back, pointing an ear in her direction.

"I knew you'd come. You couldn't not. You're as tied to this place as I am. This is where you were born, Annie. Where you became what you are. The key to our salvation."

Anne resisted the urge to tell him to go fuck himself. Stepping fully into the chamber, she kept her distance as the old man rose to his feet and turned to face her. The expression he wore wasn't the same one she'd seen the last time she'd laid eyes on him: gone was his mania, his rage, his poisonous fucking ego. Standing before his precious icon, here at the end of everything, the old man looked calm, even if his eyes still blazed with that same unshakable self-conviction.

"I heard the shooting," he said, gesturing toward the ceiling. "Out there. John and the rest. Are they dead?"

Anne didn't say anything. She didn't have to. Win let his head fall.

"It didn't have to happen like this. I hope you know that. You didn't have to kill them."

"I mean, if we're keeping score as to who's killed more of your people . . ." Anne said, nodding to the corridor behind her and all the bodies that waited there.

Win's eyes narrowed to razor slits in the lamplight, his fury returning to him.

"How fucking dare you!" he growled. "How dare you impugn their sacrifice!" He started forward, balling his cracked old hands into knobby fists. "I should—"

Without blinking, Anne pointed the gun at his face. Win skidded to a halt and dropped his fists.

"So that's what it is, then," he said. "Your great plan. Kill us all, let God sort us out?"

"I've heard worse," Anne told him.

The old man smirked. "Of course. I should have guessed. You could have had eternity, all the gifts of heaven and more. You could have become a part of the infinite. But you're a brute, no vision to you at all. Just like your cowardly bitch of a mother."

The gun kicked in her hand and one of Win's legs went out from under him in a burst of bright red. Blood and flecks of bone sprayed against the base of the icon, staining it crimson. Screeching, the old man collapsed to the floor, both hands clasped tightly to his knee in a futile attempt to stop the bleeding. Over the crest of his shoulder, Anne swore she could see the pale surface of the icon start to throb and ripple like flesh. The whispering inside her head warped into a high-pitched whine, like someone using a dentist's drill in the next room over. She blinked watering eyes and shook her head, trying to clear the sound.

Sprawled bleeding on the ground, the old man chuckled at her despite his obvious pain. There was no joy to it, no humor, just cruel, sick self-satisfaction.

"You're starting to hear it now, aren't you? The way it speaks to you. The way it whispers in your head. Everyone hears it eventually."

His words unraveled into a wet coughing fit that Anne barely heard over the thin, silver drone buzzing between her ears. It fizzled in the hinges of her jaw, and she tasted a kind of dead electric inversion, as if she'd licked the head of a nine-volt battery. Win's blood seeped into the flesh of the icon like water into fertile soil and the white stone—no, not stone—quivered again as thick, cabled veins started to spread under its alabaster surface.

How many innocent people had the old man and his cultists fed to the icon over the years? How many people had to die for Win to finally get what he'd been desperate for ever since that night? Anne winced as the drone inside her head grew louder.

But then it wasn't a drone anymore. It was words, a low, unbroken litany whispered in a voice that sounded to Anne so much like her own, save for the fact that it spoke in a language that she didn't. A language that wasn't human at all. She didn't recognize it but still understood perfectly. Its meaning came in images and sensations, scraps of memory and unfamiliar tastes. The icon spoke to her in emotions and colors, pouring itself into her like she was trying to drink from a fire hose. It overwhelmed her, pulled her under in a crush of that pale black, dark-white light, and she finally saw.

The icon and the ravenous existence that lay past it, through it, between it, was so far beyond what they could truly comprehend. So much larger than their limited animal capacity could ever hope to see. The icon was a part of it, but only in the sense that a single water molecule was part of an ocean. Trying to understand it all was like a sparrow attempting to learn quantum physics. It was entirely beyond their capacity and always would be.

No wonder Win and Darlene had thought of it as the voice of God. No wonder touching it had warped Darlene into that slavering, shape-shifting monster.

Nausea pinballed around inside Anne's belly and she stumbled back, trying not to vomit. Her palms were starting to tingle and burn. Her head pounded like a drum from the icon's unwelcome, unavoidable broadcast. Her eyes filled with tears, blurring her vision to the point of blindness. It was too much. She was overloading. In a second or two, she'd pass out and die, and that would be that.

On the ground in front of the icon, the old man had gone curiously silent, but Anne didn't notice. She didn't hear the heavy footsteps in the corridor at her back, didn't hear Win whisper, *Darlin'*.

But then something big hit her from behind, and she knew for sure it was all over.

54

Her face hit the ground first, bouncing off the cold stone with a hollow, concussive sound not unlike a gunshot. Anne felt the train-track stitches traveling her cheek strain and pull, threatening to pop. Her arm crashed down next, then the bloody hole in her side where the girl had shot her. A field of white stars exploded behind her eyelids, and she cried out in a hoarse mangle of pain.

Only a few feet away, the old man started to laugh and cheer like a little kid on the Fourth of July, all exultance and glory.

"Do you see?" he crowed. "Do you see now, Annie?"

She pressed off the ground with her gun hand and rolled over unsteadily, rising onto her shoulder and then down onto her back. Drawing breath was agony, but she filled her lungs anyway, blinking until her vision cleared. When it finally did, she wished to hell that she'd gone blind instead.

Darlene loomed over her like a living nightmare, a mane of fire-red hair wreathed around a face that Anne hadn't looked upon in twenty-five years. Her heart crumpled at the sight. She knew it wasn't her, but that didn't stop the word from forming on her lips, driven out of her mouth by childhood pain that had never healed over quite right:

"—Mom—"

For a single moment, Beverly Heller's face looked down at her just like she used to, back when Anne was still Annie. But it didn't last. None of Darlene's masks ever did. It happened in her eyes first, water blue giving way to empty white, glowing with that same horrible light from the void within the icon. It floated like smoke around her face, rising in wisps and curls as her lips pulled back into that familiar rictus grin, revealing row after row of wretched teeth and all the faces she had yet to wear, growing like foul cysts just beneath the surface. Fat blackflies crawled and hummed over her skin, bursting from swollen pores that bulged and split in spurts of bloody pus. They wriggled out of her flesh and took flight, swarming around her head like a rotting halo.

Anne heard herself scream. The Glock was still in her hand, and she watched it float up at the end of her arm, held in a fist she no longer recognized as her own. There was a cold, alien feeling rising in her ribs. She was outside her body as much as she was trapped within it, untethered from everything, and all she wanted in the world was for that ugly fucking thing to stop wearing her mom's face.

The Glock shook and jumped in her-not-her hand as flame belched from the muzzle. Anne didn't remember how many rounds she had left in the magazine, and she didn't really care. She'd use them all if it meant banishing the Beverly mask from Darlene's twisted skull.

Blood flew from the shape-shifter's wounds as Anne drilled round after round into her, but she stayed standing, barely noticing that she was being shot. Still Anne fired on the thing, pulling the trigger until the gun clacked empty, the slide snapping back and locking in place.

Darlene swung a claw out and slapped the useless pistol from Anne's hand. The strip of shirtsleeve that she'd used to bandage the gash from Iris's knife came with it, unzipping the wound beneath with a ripping noise that Anne heard more than felt.

"You can't stop her," Win wheezed from somewhere behind her. "You never could. No one . . . You were always coming back here, Annie. Always."

Anne could only lie there and watch as the gunshot wounds in Darlene's head and neck started to heal over again, knitting themselves together with new flesh and bone, the hideous caricature of Beverly reasserting itself from underneath the damage. The shape-shifter clicked and clacked its endless nightmare mouth at her, the sound like a baby's rattle made of bone and meat. Anne raised her wounded hand to shield her face from what came next.

But then a low, seismic rumble shook the chamber, rising up from somewhere deep underneath the rock floor, a sleeping giant waking abruptly. It drowned out Win's damp wheezing, the thrum of Anne's pulse in her temples, the chatter of Darlene's teeth. Perched above her, poised like some massive bird of prey seconds from striking, the shape-shifter froze, transfixed by that great tectonic roaring from below.

It transcended sound, transcended physical sensation. It was everywhere and everything, so all-encompassing that at first Anne didn't even realize that it was coming from the icon. She clenched her eyes shut like a child trying to hide inside herself, but the rumble wouldn't stop. It couldn't. Not now. Her hand turned cold and stayed that way.

What . . . ?

When she opened her eyes again, she saw the blood rising from her open palm in strings and spiraling cords.

It didn't hurt. It didn't really feel like anything. That cold that she felt—in her hand, in her face, in her ribs—was it. A faint numbness, a hint of a chill as the blood was pulled from her body and all its many wounds.

She lay there and watched her blood float through the air, drawn along by some imperceptible gravity, tracing its path toward the powdery, skin-like surface of the icon. It splattered across its face in strange patterns, sluicing back and forth in red curls and spirals that made Anne dizzy to look at too closely. The blood sank into the icon's surface like Win's before it, but this time, the stone didn't shiver, it didn't ripple. It cracked.

With a wet ripping noise, the front of the icon split in a scything diagonal curve, half-fissure, half-wound. Anne watched her blood rise weightlessly into the tear, feeding it, and the more the breach was fed, the more it spread. Anne started to crawl away. She knew what was going to happen next, and she couldn't—

The icon imploded, its fleshy surface crumpling inward as the gravity well within tore its façade away, revealing the great, bleeding horror that waited in its center.

A freezing wind blew through the little chamber, bitter and

brutal enough to make Anne's skin ache. The cold of the void, of deep space. Absolute zero, screaming out of the icon's heart. Anne pressed herself to the ground and closed her eyes again, trying to shield herself as it sheared through her. Somewhere near and yet very far away, she heard Win cackling at the top of his lungs, overjoyed, victorious.

Anne looked and saw him in supplication before the void, arms thrown wide as he stared unblinkingly at the churning luminescence that lay beyond.

After all these years, the door was finally open. The light was coming through.

It was just like it had been in Anne's memories, just like it had been in her nightmares. Not white and not black and yet too much of both like the first blossoms of a crippling migraine, it bled from the fissure—the doorway—like blood from a wound, twisting and churning, a living thing. The drone inside her head was deafening now. It filled her up and held her in place as she wept freely and beheld the light and all the horrors that thrashed within its everlasting gaze. There were teeth and claws and tumors and eyes—too many eyes. Rheumy and bloodshot and mismatched, they stared in every direction all at once, boring into the very heart of her. She saw mouths the size of planets and worlds as small as pinheads. She saw veins and calcified arteries like endless superhighways, clogged with twined black clots hundreds of miles long. It was every horrible thought she'd ever had come to life at once, and as it streamed out of the icon, it curled itself around Win in waves and formless tendrils, lifting him up off the ground and drawing him through the door, into its freezing embrace.

Anne watched the old man float through the icon's heart into that other place, carried by its hideous light, still laughing, still cackling. Through his madman's laughter, she thought she heard him speak three words:

"—behold the Revelation—"

The words rang something inside her like a bell, another memory long dormant. She felt herself grasp for it as it flitted through her mind, trying to conjure up the image in full, but there was no time.

Inside the light, Win was coming apart.

It started at his spine, slicing down from the base of his skull in a thin, glowing line, as if he were being butchered from the inside out. His limbs split at the joints and disassembled themselves— first his hands, then his arms, then his bare feet moving up to his legs. His back flayed itself along that perfect line, the skin peeling out and spreading like a pair of grotesque angel's wings above twin ladders of bloody ribs. Black cancers blistered along his raw musculature like a spreading flame. The hair on his head crumbled like cigarette ash as the skin beneath cracked and flaked away, exposing sickening white patches of skull beneath.

Anne tore her eyes away to look at Darlene: Standing before that bright, corrupting emptiness, the shape-shifter was transfixed. She stared blankly into the living light boiling in the heart of the icon, then lurched suddenly forward, as if pulled by a tether, until she stood mere inches from the light. Too close.

Darlene's body started to warp and shift again in the radiation of the light, not exactly changing shape but, rather, losing it. Her skin melted and ran as all her masks bled away, giving way to a twisted, malignant, and frail thing underneath, a human shape drained of all essence and vitality. Darlene hardly seemed to notice. She was too busy leering at the void, at Win.

The old man rose higher and higher as he sank farther into the light, and as he drifted slowly around to face Anne and Darlene and the world he'd left behind, his laughter turned to screams. The light swelled and surged around him like a pair of monstrous jaws closing tight. His voice rose in pitch until it was impossible to differentiate it from the howl of the abyss still so loud inside Anne's head.

The last she saw of the old man before the light devoured him entirely were his eyes, catching like lanterns inside his peeled skull.

Then the light snapped down around him, and in a spray of blood and pulped meat, he was gone.

Around the edges of the hole in the icon, the rock started to tremble and quake, the light from within framing Darlene's drained form in perfect silhouette. But it was already starting to fade. The door was closing. Unsteadily, Anne lurched to her feet against the gun-shot wound in her side. It was nothing short of a miracle that she hadn't passed out yet. She laid her casted hand across the bloody hole, feeling the warmth ebb out of her in slowing pulses. With all the blood that the icon had already taken from her, there couldn't have been that much left.

With her free hand, she slipped Iris's little folding blade from her pocket and eased it open—it was a wide, flat jag of dark steel with a pointed gut hook along its spine like a skinning knife. It wouldn't do shit against Darlene, even now, but she wasn't trying to stab her to death. She just needed to keep her distracted.

The hole in the icon pulled itself shut a little more, the cracks in the stone already healing themselves over. It was now or never. Anne shambled ahead, her gait hitching and uneven, and thrust the knife forward as hard as she could, burying the stubby blade deep into Darlene's back. There was a burst of dark, muddy blood, and the shape-shifter screeched and thrashed away, flailing blindly at Anne, off-balancing herself.

Stubbornly, Anne held on, dragging the blade down through twisted, fouled flesh, and pushed. She threw all her weight into her shoulder, shoving against Darlene, driving her closer to the void's waiting mouth. Darlene pressed back—Christ, she was still so *strong*—but the physics weren't in her favor. She was too unsteady. Screaming at the top of her lungs, Anne pushed for all she was worth, for her mom and Gemma and Jessup and Lisa and Dutch and everyone else, clutching the knife's handle tight as the blade sawed through withered skin and rotten meat, bracing herself against the frantic thrash of Darlene's arms.

For a second, it didn't seem like it was going to work. The hole in the icon had shrunk too much. Anne was too weak, and even damaged and depleted, the shape-shifter was solid in a way that most bodies weren't. There was no way. She couldn't—

But then, it happened.

She felt Darlene's body leave the ground, lifted by the impossible gravity of the void. Darlene's howling grew louder, her flailing more insistent. She clawed at the icon as it drew her in, the living light ripping through her withered body like invisible teeth. A hand, an arm, one leg, then two. The icon inhaled her. It didn't matter how much she fought.

Half in and half out of that terrible void, Darlene wailed and twisted around to glower at Anne. Her face was like nothing Anne had ever seen in her life, burned and cracked and bleeding from underneath, but somehow, impossibly, looking more like herself than she ever had. Gone were the masks and their rot, all those stolen faces. Inside the blood and scorched skin, here, now, Anne saw the face of the woman she'd tried to save that night, way back when. Her eyes still glowed, her expression still burned with ravenous hatred, but it was truly, finally her.

"Darlene—" Anne gasped.

The woman snapped her remaining hand out and seized Anne's shattered arm in a vise grip that crushed the remains of the broken cast to shards. Unbelievable pain ripped its way past Anne's shoulder and bored directly into her brain. Her heels skidded against the stone floor as she was dragged toward the void, and that was when she understood: Darlene was going to pull her through.

Anne screamed and tried to yank herself away, feeling the sharp splinters of bone floating in her arm dig deeper into the infected meat surrounding them. It was the worst pain she'd ever felt in her life, but still she pulled. If she was going to die down here, she was going to die on this side of the door.

Flies burst from Darlene's body in black waves, and the shapeshifter jerked back again as she sank farther into the light, dragging Anne forward another step, then another. Inside Darlene's iron grasp, Anne's arm hummed and buzzed just like her palms had all those years ago, and then the skin was splitting like an overcooked sausage inside the ruins of her cast. Blood glurged out of the cracks in the red fiberglass, and for a moment, the briefest of moments, Anne faltered. That was all it took.

Darlene screeched again and was sucked back through the door, taking Anne with her. Anne threw her other arm out to catch herself against the edge of the icon, slapping her bare, bloody palm painfully against the white stone. It was enough to keep her from going through—just not all of her.

Anne's ruined arm plunged into the glow, almost all the way up to the shoulder, and Anne felt—nothing. Nothing at all. Not heat, not cold, but pure, unadulterated nothingness. It was as if her arm with all its pains and wounds had been struck instantly numb, but even that word—*numb*—didn't do the sensation justice. With numbness, there was still some vestigial sense of presence, some blank nervous system signal that even lacking sensation, all of you was still intact.

This wasn't like that at all. As Anne's arm disappeared through the door, it wasn't like losing sensation so much as reality being rewritten around her so that she'd never had sensation there in the first place. As if she'd been born without it.

Inside the light, Darlene wailed one last time and then went curiously, horribly quiet. The icon shook from within, from below, from everywhere. Anne didn't even realize it was happening until it had already happened: the white stone surged around her arm, then snapped shut.

She tried to scream, but the scream wouldn't come. Darkness swarmed her vision, burned through with kaleidoscopic afterimages of the poison light pouring from the void. Her head rang with sudden silence. Her feet skated against the chamber's smooth stone floor, trying to find purchase, then went out from under her entirely. She didn't feel it at all when she hit the ground.

55

The chamber was dark when she finally came to again. The old man's torches must have gone out at some point, but she couldn't tell when. All she knew was that she was freezing. Every part of her body hurt. Her lungs were tight and pinched from the cold, refusing to fill no matter how hard she breathed in. She didn't know how long she'd been out or how much blood she'd lost, but she was still here. There was still some life left inside her.

Telling herself that she wasn't as scared as she really was, she reached her right arm over to feel the place where her left had been. She knew from the second she'd awoken that it was gone, snapped off by the closing icon as if it had been bitten away, but she didn't know the extent of the damage. She'd expected a seeping, infected wound at the end of a knobbly stump; she'd expected raw nerves, exposed bone, torn flaps of skin. But what she found there was only scar tissue, ribbed and ridged. Healed over while she was sleeping. She imagined her own skin melting and re-forming itself under the power of that heinous light, healing itself just like Darlene's had. It was a mercy. She saw that now.

But of course, that same otherworldly mercy hadn't extended itself to the rest of her body.

The bullet hole in her side ground against itself and vomited blood as she rose to her feet, but she bore it. There was no other choice. She thought briefly about hunting around in the darkness for her Glock, but what would be the point? Anybody she'd use it on was already dead.

All around her, the mine was silent. She couldn't even hear the whispers from the icon anymore. The massive white slab had gone as quiet as the rest of Ballmer's Hope. She didn't know why, and she really didn't care. She just wanted out.

Idly, her hand found the chain around her neck, with its simple pendant, a cursive *B* engraved in its face. The metal was warm to the touch, as if someone had been clutching it tightly in their hands only moments earlier. Anne traced the letter's loops with the point of her thumbnail, fixing their shape in her mind, imagining that it was somehow her mother who'd left her warmth behind in the pendant's simple silver, a thread tying them together, a beacon to guide her up and out of this forsaken place.

Letting the pendant lie flat against her skin, she pressed her hand flat against the wound in her ribs and started for the surface.

Cold air licked at her skin as she emerged from the mine, hunched over and limping. The hills loomed high around her, a swelling sea of shadows threatening to swallow her whole. Overhead, high above the sawtooth ridge to the east, the sky was filled with stars, twinkling bright, battling the darkness back. She'd been underneath this night sky so many times before, but she didn't think it had ever been this beautiful, this bright.

Something chittered in the trees. Something raced across the fallen pine needles. A flock of birds took flight and disappeared.

All around her, the burned forest was filled with life.

Aching and exhausted but stubbornly not dead, Anne Heller started walking down the hill to where the slope met the dirt road, then kept on going. She didn't know how long of a walk it was back to the car and the rest of the world, to a hospital, to anybody at all, but that hardly seemed to matter now. She'd come this far. She thought she could probably go a little farther.

Godzilla

The sound of the rain pounding against the windows woke her, but she didn't open her eyes until the alarm on her phone started going off. Rolling over under the blankets, she fumbled for her cell on the bedside table, mashing at its screen with sleep-dead hands until it stopped making noise. Then it was just her, and the darkness, and the sound of the rain.

She lay there for another few minutes, trying to remember her dreams as she listened to the cars sluicing down the waterlogged street outside. She'd never been a heavy sleeper, never was much of a dreamer, either, but that had all changed once she'd made it to the city. Now it seemed like every night she slept like a rock, slipping into vivid, interconnected dreams that faded from her mind the second she awoke. She didn't mind not remembering. It wasn't that much different from how life had been before, and anyway, it was a small price to pay. It felt like it had been years since real, actual sleep had been a part of her life. What were a few dreams she'd never remember?

Outside, a fire engine blew past the apartment building, its sirens loud enough to rattle the glass in the windows. An ambulance followed behind it, chased by a couple of cop cars. She'd been here for long enough that she'd mostly managed to convince herself that not every siren meant certain doom, but the sound still left her uneasy: It was an echo from another life, another her. A world she'd left behind.

Throwing the blankets to one side, she rose from her bed and went to the nearest window to watch. Three stories down, Thirty-Third Street was already choked with morning traffic; the rainstorm had only made it worse. The emergency vehicles had hit a logjam. There was no getting through, no matter how loudly they blared their sirens. People in their cars laid on their horns. Others started screaming at one another at the top of their lungs. Overhead, the rain surged and started coming down in sheets again.

Another beautiful day in New York.

In the corner of the room, a pair of wide green eyes hinged open to regard her from the top of the carpet-and-sisal tree she'd spent three goddamn hours putting together after they'd first moved in. It hadn't exactly been an easy transition for either of them, but Murphy had definitely had the harder go of it. He was a creature of habit, and it wasn't like he'd signed up to have his ass carted halfway across the country. She went over to him and scratched his cheeks, his chin, the gossamer fur behind his ears.

"I know, buddy," she said. "I know. Sorry about them."

Murphy purred and leaned into her touch.

"Listen, I'm going to go get some coffee, okay? I'll be right back, promise."

The big tabby gave her a look like she was crazy to go outside with the rain like this, but he didn't say anything about it, either.

From the hallway closet, she grabbed a pair of olive-drab khakis and a black T-shirt, socks, her raincoat, her hat, and her waterproof boots from the shelf below. She changed then and there, pausing only a moment to glance at the mirror mounted on the inside of the closet door, at the lattice of scars covering her stomach. They'd healed over well enough the past few months, but she'd long given up hope of them ever fading completely. Another part of her new life to get used to, she supposed.

Laces tied tight, raincoat zipped up to the hollow of her throat, she paused at the front door to fix her braids back into a loose ponytail with the elastic from around her wrist as she braced herself to walk into the storm.

Outside, thunder crashed overhead, hard and close enough that she felt it in the floor under her feet. It had been like this all week. The bodega was only a three-minute walk from here, but with the rain coming down like a typhoon, she was sure she'd end up drenched anyway. She still needed to replace her umbrella after the last one had fallen apart a few weeks back.

Still, the downpour wasn't letting up, and there was no time like the present and all that happy horseshit. So, pulling her apartment door shut after her, Gemma Poe hunched her shoulders up around her ears and headed out into the world once again.

After the worst of the fever had burned off, all that was left were her wounds, the motel room, the cat, and the note.

Well, all that and the money. She couldn't forget about the money. But the money came later.

She'd surfaced slowly, painfully, all the feeling in her body returning to her in a fuzzy, pins-and-needles wave that rolled through her from top to toes. The last thing she remembered clearly was running through the snow back at Lisa's after shooting at something that looked like her, but wasn't. It had lunged at her, gotten in close, and slashed her stomach to ribbons. She wasn't stupid; she'd seen what had happened when somebody tried to fight that thing. So instead, she'd run, as hard and as fast as she could.

After that, time had gotten all weird and out of order, like a deck of playing cards thrown to the ground, and so for a while there, her life had turned into a game of fifty-two pickup. She remembered a long car ride, then another; she remembered the sun going both ways across the sky. She remembered Anne lifting her out of the snow and the feel of the cheap motel blankets and the name *Dr. Rebecca*. Anne holding her hand and whispering, *Please don't die*, alongside the memory of a soft, gentle kiss that might have just been a fever dream. But maybe more than anything, she remembered the pain. It was still there, threaded through her body like it was the stitching holding her together, but it had been so much worse then than it was now. She supposed she had Anne to thank for that, too.

Except Anne was gone. Because of course she was. All that was left in the motel room to show she'd ever been there was the medicine, the note, a little bit of food, Gem's High Power and the Kimber she'd taken off that kid in Cabot, and, of course, Murph. The cat seemed to be as irritated as Gem that they'd been dumped here, but he was fine beyond that: fed, watered, warm, safe. Gem didn't recognize any of the medicine, but Anne had left it all clustered together on the table by the window with clear instructions on administering each. The note, though? That was the real kicker. There wasn't much to it, really—four lines and a quick signature, but it was enough to nearly punch a hole through Gem's chest:

> Had to go deal with a thing.
> Left you some money for cat food.
> I'll see you in New York.
> I'm sorry.
>
> —A.

I'm sorry. Gem couldn't remember Anne Heller ever apologizing for anything in her life. Not really. She might as well have left a big red cartoon sign that said, *Gone to kill myself, see you in the next world.* Gemma had cried so hard when she first read the note, curled up in those scratchy motel sheets, Murphy nuzzling insistently at her legs. She was pissed, and she was heartbroken, and she didn't know what to do with either of those things. The sorrow was like a rock in her chest, pressing on her heart as it dragged her further and further down.

How dare she pull this shit? After everything they'd been through together, she just dumped her here and headed off on some delusional suicide mission? How selfish could one person be? Gem so badly wanted to stay pissed at Anne, but the longer she sat there, reading through the note again and again, the more impossible it became. Gem knew that she'd been deadweight. That was why Anne had left her here. She wanted to tell herself that she could have helped somehow, backed her up, maybe even kept her from dying, but that was all just self-flattery. Unconscious from blood loss and fever, she wasn't any good to anyone. Just like that, her anger evaporated like fog in the morning sun, and all that was left was the heartache of losing her. *I'll see you in New York* wasn't a promise or a plan. It was a dying wish.

Gem sat there weeping into her hands for a long time, and when her tears finally subsided, she rose slowly from the bed and went to the grubby little bathroom to inspect the claw marks in her stomach. They weren't good, but they could have been a lot worse, too. Someone had done a handy job of stitching them up while she'd been under, which meant that it had been anyone but Anne doing the stitching. She traced the lines of each furrow with a fingertip. There'd be scars there for the rest of her life, but it was a whole lot better than waking up dead.

Emerging from the bathroom again, she stood for a moment in the middle of the motel room, trying to get a feel for being upright again after she didn't know how long she'd spent horizontal. She was unsteady, but she was pretty sure she wasn't about to go toppling over, either. In the middle of the mattress, Murphy stood and stretched, arching his back, then hopped down to the carpet to start padding around the room. Gem followed his movement with her eyes, the way he stopped and sniffed and stared off into space like a chubby little psychopath. That was when she saw the bank bag tucked under the bed.

Left you some money for cat food.

Oh.

She'd found her way to the East Coast in a fifth-hand Honda that she'd bought for a thousand dollars cash from the used lot two blocks over from the motel. It only cost her another five hundred for the friendly salesman to dummy up a set of fake credentials for the title and registration. Nice guy, really. After that, she packed up Murph, the cash, the guns, and the rest of her stuff, and then they were on the road again, first back up to the Happy Trails Motel and the plastic bag that waited for her inside the heat vent of room 117, then due east as fast as the car would take them.

The trip had only taken a few days with some stops in between, but there hadn't been any trouble to it, really. The farther she got from Colorado, the less the news stations mentioned bank robberies or wildfires or shoot-outs. She was well past the Mississippi River by the time the reports died out completely, subsumed by the

endless chatter of more immediately local stories and forgotten altogether. Travis's last prediction had come true, after all. Wonders
never ceased.

Her path had taken her through Kansas and Missouri and the
rest of the big empty called the Midwest to coast along the northern side of Pennsylvania, then straight across New Jersey into New
York. Most of the route was flat and desolate—not exactly what
she'd have called *scenic*—but New Jersey in particular was a lot
prettier than people gave it credit for.

Then, the city: an endless crush of buildings and bodies reaching
well past the horizon, a patchwork machine of incomprehensible
enormity that never stopped moving. It was overwhelming at first,
all the noise and sights and smells and people. Gemma had never
felt so small in all her life. But eventually, the crush of it eased back,
and she learned to focus on the immediate, the necessary. The city
was too big to take in all at once. You had to stay focused on what
was in front of you.

Eventually, Gem found herself setting up shop in the borough
of Queens, on the eastern side of the city, in a little neighborhood
called Astoria. It was a nice place, not too loud and not too quiet,
and the people—some of whom had lived there for half a century
or more—were friendly enough, but they had a way of leaving you
the hell alone. It was perfect.

She sold the car. Found an apartment. Got to work becoming
someone new.

It wasn't that hard, settling into the rhythms of her new life.
New York was a universe unto itself, a side reality rarely intruded
on by the world that existed beyond its limits. There was enough
to do, and see, and learn in the city to keep her busy for decades. It
didn't take much to understand how people spent their whole lives
without ever leaving its bounds. Building a life in this place wasn't
hard because no one ever looked at you while you were doing it.
Your life could be as big or as small as you wanted it to be, and nobody would give a shit. You stayed in your lane and minded your
business and everybody else did the same. It was the only way to
get by in a city of nearly nine million people packed into three

hundred square miles—a space roughly a twenty-sixth the size of the valley. There was safety in anonymity, after all, and everyone was anonymous in this town.

For the first couple of months, she checked the news every day just to be sure, scouring the internet for any mention of arrests made in connection with the bank robbery in Durango or the shoot-out in Alamosa, the wildfires, the explosions, all the dead people they'd left in their wake. There had been a few references early on—brief footnotes about a fire on a burned-out ranch and dozens of bodies discovered in a mine deep in the hills—but they'd largely been treated as local curiosities, rural Colorado being rural Colorado, and they'd fizzled out as such. The world had so many bigger things to worry about, after all: civil rights being eroded by the aging, angry white elite, nazis marching in the streets, the death throes of end-stage capitalism pushing the world deeper into irreversible dystopia. A few bloody dustups and dead cult freaks in some backwater most people had never heard of hardly ranked mention.

That was just fine as far as Gemma was concerned. She kept her life small by design—her place, her cat, a job tending bar in the afternoons a couple of days a week, and a stack of paperback books on her shelf that she was constantly replenishing as she worked through the volumes among its number.

It wasn't much, but it was enough, and it was hers.

And then, one day, it all fell apart.

Halsey's was a neighborhood bar through and through: a row of creaky stools lining a beat-up stretch of pine, a few high-tops and a couple of booths, TVs on the walls, boozy bingo on Tuesdays, drag brunch on Saturdays. Gemma had first wandered in for a beer a few weeks after moving into her place and walked out an hour and a half later with a part-time job. The manager needed someone to cover a couple of the slow day shifts, and Gem needed something to get her out of the apartment from time to time. It was a win-win for everybody.

The job at the bar wasn't particularly hard—day shifts during the weekdays were generally pretty dead, and even when they weren't, people were usually pretty friendly. It didn't hurt that Halsey's was relatively out of the way, as far as the subway was concerned. Nobody who stopped in was ever in any great hurry. Most of the patrons were regulars, and all the regulars were folks from the neighborhood who always played nice and tipped well. Not that she needed the money, of course, but it was still a nice gesture.

Halsey's was a lot busier than usual when Gemma came in from the rain for her shift that day, most of the tables taken, the barstools filled from end to end. Big groups of people still weren't Gemma's favorite thing in the world—after however many months it had been since she'd left the west behind, some part of her stubbornly expected to see Darlene emerging from every crowd, mouth yawning wide, overflowing with teeth. But today, nobody in the bar looked at her twice.

Down at the far end of the pine, Logan, the other daytime bartender, waved and walked over to her as she stripped off her hat and her raincoat and hung them on the hooks next to the register.

"Hey," he said.

"Hey yourself." Gemma jerked her chin toward the crowd. "What's all this about?"

Logan shrugged and shook his head. He was a skinny little thing, with shoulder-length auburn hair and arms filled with ratty tattoos. He looked like a piece-of-shit crust punk, but he was a sweet kid. Gemma liked him a lot.

"No clue," Logan told her. "Just one of those days, I guess. Maybe they're all hiding from the storm, I dunno."

"Yeah, maybe."

"You want me to stick around, help out until it clears out some? I've got a couple hours until I need to be at the bookstore for my shift, and Brendan isn't going to be home until late, anyway, so no reason for me to head back if you need me here."

Gemma waved him off. "Don't worry about it, I've got this. You can get out of here, go home, get some sleep, whatever."

"You sure?"

She gave him a warm-but-firm look, the same one that her mom used to stick her with when she was young and thought she knew everything about everything. Logan meant well, but he had plenty of his own shit to deal with. He and his boyfriend were already both working two jobs apiece just to make rent in this town. She didn't need him pushing himself any closer to burnout just because the bar was short-staffed.

"Yeah," Gem said. "I'm sure. Go on now. I'll be fine. Promise."

"Oh-kaaay," Logan said, his voice skeptically singsong. From behind the bar, Gem watched him bundle up in his own rainy-day gear, then turn back and smile at her. "I'll see you tomorrow, yeah?"

"Oh yeah," she said. "Another day in paradise. Wouldn't miss it."

Logan nodded one last time, then charged half-heartedly out the door and into the rain, turning right and jogging up Thirty-Third toward the Thirtieth Avenue subway station. Then it was just Gemma and the crowd.

She threw a bar towel over her shoulder and got to work.

The storm outside dumped harder and harder, making the gutters swell and overflow. Storms in New York were like this sometimes; either they'd rage themselves out in five minutes, or they'd last for weeks on end. Right now, they were in the *weeks* phase. Felt like it had been forever since Gemma had seen the sun.

By the time the first hour of her shift was over, most of the drinkers had cleared out, except for a young couple mooning at each other over at one of the high-tops, a big guy with his nose buried in a book near the door, and a chick with a buzz cut at the far end of the bar. Gemma set the big guy up with another pint of stout, cruised past the young lovers, then drifted back around the bar to check in on Buzz Cut.

She'd been sitting there since Gem had gotten in, had barely looked up from her phone when she'd ordered another round. Gemma hadn't paid her much mind; she was quiet, unfussy, and out of the way. The perfect customer during a rush, as far as Gem was concerned.

Gem pitched her hip against the inside lip of the bar and gently laid a hand on the wood between them.

"Something else I can get you?"

The woman set her phone aside and looked up, and Gemma's heart nearly stopped. For a second, the world inverted itself around her, and she realized that she hadn't really looked at the woman at all before this moment. She hadn't seen the long, thick scar traveling horizontally across her face, the way her left sleeve was pinned up over the place her arm used to be, or the fire-red tinge to her buzzed-back hair.

She hadn't seen her at all.

But there was no way. It wasn't possible. Gemma's first thought was that she wished she had one of her guns—it was some trick, it had to be. Another one of Darlene's masks, another cruel feint. But then the woman smiled, and Gem knew that it was really her, solid and true and big as life.

The name fell from Gemma's lips unbidden:

"Anne."

On the other side of the bar, Anne Heller smiled wider, and Gemma realized that she could see tears twinkling in the corners of her eyes. She was so beautiful when she smiled. The most beautiful thing Gemma had ever seen.

"Hey," Anne said. "I kept you waiting. I'm sorry."

Wild excitement exploded inside Gemma like a flurry of wings beating inside her chest. Tears prickled at her eyes. Her head spun like a top. Beyond the doors, the sound of the rain against the street eased back to a gentle hiss. Anne closed her hand around Gemma's, squeezing, and Gemma squeezed back, trying not to scream with joy and shock and wonder—but mostly joy.

Outside, just for a moment, the sun poked through the clouds, illuminating the city, with all its scars and messy beauty and perfect imperfection.

The storm was finally letting up.

ACKNOWLEDGMENTS

This was originally going to be a way, way different book than the one it turned out to be, but I'm starting to realize that's just the nature of the beast. Sometimes stories change themselves around when you're not looking. The road you're on doesn't always take you where you think you're going.

Luckily, I didn't have to take that trip alone.

All my love and thanks go to the amazing people whose endless patience, support, and kindness helped make this book what it is: Chelsey Emmelhainz, Kevin and Amy Sims, Rebecca Agatstein and Dragan Radovanovic, Emma Price, Jon Davies, Alex Linek, Lindsay King-Miller, Elizabeth Copps and Anthony Muller, Emily Hughes, Jordan Hanley, Figbar Lonesome, Melinda Hervey, Carley Johnson, Rick and Val Emmelhainz, Ashley Marudas, Liz Claps, Daryl Winstone, and David Whitney. You're all truly incredible, and I sure as hell don't know what I did to deserve any of you, but I'm so fucking grateful to have you in my corner nonetheless.

To my family—Lynn Lyons, Lucy and Jeremy Druckman, Steve Merritt and Anne Lang, Aaron Merritt, and Dave and Kris Merritt—this story, just like all the others, simply wouldn't exist without you. I love you all dearly. Thank you.

To my marvelous agent, Nicole Resciniti: I count myself as immeasurably lucky to get to work with you. I'm humbled every day by your grit and your kindness, your patience and your drive. Thank you, thank you, thank you, Nic.

To my brilliant and talented editor, Kristin Temple: I really can't thank you enough—your insight, creativity, sense of humor, and sheer enthusiasm for the kind of abject mayhem that I put on the page have made this story infinitely better at every turn. Thank you for helping me get Anne and Gemma where they needed to be, and for everything else. It means the entire goddamn world.

A special callout is also due to the entire Nightfire team, dedicated folks who worked tirelessly to get this book into your hands: Kelly Lonesome, Gertrude King, Alexis Saarela and Khadija Lokhandwala, Esther Kim, Heather Saunders, Jeff LaSala, Steven Bucsok, Rafal Gibek, and Valeria Castorena. Thank you all so much.

My sincerest thanks also to Veronica at Salt and Sage Books for the astute and in-depth sensitivity read, as well as Sam Wolfe Connelly for the beautiful, haunting, profoundly gross cover art.

A few musicians and bands that were crucial to the writing of this book: Wayfarer, PJ Harvey, Queens of the Stone Age, Filth Is Eternal, Emma Ruth Rundle, Monster Magnet, Buddy Miles, Gloomseeker, Wu-Tang Clan, Failure, Lucy Kruger & The Lost Boys, Death on Cassette, and honestly so many more than I reasonably have time or space to list here.

Colorado's San Luis Valley is legitimately one of the most gorgeous places in the world, and also one of the spookiest—you don't have to look very hard to realize that there are a million other horror stories out there in the shadow of Blanca Peak, just waiting to be told. If you're ever in Denver, the valley's startling beauty and undeniable charm—as well as its deep weirdness—are well worth the four- or five-hour drive south.

Just be careful about which ghost towns you go exploring while you're there.

You never know what you might unearth.

ABOUT THE AUTHOR

MATTHEW LYONS is the author of the novels *A Mask of Flies,* *A Black and Endless Sky,* and *The Night Will Find Us,* as well as over three dozen short stories, appearing in the 2018 edition of Best American Short Stories, *Tough, Southwest Review,* and more.